# JUDGMENT

Alien Invasion Book Five

---

AVERY BLAKE

JOHNNY B. TRUANT

STERLING & STONE

*To YOU, the reader.*
*Thank you for taking a chance on us.*
*Thank you for your support.*
*Thank you for the emails.*
*Thank you for the reviews.*
*Thank you for reading and joining us on this road.*

# JUDGMENT

# Eleven Years Before Astral Day

# Prologue

"Right or left?"

Cameron looked up at his father then down at his napkin. The words *Nile Cafe* edged the corner, and to Cameron they looked distinctly hand-stamped, as if the proprietor had purchased generic napkins and decided it was worth marking them manually. In the napkin's middle was a network of lines that looked like the bodies of massacred stick people stacked haphazardly atop each other. It had made sense when the man in the cafe had explained the tunnels, thick coffee in small cups between them, the man's eyebrows raised at this fifteen-year-old kid who dared to ask such adult questions. But now, in the stale underground air, it was hard for Cameron to remember which line corresponded to which passageway. Any one of them could be anything.

"Go right," Cameron said, then turned the napkin 90 degrees and nodded to himself. "Yes. Right."

Benjamin hesitated then turned right. Cameron followed, limestone brushing each of his arms. Cameron wasn't usually claustrophobic, but the tunnels were reversing that. It wasn't the confined space — it was that this part of the tunnels was off limits for a reason, and although his father figured the Egyptians were keeping secrets, Cameron thought the prohibition might be for a far simpler reason: Maybe the tiny tunnels were unsafe. Maybe they were unsound and might collapse. Closed spaces required vents and chimneys for oxygen to come in and carbon dioxide to be wafted away. The shafts here were mostly plugged with sand. That's one reason most of these types of explorations were done by robots, or by adventurous humans donned in breathing gear. Maybe they wouldn't be crushed after all. They could suffocate instead.

"Wait," Cameron said a minute later.

Benjamin peeked over his shoulder, the lantern's light throwing his shadow harshly against the stone wall.

"I meant left."

"Left now, or left back when you said 'right'?"

"Back there."

"So I should turn around."

"Yes," Cameron said, though he wasn't sure. This place was creeping him out. It wasn't only the claustrophobia — the Mullah were famously averse to visitors getting close to their secrets.

Benjamin extended his hand. "Let me see the map."

Cameron handed him the napkin.

"This is just a mess of lines," Benjamin said after thirty seconds of looking it over. "You should have had him make a map we could actually read."

"I can read it."

"Oh come on. *I* can't even read it."

Cameron snatched the napkin back. He didn't want more of this bullshit. Not now. Not after three weeks of exploring caves and talking to men who required bribes just to whisper, always feeling like the two of them might at any time be abducted and held for ransom. Not after trekking and sweating and sleeping on mattresses that Cameron felt sure were infected with insects — a fear so vivid that he swore he could feel the bugs moving at night. Not after thrice-daily lectures, delivered by his father during every meal. He said they were partners in this round of exploration, but Cameron was treated as *less* than an assistant. More like a pupil. A rather *dim* pupil who never did his homework or remembered his lessons.

"I can read it," he said.

"How can you *possibly* …"

Cameron pointed at the map, his temper rising like a tide. "This is the main shaft, where we came in. And this is that branch we ran into — see, like a Y? So this must be where we are now, which puts the Sun Chamber *here*."

Benjamin raised his eyebrows and repeated, *"Must be* where we are?"

*"Is,"* Cameron asserted. "This *is* where we are."

"You're sure?"

*No.* The answer was no.

"Will you just trust me?" Cameron said instead.

"So … left? Then you need to back up so I can turn around. Unless you want to lead?"

Benjamin indicated the narrow stone passage behind them. Cameron tried to see the gesture as a measure of trust but couldn't shed the thought of ancient booby traps springing and impaling him. It seemed like a long shot seeing as such things were for Hollywood more than reality (the Mullah preferred a more direct approach), but he still didn't want to go first. The initial set of tunnels they'd bribed their way into had been restricted, but this part was supposedly unknown except to those who obviously knew it best. Anything could be in here. Anything at all.

"No thanks. You're the 'expert.'" To get his dig on Benjamin, Cameron made the quotes around "expert" audible. Then he inched backward to the T junction and let his father pass.

"Right or straight ahead?" Benjamin asked a few minutes later.

The map showed no junction.

"Straight … straight ahead," Cameron stammered.

"Are you sure?"

"Yes, I'm sure."

Benjamin bit his lip, lowered the lantern, turned, and faced his son.

"Tell me if you don't know, Cam. I don't want to get lost down here."

"I know! I said straight!"

Benjamin looked like he might persist but then just sighed and turned.

Cameron followed, holding the map with both hands, shining his headlamp down while trying to resist the headache that came with the bouncing glow. He was pretty sure this was correct. Almost entirely. Yusef hadn't marked the right-branching passage they'd just passed, probably because he was giving them a way to reach the chamber directly without all the alternative approaches. You don't tell someone every street they'll cross on the way to the post office; you just tell them to cross the big intersection with the Kmart on the corner before turning.

Benjamin's voice came back at Cameron from over forward-facing shoulders. Sound was odd in here. The rock funneled voices toward the speaker's head, leaving a scant fraction of normal volume to echo backward.

"How do you think these passages were carved, Cameron? Hard to imagine humans doing this by hand, right?"

Cameron pretended not to hear.

"Cam?"

"It should be just up here, Dad."

"Did you hear what I said about the—"

"Yes."

"So how do you think they were carved?"

Cameron sighed loudly enough to be obvious.

Benjamin turned his head. "So you don't know that, either."

*Either.* So clearly Benjamin didn't trust his map reading even after the assurances.

"I know it, Dad."

"So why don't you just tell me?"

"Because you know I know."

"How do I know you know if you won't answer the question?"

"Gee, I don't know. Maybe because you've told me, like, a hundred times?"

"I guess it wasn't often enough," Benjamin said with false regret.

"Or maybe it's because when most kids were getting bedtime stories, I was learning about the tools and excavation methods of ancient people. Maybe I don't want to answer your question because I've already answered it a thousand times, like every day of my life is some stupid quiz."

"That's *so* not how it was, and you know it."

"Really? What did we talk about at breakfast?"

Benjamin said nothing.

"It's really too bad we split up at lunch so I could get the map from Yusef. If we'd eaten together, I'd probably be able to pass this test." He snapped in the reverberating stone hallway. *"Damn."*

"Forgive me for educating you. Most sixteen-year-olds don't get opportunities like this to—"

Cameron rolled his eyes. "Oh, for fuck's sake."

*"Cameron!"*

*"Really,* Dad? I'm old enough to fly around the world with you and break into deathtraps by your side but not old enough to swear? I thought the aliens taught us language? Shouldn't I glory in its many colorful aspects?"

Benjamin didn't reply. He seemed to be pouting, but that was fine with Cameron. It was bad enough that his father's obsession had been forced upon him as if it were *Cameron's* passion, too. Worse that the same obsession had driven his mother from their marriage. The constant lectures about aliens and conspiracy theories had replaced board games and tossing a ball in the yard. Benjamin hadn't made it to a single one of Cameron's band recitals in middle school — but Cameron had definitely made it to Machu Picchu and to meet the hunched-over shaman who couldn't wait to talk about little green men. If Benjamin wanted to feel butt-hurt over Cameron's jabs about their shared past, so be it. Someone needed to knock the man down a few pegs every once in a while — to remind him that archaeology and aliens didn't single-mindedly interest everyone the way they interested him.

But Cameron was vindicated a few minutes later. As assured, the narrow hallway yawned into a wide chamber in the ancient structure's central base — a place that was supposed to be caved in but turned out fine, just like Yusef promised.

Benjamin went ahead, spreading out, still conspicuously silent. His headlamp played along the walls, in many small cubbies like ancient shelves. Cameron watched him circulate, shining the lantern on everything. Finally Benjamin stooped to pick something up — a small item, the size of a coin. He looked up, and Cameron waited for his thanks and congratulations, waited for his father to tell him he wasn't an idiot after all.

"This isn't the right chamber," Benjamin said.

"What? Of course it is!"

"No, it's not." Benjamin shook his head. "See that?"

Cameron followed his father's gesture and found a pencil-thin spear of sunlight shining through the rock above.

"Anything seem wrong with that light to you?"

Cameron didn't want to answer. The question was obviously loaded.

"Does that look like a northern-facing shaft?" Benjamin asked, still pointing. "You know ... for the *Sun Chamber*?"

"Um ..."

"Hell, Cam. Of course it's not."

"But it's the chamber on the map!"

"It's just a room." Benjamin swore under his breath. It wasn't easy to move around undetected. If the Mullah caught wind that outsiders were snooping, there'd be hell to pay. Lucky that this was a minor outpost so their presence would be light — not much, globally speaking, to see here.

"Look at the ornamentation, Dad!" Cameron pointed around the chamber. There were symbols everywhere and a round object made of stone or ceramic lying flat, not entirely visible, on a raised podium. "It's obviously *something*. Yusef must've—"

Benjamin reached for the napkin. Cameron, more out of reflex than sense, tried to snatch it away. Benjamin caught a pinch, and the napkin tore neatly in two.

"Great. Just great." Benjamin held out his hand, and Cameron dutifully handed over the napkin's second half.

His mood had gone from triumphant to chastised in thirty short seconds.

Benjamin looked over the torn napkin. "Like I said. Not the Sun Chamber. This is either drawn wrong or you're reading it wrong. Although how *that* could possibly happen with such excellent cartography, I can't imagine."

"Well, then let's just figure out what *this* place is. You didn't even know this chamber was here, did you? Lemons from lemonade, Dad."

Benjamin was shaking his head. Pouting, Cameron thought. Now that they were here, they'd explore the chamber, all right, but not until his dad got his passive-aggressive digs in. The great Benjamin Bannister didn't like arriving at sites unprepared — and whatever this strange ceremonial room was, it hadn't been researched. It could be anything, and without knowing what he was looking for or at, he'd miss the obvious. But in Cameron's mind, this was a case of getting *more* than they'd bargained for, not less. They'd check their current chamber out *then* find the Sun Chamber. Two chambers for the price of one.

Benjamin shook his head at the napkin halves, not dignifying Cameron's words with a response, and resumed mumbling.

As his father turned and seemed to be fishing for his bearings, Cameron shone the lantern around, exploring. He approached the podium, glancing up to get a better look at the round object that was this room's clear focal point, but footsteps on the stone behind him caught his attention before he could zero in.

"Cameron."

Cameron turned. Benjamin came forward and slapped the coin thing he'd picked up earlier into his palm.

"What's this?"

"A souvenir. So you'll always remember your inability to admit when you don't know what you're doing."

"We found a new chamber! What's the problem?"

"And we'll look it over. Then we'll try to salvage the situation before the authorities or the Mullah knows we're here. But dammit, Cam, if you'd just listened …"

"Dad, I'm telling you—"

"*What? What* are you telling me? That Yusef got it wrong, not you? Or that the tunnels and chambers have moved around since he drew you the map?"

Cameron shook his head. He wanted to be angry, but the obvious error had taken the wind from his sails.

"You're just like your mother. Your ego is so fragile, you can't ask for help. We paid Yusef well. I told you to make sure you got all we paid for. I trusted you with this *one thing,* Cam."

But Cameron remembered the way the man had eyed him in the Nile Cafe. He'd seemed to resent speaking to the American kid — divulging secrets that, if Benjamin was correct, were known only to a tiny inside circle. Many palms had been greased and several connections uncovered to find the Sun Chamber, and yet *this* was what Yusef had ended up facing? Some stupid kid? Cameron had felt every ounce of the man's irritation. And so, yes, to compensate, maybe he'd puffed his chest a bit more than he should have.

And maybe — just maybe — Cameron had said, "Yes, *of course*" when Yusef had snapped, *"You understand?"* a bit too readily, as if he'd had something to prove.

Benjamin put his hand on Cameron's shoulder. The contact seemed to surprise them both. The hand dropped, and his voice was softer, lower, when he spoke again.

"I don't expect you to know everything, Cameron. I just wish you'd admit when you *don't.* Yusef explained it to you and not me, fine. But if you'd told me he'd been less than forthcoming, I'd at least have known what I was dealing with. If you'd said upfront that you weren't entirely sure of the directions—"

"But I *was* sure! Yusef showed me what all of these—!"

"If you'd just told me you weren't sure of the directions," Benjamin patiently repeated, "I'd have taken the time to search for glyphs in the tunnels. We'd have taken longer, but we'd at least have found what we were looking for." Another sigh then a lift in his voice. "Come on. Let's look around, take some photos. Then we'll just retrace our steps."

As Benjamin began making his way around the room's edge, Cameron looked at the small object his father had given him. It *was* a coin, apparently — about the size of a half dollar. It seemed to be made of an unknown brown metal, battered, with a square hole in its center. Cameron turned it over, wondering if his father expected him to theorize on the coin's origin or maybe on its extraterrestrial forging methods.

It was moot. He turned back into the chamber and was about to put it back down when his father stopped him with a glance.

"Keep it. Only the Mullah come here, and if they cared about it, they'd have taken it already. Like I said, a souvenir."

Cameron nodded then turned to the other side of the room and the raised platform that had seemed to be calling his name. He peered at his father, who was exploring a cubby. Then, without knowing why, he reached up and touched the round thing on its top. He felt a shock, like static, and practically jumped away.

Benjamin turned back, seeing him totter.

"Did you slip?"

"Just a little."

"You okay?"

"Yeah, I'm …"

What was he, exactly? Despite the shock — despite the fact that ceramic objects weren't supposed to *issue* shocks — Cameron wanted to climb back up and touch the thing again. He still couldn't see it properly without climbing onto the platform, but he could glimpse its edge. It had almost seemed to respond, conforming to his finger like dipping it in gel, despite the thing's obvious solidity.

"Cameron?"

"Nothing. It's nothing." Then he squinted back up at the thing, which he'd swear was now glowing in the gloom. But that couldn't be, and if it was, his father would say something. "But I could've sworn that—"

Benjamin cut him off, holding up a finger. Listening. Then, with something urgent invading his manner, Benjamin looked down at the napkin, turning it in circles, trying to make magic by mating the halves.

"Which way is out, Cameron?"

Cameron pointed the way they'd come.

"A *different* way. On here. Is this an exit? Is it this symbol here?"

Cameron followed his father's finger. "I … yes, that's the way out."

"You're sure?"

This time, yes. Of course he was. He had to be, or else he was a total failure.

"Yeah. But Dad, what's — ?"

A mumbling. A grumbling. Coming from all around them. And then above, around, rock walls seemed to shift like some bizarre Rubik's Cube changing configurations.

And then there was shouting.

The sound of rushing feet.

"What's — ?" Cameron blurted suddenly terrified.

"*Go.* Just go!" Benjamin pointed to Cameron's indicated path.

The walls continued to shift. Sand grated down from above. Benjamin shouted for directions, finally trusting Cameron, under duress, to read the map. Behind them, something collapsed. They heard Mullah shout.

"*Which way?*" Benjamin yelled back as they approached a fork, hurried feet behind them, chattering on in a language Cameron didn't understand.

"Right. I mean left!"

"Are you positive?"

"Yes!"

Cameron looked back, saw something crash to the ground. The world was coming apart behind them.

"Dad, what's happening?"

Still running, trying to hold his breath, Benjamin said, "Did Yusef say anything about a 'Key Chamber'?"

"I don't think so!"

"That's what they're shouting about." Benjamin pointed back, leaping rubble. "'Key Chamber.'"

"I don't know anything about it!"

"Well, doesn't matter. I think it's gone now. You didn't touch anything back there, did you? Before they came, before the walls started to shift?"

"No!" The word was out before Cameron realized it was a lie. And in his next blink he saw the thing on the podium, glowing serenely, begging him to touch it again, calling out to him even now.

The sounds were growing louder. Looking back, Cameron could see the first flashes of torchlight — not flashlights but real flames on burning sticks. Apparently the air in here wasn't ignitable after all, and the Mullah, unlike Team Bannister, weren't worried about burning all of the room's oxygen. Because they knew the tunnels and exits. Just like Cameron sort of did.

Robe-clad Mullah knights spilled into the shaft from behind, but then something fell from above and blocked their way.

They ran fast, somehow finding the original shaft as if by a miracle and heading back the way they'd come, praying for faithful memory, luck, and daylight.

# Seven Years After Astral Day

# Chapter One

Up the tunnels. Past portals and doorways guarded by immense round rock doors. Cameron was panting, heaving, the lanyard around his neck with its small metallic bounty pasted with sweat to the skin of his upper chest. Jeanine Coffey was behind him, shouting in harsh whispers. The Reptar purr was no longer audible, but Cameron thought he could still hear Titan feet on the rock-hewn stairs. Titans could move quickly if they needed, or *wanted* to. The lines blurred anyway, seeing as one type of Astral could become the other — or even a spare viceroy, as it turned out.

"Which way?" Jeanine shouted.

"This way!"

"That's down. We need up."

A sudden sound cut the air, and Cameron reacted just in time, grabbing Jeanine by the shoulder of her jacket and pulling her around a corner, into what once might have been an underground bedroom. The place was like an enormous buried anthill or rabbit warren. Even if he'd had a map, it wouldn't have helped in this unfathomable maze.

Jeanine's eyes lit with anger. She seemed about to yell at Cameron for daring to drag her anywhere when he pressed his hand flat against her mouth. Outside in the passageway, feet scampered past — too agile and fast for a Titan, too few in number to be the paws of a Reptar. And although Cameron saw little as he pressed Jeanine against the wall to silence her, the woman's amber eyes lit with alarm as she seemed to notice something flap past them in the recently abandoned corridor.

When their pursuer was gone, Jeanine said, "That was a human."

"I know."

"*Mullah?*" she whispered.

"Makes sense."

"I thought we lost them."

"They're as old as the Templars. I don't think they *lose* easily."

Jeanine, usually tough and unflappable, seemed clearly flustered. Her eyes stayed on the stone hall's doorway. "Jesus Christ. Haven't they taken their pound of flesh already? We're not even trying to find it anymore. So what's their problem?"

"Ask my father." It came out automatically and only slapped Cameron with a cold hand once out of his mouth. Even five years after Benjamin's death, his absence still hurt like it happened yesterday.

"Wait. That might *not* have been a human. The place is lousy with Astrals. It might have been one of them, changed into human form. Like Kindred."

"You know that's not how it works."

"Maybe they have one of those generator people, to *make* it work."

"*Progenitor,*" Cameron corrected, using Kindred's word for a shapeshifter's donor. They'd seen plenty in the cities and deserts they'd been forced to wander before leaving them behind, but no evidence that Titans and Reptars could borrow a non-Astral shape without a progenitor and time to nurture the process. Even then their group had Kindred as a doppelgänger failsafe, able to tell a genuine human from an alien in her skin. They were otherwise impossible to spot. Good thing the real Meyer had been so bedraggled and emaciated when they'd found him. It gave the group time to get comfortable with a pair of them before Original Meyer regained his old body and musculature, at which point the two beings had become more than twins. Years later Cameron still kept wanting to tag one to tell the two apart, like a rancher branding cattle.

"Right," Jeanine said. "That's what I'm saying. The Astrals kidnap one of the Mullah, then copy him like Kindred copied Meyer. *That guy* could be their generator."

This time Cameron didn't bother to correct her. Jeanine wasn't making a mistake; she was being intentionally annoying. She didn't get outwardly nervous often, and always covered it by becoming a wiseass when she did.

"Then who cares? Swap one foe for another. What's the difference?"

Jeanine was clearly distracted. For the first time, Cameron let himself wonder what had become of their remaining party, likely still several floors down in this strange place.

"I lost them," Jeanine said. "When the Reptars came—"

"*Shh!*"

Cameron raised a finger. He could tell from her eyes that he'd pay for shushing Jeanine, but even after assuring himself that there were no pursuers behind them, he still had to concentrate. Even Derinkuyu's touristy sections, back when there had been tourists, were confusing. The ancient underground city — sort of like an apartment building sunken into the rock — had thirteen underground floors, room for a city of twenty thousand people, plus all of the animals and supplies required for a happily ever after. It would have made a great hideout if it hadn't been infested. But of course it was, so now they'd need to move on, to try and find somewhere else away from the horde. But really, how was that different from every day since they'd arrived at Mount Horeb in the shuttle and faced —

Well, he definitely didn't want to think about *that*.

Cameron listened, but nothing came. He'd heard a phantom sound, or perhaps whoever was out there had finally found them, and was now in hiding, waiting for them to emerge.

"Maybe it was Charlie," Cameron said. "Maybe he got around the Titans and you saw him, on his way to the surface."

Jeanine shook her head. "No. That guy was wearing a robe."

"Mullah," Cameron muttered.

"But the Astrals … You know what they say about the enemy of my enemy being my friend."

"The Mullah have spent the entire occupation avoiding the Astrals. More than seven years of running and hiding. I don't think they'll engage, even if we ask nicely." Cameron crossed the chamber and peeked slowly into the passageway. "It's clear. Let's go."

"You were going down before we came in here," Jeanine said.

"I know where I was going."

"The exit is up."

"*Our people* are down."

Jeanine was still shaking her head, now at the idea of moving farther into the warren instead of up toward open air. Despite obvious guilt over losing the others in the melee below, her action plan was apparently diametrically opposed to her regrets. For the former right hand of the late Nathan Andreus, strategy always trumped empathy.

"Yes. And they'll head toward the exit, so we can meet them there."

"I'm not going to leave them behind with the Astrals and trust they can make it out, Jeanine. Even you're not that cold blooded."

She actually laughed — too loud, in Cameron's adrenaline-fueled opinion.

"And I suppose if they're besieged, *we're* going to save them?"

Cameron didn't reply. Was that actually a question?

"Kindred can see into their group mind," Jeanine went on. "He'll know where the Astrals are. He can lose them in this maze then avoid them until the group finds the main exit, or even a chimney to shimmy up."

"And the Mullah?"

"We're just two people," she replied. "But they have Christopher. And the Pall."

"The Pall stayed topside," Cameron said.

But she was set now, unperturbed by anything that contradicted her rapidly congealing battle plan. "If the Pall saw anything head into the cave after us, it'd do its smoke thing and head down past any Astrals to help. Create darkness like it did in Heaven's Veil, so the Astrals couldn't find them. Or take a form and fight."

"What form have you seen the Pall take that would be any good in a fight? Heather Hawthorne, maybe?"

"They'll be fine, Cameron. *We're* in trouble."

"Trouble? *You?*"

Jeanine rolled her eyes. "We're not going to find out just sitting here. We go up, not down." She said it with finality as if *she* led the group rather than Cameron — which, in times of crisis, she mostly did. "If they can get out, they'll do it without our help. If they can't, we'll make no difference, and heading up is triage. Either way, our course of action's the same. I'll lead, if you want to be a pussy about it."

Cameron grunted.

"Want one of my guns?"

"No."

She was handing him a pistol anyway. A Beretta and a spare clip filled with self-packed bullets.

"I said no."

"Don't be an asshole, Cameron."

"No guns."

"What do you plan to use if we run into Mullah or Astrals? Your charming personality?"

*"No guns,"* Cameron repeated. He hadn't touched one in years. Not since Sinai. And never again.

Jeanine's look was either sympathetic or impatient. But she didn't understand and would never be able to, beyond the tangential blast given by the archive that day. It had been a thousand times worse for Cameron.

He'd never touch a gun again. That's what nobody truly got. His opinion was cast in cement. If he couldn't change the past, at least he'd shape his future.

Jeanine put the gun away, not saying what was clearly on her mind. *It wasn't your fault, and you're handicapping all of us by being stubborn.* It was true but altered nothing.

"Fine. Stay behind me. But if someone comes from the rear, you'd better make like a human shield. I don't intend to get shot, diced with a scimitar, or eaten just because of your hang-ups and refusal to be rational."

They left the chamber, moving into the rock passage. Cameron didn't like small spaces — hadn't since the day he and his father had barely escaped the Mullah in Giza. But unlike those ancient hallways, Derinkuyu's corridors were rounded by time and excavation, eroded by time as if by water. There was an openness here, even underground, that most confined sites lacked. He could have abided this place. It was almost too bad the hunch had been wrong — or that someone in the dusty burgs along the way had guessed their destination and ratted them out.

They reached the stairs. Without flinching, Jeanine moved upward. She had a small lantern in her left hand, a gun raised in the other.

But two steps up, Jeanine and Cameron both froze as they heard a scratching behind them.

Cameron turned. Piper was standing in the dim stone hallway behind them, her fingernails raking the rock wall.

"Piper!" he whisper-shouted, relief flooding his chest, moving forward. "Where are the others? Did you all get away? Are Lila and Christopher with you? Is — ?"

Instead of replying, Piper held up a hand then gestured for them to follow. She didn't come forward to meet Cameron's rushing embrace. She simply turned on her heel.

"That's not Piper," Jeanine said.

But of course Cameron had figured that out. Piper had been wearing a pair of scavenged jeans and a sweater that was coming unraveled at the sleeve. The woman ahead of them was in a pristine white gown, like Piper used to wear while living in Heaven's Veil.

"Hey," Cameron said.

Piper turned to look at him.

"I hate when you do that."

With a relaxing breath, Piper dissolved into the boiling, multicolored smoke that they'd come to know as the Pall's default shape. Unlike Astral shapeshifters, the Pall could become a mute version of anyone it touched. But it required tremendous energy, and freaked everyone out — especially Meyer.

Jeanine was still frozen on the steps.

"Come on," Cameron said. "It wants us to follow."

Still with her gun out. Still poised to move upward, toward the exit. "It's going to lead us deeper into the tunnels."

"It'll protect us. It wouldn't call us if there wasn't a reason."

At the end of the hallway, the Pall's smoke became a large, malformed appendage, like an enormous reaching hand, and beckoned again.

Jeanine sighed and stepped down, moving to follow. "It's like taking directions from Lassie," she said.

## Chapter Two

Meyer or Kindred — or Meyer and Meyer, as Piper thought of them, even now — were ducked low in a chamber across the squat, brown-rock hallway. Piper could feel their energy just as she could feel Lila's beside and behind her.

The Meyers were strange, even after years of knowing them both — even after years spent trying alternative relationships, where she was *with* them both. They weren't like twins: two brothers who happened to share identical genetics. They were like the same man, split in two. It had never felt like Kindred and Meyer shared her. It had never felt any more polygamous than it would feel to love one man, *and* his reflection.

But it must have been different on some level because even though they were the same man, they also *weren't*. And still, even now with her heart beating and peril so familiar in her veins, Piper could feel them appraising their situation. Could feel each man's reaction — the same yet nearly opposite. Fused into one thing, bickering like an old married couple.

The sense didn't reach Piper in words. It came as a gatling blast of emotions.

*Yes.*

*No.*

*Up.*

*Down.*

*Told you so. Told you this was a bad idea.*

*Told you so. Told you this was a good idea.*

But the warring and yet somehow integrated contention coming from the Meyers changed nothing. They were still pinned down. Still trapped.

Piper turned to Lila. Clara was beside her. In the past, Lila would have been tightly holding her child, but those days were long behind them. Now Lila was upright, concerned but not panicked, seeming eighty instead of still in her twenties. Piper imagined they must all seem that old, and thought as much whenever she looked in a mirror.

And Clara, beside but not entangled with her mother, seemed unfazed as ever. Calm, unaffected, almost jaded, just like the other Lightborn child they'd run across. Once an anomaly, Clara's strange prescience and adult demeanor now seemed *almost* normal. Odd to believe there had once been a world where Clara appeared precocious. A world where seven-year-old girls still played with dolls and didn't hint at hidden eternal knowledge.

"Why did they stop attacking?" Lila asked.

Clara shrugged. She got her flashes, but the girl didn't know everything. Heaven's Veil had changed her. Maybe destroyed the source of her power's sharpest edge. And encountering the Ark at Mount Horeb, Mount Sinai? That had changed them all.

"I don't know," Piper answered when Clara didn't.

"They came in like gangbusters," Lila said. "I figured we were toast."

Yes. Piper had thought that, too. Even Charlie had yelped like a frightened dog when the Reptars swarmed down from above. Most of ancient Cappadocia was supposed to have been abandoned in favor of the cities, at least as far as they'd heard across the outlands. The buried Turkish stronghold of Derinkuyu had dawned on Cameron like a benevolent bolt of lightning. If nobody had claimed it, the place would be the perfect resting spot or semi-permanent residence. Or if a community had formed in Derinkuyu, as many rumors claimed, that would be even better. But they hadn't found a community of human border dwellers or a hive claimed by Astrals. They'd found an empty shell. Until they'd made their way to the bottom and invaders descended.

There was movement from across the chamber. Light was scant, especially with half their lanterns and lights muted during their flight from the Astrals, so what came looked like a shadow. But it was only Charlie.

"Christopher ran up."

Piper waited for more. But Charlie had said the unhelpful thing and was now waiting for her response, oblivious to the fact that those three simple words had offered nothing meaningful. Even years spent touring the Astral capitals and smaller outposts (some as bad as Heaven's Veil, most worse, and much of the badlands between uncrossable) hadn't softened Charlie.

"Up where?"

"To the stone door."

"He didn't ..."

Charlie's eyes, in the semi-dark, speared Lila like a sword. She stopped speaking as if chastised.

"Of course not. The door weighs eleven hundred pounds even if it weren't cemented in place. I wasn't going to help him close it, and neither were the Meyers."

Lila said nothing as if he'd misunderstood. But Piper could feel her emotion, same as always, and yes, that had been her concern. Christopher wanted to close the door to keep the Astrals out. It's how Derinkuyu had been designed, he claimed, but all Lila could think of was suffocation, of the door jamming and trapping them down here forever.

"He's back," Charlie said.

Piper waited a beat for more then said, "And?"

"He says they're just sitting there."

"Who?" Lila asked.

"The Astrals. Reptars and Titans. At the choke point. They're not trying to force their way in."

"They must think we're heavily armed."

"Because that's stopped them in the past. Like the time in Roman Sands, when we still had Terrence's big gun. They still came even when the gate choked with Reptar bodies."

"Well then, why the hell do *you* think they aren't coming at us, Charlie?" Lila demanded.

Charlie's face froze. His bangs were uneven. He didn't even use a mirror to cut his hair. It just came off then piled up into a sharp-edged bowl until he looked pre-Astral Amish.

Piper willed Lila to say nothing. Thankfully, she didn't. The group had seen more than their share of arguments. There was Meyer against Kindred, Charlie against Cameron, Jeanine against everyone, and the unlikely spats where the sides were the group versus Charlie and Kindred. Charlie didn't want to be on Kindred's side any more than the man who was once Heaven's Veil's viceroy wanted to be on the side of Benjamin's stodgy and unkempt right-hand man — who, he hadn't forgotten, had urged many attacks on Heaven's Veil before its annihilation. But Charlie and Kindred were alone with their desire to go back after the Ark. Back after the archive. Back, as things had settled, to the fearful city of Ember Flats, to face what they'd fled years ago.

The air seemed to thicken as if a fog were rolling in. At first, Lila thought the lights were dying. Her second thought was that the Astrals had turned from their usual brute force and decided to attack like old-fashioned human riot police: rolling tear gas canisters into the lower levels where they'd once thought they could make their home underground, attempting to smoke them out.

But then the building mist coalesced into a dense, multicolored, shifting cloud of smoke. Then the smoke pressed itself together, and Piper found herself staring into the face of Original Meyer's late ex-wife, Heather Hawthorne.

Heather smirked but said nothing as she crossed to the doorway, toward the hallway whose end was thick with Astral soldiers that, if Christopher was to be believed, were merely waiting.

The Pall, as Heather, raised a finger and hooked it into a come-here gesture.

"I hate it when it does that," Lila said.

# Chapter Three

Jeanine was stopped at a fork in the passageway, half-stooped under the low ceiling. Cameron came up beside her. As she shone her flashlight ahead, toward the rounded hallways, the spherical room portals, and the holes and grooves in the floor and walls, he got the curious sensation of exploring the interior nooks of a natural sponge.

"It went that way." Cameron pointed to the left.

"I know where it went."

Jeanine's answer was so flat and inflectionless that Cameron gave her a moment. She was clearly processing something. Either that or being defiant for the hell of it — something Nathan Andreus had encouraged in his lieutenant even if it meant she heeded a troublesome mind of her own.

"We followed it this far," Cameron said.

"I don't take orders from the Pall."

Cameron looked at Jeanine's face, glaring at the twin passages as if deciding which to take, her jaw subtly working. If her hands hadn't been occupied, Cameron knew she'd be chewing at her short, tortured fingernails. It was how she showed nerves even though the group's fearless commando officially had none. For a second, he saw her as the woman she must have been before the Astrals arrival. She was thirty at most, and pretty beneath all the grit and strife that coated her in equal measure. She wore her need for vengeance — for Nathan, for their other friends, for all the massacred innocents in the Heaven's Veil apocalypse — like armor. Without it, Cameron suspected, Jeanine Coffey might be beautiful. Or with it, maybe more so.

"We followed it, Jeanine. You agreed."

"I don't trust it."

"It's been with us for five years."

"The Astrals don't count time like we do. It could be a long con."

But her words were bullshit. Jeanine didn't believe this was a double-cross, here and now and out of the blue. The Pall had come from the Astral mind, like Kindred had come from the Astral body. But Kindred was one of them now, and so was this silent, dark, and mysterious thing — this *purged remainder from the mind* from the first dead Meyer clone, if Kindred was to be believed. Or, if Cameron listened to his instincts, raw humanity in its natural form. This was what they all looked like once forced through the Astral filter, deemed unworthy of inclusion in their mind and forced to escape as something new.

Jeanine was just scared of the unknown and of the way things had changed. Ever since they'd seen what they had through the Ark's eye, their world had been different. It was no longer precisely humans versus aliens. The Astrals followed, yes. And sure, they killed. But despite Jeanine's claim, Cameron increasingly felt more watched than stalked. More examined than hunted.

Before Cameron could say more, Jeanine turned to him. He saw fear in her eyes, knowing she must see the same in his. Not because they were in danger — they'd been in mortal danger for nearly a decade now. Eventually fear of death became the norm, and you stopped dreading it. This was something else.

"It's never helped us, Cameron."

"It helped us in Heaven's Veil."

"It *got us out.* That's different."

Cameron wanted to argue *(How is "getting us out" not helping us?)*, but he knew exactly what she meant. And this was hardly the time to discuss it. Unless this — with the Pall beckoning them into danger with its silent understanding — was *exactly* when it mattered most.

"Who was that man, Cameron? The human I saw? How could it be Mullah if there was only one of them?"

From the left-side passage, a black-headed Reptar emerged. Slowly, and in no rush. Cameron and Jeanine ducked behind a rock wall, but it wasn't looking in their direction. If it had been a human, Cameron could almost have believed it had left the rest of its group to smoke a cigarette and pass the time.

And now here came the smoke as if plucked from Cameron's imagination.

Swirling slowly around them.

Raising Jeanine's gun arm, commanding the movement of her hand.

Jeanine looked over at Cameron, eyes wide.

The gun leveled at the Reptar.

And then the Pall squeezed Jeanine's hand in its smoky fist, pulling the trigger, shooting the Reptar in the side of its panther-like head.

"I … I didn't mean to …"

Jeanine didn't need to finish. Every Astral in the choke point was spilling toward them like hornets disturbed.

*"Run!"* Cameron shouted, bolting up from his crouch.

So they ran.

# Chapter Four

PIPER HEARD THE GUNSHOT. For a second she was back with Meyer before this had all started, in Vail when it had still been Vail, firing the slug that had ended Garth's life outside the Axis Mundi. Then she was in the cave at Mount Horeb, which Charlie said was the same as Mount Sinai, where Moses had received the Ten Commandments from God and the smashed pieces of those original judgments had once been entombed in the Ark. Where, Cameron seemed to believe, the Astral Archive birthed its most famous legend.

But then the instinctual, gut-deep memories were gone, and Piper was back in the caves with Lila and Charlie and Clara behind her, with Christopher and the Brothers Dempsey spilling from the opposite chamber.

"Was that a gun?" Christopher asked, staring at Piper.

She didn't answer. Piper was in the stone hallway where the Pall had beckoned her. She wasn't the logical leader of this party with Cameron gone but was at the group's head, all of them unsure whether to proceed or duck back into their holes.

Ahead, Piper saw Astrals. *Lots* of Astrals. Spilling away from the choke point by the huge round stone door like water down a drain. Apparently keeping Piper's group trapped was no longer interesting. Only whatever had fired the gun seemed to matter now.

*"Psst!"*

Piper's head turned. She saw a very thin, very tall man with a wispy brown mustache beyond the choke point, hiding behind a rock wall as the Astral outflow began to dissipate.

The man looked directly at Piper and waved her forward. As Reptars and Titans poured from the funnel, Piper realized she could follow. But should she? Was it the Pall again? It had vanished just before the gunshot, dissolving into a thin, nearly invisible mist so it could sneak back past the Astral blockade.

But no, she didn't think the Pall had ever sampled a thin man with a mustache. And besides, this man was making sounds, whereas the Pall was only gestures — and (when it took the effort required to maintain a shape) facial expressions.

*"Psst! This way!"*

Kindred put a hand on Piper's shoulder. Meyer, in parallel, put a hand on her other shoulder. Piper felt like a tome between matching bookends. Meyer had grown a beard and Kindred was clean shaven, but if not for the facial hair, it would have been impossible to tell them apart.

"Don't," Kindred said.

And Meyer, in Piper's other ear, said, "For once, we're in agreement."

But Piper was thinking of the Pall. It had taken form in her stone room a few minutes ago, not Meyer and Kindred's. Both Meyers seemed to have a trusting yet suspicious relationship with the Pall, not all that different from the oddly fraternal relationship they had with each other. On one hand, Kindred and Meyer had been the strongest voices for its inclusion in the group, back when they could have abandoned it at the Utah ranch. But on the other hand, it had changed since then, like everyone else. Now Piper seemed to sense it most. Piper who, despite the Pall's maddeningly neutral behavior, still believed it was around for a reason.

Whoever this man was, the Pall had known he was was out here. And it had wanted the group to find him.

"Piper!" Meyer hissed.

She slipped her shoulders from both of their warning hands. Lila was behind her, Clara at her back. The women were leading while the men stayed in the rear. They were being either bold or foolish; she'd find out which in no time.

"This way," the man repeated as Piper approached, moving toward the passage opposite the one taken by Astrals. There was a startled gasp from her back, and Lila skittered sideways, away from the body of a fallen Reptar.

The man vanished down the passage. After a moment's hesitation, Piper raised her flashlight and followed.

She almost lost their guide several times in the next sixty seconds, but he kept stopping, giving her time to follow his glow. The group was sticking close, mumbling but saying nothing, apparently having decided that anything that drew an Astral platoon away had earned benefit of the doubt. They'd been trapped; now they weren't. Maybe this strange man was trouble, but he was leading them into a lateral move at best.

"We'll wait a moment." His words were oddly formal, and Piper realized for the first time that he seemed to have a British accent.

"Why?"

He waved them back against the wall, stowing his light. Two Reptars passed.

"That's why."

"Who are you?"

"My name is Aubrey Davis."

Piper waited, but apparently he was finished.

"Why did you come for us?"

"It seemed likely that you'd steered into some trouble."

"But how … ?" She didn't even know what to ask. *What? Where? When? And why?* But she settled for the topmost question in her mind: "Who told you we were down there? How did you even—"

"My employer and I sometimes use these caves for storage. We considered using the place as sanctuary but discovered its unfortunate shortfall as you seem to have."

"Which is … ?"

"That there's only one entrance."

"We thought a single entrance would make it easier to defend."

"Yes. Well. How would you say that has worked out?"

Aubrey was looking into the hallway, still pinned around the corner. It seemed empty to Piper, but he appeared to be waiting for something.

"We heard there was a colony here. A community of humans." That was sort of a lie. In truth, Cameron had remembered the place and its honeycombed grandeur and thought its location would be a perfect place to establish residence, and for once to be able to flee the endless sun and exposure. Sure, they'd heard rumors of communities, and if others knew of Derinkuyu, it'd make a perfect spot. Especially since the Astrals were far less intent on hunting humans lately. At least everyone but the Dempsey/Bannister clan.

"We saw you go in," Aubrey told her in his crisp accent, still looking around the corner. "Unfortunately the Astrals watch this quarter as well. Often they let humans come and go, but they went right after you. Any idea why?"

*Yes, sure,* Piper thought. *We're carrying a key that we thought would deactivate an alien doomsday device. But of course, once we realized it was an archive rather than a weapon, the Astrals were no less interested in pursuit. From Little Cottonwood Canyon to Heaven's Veil to Mount Sinai to cities under Turkey, we've stayed interesting as long as we're still holding the ball.*

But on the heels of that thought were a dozen others the group had endlessly debated.

So why not leave the key behind and let them have it?

Why not smash the key so that no one could use it?

And since the Astrals seemed truly unable to open the archive without the key even after they'd followed the Heaven's Veil scream to find it, would it really be that big of a deal to just let them have it — and unarchive what they seemed to want?

Charlie arguing one way.

Cameron arguing another.

And, still present even after his death, Benjamin Bannister's ghost seemed to argue yet a different path.

"No," Piper lied. "But our group ... we got separated from—"

But now there was sound from behind them again. The Astrals had circled around, and Piper could hear them spilling upward, still in pursuit of their alien plate — the key to unlocking God knew what evidence in advance of humanity's trial.

"Brilliant," Aubrey muttered, looking back. "I do love an exciting finish."

# Chapter Five

"Stop and wait," said the man with dreadlocks.

Cameron looked at Jeanine, their lights extinguished, crouching in the dark. They'd ducked away from the pursuing Astrals, turning back to the lower floor where they'd lost Piper and the others following the strange man's appearance. He hadn't seemed surprised to see them. He was wearing the same desert robes reported by Jeanine. But this man was definitely not Mullah.

"We have to go back down," Cameron said.

*"Down?"* He actually laughed. The man had a broad, dark face and seemed like a Middle-Easterner, but his speech was clipped and precise — far higher English, Cameron thought, than his own. "From where you shot the alien? No, I don't believe so."

"I didn't — !"

Cameron raised a hand to cut Jeanine off. They didn't know who this man was, where he'd come from, or what he wanted with them. Giving him clues that might lead to the Pall — possibly still an ace in the hole — seemed like a terrible idea.

But the dreadlocked man either didn't hear her, or didn't care.

"Listen," he said. "You're lucky to have got away from there. I wasn't sure how I was going to extract you and your others without the distraction."

Meaning the gunshot. Jeanine looked up, but again Cameron's eyes silenced her.

"Our others. That's what I'm talking about. We have to find them."

"No worries. My friend was in the opposite tunnel. I followed you; he meant to go in after them."

"They could be in trouble."

"You were the ones in trouble, my friend. Still are." He seemed to perk his ears, listening for alien sounds echoing through the hallways.

Cameron flinched. Something cold touched his bare arm. It took him a moment, in the dark, to realize it had been the wet nose of a dog sitting silently by his side. A large black lab that seemed to belong to their new guide. But the dog required no instructions and behaved like a human. Cameron wasn't sure if the animal was shepherding their group of three or herding it. It seemed calm enough, but Cameron wondered if that would change if he tried something the dreadlocked man didn't want, like fleeing in pursuit of his friends.

"I have a vehicle outside. It is sufficiently hidden. You were not going to escape on foot, as we saw you come. I am fairly confident that my friend has already ushered the rest of your people from the lower level. Go back now, and you will only increase your chances for peril. I am a competitive man. If my assistant returns with a greater percentage of those he was charged to save, I will be disappointed. So please, stay close. Even one of you getting eaten takes my record down to 50 percent."

Cameron's brow furrowed. He looked past Jeanine's questioning face to the man's, but his head was still forward.

"Why are you doing this?" In Cameron's mind, nobody in the modern world acted out of kindness. They'd seen oppression in Heaven's Veil, tyranny in Roman Sands, and nothing but defensive selfishness everywhere else they'd gone. To Cameron, these caves were supposed to be a hideout for their group and their group alone. Piper held the naive belief that they might find people here — and that if they did, those people would welcome their presence instead of killing them outright as threats.

"My dog likes you."

Beside Cameron, the dog licked its lips, watching him with big, placid brown eyes.

"Come. The way is clear."

The man walked. Cameron followed first with Coffey behind him. The dog, true to the man's words, padded along silently at his side as if on a leash.

"Who are you?"

"My name is Peers."

"Is that a first or last name?"

"I prefer the allure of a single name. Like Madonna."

"What?"

"Basara," Peers said.

Cameron assumed he'd just been given the man's last name, though he could have it backward. Neither order was more obviously correct.

"Come. We need to keep moving."

Jeanine gripped Cameron's arm. Their quarters were too tight for her to say anything unheard, but the grip and her eyes broadcast enough.

And Cameron attempted to silently answer: *What's our alternative? Being killed by Astrals?*

As if in answer, a sound percolated through the stone, its direction impossible to pinpoint. Tunnels went up, down, and to all sides. Echoes formed a soup.

They moved through the nexus, past an obvious upward staircase, and to another upward staircase farther on. Each of Peers's turns had purpose as if he knew the place well. It took long minutes before they reached their first hint of daylight, and several times Cameron had been sure, based on sound, that Peers had been leading them into a den of purring Reptars. They stopped and went, ducked and trudged forward. Whenever they paused, the black dog sat at Cameron's side and looked up at him.

Peers was first up the next stairway, same as the other times, but now he stopped, peeked back down, and seemed to think.

"What is it?" Jeanine asked.

"Tell me you are accomplished runners," Peers said. "You needn't be marathoners, per se, but perhaps you enjoy a sprint over shorter distances. You know. For fun."

Instead of answering, Cameron moved past Peers and peeked up the staircase. There was a large anteroom in the rock. Past that was the cave's front entrance, and abundant sunlight beyond. They had maybe twenty yards to cover, and that wasn't a problem. The thirty or more Reptars milling the area's recesses were.

"Just a straight jaunt through the center, don't you think?" Peers said, rustling his robes as if to loosen his joints.

"You can't be suggesting ..." Cameron began.

But then Peers shot up the steps. The dog nipped Cameron's heel; then they were running. Every black alien head turned, rising from a semi-crouch and turning to follow.

They could never make it. Not in a thousand years.

The way was clear up top, but they'd be in the wide open. Reptars were faster than people in a straight sprint. They'd be pinned seconds after arriving topside. Then the Astrals would steal the archive key or kill them. Probably both.

But when Cameron arrived in the sun with Peers, Jeanine, and the dog ahead of him, he saw Piper standing off to one side. A reinforced vehicle that had once been a Honda Accord screamed toward him from the other side.

Cameron dodged just in time. The car missed him by two feet at most then gunned hard at the cave entrance. There was a crunch, a bang, and a visible poof of white airbags as the car's front end smashed into a hole in the hillside. No glass shattered; the car had no windshield or windows.

A thin man was unbuckling, pushing at the deflating airbag and extricating himself from the smashed vehicle with amusing delicacy. When he finally jumped from the trunk end to the ground, Cameron saw that he had a small mustache and was wearing a crash helmet.

Peers took Cameron and Coffey by the arm and led them toward Piper and the others — who, it turned out, were standing in front of what looked like an armor-reinforced urban tank that might once have been a city bus. He nodded toward the man with the helmet.

"That's Aubrey," Peers said. "But I wouldn't talk to him right now. He'll be peeved about losing his car whether he volunteered it or not."

"But—"

Toward the bus's door. Shoved inside while the man called Aubrey shooed Meyer, Kindred, and Clara in from an added entrance on its other side.

"You'd better have your ticket out and ready to be stamped," Peers told them.

Up the steps. Into what was, yes, indeed a converted

bus armed with gun turrets. Studded with spikes and wrapped in razor wire.

"I'm just kidding," Peers said. "We don't stamp tickets anymore."

The engine revved as the man with the mustache plopped into the driver's seat. Peers stood beside him, holding a vertical handrail. The bus lurched. Swung in a half circle. Then peeled out through ancient stone streets and hills while the Astrals poked futilely around their new prison's plugged hole, their spherical silver shuttle hovering without a pilot nearby.

After the rattling streets gave way to open roads, Cameron finally peeled his eyes, steeped in terror, from the windows.

Then he turned and saw that someone was already sitting beside him.

It was the dog.

# Chapter Six



THE TRAVELERS WOULDN'T SLEEP.

That didn't surprise Peers. When he and Aubrey had first made their way out of London, in the occupation's earliest days, a charismatic man named Saul had taken them into what turned out to be more cult than caravan. Peers hadn't slept for the first night they'd been in Saul's too-good-to-be-true protection, nor had he slept on the second. Not since university had he stayed up for so many hours, and the longer he'd stayed awake, the greater his paranoia. Sleep was the enemy. If he'd lowered his guard, something awful would happen. But as luck had it, something horrible had happened anyway, and the next day Peers and Aubrey were back on their own with blood soaking their clothing and hands.

He understood why Cameron and the others didn't sleep, and why the one they called Kindred seemed so uncertain of him. To Peers, Kindred looked exactly like Meyer Dempsey, Heaven's Veil's supposedly dead viceroy. That would have been fine if not for the group's second Meyer Dempsey — this one simply called "Meyer." But

Peers thought he knew what this was. Astrals were shapeshifters. It seemed that Kindred had once been Astral, and was now stuck in human form. Surely he'd eye Peers with a raised brow, but no matter his suspicions he wouldn't truly know anything beyond the fact that Peers wasn't Astral.

It would take time. And that was fine.

A half hour expired, and the questions got started. They asked Peers how he knew they were in Derinkuyu when they really wanted to know why he was looking for them in the first place, especially the farther they got from the ancient Cappadocian city. Hours passed, and it was obvious that the honeycomb was far from Peers's home base. *Why* had he and his assistant trucked all the way out to that specific point to rather coincidentally save them? If pressed, he'd tell them he knew they had the archive key, and that the Astrals were after it. But he wouldn't say anything until he had to. Secrets had to be rationed.

Evening slowly replaced afternoon. The crew became restless, unwilling to close their eyes despite obvious fatigue. Perhaps it was dawning on them that their saviors had captured them, too. They weren't in chains and Peers wouldn't use force to hold them, but those on the bus had entered a quiet standoff. While the vehicle was in motion, everyone on board was more or less stuck. All eyes seemed to be weighing the situation, frying pan versus fire. They could ask to get off, yes. But why? The outlands offered no cover, and Peers had given no reason to doubt his intentions.

Except for his and Aubrey's appearance being so highly, *highly* coincidental.

Peers shifted attention between his new charges and the road. The Den was another half hour away, and the only customs or border patrols still in these parts were those that wandered everywhere, regardless of the old, pre-Astral map. And besides, he had help keeping this stretch clean, so Peers had little reason to worry. They'd be there soon — no need to press things beforehand.

But something itched at him. Something that felt forgotten. He'd known the group's composition, and they were all now in the bus. Kindred; Meyer; Cameron Bannister and his apparent wife, Piper; Meyer's daughter, Lila; and her obviously Lightborn daughter, Clara. The blue-eyed man with the dark stubble seemed to be with Lila, and though Peers wasn't good with names, he seemed to remember their brief introductions naming him Christopher. There was a stern-faced man in a button-up shirt and brown slacks named Charlie, and the hard-edged woman with the brown ponytail was the group's militant: Janet, or something.

And that was everyone. All the spotters had seen — everyone Peers had background on, if he cared enough to look.

So why did he feel like something had been left behind? Something that might come back to bite him?

And why, several times now, did he seem to see something in the corner of his eye, like an animal running along beside the bus?

"You know us, don't you?"

Peers felt his attention snap. He looked down to see the little girl. Glancing back, he saw her mother watching them both from a few rows back. Clara was seated across the aisle from Peers, watching him with unconcerned eyes.

"I do now." Peers tried to affect a smile, but Lightborn gazes were so unsettling. Rumor had it they could talk across distances. Intuit the future. Peers believed it, too. In the past, Astral incursions had resulted in highly spiritual societies that connected mind to mind. Ironic that in the modern world it had taken drug users to open those particular doors to the aliens.

"But you knew us before. You knew we were in those caves."

"We saw you go in." Peers regretted the words as he said them. He was treating Clara as if she were a seven-year-old kid because she biologically was one. But Clara was big for her age, seeming almost preteen. And there was nothing naive or innocent about her eyes.

"My mom didn't want to ask you, but I know you won't mind answering."

"Okay. Shoot."

"Why haven't the Astrals followed us?"

"Because we plugged them in with Aubrey's car."

"Damn right we did," Aubrey muttered from the driver's seat.

"But there should be others. They think in a network. Why didn't they call to another shuttle and follow us?"

"I assume we got lucky." But Peers could hear the tone of his voice. *This isn't a child,* he told himself. *Not in any of the ways that matter.*

Clara appeared to chew on the statement. He'd never seen a Lightborn so close. Never had a conversation with one. Supposedly children born near Astral network hubs, in those vital early days, weren't entirely impossible to find, though they were definitely rare. He'd researched, sure. But nothing could prepare him for Clara's assessing stare. Some rumors said they could read minds. Was it true, or just more bullshit mysticism?

"We've been lucky," Clara said.

"Exactly."

"I mean all along. Every day."

"Nobody's lucky all the time."

"I suppose not," Clara said. "My dad and grandma

died in Heaven's Veil. Lots of our friends, too. Even some of the people who got out of the city died later, like it didn't matter. A policeman, Chief Jons. And this girl, named Grace. It's been hard since we left."

"I see."

Clara's head tilted. Then, without accusation, she said, "See? You do know who we are."

"I do?"

"Well, you're not surprised that we came from Heaven's Veil. Or that we crossed the ocean."

"Maybe I just hide it well." Peers meant it as a joke, but the girl just kept watching him.

"You don't hide anything particularly well. I can feel your surprise." Then the girl did something that made Peers jump in his seat. She reached across the aisle and touched the back of his hand.

"If you let me in, we can get to know each other more easily."

With the girl's words, Peers felt the most curious sensation, like someone palming his brain, squeezing it gently, curious about what was inside.

"My mom doesn't trust you …" She trailed off, waiting for Peers to repeat his name.

"Peers."

"*Peers,*" Clara repeated. But he was sure she'd known it already, and that this was a link in a long chain of subtle manipulation. Some of the region's guerrillas were excellent at building false trust, and this felt the same. "She doesn't trust you. But you don't scare me, Peers."

"That's good. I'm not a scary person."

"If you let me in," she said as the gentle pressure inside his skull reasserted itself, "I can tell that to the others, and they'll believe me."

Peers flexed a tiny interior muscle. He felt Clara's

probing mental hand forced back.

"I'd really rather not. Nothing personal. But I believe intentions are best demonstrated the old-fashioned way."

He thought Clara might protest — or possibly sound an alarm that their abductor was not to be trusted — but instead her body relaxed and the hand retreated, both from atop his own and from inside his mind. Then she was just another girl, half-slouched in the seat across from him.

"It's Clara, right?" he said.

Clara nodded.

"I'll tell you a secret if you'd like."

"Do I have to keep it quiet?"

"Only if you choose to."

"Then it's not much of a secret, is it?"

"That's for you to decide."

Clara straightened, clearly interested.

"I do know who you are. And I did know you were in that cave."

He thought Clara might react with suspicion, but she merely raised her eyebrows quizzically. Their voices were low, and the row behind them was empty. This truly was a secret for as long as Clara wished it to be.

"I have friends who know far more than I do. I met many of them in England, while at Oxford."

"I've never been to London," Clara said, somehow delighted by the notion of another strange land.

"It used to be a beautiful place, like your Heaven's Veil. And my friends, they shared many images when the Internet was still open and free. Some small computer networks — not many, but some — are still active. And my friends, they told us about you."

"What did they tell you?"

Peers nodded toward the back of the bus.

"That man there is Cameron Bannister. His father was

Benjamin Bannister."

"He still has nightmares about his father."

Somehow Peers felt sure that she wasn't speaking from conversations with Cameron or overheard nighttime voices but as someone who'd sampled those dreams in her mind.

"Benjamin was an important man. He sent a lot of information to my friends. And so we know." Peers paused, reminding himself that Clara had probably already figured out what he was about to admit. "We know about the key Cameron found. To the Ark."

"Oh," Clara said.

"That doesn't surprise you? I'm doing my best with this secret, you know." He put on a playful smile, but Clara only returned it out of obligation.

"Is that why you came? Have you been following us? Did you help us escape the Astrals because of the key?"

"Partially," Peers said. "But there are other reasons. Your grandfather, there, for instance? He knows things that my friends might very much like to hear, about the Astrals."

Clara finally laughed, pointing away from where Peers held his finger.

"*That's* my grandfather. The other one is Kindred."

"See, Clara? This is why it's good we've met."

"Kindred used to be one of them. But they changed him. He's let me in, all the way. So I know he can still sense the Astrals, but I also know he can't go back, or maybe *wouldn't* go back. His body could change if it wanted, but he's human now in all the ways that count, and so he won't ever do it. He's angry, and would never join them again."

"What's he angry about?"

"The Astrals killed his son. My uncle. And they killed my grandma. He used to be married to her a long time ago."

"But wasn't it Meyer's son? The human Meyer? And it was the human Meyer who was married to your grandmother."

Clara shook her head. "It doesn't matter. They're the same person, inside and out. He's the same as my grandpa. They *both* married my grandma. They *both* had a son who was killed."

"That must make for strange family reunions."

"They both were married to Grandma Piper," Clara said, as if this explained the situation, or gave it a finer point. "And now that she's married to Cameron, they both still love her."

Peers decided not to pry. He should keep his distance from these people, hard as it would be.

"So that's why you're here." Clara's hands were folded in her lap and she'd looked down while speaking, as if some horrid realization had dawned, and turned her into a child again.

"Why do you feel I'm here?" Peers asked.

"To make us go back."

"Back where?"

"To the Ark."

"*Back?*" Peers repeated. "So you've been there before? To Ember Flats?"

Clara's brow wrinkled, looking as though she didn't know where the Astrals had taken the Archive after they'd followed its scream to Mount Sinai, where the Templars had stowed it — probably with some sense of historical irony. But everyone knew the Ark was in Ember Flats. If the world had a logo these days, that was it: the Ark on its enormous stone plinth in the city's center, waiting to be unlocked like Excalibur waiting to be pulled from the stone. Peers had friends who'd tried to protect the Ark in its old location, to beat the Astrals to it once it had screamed with Heaven's Veil's death, as a tidal wave of agony had rushed toward the ancient recording device. But you didn't need to have seen it carted off to know its location. The Astrals weren't hiding it. Anyone who could fight their way into Ember Flats could walk right up to the thing and touch it.

"No. We went to the old place."

"To Mount Horeb?"

Clara nodded. "Cameron and his dad thought of it as Mount Sinai, but yes."

Peers was floored. The scholars had been right all along. The Bannisters had found the key where the Templars had hidden it, and they'd reached the similarly hidden Ark before the Astrals had triangulated on the Heaven's Veil scream. Some claimed the Bannister group didn't actually reach the Ark first, and that the Astrals had stepped out of the way to let them at it. Only the Mullah would have stood in their way, and if Clara was telling the truth, they'd actually made it.

They'd reached the Ark. They'd stood in front of it in its ancient resting place and the birthplace of its legend.

But if that was true, why was the key still unused in Bannister's satchel?

Before Peers could ask for more, he he saw Clara's hands knot more rapidly in her lap and a tear drip down her cheek.

She looked up. "Don't take us to the Ark, Mr. Peers. Anything but that."

He looked from the girl to the road ahead then toward the side of the bus where something again seemed to race past in the corner of his eye.

"We'll be at my place soon," Peers told her, his gut somehow troubled. "And then we can rest."

# Chapter Seven

Piper looked across the aisle at Lila then at Clara asleep against her mother's side. Lila looked over, but the two women said nothing. There was a quiet spell over the bus.

Nobody seemed to know if they'd done the right or wrong thing in climbing aboard. There'd always been a 50/50 chance that the junker who'd ferried them to the ancient city would have stuck around as Cameron had asked, and those odds had grown substantially worse, Piper felt sure, when the shuttle full of Astrals had plopped its fat silver body down at the cave's mouth. Maybe the aliens had killed the man out of hand. But more likely, he'd simply run back to his quasi-legal business and left their group stranded.

They were supposed to be able to live there. Either the underground city was occupied by the rumored community, or it was empty, in which case their motley crew would have made it home for a while — far enough from their troubles to almost forget them, never close enough to their old homes overseas to merit much fussing. Piper felt sure she'd die over here somewhere — maybe soon, or maybe in decades. Either way she'd seen the last of America. It was silly to let that bother her. There wasn't any America anymore, anyway.

Piling into Peers's armored bus had been their only option. He and Aubrey seemed like respectable enough men. Even the dog — Nocturne — had spent a good portion of the trip patrolling the aisles, licking hands to welcome the visitors, curled up on the floor beside Charlie, who turned out to have a surprising fondness for animals. Better with them than humans, anyway.

Clara blinked awake as if feeling Piper's glance. Lila looked over as well. Piper didn't need to see their eyes to sense their emotions. The feeling was bone deep.

"Have a good nap, kiddo?" Piper asked.

Clara nodded against Lila's side. It would have been easy, in this moment, to believe Clara was just another seven-year-old kid. But it wasn't Clara's simple nod that stopped her. It was her own use of the word "kiddo." An older one of her words — one she'd sometimes used with Trevor, back before the world had gone sour.

"Saw you talking to Mr. Peers before."

"It's just Peers, Piper."

Piper let a smile touch her lips. It was so easy to speak to Clara like a child, but she seldom replied as one.

"What did you talk about?"

"Nothing."

Piper turned to Cameron, on her other side. She was about to speak, but Cameron was already in her head.

"My gut says he's safe," he said.

"Think so, do you?"

"They let us keep our weapons. There are seven adults in our group and only two of them. And we still have ..." He trailed off, ticking his head toward the window, seeming to indicate the silent and only probable presence of the

Pall outside. "That dog's not exactly a killer, either. So if Peers intends to shanghai us, he's not going about it intelligently. And he did get us out of there."

"He could be Mullah."

Cameron patted his satchel, which still contained the stone disk. "If he were Mullah, he would have already taken what we have."

"You sure about that?"

Cameron's hand moved to his chest. He probably didn't even realize what he was doing, but Piper had spotted him doing it more and more as they retraced the old archaeological stomping grounds he'd once trod with his father. He was touching that charm he wore around his neck, the old coin with the square hole in its center, dangling from a leather lanyard. The coin Charlie had found in the tiny cache of Benjamin's belongings, and Cameron had pounced upon like Gollum to his Precious.

"I'm sure."

But he wasn't. He didn't know more than any of them.

Cameron took Piper's hand. "All I know is that Derinkuyu was a bad end. If Peers says he has a hideout and wants to take us there, maybe it'll be what we need."

Piper wasn't as sure. Derinkuyu hadn't been a bad end until the aliens had poured inside it. And nothing about the encounter felt entirely right. The Astrals' pursuit felt wrong, seeing as they'd already gone to the archive and then let them be. And the way they'd simply backed off, after pinning them in the caves? That didn't feel right, either. The sudden and fortuitous appearance of their rescuers was another itch atop many. But as the Astrals worked with the remaining capitals and the mind network had strengthened, coincidence had become more the norm than an oddity.

Piper let it go, watching the parched land surrender to

even more withered, shriveled desert. There were no gangs, no marauders, no pirate groups come to steal their precious weapons and fuel. But that was another question: Unless Peers had shady connections, how did he get the gas required to drive his rig?

They saw no other vehicles despite the rumors of this land being a hotspot. They saw no shuttles. They'd have easily been visible from space. Before the Astrals had recalled the shuttle Kindred used to ferry them across the ocean, they'd at least had the benefit of traveling like the aliens. Nowadays, expeditions required stealth, stowing away in known and innocuous vehicles. Nowadays it required luck. Why Astral eyes had no interest in this death wagon, Piper had no clue.

But they reached a cliffside without incident, then both men were leaving the bus to raise a camouflage drape. There was some sort of a stronghold beyond, and to Piper it looked like something hollowed out and made to work rather than something discovered. There were large metal doors, inexpertly jammed into the rock, edges crumbling around the periphery. There was a mass of circuitry half hanging in a small alcove to one side, not even properly bolted down. Thick cables ran from the back. And judging by the spotlights — dim in the daytime — that had lit with their approach, the place had plenty of power.

Aubrey drove the bus through the entrance as the doors peeled open, killing the engine once they'd entered a cavernous, hollowed-out space like a garage missing its front, spilling out into what could only be described as a massive cave. But this wasn't like Derinkuyu, thousands of years old and etched by time. This was something natural, recently expanded, and held up from collapse by what seemed to be nothing more than positive thinking.

Peers did something more at the panel, and the doors

closed behind them. He rushed back and dropped the camouflage drape, scampering through the doors before they sealed. Piper was reminded of their bunker under Meyer's old Axis Mundi, back when there'd only been one of him. That bunker was polished, not roughly assembled as this one appeared to be. But then again, look how it had turned out.

Peers reappeared at the bus door then climbed the three stairs to stand at the front of the long aisle like a guide about to give excursion instructions to a group of tourists.

"Welcome, my friends," he said, "to the Den."

# Chapter Eight

THEY WATCHED LILA, Piper, and Clara file out. They were preceded by Christopher (who seemed to feel a manly need to protect them and go first) and Jeanine Coffey (who, as the group's fiercest member, seemed to resent Christopher's gallant but misguided chivalry). Charlie and Cameron took the rear, discussing Benjamin's research and wondering aloud what this place was or had ever been. Peers's Den was too large, Charlie said, to have been carved with human tools, its throat held open without visible girders. But they only mumbled, and Cameron shooed Charlie from behind, seemingly as concerned with appearing rude as with getting to the bottom of whatever truth might be waiting.

Then Kindred, upon setting his feet on the Den's rough rock floor, yanked Meyer back and began speaking fast and low. He spoke to Meyer without thinking — Peers had been told that when the two of them went deep; their dialect was practically another language. A shorthand with higher context, silent but forever present between them. Piper had told them as much during their failed triad

59

marriage. Sometimes Kindred wondered if it wasn't the impossibility of three-way love that stymied Piper's heart so much as a conviction that she was being deliberately excluded from what passed between her husbands.

"This is Astral," Kindred told Meyer.

"Are you saying — ?"

"Peers isn't Astral. I would know."

"And Aubrey?"

"No."

"Nocturne?"

"Not the dog."

"Where is it?"

Anyone listening would probably assume Meyer was asking for the dog's whereabouts, but Kindred saw a deductive flash inside his mind. It wasn't really telepathy so much as the product of identical brains reaching uniform conclusions.

*The Pall. Where is the Pall?*

"I haven't seen it."

"Can't you feel it? You're one of them."

Kindred hit Meyer lightly in the chest. It wasn't actually an assault. It was another of their two-bodies, single-mind bits of shorthand. Sometimes Kindred felt that he wasn't really himself; he was half of a larger whole. The truth, he suspected, was that both things were true.

The jab said, *I'm not Astral, and you know that because you're half of me, so stop being an asshole because it makes me half an asshole, too.* It felt to Kindred — and to Meyer, according to the times Kindred sampled his thoughts — like slapping your right hand with your left when it reached for a cookie it wasn't supposed to take.

"I can't feel it. I've never *felt* it."

"Do you think *he* felt it?"

Meaning the other Meyer. The first copy, before

Kindred's creation. The Meyer whom Raj had shot dead, whose unfurling humanity and conflicting emotion had first torn into the Astral consciousness. Divinity believed it had purged the troublesome human doublethink from the Astral stream before creating Kindred. But that's not what happened. The rift remained then spread. Five years had been plenty of time for the Astral hive mind to occasionally face its emotions with all the tools of a moody adolescent.

*And* it had created the Pall. The waste squeezed from Meyer Dempsey's mindstream was supposed to have gone nowhere, but it hadn't. Those "problematic" emotional bits had become their own thing, refusing to die. Once outside the Astral collective, those leftover bits had taken shape. But the Pall, like everything, had changed since Sinai.

Kindred and Meyer (and the conjoined thing that emerged as Kindred-Meyer) sometimes wondered if the Pall was now something new. Something that spoke to the archive like the scream through Heaven's Veil's death.

"It's irrelevant," Kindred answered. "It's what drove the unspooling. It helps us."

Meyer looked into Kindred's eyes. The glance said a thousand things.

"But this place," Kindred continued. "I can practically feel their hands on it."

"The power, you mean?"

"The structure. The way it was built. The movement of giant objects, like the sandstone in the pyramids. There is no capital in Turkey."

"Of course not."

"But you agree this is recent."

Meyer nodded. "It's recent."

"Why would they have carved it? Where does Peers draw his power from?"

"Generators."

"Who refines his fuel?"

"He must trade for it." Meyer's manner had become clipped, short, much like the old Meyer. He was impatient; Kindred could feel it from the inside. But between the two of them, neither was in charge.

"He knows we have the key."

"Of course he knows."

"Do you feel that he wants it?" Kindred asked.

"Feeling is your thing."

"But reasoning is *ours*."

"I don't know," Meyer answered, running a hand over his salt-and-pepper beard. "I don't have enough information."

"You have all the same information that I do."

Now Meyer seemed outright annoyed. The rest of the group had moved away, following Peers and Aubrey. Soon they'd be conspicuous in their absence.

"If you want to know so badly, call home to the mothership."

Kindred didn't bother responding. Meyer knew perfectly well that although Kindred could sense Astral hands and sniff out shapeshifters in disguise, he could only feel the collective in the slightest of ways. His jab was purely human — the kind of verbal weapon he'd often used when they'd been fighting for Piper's primary favor, before they'd given it up and made the torturous decision to let Cameron offer Piper his hand.

"I need your half," Kindred said.

"I have nothing to offer," Meyer replied, his eyes still on the departing group.

"Does it make human sense to you, Meyer?"

"Does it make human sense to *you, Meyer*?" Meyer spat back.

"There's no need to become emotional."

"There sure isn't, *Meyer.*"

Kindred bit his tongue. He was as much Meyer as Meyer Dempsey himself. He knew, intellectually, that he hadn't grown up as a human boy, that he hadn't created and run several successful businesses or produced many major films, that he hadn't loved Heather before loving Piper. Those things made logical sense, but he still didn't believe them on the deepest level. And Meyer's impatience, imperiousness, and temper was part of that same mental stew. Together, Meyer and Kindred formed a sort of mortal super-being. But that didn't stop Meyer from being an arrogant cocksucker — or make Kindred want to resist being an arrogant asshole right back.

"I don't sense danger," Kindred said, forcing a slow breath, trying to find an elusive center. Piper thought it was both hilarious and adorable, but the two men had taken up meditation to soften the sharpest edges of their mutual tempers. It was the only way they could survive each other — necessary since each was more or less half of the other.

When Kindred looked at Meyer, he saw that the other man was also slowing his breath, to calm the argument just the same.

"I don't necessarily assume danger either," Meyer said. "But I do intuit a secret being kept. And I'd urge caution."

Kindred couldn't help but look back at the large metal doors — doors that Peers and Aubrey couldn't have moved into place by themselves.

"Caution," he repeated.

But even as they turned to follow the group, Kindred couldn't help feeling that caution was futile. They were inside with the doors locked, one cave-born trap potentially traded for another.

# Chapter Nine

The Den was intimidating.

Cameron tried to play it cool as if none of this were a big deal, but he couldn't keep his eyes from looking around. And because the place was so massive — in area, yes, but also in height — his head had to ferry his eyes where they wanted to go. He surely looked like a slack-jawed tourist seeing the big city for the first time. It didn't matter. The Den was fascinating. It demanded attention, and if he had to appear a naive dullard to take in all there was, then so be it.

Immediately, Cameron was reminded of the ranch his father and Charlie had built inside the rock face in Moab, Utah. The Den was stuffed with scientific equipment, all of it lighting up and flashing, occasionally beeping and churning, vast wet benches like the one Charlie and his assistants used to man while searching for evidence of panspermia. Peers told the group as he toured them around that he'd been obsessed with aliens since before aliens were a genuine thing — and that, too, reminded Cameron of his father. He could imagine their dreadlocked leader in his desert robes like a Benjamin Bannister of a different flavor: drawn to ancient aliens sites, both men mildly (or clinically) obsessed with solving some of the world's oldest mysteries. Peers told them about excursions in his youth to predictable sites like the Giza pyramids and the Sphinx, alongside lesser-known sites like Palenque, and modern-day curiosities like the Coral Castle and the Georgia Guidestones.

Cameron recognized every one of the names. He'd forgotten so much, but Benjamin's notebooks — pulled from the same Bannister souvenir stash as the coin he now wore around his neck — helped him to remember. Part was practical: knowledge needed to defeat the Astral menace back when he'd believed that were possible. But most was penance, flogging himself with his father's obvious, after-the-fact veracity, weighed heavy against Teenage Cameron's skepticism, shame, and venomous resentment.

But the Den differed from the Utah lab in three obvious ways.

The first was its sheer size. Moab had been a modest lab with a house of about the same square footage across a small lawn — the Den was a flat-out Bat Cave. Titanic, with high ceilings, hints of fathomless depths below, and a footprint that seemed to sprawl forever.

The second was its depth of equipment and supply. Plenty of the Den seemed to be quarters and shared spaces devoid of gadgets, but the enormous central space, like an elongated blimp hangar, was edge-to-edge with consoles, detectors, and God knew what else. All of it was on, functioning as if Middle East Electric still sent this place a generous 120-volt supply line — or whatever the voltage had once been in this part of the world. Moab, by comparison, had felt like Geppetto's wood shop.

But the third and most disquieting difference between

the Den and Benjamin's old lab was that no one seemed to be present. Just Peers, Aubrey, and Nocturne the lab. Of the three of them, only Aubrey — with his upright manner, crisp London accent, and tidy mustache — looked like he belonged. Moab had been entirely different. While up and running, the lab had been fully staffed: assistants, techs, the apocalypse equivalent of graduate students, even nomads who'd ended up joining the lab by default, like Ivan and his team of militants. But here there was no team.

"We found this place eight months ago," Peers said as they moved from the huge central space into a smaller, cozier conference-type area — where, thankfully, his voice finally shed its echo. "Aubrey and I had been wandering, as I gather you have. We'd been up near Ankara, headed south toward the Israeli coast. We had no specific aims beyond the obvious: the cradle of civilization, the Holy Land ... searching for who knows what to aid us in our Astral quest. Then one day we saw this portal in the rock, and came closer. The doors were open. We added locks to make it more secure, but otherwise the place is as we found it. Something they made, then abandoned."

"Just like that?" Jeanine asked.

Peers nodded, unfazed by her obvious doubt. "Just like that. We've swept it in every way we know. Got the power back up. It's possible they're still monitoring this place, but I see no reason why. So we took it over. And now all of this equipment? It's ours to monitor what we can. To watch *them*, for a change."

"What do you 'watch'?" Piper asked.

"That's a question for later. For now, all that matters is that it's home, with beds to lie upon and food to eat. Security so you can properly rest."

"But is it ... networked?" Cameron asked, thinking of

the past and things long forgotten. If any place had a way to reach the outside world — not that they needed it much these days — the Den was it.

"Not in the way you mean, unfortunately," Peers said, pursing his lips in a miniature frown. We had a network for a while, but not since I've been here. It was back in my Oxford days, when Aubrey served as my assistant. Years ago, when the Internet was still chugging along."

Peers raised an eyebrow as if not yet finished. And maybe there was more, Cameron thought. It seemed likely that the Internet would have eventually died under Astral occupation given that the aliens didn't seem to get it, but that very understanding — the Astrals wanting to investigate humanity's "external brain," according to what Piper said the monks in Heaven's Veil had told her — might have kept it going if Terrence hadn't botched the network for everyone. The Canned Heat virus had opened a tiny window and might have enabled Peers's friends to talk to Cameron's. But over time Canned Heat had won, and the Astrals alongside decreasingly numerous human techs had lost. The world's information net had darkened again. So the blackout Peers was lamenting? Cameron might have had a hand in it. He might have been on the side of the man who'd unleashed the virus, and caused the collapse.

"It's time I admit something to all of you," Peers said, meeting Cameron's eyes as if tasting the flavor of his thoughts. He looked at Clara then back at Cameron. "I've been following you, using the means at my disposal." His eyes took in the space around him. "And when I came to those caves, it wasn't entirely coincidental, though it was fortuitous. The truth is, I've been *hoping* to meet you."

Jeanine flinched. Her hand hitched toward her weapon, then she relaxed, catching herself. They were all scarred by time, and Jeanine always ticked for her gun.

Cameron had made that mistake once, and wouldn't make it again.

"My friends were in contact with a group in America that I believe you may represent. We were part of what was once thought of optimistically as a worldwide resistance. I was always skeptical of that way of thinking: that we needed to *resist* the Astrals. But you remember how things were back then."

"I remember the ship that destroyed Heaven's Veil," Piper said, her voice uncharacteristically cold.

"And you know why it did that," Peers said. "Don't you?"

Cameron watched Piper. She said nothing, but Charlie came unexpectedly to life and answered for her.

"They wanted to find the judgment archive."

"That's right," Peers said. "Before the network went dark, our circle was sharing such a conclusion. It wasn't clear if you'd reached the same deduction at first, when we lost sight of you and then communication with each other."

"We figured it out," Charlie said.

"*I* figured it out," Kindred corrected.

Cameron remembered that, too. Kindred had piloted their shuttle eastward for as long as his all-too-human shock response buoyed him, but then the wave struck and laid the man flat. Kindred was human now, but had shared most of the Astral mind at the time. The *scream* had nearly overwhelmed him.

"I've never understood this part of events," said Aubrey, entering the room. Cameron was amused to see him holding what appeared to be a cup of tea.

Charlie watched Peers. He seemed to be assessing the man, determining if this was a ploy to make their group divulge something they shouldn't. But there were no true secrets anymore. They knew, and the Astrals knew that they knew.

"The Ark," said Peers, seeing Charlie's hesitation. "You know about the Ark. That it is an archive of humanity."

"Human *events*," Charlie clarified. "Thoughts. Emotions."

"So why destroy Heaven's Veil?" Aubrey asked.

Charlie looked from Peers to Cameron. His eyes were suspicious. But then again, Charlie was always suspicious.

"You don't trust me," Peers said.

"It's hard to trust anyone," Cameron replied. "Charlie's just being cautious."

Peers settled back in what seemed to be a transplanted wooden chair. His glance invited the others to join him around the heavy table, but only Clara did.

"The man we were in touch with in America," Peers said. "His name was Benjamin Bannister. He sent a group out to a location believed to contain an important relic hidden by the Templars. A sort of key."

"Interesting," Cameron said. Peers raised his eyebrows, but Cameron refused to bite at the man's dangling bait.

Peers shrugged. "I met Benjamin once. In person, in Tunisia, on a dig. We retired for drinks afterward and had a nice long chat."

"Hmm. Good for you."

"It's an interesting charm you carry," Peers said.

Cameron blinked at the sudden change in topic. "What?"

Peers stood from his chair and stepped forward. "May I?"

Before Cameron could answer or ask for clarification, Peers reached out and pulled the leather lanyard from Cameron's neck into the open. He set the small coin on its end into the cup of his palm. He eyed it for a moment, then his brown eyes went to his face. "Benjamin told me his work was his greatest accomplishment, and that he was proud of it."

Cameron felt the leather tug at the back of his neck. He wanted to back away, but the moment was too awkward, and everyone was watching.

"He was driven."

"He confessed to a single regret: that he always put work before family. In Tunisia, Benjamin showed me a coin. A coin like this one." Peers turned it over, inspecting its back. "And he told me, 'This is my ball and chain.'"

Cameron swallowed. He'd heard his father use the phrase in Moab but assumed it was in jest, the way Benjamin joked about most things. He was talking about Charlie as weighing him down, maybe. But as Cameron thought back, he recalled the way his father had always seemed on the edge of saying more, reaching into his pocket whenever he said it, as if his fingers sought the object of his expression.

Cameron had never asked Charlie where, specifically, he'd found the coin that had made its way into Benjamin's belongings. Or what it might have meant to his father between the day they'd found it and the one when Cameron had run a lanyard through the coin and hung it around his own neck.

"He told me a story. About the coin he wouldn't even let me hold and see. He said that he'd offered it to his son in spite, during a moment of anger. The coin was meant as a token for his boy. A souvenir of the fact that the son was bullheaded and could never admit when he didn't know which path to follow or which choice to make. But after the boy left, Benjamin said he found it on his dresser. And he took it for himself and had carried it every day since."

Cameron had never heard this part of the story. "Why?" he said, before managing to stop himself.

"He said, 'It wasn't my son who needed the reminder to be humble — to admit when he was over his head and had no idea what to do next. It's me who needs it, and that means it's my burden to carry.'"

Cameron swallowed.

"It's your choice whether or not to trust me. And if you are not sure which path to take ..." Peers let go of the coin, and it fell against Cameron's shirt like a nudge. "Then believe me, Cameron Bannister: of all people, having met your father and hearing his story, I will understand."

# Chapter Ten

Charlie found Cameron alone, outside the Den in the desiccated land, around the corner from the doors, as night approached with the unblemished and cloudless sky stretching overhead. It was cold. A few in the party had seen Cameron leave, but none had asked why or where he was going. Peers had made it obvious that the doors were closed, not locked. An unspoken agreement shivered through the group: some unknown ball had rolled into Cameron's court, and all anyone could do was to wait for him to decide whether to hit it back.

"It's in Ember Flats," Charlie said.

Cameron looked up. He was sitting in a plastic chair, wrapped in a blanket. It was a pouting, petulant little nest he'd made himself. He couldn't stay out here and knew it. Maybe they *were* free to go, not pinned in the cave. But what option, other than staying and joining this new cause, was there? To sleep in the sands and freezing? To keep on wandering — with no direction in mind beyond *away*?

Cameron didn't bother to ask what Charlie was refer-ring to. This was far from the first time he'd brought it up.

"I know it's in Ember Flats."

"Peers knows we have the key."

"Good for Peers."

"It's why he's been watching and following us."

"I thought it was because he was my father's best friend?"

Charlie took a long look at Cameron. Then, seeming to reach an incredibly difficult decision, he pulled over another plastic chair from near the rock and sat beside him. His posture didn't look remotely comfortable. He sat ramrod straight, head high, knees together, hands on thighs. Whatever Charlie was affecting, it was an attempt at something unnatural. A parody of companionship, trying to be friendly in a way he'd seen in a video, or read in an instruction manual.

"Nobody knew Benjamin better than me."

"Charlie, I'm—"

"*Nobody,*" Charlie interrupted. "You spent the first part of your life tolerating him and trying to get away. Once I caught wind of his reputation, I spent most of my time trying to work with him then hooked my wagon to his. I'm a good partner to the right person. I'm not as good on my own."

Cameron looked over at Charlie in the dim, seeing his neutral, forward-facing stare. There was a single exterior light on the Den, and Cameron had the distinct impression Peers was only allowing it to pacify Cameron. It wasn't wise to draw attention, even out in the middle of nowhere.

"I keep telling you," Charlie continued, "that Benjamin wanted us to find the archive."

"We *found* the archive."

"Find it and unlock it," Charlie corrected. "The Templars separated the key and the Ark for a reason, but it was to keep them both away from Astrals, not human hands."

"You can't know that. You saw what happened at Sinai." He looked at Charlie, trying to imagine emotion in the stoic man. "You even *felt* it, same as the rest of us."

"You can't let your personal baggage get in the way of—"

"Then *you* take it, Charlie! You and Peers. Take the key and march right into Ember Flats and complete my father's exalted mission. Peers showed me some of his satellite imagery. If I had to guess, he's like Nathan — one of the privileged few the Astrals granted access and control so they could keep order. Either way, he's got some pretty pictures. And not just satellite, or shots from above. It's like someone stood right in front of the goddamned mega-platform they built for the Ark and took souvenir photos then emailed them over to Peers."

"He says it's Astral technology, and that he's hijacked it."

Cameron shook his head. Charlie never seemed to accept nuance, or get a subtle point.

"It's right there in the Ember Flats town square," Cameron said, suddenly tired. "I can even see the impression, where the key must fit into its front. I don't think anyone would stop you if you walked right up to the thing and opened it up. It's like they're waiting for it to happen."

"That's exactly my point, Cameron. They're waiting for you to go in and do what needs to be done."

Cameron sighed. He'd been hearing this same argument for five long years. Charlie had barely wavered, and neither had Kindred — Charlie's unlikely ally. Charlie wanted to insert the key and open the Ark because it's what Benjamin's research seemed to suggest. Kindred wanted the same thing because he sensed something in the

Astral collective that suggested breath was being held on both sides, and would be until the deed was done. Delaying, Kindred said, was like a kid locking himself in his room because he was in trouble, hoping in vain that the problem might have disappeared when he finally came out.

But the situation was frustratingly rigid. No matter how many times Cameron suggested the group split so that each contingent could do what they felt they must, Charlie and Kindred refused. They wouldn't take the key to the Ark. They'd stick around and keep insisting that Cameron do it.

"Fuck that, Charlie."

"You should talk to Peers about this."

"Well, fuck Peers, too."

"He's been attacking the same puzzles as we were. Only he's been able to incorporate new information and keep working these past years instead of merely running." Charlie looked quickly at Cameron, eyes behind thick glasses and clearly attempting to take the implied reproach from his words. "Because he's English, he's got a slightly different perspective. You may want to hear it."

"Stonehenge, I suppose."

"Arthurian legend," Charlie replied.

Cameron barked a small laugh. "Well, that makes sense. *Camelot*. You really are becoming the new Benjamin Bannister. I suppose an alien sat around the Round Table?"

"You know how myths are. Over time, they become more symbolic than literally true. Some event happened, and the people of the time built a moralistic story around it. Myths aren't history; they're closer to parables. In this case, it's the myth of the sword in the stone."

Cameron laughed again.

"How long has it been since we've been in danger from Astrals seeking the key, Cameron?"

Cameron pretended to look at an invisible watch. "Hours?"

"They pinned us down but didn't attack. You and Jeanine were separated from the rest of us and they chased both groups, but did they ever *truly* pursue us?"

Cameron wanted to give an obvious yes, possibly with an insulting eye roll. But he paused a second too long, and Charlie's words began to tumble through his head. They'd been in danger plenty, but not from the Astrals. The only verifiable danger came from the Mullah — the radical branch of Templars who had different views on how history was supposed to unfold. The Astrals always showed, swarmed, and flashed their teeth, but they hadn't lost anyone since Nathan Andreus's daughter, Grace. And the aliens weren't the ones who had ended her life.

"What Peers has been telling me makes sense," Charlie proceeded into Cameron's silence. "Beings came from the sky, and humanity cowered. But in the past, there's always been evidence of societies built together, not conquest."

"Aren't you the one who said back in Moab that colonization came first, and annihilation followed?"

"Matter of perspective, maybe."

"And Heaven's Veil? Was that a matter of perspective, Charlie?"

"If you're objective, yes. They needed to find the archive, after the Templars hid it, because what it contains is necessary for their next stage on Earth. But they're making this up as they go too, Cameron. If they've always left a device behind to record what humanity did in their absence between epochs — like security camera footage to be reviewed the next day for patterns — then it makes sense that they tried to find it first thing. It was supposed to be under Vail, below the Apex pyramid. In the past, it seems to have always been left at one of the nexus points. But the Templars had a sense of humor last time. They took the Ark from where the Astrals left it and stowed it where it had famously judged humanity in the past. But the Astrals didn't know the Templars had found it, and when they saw that the key had been removed and stored separately, back in Cottonwood, I imagine that made them nervous. So they followed us, assuming we'd lead them to it. When that didn't work, they powered up the grid in Heaven's Veil, turning on what Clara called the 'spotlight.' We put an end to that, too, by blowing up the Apex. What choice did we leave them?"

"You're right, Charlie. Obliterating an entire city full of hundreds of thousands of people was really sensible once you look at it that way."

"Don't be dense," Charlie snapped, surprising Cameron. "This is a race that's been around for hundreds of thousands of years at least, possibly millions, or billions. Cosmologically speaking, there's room on the timeline for a species nearly that old given the right circumstances. They seeded life throughout the galaxy, maybe *many* galaxies. They've likely had the capacity for intergalactic travel since before humanity was a gleam in evolution's eye. We don't know how long their natural lifespans are as individuals, but I don't think it matters because they're barely individuals. You've heard how Kindred talks about his nightmares."

Cameron had. Kindred was Meyer Dempsey through and through, but some part of his higher mind must have held bits of his former Titan self. He sometimes had night terrors of the day he was changed, and of how petrified he felt to be cut from their collective.

"They don't think the way we do," Charlie said, his

intensity fully returned. "It's stupid and arrogant to attribute human thought to beings that might, for all intents and purposes, think of themselves as timeless — in a single unbroken mind, if not in body. When you're that old, you don't worry about whether your meal at a restaurant is five minutes late or lose your Zen when the person in front of you at the ten-items-or-less line has fifty items. So yes, Cameron. To them, destroying Heaven's Veil might have seemed perfectly sensible. If we killed as many Astrals as they killed humans, they'd shrug it off and keep ticking. It's possible they feel it was no big deal. And by doing it, they generated an emotional signal — from the dying but also from anyone who saw or heard about it — that would have to stream out and into their lost archive. They tried to find it through more peaceful means, but humanity kept it hidden. They need it to do their work. So in their shoes, what choice did they have?"

Cameron just stared. "So we had it coming? That's great, Charlie. Now can you explain why 'inferior' races are just begging for ethnic cleansing, or why women who dress provocatively have a justifiable rape coming?"

"Stay in your shell, Cameron. Keep applying your own way of seeing the world to the Astrals. See how far it gets you. Or how much further it gets you than the past five years of running away."

Cameron glared at the scientist. Charlie was normally comically stodgy, so stiff and divorced from the normal rules of social intelligence that he couldn't be convincingly angry or offensive. But this was a new Charlie, and Cameron saw determination in the set of his jaw as they sat in the near-dark. For decades, Cameron had known him as his father's straight man — someone everyone dismissed because it was only Charlie — too oblivious to know any better. But he had several PhDs and knew more, by far, than anyone else in their longtime group. Speaking with Peers — and incorporating whatever the man had told him — seemed to have finally snapped Charlie out of complacency. Cameron didn't have to listen, but doing so now felt like deliberately burying his head in the sand. And this time, if he refused to hear Charlie, he felt somehow sure the group would split, and the division would be permanent.

"The sword in the stone, huh?"

"That's what Peers thinks," Charlie said, an edge still in his voice.

"So what does it mean? What comes next?"

"You know what comes next." Charlie fixed Cameron in his hard stare. "Nobody could pull Excalibur from the stone, even as it sat there in the middle of the town square for anyone to try. Nobody but Arthur."

"If you think it's right," Cameron said, "I'm willing to trust him. I'll give him the key, and he can open it … and God help us all if the Astrals don't like what they see we've done while they've been away." Cameron thought of Hitler. He thought of cults led by deadly leaders. He thought of poverty, starvation, apathy, hatred. It wasn't a pretty picture, but if Charlie was right, the Astrals had all the time in the world. They'd wait as long as humanity required to make up their minds and face the jury.

"Based on all Peers showed me, that's not how it works," Charlie said. "You touched the key first, inside the Cottonwood archives."

But Cameron couldn't go back. He *wouldn't* go back. Not ever.

"You're King Arthur in this tale," Charlie said, "and it's time to pull Excalibur from the stone."

# Chapter Eleven

"I'M GOING."

Meyer stopped, Lila's back to him. He thought he'd been quiet, even on the Den's stone floors. The place was a study in opposites, stocked to the rafters with technological equipment — damn near a post-Astral version of NORAD at Cheyenne Mountain — but there were no niceties to go with all the doodads. Charlie might as well have designed the place. It was eminently practical and not at all warm. The perfect hideout for a logical pragmatist. If they weren't planning to leave immediately, Charlie would be happy here. As might Kindred, with all the Astrals in the air.

"I hope you don't mean what I think you do."

Lila turned to face her father. "I suppose you're going to ground me?"

"Maybe." But he allowed a smile. He saw Lila almost smile back. Smiles from her father were still disarming. Time was, he barely ever smiled or laughed. But that was before he was confined for two full years, forced to confront his humanity first, his sanity and survival second.

"Dad, I'm twenty-four years old. You can't tell me what to do."

"I don't think I've told you to do anything. All I did was walk into the room." He looked around. "Is Christopher here?"

"He's with Clara. She wanted to explore."

"Did Peers say it was okay?"

Lila nodded. "They're with Aubrey. I told him not to show Clara where they kept their enemies' severed heads."

"Please tell me that's a joke." But the smile was larger now.

"Don't try to soften me up. I said I'm going."

Meyer entered the small room. It probably hadn't been intended as a bedroom, but it had become one. There were three skinny collapsible cots against the walls. Two had been pushed together. Meyer felt a curious unpleasant sensation and marveled at himself for a moment from the outside. Even after all that had happened, the idea of his adult daughter sleeping beside a man still gave his stomach a quiet punch.

"I'm just checking out the digs." Meyer circled the room. It was *so* blank. Three cots, accompanying bedclothes, and nothing else. They'd been wearing their travel backpacks in Derinkuyu when the Astrals arrived, but Lila had handed hers off to Christopher once it became too unwieldy in the tight passages. He'd lost it in the exodus, and now it seemed Lila would need to share Piper's clothes until they found another former human spot to raid.

"You were easier when you were a hardass." Lila said it without any edge.

Meyer sat on a cot. "That was the old Meyer Dempsey."

"I'm pretty sure you're still the old Meyer Dempsey. We have a new one, too."

"*Original*, not *old*," Meyer clarified. "Now I'm the kind-hearted father you've always deserved."

"You still wear suits."

"The coats are warm. I don't wear them for fashion."

"If you shaved that beard," Lila said, now poking in a minuscule pile of loaned belongings, "I'd never be able to tell you apart from Kindred."

"See? That's exactly what I'm talking about, right there. You didn't just recapture the caring side of your father. You got a second caring father, too."

Lila rolled her eyes. It had become an unfunny joke. Meyer knew he'd never fully have his daughter back — not as long as Kindred was around. Everyone knew the group contained one Meyer and a copy, but Kindred had all of Meyer's memories up to the point they'd split. It was only a semantic matter to say that Lila wasn't his daughter, that Clara wasn't his granddaughter, that Piper hadn't once been his wife, and that he hadn't lost a son — and a good friend and secret lover — to the Astrals.

"Stop it, Dad."

"I'm not doing anything."

"You're going to try and convince me that I shouldn't go to Ember Flats."

"I haven't said anything of the kind."

"That's why I said, 'going to.'"

Meyer watched Lila for a long, quiet moment. Then: "So do you think Aubrey grew that little mustache on purpose, or has he just been missing the same spot for months?"

"*I'm not going to change my mind!*" Lila snapped. And in the sentence, Meyer heard all the petulance he'd grown used to through her spoiled teen years. She wasn't coddled these days, and her words rang in his ears as almost funny.

"It's too dangerous, Lila," Meyer said, giving up.

"Then none of us should go."

"Some of us need to."

"And that 'some' includes you and Kindred."

"Ember Flats has a viceroy we may need to talk to. I was a viceroy." He corrected himself. Their memory sharing only went one way, but sometimes it was hard to disentangle himself from his doppelgänger regardless. "Well, you know what I mean. He was. I'm his other half, yada yada."

Lila put a fist on her hip. Technically, it was true. When Meyer and Kindred could stop arguing and put themselves on the same wavelength, some trick of the collective gave them deductive and mental abilities Sherlock Holmes would envy. But really Meyer was going in addition to Lila because he was Meyer, and Meyer Dempsey didn't stand at the back of any line.

"And Clara ... hell, you know I wish she didn't have to go. But you know how she is and the kinds of things she can see. If there are other Lightborn children there, then I guess it's moot, but ... Piper is staying," he said, changing tacks.

"No she's not."

"Yes, she is."

"I just talked to her five minutes ago, Dad. Don't lie to me."

"Damn. I knew I should have stealthily manipulated her first."

Lila sat. She exhaled slowly. After a bit, Meyer sat beside her.

"Dad. *Daddy*," she said, putting a hand over her father's.

"Don't use 'Daddy' on me."

"I'm not the bratty little rich girl I used to be. The world isn't what it was. Once upon a time, it was your job to protect me. But I have my own job to do."

"It'll never stop being my job to protect you."

"Then protect me on the road. Protect me in Ember Flats. I can't just stay here. How does that make sense? You're going. You need Clara. Chris won't stay, and good luck convincing Piper. So am I supposed to stay by myself? Maybe with Aubrey? How is that preferable to …"

She wouldn't finish the sentence, but Meyer knew what she'd almost said: *How is that preferable to dying in Hell's Corridor?* It should have sounded like a rhetorical question, but it wasn't. The world was so upside down now that death with family might be better than living alone.

"It's a suicide mission, Lila," he said anyway.

"Then don't go."

Meyer felt his face work, trying to find a way through the bind she'd put him in. But there was no escape; Lila was telling the truth that she was no longer who she'd been. None of them were. The Meyer of seven years ago would have kicked the Meyer of today right in the balls for being emotional: weak, human, vulnerable — more compassionate in a world where hardness was perhaps needed more.

"I know how you are, Dad. And I know how you are when you work with Kindred. You don't believe it's a suicide mission. Not for the mission as a whole, at least. I'm not stupid. I've heard all the same things about Ember Flats as the rest of you. And it feels like there's nobody, anywhere, who hasn't heard rumors of the freaks and cannibals in Hell's Corridor. But you wouldn't do this if you didn't think it could succeed. You're too logical, even now, to be content with a heroic gesture. And you wouldn't even consider it if you didn't think it was important. Vital, even."

Meyer said nothing.

"Yesterday, this group was running from the Ark. It felt like Cameron had a compass that told him nothing other than when the Ark was at his back, and he always wanted to get as far away as he could. The rest of us felt the same. Charlie and Kindred complained, but we've been ignoring them forever. But I've been watching you change. All of you, one by one. Now it's like this sense of grim duty. So tell me, father of mine: tell me how, when everyone else suddenly sees such importance in this mission that all minds have changed 180 degrees, I'm supposed to be the one stubborn holdout who refuses to believe."

He shook his head. "We won't all make it. Maybe through the badlands outside Ember Flats, in Peers's outfitted bus. *Maybe*. But I've seen enough cities to never want to see one again. There's been anarchy since Heaven's Veil fell. They'll see us coming. There's no way to sneak in — not the way we'll be hightailing and hauling ass through Hell's Corridor with road warriors screaming behind us. Between Kindred and me, maybe we can talk our way in. Peers thinks the Astrals actually want Cameron to open the Ark, and the more Kindred and I think on this, it almost makes sense. So maybe the mission succeeds. But why risk bringing extras? You'll be …*fodder*, Lila."

"Chattel with my family over staying here alone."

"You might have Aubrey."

"But he can't even shave properly, Dad. He's been missing the same spot on his upper lip for months."

Something inside him ached, but Meyer laughed anyway.

"Peers says he can clear us to take most of the main roads, but it's still over a thousand miles."

"Oh, you didn't mention a long car ride. My mind is totally changed."

"It's going to take days to get there."

"I had fun the last time we took a road trip," Lila said.

"When the Astrals invaded? The trip that ended with us shooting our way into a bunker then practically being smoked out before I was abducted?"

"Good times," Lila said, leaning against her father's side.

"If the Astrals abduct us again, you might not get your own room."

Lila giggled.

"They'll probably probe the shit out of us, too."

"I've got Christopher for that," Lila said.

"Dammit, Lila. Don't ever say that sort of thing to your father."

She laughed again, and for a moment it seemed like everything might be okay.

But they wouldn't be, and Meyer — with Kindred's help — already knew it.

There would be blood on the way to Ember Flats.

There would be death.

The logic said so, and the logic never lied.

# Chapter Twelve

CAMERON FELT the repulsion of Giza the moment they all
piled on to the bus for their journey. It was as if he'd been
walking away from the wind for so long, he'd grown used
to its subtle nudge at his back. Now he was a long way
from home, turning around to retrace his steps. And even
though he'd been told he needed to return, the wind's
insistent hand, shoving him away, said otherwise.

Everyone boarded the bus. No one stayed behind, as if
they'd decided to take a family road trip rather than
barreling into the monster's mouth.

Cameron *had* to go. Peers said he was the one chosen
by both key and Ark to pull the metaphorical sword from
the stone. Once he looked the issue in its eye, he had to
admit he'd been feeling the pull for a while. He had
dreams about finding the Ark again, even though word had
clearly been passed around that it was right there, smack
dab in the center of Ember Flats. Until the Den and its
overabundance of information, Cameron hadn't actually
seen the thing on its enormous plinth, but every traveler
knew where the archive rested. Every barman in every

backwoods watering hole knew where it stood. In every city they'd fought through — every burg they'd eventually fled, holding their belongings and female members close — people had known where the Astrals had taken the prize they'd finally found in Horeb's guts. But so many other things made sense, too — like why the Astrals hounded them constantly but never truly attacked them anymore. Why the Mullah, who opposed the Astrals, did. And why Cameron increasingly sensed that running from what had happened was only delaying the inevitable.

Meyer had to go, with Kindred by his side. The two halves — Kindred able to sense the Astral collective and Meyer with his former prisoner's knowledge — would be needed if they faced the Ember Flats viceroy. The network was severed; they had no idea how the other capitals had fared or how far they'd fallen. They'd found a tyrant viceroy in Roman Sands, the Astral duplicate of some famous human soured — the opposite of Kindred's softening. He'd told the others, as they'd run from those guarded walls, not to judge the Astrals harshly for that one. Kindred had discovered he wasn't truly Meyer Dempsey, but it was unlikely the same would happen for others. The Roman Sands viceroy probably thought she was the real Liza Knight. The human had gone bad, not the Titan who'd assumed her shape.

Clara had to go because she was Lightborn. Cameron liked that least of all but knew it was true. She could see the path ahead, at least a little, and speak to what lay beneath the surface of Astral consciousness.

And because Clara was going, Lila and Christopher were, too. Because Lila and Clara were going, so was Piper. Charlie was their analyst and Jeanine their militant, having effortlessly stepped into Nathan's cruel shoes. And after that there was nobody left besides the Pall, now unseen for the trio of days spent in the Den refueling, resting, deciding to trust the man who'd been watching, who'd saved them from what may or may not have been an actual Astral siege.

"I don't understand why we're not being followed," Cameron said, looking through slats in the bus's sides, where windows should have been.

Jeanine was beside him. Cameron would rather have had Piper at his side, but that would mean accepting her presence, and he was still hoping that at some point before hitting Hell's Corridor he'd manage to shoo her and a few of the others off the bus.

"He has satellite feeds, like Nathan had," Jeanine said. "And I get the feeling he's made deals with whoever's controlling these roads. Or maybe he's the one who controls them."

But the difference between Andreus and Peers was that Nathan had built himself an army. Peers had only Aubrey. Two mild-mannered Brits, controlling the Middle East by themselves.

"Nathan had access to satellites because the Astrals *gave* him access in trade," Cameron said.

Jeanine didn't answer. There was no good answer to most of what was happening. They could believe Peers just so happened to keep an eye on their group despite the effort they'd taken to hide themselves, the many waypoints they'd taken over the years, and the month they'd spent in a massive junkyard of entirely defunct vehicles, pinned down, subsisting mostly by hunting rats. They could believe that Peers got the gasoline to run his hybrid bus by raiding a mostly unguarded Astral refining station in the desert as he claimed — and that he and Aubrey had modified the bus by themselves, including adding the four thirty-gallon tanks behind the rear partition. It might be true.

Lies were being told; Cameron wouldn't allow himself the luxurious stupidity of pretending they weren't. But Kindred said that Peers wasn't Astral, and neither were Aubrey or Nocturne, both of whom had come along as well because a party isn't a party without a butler and a dog. But Cameron couldn't work out a harmful angle to the possible lies. Hell's Corridor took no bribes. If they were overtaken, the painted cannibals would devour Peers and Aubrey just the same.

"You should talk to him, Cameron," Jeanine finally said.

"Peers?"

"Yes."

"About what? Benjamin?"

"About this. About *all* of this." She gestured to indicate the bus, the fortunate fuel, the lack of pursuit by Astral shuttles or road warriors, the fact that they'd been talked into going at all.

"I'm not sure what you mean."

"Ask him if he's telling the truth."

Cameron thought she must be kidding, but Jeanine's eyes were hard and serious.

"Right."

"You'd be amazed what happens when you're straight with people. One day, a man came into the Republic claiming to be lost. And Nathan said to him, perfectly reasonably, 'Tell me something. Are you telling the truth?' He blurted out that he'd been sent to kill Nathan, then he became one of his best lieutenants."

Cameron looked back out the window. Something flashed in the corner of his eye, momentarily became a long column of shifting-color smoke, and then was gone.

Without a word, Cameron stood. He sat beside Piper

then leaned against her as the bus rumbled on. He was asleep ten minutes later.

He woke an unknown time later when Piper rose to use the onboard bathroom. The day slipped by with little conversation. Cameron milled up and down the aisle, restless, hating the quiet. Meyer and Kindred took the back seat for a pow-wow — low, subtle, quick words whispered in their strange little language. Lila and Clara had either brought or found a deck of cards because they began playing Go Fish. Piper pulled her battered Vellum from her pack, recently charged after a long quiescence in the Den's abundant power. She hadn't added new books to the thing in half a decade but always found something to read when power allowed. The same books over and over or new-to-her stories she'd stockpiled before Astral Day, Cameron never knew.

Day became evening. Opposition ignored them. Evening became night. With the sun's departure, Peers announced that the headlights made the bus too obvious a target and pulled off the road. Never mind that the bus — which was large, silver, and not silent — had been a target all day. Never mind that there was a shelter at the ready, and Peers pulled them right into it.

They made a small fire. Jeanine and Meyer stood sentry. Some hours later they traded — Kindred and Christopher took a turn. Cameron considered speaking to Piper and then Jeanine, rallying a group to mutiny or leave. Instead he found himself sitting on a rock, knowing only four things: They were headed to Ember Flats. The Ark was in Ember Flats. Cameron would need to open the thing if they could reach the city and resist arrest long enough to reach it. And Peers, no matter his motivations, would take them there.

Aubrey sat beside him.

"You're wondering about Peers."

Cameron looked over. The firelight barely reached this far, but there was a moon. He could see Christopher's arms burdened with a rifle, standing just a few dozen yards farther on.

"I don't blame you," Aubrey went on. "In your shoes, I'd wonder about Peers as well."

"The Den …" Cameron began.

"He's telling the truth about the Den. It's stuffed with Astral technology and was clearly an alien base. We found it as he said, but it was mostly dead. Filthy. None of the equipment seemed to work. Sand had drifted in. But Peers went to school for a curious combination of majors. One was as you'd suspect, which gives him his archaeological bent. But don't let his desert robe and knotty dreadlocks fool you. He's also an engineer. When I first met him, he looked like an accountant. And if Peers Basara can't clean a machine and make it run, it can't be fixed by anyone."

Cameron looked toward Peers, by the fire, chatting amiably with Meyer. Or at least Cameron thought it was Meyer; from here, what he thought was a beard might merely be shadow.

"But you wonder how we can so boldly turn toward Ember Flats. The explanation of our fuel supply doesn't sit right. You've noticed that the roads are clear as if they've been paved just for us." The thin man nodded toward the shelter's front, just beyond the fire. The entire bus had fit neatly inside. "And most of all, you're wondering about that. How we found shelter so easily, so readily."

"Okay. I've wondered."

"He's obsessed. Peers, I mean. Did he tell you we've been to Ember Flats before?"

"No."

"Years ago. Before the Ark was there. By the timeline as I understand it, before Heaven's Veil was destroyed. We knew the Templars had hidden something the Astrals needed, thanks to communication bursts your group sent our friends before the Veil went dark. It was simple — and honestly rather obvious — to conclude it must have been the archive."

"Why was that obvious?" Cameron remembered Benjamin's glee when he seemed to realize the same thing, regarding the whole thing as a big historical joke. But it had taken Charlie's analysis of Benjamin's work and Clara's plunging of Cameron's forgotten past to assemble two and two on the American end.

"Once we realized the point was judgment rather than simply blowing us all up, it was simple. The Ark of the Covenant is perhaps the most famous object in history. And like any famous historical story, it's been distorted and symbolized over time. Some ancient aliens scholars believe it was a weapon, just as we first thought the Astrals had lost a weapon. Some believed it was radioactive, that it was a machine, that carrying it could bring domination or destruction. But more famously, what is the Ark known as?"

"The resting place of the Ten Commandments."

Aubrey nodded. "Perhaps a prior set of judgments. At least history's interpretation of the story. We considered Biblical Mount Sinai, but by then the Astrals had triangulated on the emotional outcry that arose with the annihilation of Heaven's Veil, and we knew we'd never find it first."

"If the Ark wasn't in Ember Flats, yet ..."

"We still thought of it as Giza back then. Can you think of any reason why a couple of ambitious British scholars like yours truly and my mate there might want to reach Giza, as part of what used to — before the great changes — feel like a revolutionary cause?"

"You were searching for something."

"That's right. In the original pyramids, before they were made of blue glass. In those old monoliths, clichéd as they are. We were able to bribe our way in, sniffing out a trail Peers had uncovered. It was just the three of us."

"Three?"

"Me. Peers. And Peers's son, James."

Cameron looked up, surprised.

"We were captured by the Ember Flats guard. We were supposed to be taken to the viceroy, a woman named Mara Jabari. We never made it that far; I imagine she was too busy handling insurrections elsewhere. So the guard handled us on their own, with the viceroy's blessing. They wanted to know who'd sent us and what we were after. When Peers wouldn't talk, they decided to show us they were serious. So they killed James. Just shot him in the head. He was only nineteen."

Cameron looked at Peers, still by the fire but now beside Clara. They were just talking, but something hurt Cameron's chest. It wasn't about the story being told. It was more personal — another father-son bond broken, or reflected pain on the day they'd found the Ark then run with no intent to ever return.

"He'll die to reach Ember Flats again, Cameron. He does not care. He wants to look Mara Jabari in the eye then slit her throat. *That* is Peers's secret, and I thought you should know it before we go farther. It's in our mission to help you reach the Ark, if indeed that's the right choice, which I'm also not sure of. But know that Peers has vengeance on his mind. Know that he's been scouting satellite imagery, making lists of necessary supplies, even heading out to set up bivouac stations like this one.

Mapping routes. Handing out bribes. All just to get us into the city, by any means necessary."

Cameron considered. If anything, Aubrey's story made the case for following him even stronger. If Peers wanted to slit the Ember Flats viceroy's throat, he'd have done all he could to make sure he got close enough to pull his knife. Close enough to reach the Ark, as long as there were no conflicts.

"And Hell's Corridor?" Cameron said.

"The painted cannibals cannot be bribed. The peril there is all too real. And once we enter the city, it will likely be just as bad. To Peers, all of this is acceptable risk."

"And you?"

"I have stood by Peers this long. James was like a son to me as well. But perhaps even more, I believe in the archive. I believe that if it can be opened — if it *should* be opened — that this will at least end. Your man Charlie will tell you: Once the archive is unlocked, we believe the information collecting will stop, and the process of judgment will begin, like a jury retiring to reach its verdict. They may judge you as well, as the key bearer. We cannot know how long the process will take or what criteria they will use. You know as well as I do what their device must have recorded over the past epoch: humanity's best and worst, hopefully not in equal measure. But whether we are found guilty or innocent, it will be over. And *that* is why I am here. The life of a nomadic archaeologist and ancient aliens theorist may sound like it's all grand galas and parties with dancing girls, but I assure you, the reality is far less impressive. And I'm tired, Cameron. Taking you to the Ark feels a bit like playing Russian roulette. But by now I'm ready to pull the trigger even though I can't know whether it will be air or a bullet in the chamber when the hammer falls."

Cameron lifted the thermos at his side. He'd poured

some of the distilled liquid from Peers's bottles back at the Den into the dented metal tumbler and a bit more into the cap. He handed the cap to Aubrey and raised his cup for a toast.

"Amen to that, at least," Cameron said.

Cups clinked.

They drank.

# Chapter Thirteen

LILA FELT the wrap tight around her torso. She hefted the carbine's weight in her arms. Jeanine, who'd fired one before, had tried to talk Lila out of the weapon when Peers had opened the bus's equipment locker to distribute guns like deadly presents. Jeanine said its kick would "knock her tits off." But seeing as Lila — like Piper — had wrapped herself tightly enough to obscure her appearance, she figured her warning was moot.

"Just don't try to shoot through the slats," Jeanine warned. "You'll never hold it still enough and will end up cutting our ride in half."

Lila thought that was a bit of an overstatement. She could pull a trigger, especially after squeezing so many (on admittedly smaller weapons) in the past. But she'd still heed Jeanine's advice and only shoot with her upper half fully through one of the pop-up hatches, content to call the issue a draw.

Jeanine walked away, checking the others' weapons, leaning out to survey the bus's shell for obvious weaknesses, generally taking command away from Peers, who to his credit seemed willing to give it. Cameron had hinted that Peers had planned this operation in advance — but emphasized that a run down Hell's Corridor couldn't *be* planned. If Peers were as smart as Aubrey claimed, he'd take Jeanine's advice and keep his mouth shut.

Lila watched Jeanine, stuffing down a mounting sense of concern that had bloomed into terror. Jeanine looked completely at ease, even cavalier. She hadn't wrapped her torso to hide her femininity from the horde ahead. She hadn't hidden her ponytail or smeared any grease on her face. She looked, Lila thought, like she'd probably make a rather delicious target. But Jeanine had been wearing a grenade inside her vest for months, nestled between her breasts in a modified bra pouch. "Let someone try to cop a feel on me," she'd say. "Just let them *try.*" And that didn't include the second tiny grenade she had *just in case.* The little black cylinder with its short, dangling cord. "I keep that one in a seam on my pack, no one would ever look there," she'd often said, and always like a dare.

Peers had brought satellite images of the Corridor, but they showed nothing they didn't already know. Jeanine spread them on the bus's central table as their target approached, calling for a stop and a general meeting.

"The Cairo ruins still seem in need of restoration, making the area practically impassable at speed, and certainly not by an armored bus," she said, pointing at the papers in front of her for all to see. "The Nile is patrolled by what seem to be human-manned boats. I have to assume they're under the dominion of the Ember Flats central government."

She eyed Kindred. Lila turned her head to see the former viceroy nod.

"We already knew that the Abbas Bridge is the only Nile bridge still standing in the combined metro areas — Giza to Cairo — and miles to the north and south. Abbas itself is a highly trafficked, highly regulated checkpoint. That all means that Ember Flats is unapproachable from the east. So we can only make this long detour, here—" She traced a line on the map with her finger. "Around to the south, away from the Nile delta, through unincorporated, unregulated outlands. Make sense?"

Heads nodded.

"The desert to the south and west is pocked with tiny outlaw governorships — yes, like my former employer's, only with a lot less order and civility — that are rumored to be little more than competing clans who've undergone a rapid selection process, like evolution in a hurry."

"What's that mean?" Lila's eyes ticked toward her daughter, who was paying more attention than Lila wanted her to. But it's not like Clara could be protected from the truth, and never really had been.

"It means that only the most brutal survive," Jeanine said. "The clans are, as far as we can tell, entirely men. Unless you count their slaves. Which, by the way, is the reason they're all here — all these warring clans, hanging out in the desert beyond Ember Flats." Jeanine looked at Clara but didn't flinch. She spoke to Lila and Piper in her most no-bullshit of voices, as if meaning to shoot straight for their own good. "They live off of spoils tossed from the city. Best we can tell, banishment is Ember Flats's primary method of punishment . They steal the women, and eat the men."

Lila felt the wrap around her body. Was it better to be eaten than held and raped, assuming she'd be dead before the captors realized her gender? She wondered if maybe

Jeanine's grenade solution wasn't, in the end, the best way to go.

Charlie, beside Jeanine, took the ball and continued the lecture.

"Just as we'd assumed, Peers's images show that the Astrals have irrigated far outside the old valley. They don't seem to have bothered to grow palm trees around the pyramids, but they've reincorporated them into their urban sprawl. See here, and here. The footprint is mostly Old Giza, but Ember Flats proper stretches well into the previously arid region we've classically associated with ancient Egyptian society. The Great Pyramid is here. The Sphinx is here. And this" — he traced his finger in a lazy loop, hitting map markers — "is the Fibonacci spiral. They seem to have centered Ember Flats on the old blueprint from their last visit. You'll see new development here, here, and here."

"What really matters to us is this artery." Jeanine moved her finger to a line at map's lower corner, leading into Ember Flats. "Faiyum Desert Road."

"I've been on that road," Cameron said.

"I'm sure it's changed since you last saw it," Peers said. "When Aubrey and I came to the city five years ago, the Astrals were using this old stretch as its major supply artery — for anything that the humans insisted on moving without Astral help, I imagine."

Lila felt herself nod. The same thing had happened in Heaven's Veil. The Astrals could probably have waved a cosmic magic wand and made the city shape itself to their ideal, but humanity had grown a lot of pride since the old days. In what felt like a gesture of pity, she remembered her father (the man she'd thought at the time was her father, anyway) negotiating human building in addition to all that was being done by shuttles and motherships.

"They were still dealing with a lot of rebel activity at the time," Peers continued. "So it seemed they'd done massive earthmoving along the sides of the road, a few hundred yards distant, to make it into a valley. The shuttles were able to efficiently patrol the edges from the air to protect the road so that none of the human raiding parties could reach the supply caravans before they could spot them and take them out."

"But as with everything, the Astrals seemed to have stopped humoring Ember Flats once people quit constantly fighting," Charlie said. "The city stopped using the roadway. They seem to have abandoned it, probably because shuttles can easily bring whatever they need. It's fallen into disuse. We watched the road for a while before leaving the Den and didn't see a single legitimate supply vehicle."

"*Legitimate* vehicle?" Piper said, her eyebrows knitting.

Jeanine swept the big map aside and replaced it with a greatly magnified image. Lila saw the same valley roadway, now scattered with what looked like small, out-of-focus black and silver rectangles of various sizes.

"This bit of forgotten road, if you haven't connected the dots," she said, "is the stretch known as Hell's Corridor. It's the only intact and passable route to Ember Flats that's not already claimed by one of the clans. Because it was patrolled by superior Astral forces for so long, no one clan was able to claim it."

"What are all these little rectangles?" Lila asked.

"*All* of them claiming it." Jeanine laid several magnifications atop the road valley image, clearly showing the rectangles to be highly modified vehicles, each one as frighteningly armored and armed as their bus. Poking from the tops of the vehicles and surrounding them in loose groups were colored dots that Jeanine seemed to have put on the image for some reason.

"What do the dots indicate?" Piper said, pulling one forward and squinting.

"They don't *indicate* anything. You're looking at people's heads." Jeanine turned the image around, seemed to consider something, then returned it.

Lila looked again. All of the colored blobs were more oblong than circular, but they were all sorts of colors: white, blue, orange, red, green, teal, more.

"I almost wish the resolution on the Den's equipment wasn't so good," Jeanine went on. "But it looks like the rumor mill got it entirely right. The clans all shave their heads then paint themselves in their clan's color. This is as a big dustup was forming, but we clicked through images as it unfolded. When dots of different colors get near each other, they start to disappear. We think it's the clans killing each other then stealing the bodies for their own ... use."

"Use how?" Clara asked.

Lila took Clara by the shoulders, held her close, and used her eyes to beg Jeanine's silence.

"Nobody occupies the corridor," Peers said. "I've been watching it the entire time Aubrey and I have been at the Den. They only enter it like this to fight, and nobody enters it on one side without another side heading in. So they keep an eye out, but it's usually empty. If we're fast enough, we can maybe squeak through."

Meyer and Kindred both looked at Jeanine. She shook her head. Lila sensed that a question and answer had silently passed between them. Part of Jeanine's response seemed to have been, *But let's not mention that.*

"We should go around," said Cameron.

Meyer shook his head. "We can't. We've run all those scenarios. The bus won't have sure enough traction anywhere but here."

"Then we leave the bus. We go in on foot."

Kindred spoke, and Lila knew he was answering as her father's other mental half. "The scenarios predict far less success if we slow down and offer multiple targets. Some of which are … less equipped than others." *The scenarios.* The pair was always running scenarios, and their logical conclusions never seemed to be wrong. He'd looked at Lila and Clara while saying the last. It was insulting but true. Carbine or not, she'd be easily overtaken the minute the cannibals arrived and sent her into a panic.

"Can we get our hands on another shuttle?" Cameron asked, looking at Kindred.

"No. We're lucky they weren't in the shuttle I originally commandeered when the collective called it back."

"Multiple vehicles."

"We have the best chance of success with a single target."

"Multiple vehicles could draw pursuers off of the one we most need to get through the Corridor. So they won't all be on us at once."

Meyer looked pained and sympathetic at once. "And who goes in the decoy vehicle, Cameron? It can't be you. So whom do we choose to die?"

"Besides," Jeanine said, "even assuming we could get more vehicles, which I don't see how we can, there are plenty of clans watching the valley to overrun two cars, three cars, whatever. Our best shot is with a blitzkrieg run. All eggs in one basket, put the pedal to the metal, and drive like hell."

Cameron looked at Peers and Aubrey then Charlie. He seemed to decide whether he should say something then finally did. "I thought you said the Astrals *wanted* us to reach the Ark."

"That's only a guess," Aubrey pointed out. "It's in no way certain."

"And there's no 'us,'" Peers added. "You're King Arthur, remember? If anyone is supposed to reach it, it's you and you alone. But even then it feels far from a guarantee."

"Because the Astrals can't control the clans outside Ember Flats and clear us a path?" Cameron shook his head. "I don't buy that for a second."

"Because it's a test," Charlie said.

All heads turned toward Charlie.

"We're here to be judged, remember? We open the archive, and we open humanity's case file. But won't *the way we try* tell the Astrals a lot about us? If we don't make it, they've learned something about this group, as representatives who carry the key. But if we don't make it, do they really care? Maybe someone else will pick up the key and try to open the archive instead. Or maybe the Astrals will render judgment without bothering to have a trial, if that's the analogy. After all, if a defendant doesn't show up to defend himself, he loses by default."

The bus was quiet. Cameron turned to Lila and Piper with his lips pressed together, his expression grim.

"This is why you have to stay behind," he said. "This is why it's stupid for you to come."

"Maybe," Peers said. "But then again, if this is all part of a test, might our faith matter to the archive? Maybe it's interested in which choices we make about life, death — and, not to be trite, but … sticking together until the end."

Lila crossed her arms over her chest. The gun, on its strap, nestled against her.

"Cameron and Clara are going, so I'm going. If you want me to stay behind, you'll need to tie me down."

Piper put an arm around Lila's shoulders. "Me too."

Cameron gave what Lila thought was a pointedly sexist sigh as if to say: *Women.*

"We'll all be fine," Piper said. "You'll see."

Kindred looked away. So did Meyer.

Clara said, "Not all of us."

## Chapter Fourteen

THE BUS IDLED at the end of a long road, at the Corridor's southeast end, where embankments the Astrals had built to shelter the road were barely twin mounds at the sides. Ahead, the terraformed walls grew, offering protection from anyone attempting to overtake a passing convoy from the sides.

Or — for any convoys passing without the benefit of an Astral guard on the raised shoulders — offering an impossible corner.

"You're sure this is a good idea?" Peers looked over at Jeanine, who was surveying the scene from one of the bus's pop-tops using pre-Astral-Day binoculars.

"It's a terrible idea," she replied.

"Then you're sure this is the *only* way."

"If you want to get to Ember Flats, yes. But that's a question worth asking: Are we sure we *want* to? I don't know about you and Aubrey, but we've spent five years moving slowly and steadily away from the place. Fifteen hundred kilometers later, I'm not entirely convinced we haven't just wasted a lot of time and fuel. It's not too late,

Peers. We could turn around. No point in throwing good blood after bad." She lowered her binoculars, and Peers saw something curious on the pretty woman's hard face: *fear.*

"We haven't spent any blood," Peers said.

"You spent your son. Meyer spent his. Cameron's father. Clara's father. Meyer's ex-wife, Heather. My old boss's daughter. And those are just the big ones."

"I meant on the detour from where you were to where we are now. Nobody's died. No one's been hurt. We have no sunken costs in term of life or limb."

Peers wondered why he was arguing the point then realized that he was terrified, too. The ravine-shaped funnel ahead was empty, but it wouldn't stay that way. And even if they made it all the way through, then what? Every city Peers had seen and every city the new group whispered about had been worse than the last. The Astrals were building in all the capitals, according to satellite images in the Den. It was so efficient, slave labor seemed the only explanation. Just like in the days of pharaohs. Ember Flats wouldn't be a picnic. Fantasies of walking to the Ark or to the viceroy's mansion suddenly felt exactly like that: *fantasies.*

"Not yet," Jeanine said.

"Clara's just a kid. Just because she said—"

"Clara's not just a kid. She's Lightborn."

"That just means she's advanced and sensitive."

"Kindred and Meyer would tell you the same thing. You can see it in the way they skulk around, the way they won't meet your eye. It's not probable that at least some of us will die if we do this. It's inevitable. So I have to ask, why do it? Why fight a losing battle? There's no shame in walking away."

*No,* Peers thought. *There's no shame.* But if they didn't try for Ember Flats once this close, how would he look at his reflection in whichever chipped and filthy mirrors he might find in what was left of the world? And how long could he really expect to keep on breathing if they turned away now?

But Peers didn't have to answer. Didn't need to convince her, even though he himself was more uncertain than ever. He didn't believe in the powers of the Lightborn. They were simply less jaded versions of readers and psychics. But still he felt a cold hand pressing against his spine as if the future was really already written.

He didn't need to give his conflicted opinion because Jeanine spoke first.

"You're sure it's there," she said, staring forward.

"The Ark?"

"You aren't just guessing. Listening to the same rumors we've all heard. You have proof."

"I have photos. Recent ones."

Jeanine sighed. The Corridor ahead remained far too empty. As was the land around them, back where they could still see the horizon. Some people said the cannibal tribes had made themselves comfortable in the ground they called home, burrowing tunnels over the years using scavenged Astral equipment, honeycombing the sand and rock like nests of ants. Ahead, not five miles distant, they saw the Ember Flats skyline. Stone pyramids joined by blue glass. Old temples met with new ones of rock and metal. The modern city lay beyond, closer to the Nile. But the true capital was here. The mothership, hanging just off to the side, giving the city its sunlight. Ember Flats protected an area that included both irrigated soil and arid sand, but it was in the desert that Viceroy Mara Jabari and her government made their traitorous homes. Peers could feel eyes upon him as they sat indecisive at the artificial valley's mouth. The only thing keeping the clans at bay was the knowledge that other clans were eyeing the new prey as well. The only thing keeping them temporarily safe was the fact that they were in such a fragile abundance of danger.

"When the Ark shone into us at Sinai all those years ago, I felt as if it was judging me even back then," Jeanine said. "But do you want to know something funny? I've felt ever since as if it left the seed of a challenge inside me. As if it's been watching with condescension to see if I have what it takes to meet my summons."

"What happened at Sinai?" Peers asked. Several of the group had alluded to that day, but each time it felt like a slip. They were hoarding a secret that they'd agreed to bury forever. This, here and now with Jeanine, was the first time he'd ever heard anyone break the covenant and speak so openly. It had the feel of a dare. Or, to use Jeanine's word, of a person rising to a challenge.

"Make you a deal, Peers. If you and I both make it through the next fifteen minutes or so, I'll buy you a beer and tell you the whole story."

Peers, despite his turbulent emotions, managed a small smile. "And if they don't have beer in Ember Flats?"

"They're living in pyramids. They must be on some mind-altering drug."

"Not two minutes ago, you were arguing that we should turn around and not look back."

"Yeah, well." Jeanine sighed again. "I guess I don't like the idea of some alien device thinking it got one over on me for all of eternity."

"Deal, then."

Jeanine slapped Peers's offered hand. Then her face snapped back to serious.

"Start the clock," she said.

# Chapter Fifteen

CHRISTOPHER WAS PEERING through the bus's slats, listening to its idling motor thrum like a heartbeat, watching a vulture settle near a canted road sign written in Arabic like an omen. His eyes on the tall boy with the thick eyebrows standing at its side, staring back at him.

He jumped when Lila set a hand on his shoulder. His head smacked the overhead rack. Instead of luggage, it held boxes of ammunition they'd all helped pull from the Den's stores. It was pointless. The run would be quick, like ripping off a Band-Aid. The idea of anyone but Jeanine competently reloading a military weapon in the hot mess of panic, as the bus bounced over ruts, was absurd.

"See anything?" Lila asked.

Christopher returned his eyes to the road sign. He saw the vulture, but Trevor Dempsey was gone.

"Nothing," he said.

Lila was looking at him funny. Her mouth made a curious little shape. She raised one hand and brushed hair from his forehead.

"What?"

"Nothing," he repeated.

"Chris …"

"I'm just jumpy, Lila. I think we all are."

Lila turned at a noise behind her. Christopher followed her gaze. Jeanine was pressing buttons on a large LED clock that had, once upon a time, probably spelled out the name of the bus's next stop. For reasons unknown, Peers had converted it to a multipurpose display. For the duration of the trip, it had been counting off their trip with kilometers traveled. The display had been counting backward from just under fifteen hundred — probably to give the passengers some sense of progress on the days' long journey. It had almost reached zero, but now Jeanine was resetting it to read *10:00*. She stepped back and the clock suddenly read *9:59*, then *9:58*.

"I know we're all nervous." Jeanine tapped the clock. "But the good news is that we only have to be afraid for another ten minutes. Once time runs out, this will all be over." She looked directly at Clara, and Christopher — the girl's adopted father, in spirit if not on obsolete paper — felt a pang of intense guilt. This token and the associated pep talk was for all of them, but she was offering it mostly to Clara. The girl Christopher wasn't protecting, and was shepherding into peril.

Nobody contradicted Jeanine to voice Christopher's thoughts:

*Ten minutes, unless the bus is tipped over and we have to make it on foot.*

*Ten minutes, unless Ember Flats is just as bad inside as it it outside.*

*Ten minutes … unless we're all dead in five.*

She went on, framing the talismanic clock like a seasoned leader. It was a battlefield commander telling a gutted soldier he'd be just fine, but even Christopher felt himself calming by degrees as the seconds ticked in peace. *This isn't so hard, just nine minutes and forty seconds left to go.* Then movement caught his eye, and he looked through the slats, again at the road sign.

Now Lila was standing there, with an enormous dark red stain on the front of her shirt, intestines sliding out of her abdomen with the languor of cold syrup.

Christopher rubbed his face.

And then it was Clara, equally dead.

His hand found Lila's. He squeezed it, and Lila — the real Lila — looked over at him. The bus was rolling forward as Jeanine's pep talk concluded, and as he glanced back, the road sign and the macabre figures waiting beside it like zombies at a bus stop fell out of sight.

"I thought of something," Christopher said. "The Pall. The Pall is still out there, and it will help us."

Lila seemed to take heart. She actually brightened.

No reason she shouldn't. Lila hadn't seen what their puzzling companion had shown him, and wouldn't wonder how those particular visions implied assistance rather than amusement from its place on the impartial sidelines.

## Chapter Sixteen

They came like locusts.

Aubrey, behind the wheel, put the hammer all the way down. Peers must have done something to the engine, or else buses in this part of the world had greatly improved their speed since Cameron had last taken one with his father. He felt the titanic thing rattle, shimmy, then finally find a sweet spot in resonance where everything stopped shaking as it if it might fall apart. Cameron held tight to one of the side-mounted guns, using the weapon as much for stability as defense. There was some sort of hopefully impenetrable glass above the gun's point of rotation, giving Cameron a fairly clean view of whatever he intended to kill. It was tinted slightly blue, and if they weren't being surrounded by hotrods covered in spikes and painted skulls, he would have asked: *So, Peers, is this an Astral windshield? Do you prefer it to human acrylics or polycarbonate?*

But there was a convertible thing that was probably once a Jeep ramming into their side, cutting the air with the screech of squealing metal. The innovative clan of red-painted bald men had done in life what James Bond movies had been doing in film forever and dressed their wheels with footlong spikes. The bus tires were shielded, so the spikes could only rake the metal, just as the spiked once-a-Jeep scratched long, warbling notes of protest into the armor plate along the sides.

Cameron swung the gun to fire, but the driver hit the accelerator. The car jolted forward as if from a shot of nitrous, easily dodging its swing radius. Then, with practiced precision, the red men were effortlessly jockeying into position, grabbing the bus's sides and climbing aboard.

Shots fired from above. Singles, probably a pistol. A red blur fell past Cameron's blue-tint windshield, and the bus gave a great lurch as if over a human-sized speed bump. A woman screamed, and then there were more shots. Cameron turned, but Kindred was right behind him, glaring.

"Don't leave your station. Don't you fucking dare."

"They need help!"

He looked up, but there were still three sets of legs visible beneath the open pop-ups as the bus lurched and veered. Cameron could see the black modified seat belts, tethering them to the platforms as the bus jumped. The front set of legs belonged to Christopher. The rear — the most important position, to handle the pursuit — was Jeanine. Charlie sat in the middle. The position was supposed to be Lila's, but she was inside, tasked with handling a mounted weapon. She'd been shaking too hard when the bus began rolling, and despite the side gun's vital importance and Lila's less-than-ideal experience handling anything like it, Jeanine had swapped on the grounds that given an unmounted weapon, she'd kill half their group in friendly fire. Charlie — similarly inexperienced but methodical to the point of sterility — had taken her place.

"We'll shift you if you need shifting!" Then, "The lance, Cameron!"

But the long lance protruding through the slats — the one Cameron had been clearly instructed on using to knock boarders from his gun in the event he couldn't shoot them off — had already been yanked through the slats. The cannibal who'd grabbed it — painted green, his face covered beneath the paint in jet black tattoos — was climbing topside, toward Jeanine. There was the chatter of an automatic weapon from above, and the man, with Cameron's lance, struck the dirt.

"Goddammit." Then, with an air of great impatience, Kindred reached for the trigger of Cameron's weapon and pulled. The thing chugged like clearing its throat, and the man who'd made the poor decision to try and wrench it free by hanging on its end went in two directions at once.

"Leave concerns about the others to — !"

Meyer was beside Kindred, turning him away. The pair's connection to the Astral collective would do no good out here in this swarm of humanity, but they were monitoring the situation from the peepholes around the bus, on the monitor, and from above using video from the drone Aubrey had launched once they were rolling. Knowing he was chancing being yelled at, Cameron sneaked a glance at the drone monitor. The clock was above it, showing that only thirty seconds had passed. The monitor painted a grimmer picture. Apparently fresh meat in cannibal territory had called out the clans in force. Cameron saw all the colors of the rainbow and dozens of armored vehicles swarming the bus from above, closing around it like clotting blood. Men were on the bus like dust on a staticky balloon.

"Everyone on your pads!" Peers shouted from the front, beside Aubrey.

"No, wait!" Meyer broke from Kindred and ran forward. He said something to Peers, but Cameron didn't hear it because a 1970s-era Lincoln Town Car — souped up with a blower through the hood and ornaments pocking the car's cut-away profile like grotesque art — had pulled within range. They must not have seen the big gun on the bus's side or were simply pinned in by the four other vehicles of different-color clans in close proximity because they lined themselves up nicely right in the sweet spot. By the time those in the target car were raising their weapons, Cameron was getting a satisfying look from their faces as they stared down his barrel.

Adrenaline soaring, Cameron held the handles and pulled the trigger. The car's riders burst like piñatas, spilling confetti guts into the screaming wind. The gray behemoth, suddenly driverless, slowed as it drifted sidelong into the vehicle beside it. A man hanging onto the next vehicle was speared on an adornment, and his battle-cry face became a mask of agony.

Cameron glanced back to watch Meyer converse rapid fire with Peers, whose hand was on a huge homemade knife switch like something from a Frankenstein flick. The hand kept twitching as if time were running out and Meyer was costing them minutes and lives.

"*They're all over us!*" Aubrey shouted. "Don't you bloody say he shouldn't — !"

Peers glared at Meyer. Kindred ran forward, bringing a small tablet with him. It must be the dual Meyer-Kindred logical mastermind attempting to digest all that was happening and plot the logical scenarios forward, adjusting as seconds melted, their dual brain following each action inevitably forward, trying to find consequence loopholes their group could squeeze through.

"*On your pads!*" Peers screamed.

Jeanine, Christopher, and Charlie shuffled their bodies away from the metal frame, leaning back in their harnesses. Their feet were already on rubber pads, but as Cameron's eyes flashed around he saw Clara scramble onto hers, knees to chest, youth bleeding through her usually cool, precocious facade.

"Not yet!"

To the others, ignoring the Meyers: *"Do it! Now! All of you!"*

And Kindred, to Peers: "Wait! Just another second!"

"Now," Meyer said.

*"Now!"*

Cameron barely pulled his hands from the mounted gun in time. Supposedly the mounts were mostly nonconductive, but Peers had warned him to take his hands away when they hit the pulse just the same, in case it arced. Which it might. The generator used to electrify the bus's skin was Astral technology, after all, like most things from the Den.

Every hair on Cameron's head seemed to stand on end. There was a low hum, a buzz, and a flash scent like burning meat. All the limbs he'd seen climbing the bus vanished at once, the Permaflate tires bounced across a scree of bodies, and the drone footage showed the bus swept clean as if by a powerful breeze.

But then the other thing happened, as Peers had warned it might when running so much electricity through the vehicle's frame from a mostly untested generator.

The back of the bus, near all those extra gas tanks, had caught on fire.

# Chapter Seventeen

PIPER FORGOT all about her pistol when she smelled the smoke and felt the fire's heat. What had caught fire, anyway? Weren't busses supposed to be made of plastics and metals and other things that didn't catch fire?

But the acrid black smoke filling the rear told her something far beyond normal had happened, and that it wasn't just flammables burning. It was plastic, too. The device had knocked all the clawing cannibals off their sides — a good thing because she'd seen Christopher fall and knew he'd been sliced or shot, though not enough to keep him from springing back up. Jeanine had been grabbed several times, but she had a knife and was somehow juggling firearm and blade well enough to hold her ground.

Without electrifying the bus they'd have been overtaken. But now they would burn.

Meyer shot past her. He must have been ready to grab the extinguisher because he was wielding it now, spraying a thick white cloud of carbon dioxide at the rear, chilling Piper's exposed skin with its proximity.

"Shit."

Kindred, coming closer: "What?"

"Shit."

*"What?"*

Peers, arriving, glancing at Piper as she gawked atop her rubber mat, seeming to consider a reprimand for her for no longer aiming through the metal slats.

"Where is that smoke coming from?" Peers was holding a fire extinguisher, too, but didn't seem to know where he should aim. The visible fire had gone out immediately, but smoke was still belching from somewhere far back, licking the ceiling and making a cloud.

"Something's still on fire back there."

"Where?"

"Behind the tanks. Is there insulation? Batting? Anything that could be lit on fire?"

"There's—"

Meyer cut Peers off. "You had to put the tanks inside the shell. Couldn't carry gas?"

A blue-painted hand reached through a broken slat and gripped Piper's chest as the bus trembled with speed. Wind whipped her hair, confused her distorted hearing. She reacted on impulse and fortuitously planted a slug between a pair of goggled eyes. Blood back spattered Piper's arm, and the dead body hung on for a few seconds longer before gravity raked it back and gouged its arm open on the slat's sharp edge, falling eventually away.

"Are you really going to measure dicks right now?" Piper shouted, near panic. *"Fucking fix it!"*

Piper's shrill voice must have shocked the usually unflappable Meyers because they glared back at her for a minute before Peers firmed his lip and kicked the side-rear door open to climb the armored exterior with only a fire extinguisher for protection.

"Jeanine!" Piper shouted up at the nearest legs, rear-most in the top-hatch line of three. "Peers is — !"

"I see him!"

Something at Jeanine's waist jostled. She'd taken Lila's carbine and must have somehow holstered her smaller weapon in its favor because a jarring rattle trickled down from above as Jeanine worked the rear of their ride, presumably clearing the way.

Piper couldn't keep her eyes from the clock. Impossibly, only two and a half minutes had passed. She watched until another sixty seconds was gone, hearing gunshots from all around, flinching every time the cannibals outside returned fire or rammed their accelerating sides. Peers had mostly bulletproofed the bus, but there were openings for guns — and, it turned out, for blue-armed men to reach inside. Something screamed past Piper's face and made a metal box in one of the luggage racks jump. It felt like being dive bombed by a horsefly, but the box, when she looked back, had a hole the size of a large grape.

After a long minute, Meyer went to the door on an unseen signal, pulled it open, and yanked Peers back inside, whole and seemingly unharmed. The door wouldn't close. Men with masks full of teeth and yellow eyes were halfway through until something came at them screaming, swinging at the limbs and heads with a machete, leaving dripping red marks. It took Piper a few shocked seconds to realize it was Lila, whose already-large eyes were now saucer sized once the portal was finally forced shut.

Four minutes gone.

Four and a half.

Piper watched Jeanine's pacifying clock as if it were a real thing. It meant nothing. But she looked toward the windshield and saw that Ember Flat's massive gates were much closer. They'd been an almost-invisible speck, but now she could almost see detail. Enough to think the gates were open. *Wide open,* and never mind the barbarians behind them.

Five minutes. Half their time in hell was gone, and Piper told herself it meant something.

*"Peeeers?"*

Aubrey's warning shout, drawing the man's name out, still jockeying the bus's huge horizontal wheel. And beyond the Astral glass windshield, where seconds earlier she'd seen only the end of their long and horrible rainbow, Piper now saw something new.

More cars, hideously modified into instruments of doom, swarming from the front in addition to those already crowding their sides and rear.

Reinforcements.

They were trapped.

# Chapter Eighteen

Peers rushed forward, almost colliding with the console in his clumsy dash. Staying upright as the bus stormed forward was difficult enough, but he hadn't anticipated how much worse panic would make it.

"What do I do?" Aubrey asked.

"I—"

*"What the hell I do, Peers?"*

Meyer arrived at Peers's side. But no, it was Kindred. Meyer arrived on the other, same except for his beard and eyes — quieter than Meyer Dempsey was supposed to be, even now. Perhaps Zen, maybe worried. But it was Kindred, with that partial connection to the Astral mind that seemed so like computing power in the old world's cloud. Yin and yang when working together. Good cop and bad. Heads and tails on the same exact coin.

"What should he do?"

But Kindred and Meyer were both thinking, looking around, consulting monitors and the view from the drone above.

*"What do I do, Peers? I'm almost up their asses!"*

"Stop the bus, Aubrey," Peers said.

"*Don't* stop the bus," Kindred argued.

"Don't stop?"

"Don't stop the bus," Kindred repeated.

"Goddammit, where do I — ?"

"Floor it. Right at that one in the middle. See it there?" Kindred pointed. "With the purple clan."

Peers followed Kindred's finger, but his words didn't make any sense. In its previous life, the thing had once been a pickup, but like all of the clan vehicles it had been heavily modified with — so it seemed — whatever the clans found lying around. This one had an ancient cow catcher like from a locomotive's front and skulls lined along a bar mounted above the headlights. The men in the bed and on the truck's roof looked like berserk metal fans who'd stumbled into KISS's wardrobe, wearing black armor and shoulder pads with gleaming silver spikes, their faces covered with war paint.

Peers saw it all because the truck was barreling toward them as rapidly as they were racing forward. They'd meet in the middle in a quarter minute at most, right into the thick of killer oncoming traffic.

Across the wall of vehicles, weapons were raised by shouting men.

"They want us to stop," Peers said.

"Don't stop."

"They've got guns! They'll cut us in half!"

"They won't shoot."

"Of course they'll shoot!"

"They want us alive."

"Why do they give a fuck if we're—"

Kindred cut him off. "They want Jeanine."

Peers looked up as if he could see through the roof. Jeanine, up top with her femininity in plain view.

"Aubrey," Peers said, "stop the bus."

"Don't stop the bus, Aubrey."

The gap closed.

Closer.

Closer.

"There's no possible way to get through that cluster of—"

At that moment, what looked like a large black bird slammed into the windshield of the truck where Kindred had focused Aubrey's aim. But it wasn't a bird. It was the drone, which Meyer was piloting with his tablet.

The glass turned white with spiderweb cracks, the large plane knocking the folding windshield off its adhesive seal and in toward the cab's occupants. The truck screeched hard sideways and rolled forward like tumbling dice. The others tried to compensate in both directions at once, and metal screamed as a chain reaction of crashes made its way down the spine of closely grouped vehicles.

*"Floor it!"*

Aubrey saw the gap made by the crashed vehicle and rammed the bus down its throat. The armored sides, supercharged engine, and Permaflate tires all did their jobs as the heavy bus widened the gap. Sparks flew along the bus's length, and Cameron gasped as his mounted weapon was ripped free, leaving an undefended hole. Feet hit the floor as the three snipers up top jumped inside.

For a few seconds there was only noise and darkness and fury. Then Peers felt a fresh draft at the driver's window and saw two brutes of different paint colors clamoring to climb in at the same time, both armed with pistols.

Lila managed to shoot one, and Christopher, down from the roof, shot the other.

But not before one of the intruders shot Aubrey dead, and the bus began to lurch out of control.

## Chapter Nineteen

CHRISTOPHER FOUGHT to clear his head. But Charlie reacted before he could leap into the driver's seat, jumping atop Aubrey's body and shoving it aside without any sentimentality. He jammed his foot onto the accelerator and slammed the bus through the onrushing traffic, but the bulldozer strategy was already faltering. Only seconds had passed since they'd struck the oncoming mass, but those near the rear were figuring it out, trying to close the gap, steering natural panic at the ensuing pileup into their mission's more rational thought. Only the fact that the clans didn't work as a unit (purple fought blue fought green fought black as they all grasped for the prize) kept the effort disjointed, and Charlie's path more or less true.

Openings widened. Openings closed. They were in the middle, surrounded by ten colors of warring factions charging toward them, with them, alongside them, distractedly away from them. Only confusion held their favor.

Christopher felt a hand tap his shoulder. Clara and Piper were on his sides, holding on as the bus bounced and swayed, neither paying him any attention. Christopher looked forward again, but the moment he did he felt another tap.

He moved back, looking around, curious.

And that's when he saw the final passenger. The one who hadn't boarded the bus, though Christopher had seen him on the roadside.

*"Trevor?"*

Trevor smiled.

But of course, it wasn't Trevor.

Shouting. Clanging metal. Gunshots. But somehow, time had stopped for Christopher, and all was quiet.

Trevor's sides puffed. His facial features became indistinct. Even his clothing seemed to dissolve. For a second, Trevor became half-human, half-smoke, then solid again.

The Pall, wearing its Trevor mask, raised its hands and turned them as if around a wheel, in a driving motion.

Then it made both hands into a tight ball and whipped them rapidly apart, like something exploding.

It made the driving motion.

It made the exploding motion.

And Christopher understood.

# Chapter Twenty

LILA WATCHED THE CROWD. She heard the shots and the screaming. Smelled the reek of fear in the air as Jeanine said to Kindred, "Time to use the car."

"No. It's pointless."

"We're getting flattened!" She looked back at Cameron. "Open the emergency hatch in the middle of the floor. Climb down into the—"

"I said no!" Kindred barked.

The bus lurched. Was kicked sideways. Lila's eyes fell on the huge knife switch that had electrified the bus earlier, but Peers was right beside it, shaking his head. That either meant *It won't work a second time* or *It'll burn us alive if we use it again,* but the simple gesture made Lila's gut sink as time ticked away. It was over. They weren't going to make it. They'd be enslaved at best, and likely eaten alive. She suddenly felt all girl as if her body wrapping fooled no one. Suddenly Jeanine's grenade strategy made a lot of sense. Lila only hoped she'd been polite enough to bring suicide for them all.

Jeanine said, "Cameron, there's a low, flat escape

vehicle attached to the bottom of the bus just below the hatch. Peers showed me. Take the satchel and—"

"No, goddammit!"

Jeanine turned on Meyer like a striking snake.

"There's no way out! Do you hear me! You don't even have your sky view anymore! You can't predict your way out of a no-win scenario!"

"Jeanine," Meyer said.

*"Fuck both of you!"* She shoved Meyer in the chest. Then Kindred. Her face was flushed, furious, eyes brimming. "Strategize this: *We're fucked!* All we can do now is get Cameron into the city!"

The bus was noticeably slowing. Cameron seemed to have shut the pop-ups when Jeanine, Charlie, and Christopher had come down, but up top Lila could now clearly hear —

Wait. *Christopher.* He'd been right beside her a minute ago.

"Cameron, take the Ark key, and get into the escape car. Peers said it drives like a go-kart. They'll be focused on us." Her features hardened. "Especially when we detonate the bus behind you."

Eyes spun to Peers.

"They won't notice your little car when the whole fucking thing goes up from the C-4 in the luggage compartments."

Lila's attention snapped. She felt suddenly cold, knowing this was serious, this was real — this was finally over.

Jeanine continued, her eyes strained and reddening. "The escape car is really low, only big enough for one person. You can probably get under half of their wheels. The Ember Flats gates are wide open. The clans must know not to enter, but you can! With luck, once we blow it, there'll be enough confusion that you'll be able to—"

"*No*, Jeanine!" Meyer held her arm, which tried to strike him.

"Clara," said Lila, swallowing. "Send Clara."

Cameron nodded. "Yes. That's it. Send Clara."

Banging from above. Banging from the sides. Charlie shouted from behind the wheel; Lila watched the speedometer drop to 30 kilometers per hour, lower.

"It can't be Clara!" Kindred shouted. "It has to be Cameron. It has to be — !"

Jeanine pushed herself away from the others. Drew her sidearm. Pointed it at Cameron's chest, flicking it toward the others in warning. The jostling bus didn't falter her aim.

"He's right, Cameron. It has to be you. Now go."

"Jeanine, I can't just ..." Lila watched him swallow, noticed his control slip a notch. "Dammit, Jeanine, I can't. Not after Grace! Not if I have to go into the city and stand in front of that thing and — !"

She cocked the gun as the bus's front collided with one of the vehicles, slowing its forward march to a crawl.

"I'm sorry, Cameron."

He turned. Slowly. But then he stopped, and Lila realized why when she looked down and saw that the floor hatch had already been popped, and that whatever had been under the bus was gone.

Two of the luggage compartments were open as well, loose wires dangling.

And both were empty.

## Chapter Twenty-One

THE EXPLOSION SENT an earthquake through the bus floor. For what felt like solid seconds, Cameron thought the world beneath him might open to swallow them whole. But the tumult wasn't ahead or underneath them — a bright flower that was partially orange flame but mostly brown sand. Vehicles seemed to pop up and tip over not far away. Machine parts rained. And Cameron knew that he'd finally shed his old life once and for all. Benjamin had Charlie, but Cameron came into this with Dan, Vincent, Terrence, and Christopher, who was now gone for reasons unknown.

The moving clans screeched around them, more distracted than when the drone had crippled the lead truck. Wheels squealed, collisions ignited around them in a circle. The entire jam seemed to pulse and open like a heartbeat, but it was too little, too far. The explosion had probably been big enough to clear a patch beyond their current fix. But the bus's front was still jammed against a clan vehicle, and they were still sown in.

"Floor it, Charlie," Cameron said.

"There's nowhere to go."

"There's a hole farther up now. Look at them. They think we have allies."

And it was true. Swarms of cars were suddenly uncertain. Heads in the trucks and other vehicles were looking up, backward, toward the sky. Something kept them out of Ember Flats through those big open gates, and that meant that even the horde feared whatever the capital had inside. There was an uneasy truce, and Christopher's act of heroism had reminded every clan. This wasn't just all of them versus one helpless bus. There were other forces in play, with explosives at their disposal.

"Come on, Charlie. Floor it."

"There's nowhere. Look. See?"

"Get up," said a voice at Cameron's side: Lila.

*"Get up, Charlie!"*

Charlie, shocked, shifted aside. Lila sat, dodging Aubrey's corpse without a thought. Her eyes were streaming, but she seemed not to have noticed. She'd lost her father, lost her brother, lost her mother, lost her husband, recovered her father with another to spare. Now she'd lost Christopher, and the wound would be deep. But now, in those big, brown eyes, Cameron saw only determination and absolute, total fury.

"Do you even know how to drive a—" Charlie began. But Lila had slammed the bus into reverse and jockeyed it into what had seemed a minuscule gap in the rearview mirror. Charlie fell over Aubrey's legs, banging his head.

Lila steamed forward. Hit a truck broadside. Consulted her mirror and saw that painted clansmen were streaming up from behind on foot, eager to take what they'd finally felled. Cameron saw a smirk touch Lila's lips. She put the bus in reverse again and swung around so she was backing right at them. The thump, when she struck the truck again, was muffled as if bodies were pinned between the vehicles. But she didn't immediately move forward again. Instead she floored the accelerator, pressing harder.

"Lila, there's nowhere to—" Charlie said as he moved to regain his feet. But there *was* somewhere to go; the mob of vehicles had left a gap near the embankment. Charlie fell again as she struck it, protesting, pointing out that it would tip if she tried to climb it. And the bus nearly did, but then Lila swung the big wheel the other way, down the embankment after five seconds' climbing, teetering on the edge of balance but sliding past the forward group's edge, slamming into the area cleared by Christopher's blast. The place was like the heart of a missile strike, debris blasted out equidistant in the pattern of a star. More cannibals on foot had stormed into the space, and it sounded like popcorn as they struck the speeding front bumper. The bus leaped as it crushed them below its Permaflate tires, and then their path was suddenly clear.

Lila didn't stop the bus until she'd crossed an invisible line past the Ember Flats gate, striking a wall made of sandstone or clay, shaking everyone aboard to their feet in a resounding and metal-rending crash, flooring the pedal until Cameron rested a hand on her shoulder and said she could stop.

Behind them, the multicolored clans lined up at the border, their faces furious. Fights sparked from clan to clan, realizing they were surrounded by enemies. They warred for mere seconds before an Astral shuttle floated overhead and a ray incinerated enough men at the front to scatter the others.

Cameron's hand was still atop Lila's hunched shoulders. On her curved back. He wouldn't move it. He knew it had to stay.

"He saved us, Lila," Cameron said. "We made it. We're safe."

Lila's shoulders hitched slowly at first then shook uncontrollably as she wept.

# Chapter Twenty-Two

AFTER THE THROTTLE stopped revving from Lila's foot on the gas and Cameron killed the engine because something mechanical seemed to have broken, with only half the drive wheels still spinning and the front end of the bus wedged into the wall, all eyes turned to Kindred.

"What now?" Cameron asked him.

"This is Peers's mission," Kindred answered. His logic had run out. As had Meyer's, where their minds touched. Kindred was no longer the conjoined thing they formed together; he was again just Kindred, and Meyer was again just Meyer. Inside, Kindred was still the man who'd led Heaven's Veil as viceroy after the mothership had returned him to the Axis Mundi, after he'd hitched himself to Heather, had two children, then divorced and married Piper. In Kindred's mind, the memories were continuous and wholly his own. The factual knowledge that claimed otherwise was impossible to reckon. Deep down, Kindred would never believe those memories and experiences didn't belong to him — even though it was obviously true.

The others were looking at him for guidance as if he

had all the answers. As if he knew more about Ember Flats and what came next than the satellite images and outland rumors had shown them. As if his sometimes-connection to the Astral collective made him one of them, when in fact, he was only a man, same as always.

Kindred looked back into the bus for Clara. He hadn't noticed her for some time, and for a horrible moment he was sure they'd lost her in the collision with the sandstone wall, if not before.

But no, she was right there: shorter than the rest of the group but standing within it. Clara was seven years old — but in other, subtler ways, she was the oldest among them.

"Any idea what we should do now?" Kindred asked her.

"I don't know" she said.

Lila was still crying, still filling the pregnant silences with the sour sounds of grief. Piper went to her, relieving Cameron, and squatted to lean in and whisper close. Clara didn't move to comfort her mother; Kindred imagined that would come later. Instead Clara stayed where she was, eyes locked with the man who masqueraded as her grandfather.

The crash had popped the unbreakable windshield from its seals. Smoke or vapor poured from the stopped engine. The bus didn't seem to have airbags; they'd all survived the crash without a cushion. They were lucky to be alive, past the gates after driving through hell.

The accordion door to the driver's right had also popped out of place. Still feeling expectant eyes upon him, Kindred moved toward the door and peeked cautiously out into the street. And it *was* a street, of sorts; the sandstone wall Lila had struck appeared to be the back of a very broad, squared-off building whose face was away from them, looking into the city beyond.

It seemed they hadn't entered the city after all — just

these long, peripheral outskirts. The open gates had let them into an empty space like that between rows of barbed wire fence surrounding a prison. The surface below Kindred's feet, as he stepped out, appeared to be concrete or finely crushed stone. It formed a road that led off in both directions around Ember Flats's periphery, between the outer wall and an inner one made from the backs of buildings. The inner wall, like the outer one, was topped with razor wire. If this was a prison, this no-man's-land would be where guards would march on patrol.

The thought made Kindred remember the shuttle that had dispatched the barbarians. It had sped off already and was nowhere in sight. The clans had remained, though — just beyond the open gate. They were standing back a handful of yards, staring at Kindred as he left the wreck, their eyes burning with hate. The bald men were grouped by color, but only in the most haphazard way. Blue-painted men were within reaching distance of teal-painted men, who on their other side were within reaching distance of black-painted men who looked like walking shadows. They knew not to come any closer. The shuttle had let the bus — not the cannibals — into the city's outer edge.

One of the red-painted men, wearing an elaborate headdress of multicolored feathers, opened his mouth to speak. Kindred half expected a strangled barbarian shout, but the man's measured and reasonable voice sounded like well-mannered words at a board meeting:

*"We will wait for you."*

Kindred said nothing. He turned from the gate. He wandered back to the bus's wreck and past it, until the street-like middle ground rounded a bend and the clans were no longer visible. He wasn't sure what he was looking for, only that he was compelled to scout the area. The sensation was like smelling the air — tuning in to the fact that he'd once had a purely Astral mind, that he'd communicated some with the Astral mind even when he'd been Meyer Dempsey, that he'd once had enough psychic sway to infiltrate the mothership and retrieve his donor. Kindred's higher brain argued that he was human and couldn't sense the Astrals any more than any other human. But he didn't have to feel the Astrals. He'd be content to feel the Pall, which had always been somewhere in the middle.

And yet he couldn't feel the Pall, and hadn't felt or seen it for days. Perhaps they'd outrun it; maybe they'd left it behind somewhere between Derinkuyu and the Den and Ember Flats. It hadn't taken a form and boarded Peers's bus. It hadn't made itself visible along the way, at least not that Kindred had seen. So where was it now? Was the Pall finally gone?

*No, it's not gone. It's just not showing itself.*

Kindred could feel its presence the way he could feel Meyer slowly closing the gap behind him. Between Meyer and Kindred — between the human and the Astral who'd become human — there was the Pall. It was as if the Meyer Dempsey who'd been shot dead by Raj was still around, his spirit now on both sides, somehow creating a link between their party and the Ark. That was the sense Kindred got, anyway, the reason he'd sided with Charlie to argue that the group needed to return and finish what it started at Sinai. Because Sinai was where the Pall had first begun to change, after it had found and touched its second source. That's when it had stopped being an ally and had become something else, something in the middle. Impartial but helpful. Assistive. But always at a price.

"How do we get into the city?" Cameron asked.

Kindred turned from his thoughts to see that the entire group had followed him. The bus was still smoking behind them, its front stuck, its axles apparently shattered. They would be on foot from this point on, for better or for worse — and God help them if they needed to run through Hell's Corridor again.

Piper, with her arm around a silent Lila, was watching the sky. "Where are the shuttles? Where are the Reptars?"

"Inside the city," Charlie said.

Meyer came up beside Kindred. He felt their minds touch, felt the synergy. Logic unfolded like an unlocking puzzle box, and indistinct questions began to become likely answers.

"They should be patrolling out here," Meyer said.

"*And* inside." Kindred nodded.

"Shuttles."

"They could make circuits. There's reason to."

"The mothership?"

"Unessential."

"Do you feel it?"

"Its presence. Not its intention."

"There's something. Something missing."

"But the wall—"

"It's just buildings."

"But it's still a wall."

"A *barrier,*" Meyer agreed.

"The only thing we can think is—"

"Obviously. But why?"

Kindred jumped from Cameron's hand on his shoulder.

"Maybe you two wouldn't mind speaking in English?"

Hadn't they been? Kindred could never tell the difference. But then again, it was possible that most of what he and Meyer had just discussed went unspoken, in their private dialect or otherwise, and had happened with their usual shuffling of mental images.

Kindred and Meyer both looked past Cameron, to Piper, to Lila beside her. Feeling the same shared thought at the same time, they both took a step forward — but seeing this, Kindred deferred. Meyer went to Lila and wrapped an overdue fatherly arm around her as Kindred held himself back, feeling his usual push-pull. It was ironic: Human Meyer's captivity on the mothership and the ensuing emotional crash course had made him more empathetic than he'd ever been before — and hence it was the copy of Meyer, in Kindred, who'd become more *Meyer* between them.

"Sorry," Kindred told Cameron. "We were just trying to theorize about the city's makeup."

"And?"

"I'd rather not say. It's ... in flux."

Cameron rolled his eyes. Charlie spoke in his place.

"Don't be obtuse. The gates were wide open. They let us walk right in, but we're in the no man's land instead of the city itself. You'll forgive me, but this all seems very familiar."

"You mean it's like Heaven's Veil."

"Which makes sense," Charlie said. "Similar defense plans for the capitals. Heaven's Veil had outlaw badlands, too, though they weren't as ... *advanced* as what we just went through. There was the entrance corridor at Heaven's Veil that was a lot like this one, and you had to go through the corridor to get into the city itself. But I also remember entering Heaven's Veil. *Twice*. And each time, the Astrals stepped aside and let one of us waltz right into a trap."

"This is different," said Kindred. Beside Lila, Meyer nodded.

"How?"

"To be blunt," Kindred said, still looking around, his mind still touching Meyer's, still looking for evidence he could add to his deductive equation, "it doesn't matter what we think because our course of action can't change."

"Are you saying it isn't a trap?"

"I'm saying it's irrelevant. Either way, we have to enter the city. We're hemmed in by the barbarians at the gate."

"That's how traps work."

Clara spoke, and heads turned. "No, he's right. This is different. I feel it too."

Kindred nodded. "They're not waiting for us to come inside so they can fool us. They're just *waiting for us to come inside.*"

"Then shouldn't we take the guns?" Lila looked at a still-fully armed Jeanine. The other weapons had been thrown about during the escape and crash; only Jeanine had thought to hold or recover hers.

"No," Kindred said.

Charlie had already turned back toward the bus. He stopped.

*"No?"*

"No." Meyer looked at Jeanine, but there was no point in arguing. If they asked Jeanine to leave hers behind with the weapons that had stayed on the bus, it would be wasted breath. But one gun (okay, two; she still had her sidearm) would change nothing except for the looks it would solicit from those inside.

Kindred watched the group, seeing their confusion. But based on the satellite images, there was an inner gate not much farther ahead, and once they reached it they'd understand.

Although even Kindred, honestly, didn't understand what the evidence and ensuing logic was telling him.

That Ember Flats wasn't what it seemed.

# Chapter Twenty-Three

PEERS HUNG BACK at the group's rear. With Aubrey dead, he was a lone stranger among family. The group was kind and courteous, but Peers had noticed the tall brunette, Jeanine, constantly glancing back at him. She kept slowing down — Peers supposed Jeanine wanted him to pass so she could position herself as rear point. But Peers slowed when she did, and the resulting nothing seemed to prove that he was at least *accepted enough*. She wouldn't force the issue and insist he walk ahead so she could keep an eye on him, but she didn't seem to trust him, either.

His hands fell to his robe, feeling for his concealed knife. It was still there, easily hidden by the voluminous fabric. They made a motley crew: most of them in assorted clothes they'd managed to keep intact, Meyer and Kindred in what could almost pass for business casual, Peers looking like a desert wanderer with a dog instead of a camel. Ideal dress for hiding weapons.

Nocturne looked up at Peers as if hearing his thoughts. The black dog was trotting in almost a heel position at Peers's side as if this were all perfectly normal. The crash had knocked them flat, but Nocturne had survived, unbruised like the rest.

"What are *you* looking at?" Peers asked.

Nocturne licked his lips.

Cameron had taken lead at the front. The twin Meyers seemed to be letting him head the group, content to hang back and play navigator. There had been several false alleyways, and already Cameron had led them down two before backtracking. There had to be a way inside, and Cameron kept saying he remembered the way from the satellite imagery. But Cameron was just trying to not lose his shit, much like Peers was doing by talking to Nocturne and touching his knife. Just as Jeanine was doing by watching the straggler, clinging to the little control she still had.

"You ever have a dog?" Peers asked Jeanine when he caught her glancing back.

"All the tough spots you described getting into, I'm impressed you didn't eat that dog."

"He is adept at finding food, so it would be foolish to use him just once," Peers said. "And besides. He is a great conversationalist."

Jeanine turned her head and kept walking.

The group stopped. The outer periphery around Ember Flats wasn't uniform; there were spots where the inner city's buildings didn't form a smooth wall and anyone walking the edges needed to detour around odd angles in the clumsily added outer shell. Peers knew every detail. He'd studied overhead photos night after night after night. For years. Grease pencil in hand, marking routes in and out. If they'd gone the other way around, there was a simpler but smaller gate they could have used. Cameron only seemed to have eyes for the large one, and Peers wasn't about to argue. But to get through some of these tough spots, you had to walk in unexpected directions. Of course Cameron kept running them into dead ends. And each time, of course he feigned exploration, insisting that he knew what he was doing.

The periphery opened again, and now Peers could see the inner door ahead. He touched his knife, feeling impotent. None of them had any idea what to expect, and they had but two firearms among them. The group sort of knew where they needed to go but not that the Ark had been moved twice. Peers hadn't told them. His theories on Ember Flats were just that: He knew the city's layout but not its makeup; he knew where the buildings lay but not the city's culture. The images always showed people, but it was never obvious, from above, who was who. Curiously, satellites saw the outlands and Hell's Corridor in crisper resolution than the city itself. *But why?* Were the Astrals hiding something?

And how were they supposed to get inside with only two guns?

Would it make any difference if they were armed to the teeth?

Maybe not. And perhaps that was Kindred's point. He'd said it wasn't precisely a trap, but he was only guessing. They'd made a lot of noise coming in, and the city leaders would be stupid if they didn't have a way to notice a bus barreling in. Someone would almost certainly be waiting at the gate, and those someones wouldn't easily be overtaken by seven adults, a kid, and a dog — no matter how heavily armed.

But they arrived to find the gate casually ajar, the way Peers's grandmother always used to prop her screen door open in summertime. There were no guards, or contingent waiting to abduct them.

"Is this it?" Jeanine asked, coming up from the rear.

"Is this what?" Cameron asked.

"The gate."

"I see an opening in the wall. I see doors. Looks like a gate to me."

But Jeanine wasn't moving closer. Lila, Piper, and Charlie were hanging instinctively back as well as if they expected something to leap through the wide-open door and bite them. They could see people passing by through the door — milling humans and giant, hairless white Titans roving by. Nobody was looking toward the door. They saw the hustle of a modern midsize metropolis, if "modern" included sandstone blocks and gleaming blue glass.

"Where are the guards?"

Cameron shrugged then looked at Jeanine as if she'd asked the world's stupidest question. "Coffee break?"

"Be serious for a second, Cameron," Charlie snapped.

Peers inched forward. They must look ridiculous from the outside. They were approaching exactly nothing with intense foreboding and drama. It was like squaring off against a sloth, fists raised, daring the sleepy thing to come at you.

"Get away from the door," Peers said.

Heads turned.

*"Get away from the door,"* he repeated.

Meyer squinted at Peers but complied. Kindred did the same. Slowly they all moved to the side, out of sight. Peers felt his pulse in his temples, certain that something was wrong. They were waiting just inside, surely to pounce.

"What is it, Peers?" Lila asked.

"Listen. Do you hear that?"

Four humans passed pushing some sort of a cart. The rapid-fire clacking of casters on stone sounded just like a Reptar's purr.

"The cart?" Lila asked, peeking past him.

"I thought it was …" He trailed off, glancing at Cameron.

"I thought the same thing," Cameron said. "Reptars."

"I don't *see* any Reptars," said Piper.

"Peers," Cameron said, his voice artificially low. "You've been here before."

"A very long time ago."

"Then you've studied the satellite photos."

"Yes, but—"

"Do you know where the peacekeeper station is? The Reptar patrols?"

"No, I'm sorry."

"I remember a cluster of buildings. That way." He pointed. "Who has the maps?"

"The bag with the maps was pinned back in the bus. I assumed we'd have to use the tablet." She looked at Meyer and Kindred.

"The tablet hit the floor in the crash," Meyer said.

"You let it break?"

"We were a little preoccupied with making sure the key didn't break in Cameron's satchel to worry about the tablet." Meyer nodded toward Cameron's waist, where they'd already verified the key, in its padding, was still intact.

"Peers," Cameron said. "You remember. You know the city."

He did. His knowledge of Ember Flats and the region as a whole — as well as his connection to the community Benjamin had been collaborating with before his death — was the main reason he was here. But he didn't just *know* the city. He'd *obsessed* over it. He'd plotted attack plans. He'd run scenarios. And yet he was already lost because by now he'd assumed they'd have gone over a wall, detouring through alleyways to lose their pursuers. Ironically, the only thing he hadn't considered was the idea of walking right through the front door unopposed.

"The Ark is that way, right?"

Peers nodded. "Last we saw."

"So how do we get to it?"

"We could *walk that way*," Charlie said, pointing where Cameron already had. "Am I missing something?"

"Where are the Reptar patrols? Where is the Ember Flats guard?" They'd inched back out, a bit in front of the open door, where the city's day-to-day activity marched on, uncaring. "Peers?" said Jeanine, trying again.

"I ... I'm not sure."

Meyer and Kindred were both watching the detente, their faces losing patience. Peers eyed them both — the former viceroy and the Astral who'd become his duplicate — feeling lost. He'd plotted this exact scenario so many times. He dreamed of Ember Flats. He knew the way from the outer gate to the inner gate to the viceroy's palace — practically right into Jabari's bedroom, where she closed her eyes at night. He'd seen the cluster of buildings around it in still images from above, watched the feed, deduced they were government houses. He'd scouted obstacles to hide behind, jumping from one to the other. But he was at a loss facing this complete and utter lack of resistance.

"It's a trap," Jeanine said. "They know we're here."

Cameron looked like he might agree. Meyer rolled his eyes and walked right through the doors, into the thronging crowd.

# Chapter Twenty-Four

CAMERON RUSHED TO KEEP UP. Once through the gate, he realized that Ember Flats was as teeming as the streets of any old-world, moderately sized city. It wasn't as big as New York or London or Berlin, and despite the Middle Eastern heat and limited desert colors it didn't strike him as Cairo before Astral Day, or Jerusalem, or Damascus, or any of the other cities in the region he'd visited with his father long ago. Ember Flats was something else. Something new, echoing the old.

Meyer and Kindred, keeping their heads down and moving quickly, forded a stream of pedestrian humans and Titans then vanished. Cameron scampered behind, hearing the others on his heels. Once past the flow of bodies, he saw the two Meyers farther on, down a third of a city block.

As he rushed to follow, Cameron couldn't help but look up, around, everywhere that caught his eye. The place was like Heaven's Veil's promise — potential the old capital never had a chance to reach. Cameron saw the same basic building schemes, the same basic geometric precision in its layout. He saw a familiar city grid here in the downtown, knowing the poorer areas would be similarly reflective of Heaven's Veil's more impoverished sections. But whereas Heaven's Veil had been immature when destroyed (hastily constructed houses, not much more than well-appointed bivouacs), Ember Flats had benefited from a half decade to grow on those same humble foundations. There were tall buildings that were like ancient/contemporary hybrids: brown stone accented with chrome and glass, dozen-story constructions that resembled primitive, smooth-walled obelisks. There were buildings that looked like architectural whimsy beside squat, practical-looking stone structures fashioned from heavy pillars. The city was somewhere between ancient and new — a tight, tidy footprint meant for walking with some hints of public transportation (Cameron saw single rails embedded in the street and rows of green or red lights arcing upward) but without the quaint and overly narrow look of streets built before cars. And yet there wasn't a single automobile. Shuttles, yes. But no cars.

And Meyer was gone again, around a corner.

Glancing back, Cameron saw most of his group. Lila was hand in hand with Clara behind him with Nocturne running beside them like an escort; Charlie looked like a hustling businessman with a filthy and highly unfashionable wardrobe; Jeanine trotted like a soldier, cradling her weapon as if it were a child, drawing frightened looks from all who saw it. But he couldn't worry too much about them. They would follow. Catching Meyer and Kindred was what mattered.

Around another corner, in time to see them vanish again, now down a narrow alleyway.

*"Meyer!"* Cameron hissed. It felt inappropriate to shout, though not for the reasons he'd originally imagined.

They'd already passed hundreds of people and dozens of Titans, but there were no Reptars or armed police — no one out to get them. Nobody, it seemed, cared that Ember Flats had been invaded. But Cameron still hiss-shouted with a sense of social propriety: anyone who'd been raised to eat with a fork knew that you should never shout in public.

*"Meyer! Kindred!"*

He practically ran into them both at the next corner. They were coming toward Cameron rather than away, and looking farther on, Cameron saw why. There was a huge green shape made of what looked like either matte-finish metal or plastic blocking the path. It looked like a monolith — but then he noticed refuse poking up in a pile at one end and realized it must be the Astral version of a dumpster.

"This way is blocked," Kindred said. "Go around."

"Are you talking to me?" Cameron looked at Kindred then at Meyer. They talked to each other plenty in addition to whatever it was they did inside their minds, and it wasn't clear if this was one of those times.

"Yes, I'm talking to you. Go around."

Cameron pointedly blocked the way. Kindred and Meyer both tried to shove past him, but then Jeanine arrived and completed the blockade.

"What the shit?" she said. "You're going to get us caught."

"Look around you, Jeanine," Kindred said. "Nobody cares that we're here."

"That doesn't make any sense. We all know what Ember Flats is like."

Cameron was still warring with what his senses were showing him. He'd heard the rumors same as anyone: *Outside the Flats is hell, and inside is worse.* Cameron had been picturing Heaven's Veil's police state, magnified by five years of fighting, distrust, and rebellion — along with the force required to quell it. In Heaven's Veil, there had been Reptars and human collaborators, oppression and murder. Everyone knew Ember Flats was the *real* capital, what with the pyramids and the Sphinx and the new monoliths anyone with a crap-resolution feed could see they were building from space. The ancient Egyptians had needed many slaves to build their tributes to god-kings. It only made sense — and the tales confirmed — that modern Egypt would be the same.

But the reality of Ember Flats was all around them.

"Obviously we were wrong," Meyer said.

"It's just a city," Kindred echoed.

"You said they were waiting for us inside," Cameron reminded them.

"They are," said Kindred.

"In the way a city used to expect the pope," Meyer added.

"But not as celebrities."

"Just as in, *They knew we'd be here.*"

"Though we are celebrities, in a way."

Jeanine was holding up a hand, trying to make sense of the rapid-fire shorthand streaming between the Meyers. "What are you talking about?"

"They know we have the key, Jeanine," said Meyer. "They know we can unlock the Ark."

Cameron slapped the satchel against himself.

Kindred shook his head. "They could have taken it a long time ago if they'd wanted. They won't steal it from us. They're waiting for us to use it."

"Then fuck that," Cameron said, unsure of why he was saying it. Any excuse to steer clear of the Ark was welcome, and avoiding something the Astrals wanted would do just fine.

Jeanine wheeled around. They were mostly concealed in the alley, but several of the passing humans saw her and scattered. Cameron spotted two Titans in the group, but neither paid the people milling in the alley any more attention than they paid those in the rest of the city.

"This is ridiculous," she said. "I feel totally exposed."

"Calm down, Jeanine."

"We need a plan."

"We have a plan," said Meyer.

"Really? Then maybe you should share it with the rest of us." She spun back to face him. At the alley's end, another two people saw her and rushed on. *It's her gun,* Cameron realized.

"Find the Ark," Kindred said. "Open it up."

"It's the same plan," Meyer added. "The same plan we had coming in, except that we won't have to fight our way to it."

But Jeanine seemed totally out of sorts. She kept looking around, clearly uneasy. She was like a balloon flying into the upper atmosphere. Freedom was pure up there, but without the surface world's usual pressure to crush her, Jeanine seemed lost. It wasn't the threats inside the city, it was the total and complete *lack* of threats now throwing her for a loop.

"Now let us past," Kindred said. "The archive building was over there on Peers's images. We just need to go one block up."

"The crowd is one block up," Jeanine argued. "Right in the thick of all those people and Titans."

"That's how we know we can get through."

"But you're running right across the open! We're defenseless!"

"There's nothing to defend against."

"Goddammit, Meyer, we … we …" But she didn't seem capable of finishing the sentence.

Kindred extended a hand. "Give me your weapon, Jeanine."

"Why?"

"You're attracting attention."

*"I'm not attracting attention!"*

Her elevated voice drew a few more eyes to the alley's mouth. A Titan glanced at her gun but then moved on.

"This is just a city."

"It's an Astral capital!"

"We can feel it, Jeanine. We thought it would be like Heaven's Veil or Roman Sands here. But it's not."

She gripped the carbine, holding it tight. Her body language clearly said that if anyone tried to take it away, they'd be in for a fight.

"Then stay back, at least," said Kindred. And before Cameron could think to stop them again, both men were past, now walking briskly. Cameron's gaze drifted toward Piper, whose color was up from the rushing and running. Her big eyes were frightened, but they were following Meyer and Kindred, urging Cameron to follow.

But instead of following, Cameron turned to Peers.

"What's going on here, Peers?"

Peers no longer resembled a man with a plan. He'd come to kill the viceroy, but now he looked like another crazy person in dreadlocks and a desert robe — an oddity from the outlands come to the big city with his dog, a new breed of urban nut job for the respectable people of Ember Flats to avoid like New Yorkers once steered clear of beggars.

"I … I don't know."

"Are they right? Are we really just … *allowed* to be

here? The gates were open. *Both* gates. Is there really no trap? Are they really going to let us walk right in and do what we came to do? For fuck's sake, there are armies of cannibals outside, not even walled off! Have you heard *anything* about Ember Flats that … that … ?"

*Explains this?*

*Justifies this?*

*Makes any fucking sense at all?*

But in the end Cameron could only let the sentence hang. No one picked it up, so it dangled, unfinished and meaningless.

"I … I have no idea," Peers stammered.

"We have to go," Piper said. "We'll lose them."

Cameron followed Meyer and Kindred to the alley-way's end then into the uncaring flow of the crowd going about its daily business, leaving Jeanine with her weapon and Peers to choke on his neutered presumptions.

## Chapter Twenty-Five

THEY EDGED INTO THE CROWD. Everyone was looking at them.

Piper could understand. She'd been a city girl once, a lifetime ago. When you lived in the city, there was a code about what you saw, what you accepted, what you ignored, and what you only pretended to disregard. She knew that the people of Ember Flats had noticed them plenty and were averting their eyes, sliding away to make room for the weirdoes among them.

Piper, Lila, and Clara might pass for normal; the city's dress code had settled somewhere between new and old, and the people wore a mishmash that wasn't new-world modern or old-world modern, nor was it ancient like Piper always somehow expected Egypt to be. Piper's worn and dirty jeans fit in, as did her still-intact button-up blouse. Meyer and Kindred, both of whom somehow kept clean and crisp even through all the grit, fit even better. Cameron was used to blending in anywhere and anonymous enough in appearance. Charlie was a sore thumb in the best of times but at least dressed normally. But Peers's desert robes and the black dog at his knee were another story — and Jeanine, with her automatic weapon, was another *world's* worth of story. The crowd was parting around her, saying nothing, murmuring once they were past. Piper felt a spotlight of attention while nobody intervened to stop them.

"This way," said Meyer, at the group's head.

They followed. Down a broad street — all pedestrians save the occasional gliding platform that seemed to serve as open-air public transportation. Past parked Astral shuttles that didn't flinch as they walked by. Down what might have passed for a New York boulevard in the 1900s, with shorter buildings, a distinctly eastern architectural style, and several enormous blue-glass pyramids visible on the pinched-down horizon — plus a few new monolithic sculptures Piper could barely see but that made her skin go cold.

Heads turned to watch them.

They passed a low gate that had been propped open, more ornamental than restrictive. The gate and its low stone wall let them into a courtyard surrounded by white buildings that reminded Piper of Washington, DC, which she'd visited as a girl but knew little about now. It had to be the government seat, and these had to be government buildings. This was a human place; Astrals didn't make buildings like this.

Meyer and Kindred stopped, seeking the next set of directions. Cameron came to join the small circle, glancing at the fewer milling pedestrians around them, Titan and human alike.

"I don't understand this place. There aren't any Reptars. None of the Titans have guns. No shuttles patrolling the sky."

"It's almost like it's just a city going about its business, isn't it?" The way Kindred said it was almost insulting, as if that had been obvious from the start. But it hadn't been; they'd all been there for Heaven's Veil, and they'd all seen the other cities and capitals. Ember Flats had a reputation, just like everywhere else: It was supposed to be a hellhole, a prison without cells, a city living under martial law, ruled by the bloodthirsty viceroy. There were supposed to be legions of slaves building effigies like the ancients. Beatings, executions, and streets filled with nothing but Astral enforcers and human turncoats. There should be death squads. Bars and barriers, surveillance and chains.

"There," Meyer said, pointing. He and Kindred started to move off again, toward an open spot that looked like some sort of sculpture patio or memorial garden — a tourist spot if ever there was one — but Cameron grabbed Meyer by the sleeve.

"I changed my mind."

"Don't be ridiculous," said Peers, speaking up from the rear. "I've already explained."

"I don't like this."

Peers looked at Kindred then Meyer. "We came here for a reason. Christopher *died* for that reason."

Cameron was ignoring Peers, appealing to Meyer. "You have to feel it. This isn't right. Come on, Meyer, I know you can feel it."

Peers answered instead. "You're just afraid."

As Cameron protested, Kindred inched forward. Meyer, guiding Cameron by his sleeve, casually followed. They were shifting around a semicircle, and now, as their perspective changed, Piper thought she spied something ahead. Something she'd seen before and naively hoped she'd never see again. They'd raised it up, built a cupola made of polished rock and a wide courtyard of flagstones. They'd put it in the spot of honor in this circle of buildings, easy to climb low steps and reach, easy to see, easy for anyone to walk up to and try their hand. It was the opposite of hidden — for the citizens of Ember Flats, but especially for them, the red carpet practically rolled out.

"Charlie," Cameron said, turning to the scientist. "Think for a second. They could have beat us to Sinai. They *let* us reach it first. Then when the crowds came to the mountain, they moved it here, put it out in the open, then practically advertised so the world would know where it was. Why do they want us to reach the Ark so badly? And should we really do what they want us to?"

"We've talked about all of this," Charlie deadpanned. "For *years*."

They could see the golden chest fully, maybe five feet off the surrounding ground, held high on its platform like something angelic. The Astrals had cleaned what was dull with dust when they'd found it the first time. The Mullah had guarded it in its old resting place but seemed to have done so through a closed door as if afraid to face or touch it, even without its activating key. Not that the Mullah had needed to worry when Cameron had come to open it, of course. They'd been dead when Piper and the others had arrived, killed as efficiently as if by an advance team of Astrals who'd come to clear a path for the crusading heroes — for King Arthur, by Peers's analogy.

"There's something wrong about this. *You* feel it, don't you?" Cameron turned to Piper, and she saw something that broke her heart: he was absolutely terrified.

Jeanine held out a hand toward his satchel. "Oh, for fuck's sake. Give me the plate. *I'll* do it."

"It won't work for you," Peers said.

"That's ridiculous." She reached, but Cameron backed away. Then: "Just give me the key, Cameron."

*"It won't work for you,"* Peers repeated, his patience obviously thin.

"Then Clara," Jeanine said. "Clara's Lightborn. She can do it."

Lila pulled Clara close, holding the girl against her, eyes wide.

"It has to be Cameron," Peers insisted.

Cameron snapped toward Peers, his fear now something sharper. "You certainly know a lot about this, don't you?"

"I'm just agreeing with Charlie's research. *Your father's* research."

"They're just making guesses. Even *he's* guessing." Cameron jabbed a finger toward Kindred, who up until now had seemed to be leading them. Piper could feel emotion rising from Cameron like heat, plenty loud enough to register on her increasingly empathic senses. He was a drowning man who'd pull anyone down to save himself. It might be ignoble, but it was intensely, horribly, irrevocably human. Even Jesus had wished for someone to take the cup from his lips, and Cameron was only a grown-up boy.

*"You,* on the other hand," Cameron continued, again indicating Peers, "seem so goddamn *sure."*

Peers blustered. "I'm just following the lore and what the Den's equipment revealed about—"

*"The Den.* Right. That convenient place filled with Astral technology that nobody ever came to claim, or kicked you out of. Right in the middle of open land we were allowed to cross without interference."

Peers suddenly puffed up, seeing all the eyes on him as the group's lone outsider. "Say it, Cameron. Just say what you need to."

Cameron jabbed a finger in Peers's face, turning to Meyer, to Kindred, to Jeanine.

"He's with them. He's with them, and we all know it."

"Bullshit!"

"You might even be one of them for all we know."

"He's not Astral," Kindred said. "And neither is his dog."

"Then you're working with them." He rounded on Peers, now very close. "What's in it for you, Peers? What did the Astrals promise you? Will they let you kill the viceroy, so you can take her place?"

"Cameron ..." Piper could feel him unraveling. He was too angry, deflecting, panicking. This wasn't about Peers. He simply made the best target.

"He showed up in Derinkuyu right as the Astrals pinned us down! Peers to the rescue! Doesn't that strike you as convenient?"

*"How dare you,"* Peers said, his voice narrow and dangerous. "My good friend lost his life getting you here. To this place that you *agreed* you needed to reach, for a second chance after whatever cowardice stopped you the first time you found the Ark at—"

"Don't you fucking talk that way to me! Don't pretend for one fucking minute that you know what you're talking about!"

"Keep your voice down." Meyer was looking around the courtyard, suddenly cleared. There were people at the periphery, beyond the buildings, looking in at them, wary.

"Go on, Cameron," Jeanine said, noticing the same wary faces. "If it has to be you, it has to be you. So man up, and do it."

Unbelievably, Cameron crossed his arms.

"Cam ..." Piper tried.

"No. Just ... no. Fuck this. Fuck *all* of it. He's wrong.

They're all wrong. You saw what it did last time. You *felt* what it did. This isn't what's supposed to happen. My father died to get this key." He patted the satchel. "They certainly didn't want us unlocking anything back then. Now they're *waiting for us to?* And that doesn't strike anyone as suspicious?"

"Goddammit, Cameron," Charlie said. "If you don't get up there soon, someone is going to show up and — !"

*"What,* Charlie? What will happen? Will they stop us from opening the Ark? No. I don't think so. Because, look: *it's right there on a silver platter, like cheese in a trap!"*

Jeanine shoved Cameron back then shot her hand into his satchel. A second later she was marching toward the raised platform, stone key firmly in hand.

Piper heard shuffling sounds behind her then a blur from all around. Jeanine paused, seeing it as well.

Human men and women with weapons, interspersed with Titan guards. Their leader appeared to be a thin black man who stepped forward and said to Jeanine, "Please, ma'am. Set that object down slowly, then raise your hands high where we can all see them."

Jeanine's eyes darted around the circle. They were outnumbered three to one, and she held the only weapons. But she raised the key rather than lowering it, her eyes seeming to say, *Let's see what happens next.*

"I'll smash it," she said.

"Go ahead. Just don't touch your weapon."

Titans and humans inched forward. Jeanine raised the key higher, but they didn't hesitate.

Beside Piper, Kindred slowly shook his head. Then as the guards reached Jeanine and began to carefully confiscate her carbine and pistol, she simply lowered it, letting the ceramic plate hang at her side.

Piper went to her knees when asked then put her hands

behind her head. The armed men and women produced rather ordinary handcuffs, and thirty seconds later everyone was wearing silver bracelets except Nocturne and Clara. The guards frisked the group, this time including Clara, and took a knife from Peers.

They each received a pair of escorts and were led out of the courtyard onto a strangely stable levitating platform.

Except Nocturne, trotting behind Peers without escorts, his tongue out and tail wagging.

# Chapter Twenty-Six

MEYER BLINKED HIMSELF AWAKE, suddenly aware of a strange sensation on his face.

He was confused by everything: the room he found himself in, the scented tinge of the air, bearing the pleasant tang of cinnamon, and definitely the wet sand-paper stir on his cheek, accompanied by a dark cloud in his peripheral vision. But most of all Meyer was confused because he didn't remember falling asleep.

He rolled his head on what seemed to be a pillow, fighting for clarity. He blinked again and realized that the big black cloud was Peers's dog, licking his face.

Meyer raised a heavy arm to shoo the dog away, but Nocturne stopped on his own before he could. Then he turned and walked through an open door into a lit hallway, his errand apparently complete.

"It's a good thing Raj isn't here," said a thin, helium voice from behind him.

Meyer rolled over. Heather was sitting on a padded armchair, her posture like a man.

"If Raj *were* here, that dog would have been dinner a long time ago."

Meyer considered pointing out that Heather's racism didn't even make sense but didn't bother once he remembered that you couldn't talk Heather Hawthorne out of being Heather Hawthorne, no matter how inappropriate she was. And also, Heather was dead.

"Don't ask if this is a dream," Heather said. "That's like something Piper would say, not you."

Meyer opened his mouth.

"Maybe we're on drugs," Heather said, preempting him. "Maybe the alien invasion never happened, and we're lying on the ground, totally high, back at the LA house."

Meyer rolled back to look at the hallway beyond the door. There was an elaborate sconce made of what looked like brushed aluminum. The top was blue glass like the Astral pyramids. He was in a king-sized bed with too much comforter amid a mountain of pillows. Lights were low, but the illuminated hallway gave him plenty to see by. The room was like something in a palace. Or like something in the mansion that Kindred had ruled in Heaven's Veil while pretending to be Meyer. Not that Meyer had ever seen that particular mansion.

"They told me you were dead," Meyer said.

"I never fucked him, you know. Either of them. The one that Raj killed or the one they sent in afterward. I'm sure all three of you fucked Piper, but isn't it nice to know there's still at least one thing you got that the other Meyers didn't?"

"How did you survive? I thought you—"

"You want to know something interesting, Meyer? The last time the Astrals came here, they found people who were connected thanks to their societies, their natural human bonds. *Each* of the last times they came, actually. So they worked with us and made everything better. By the time they judged and left us behind, survivors mostly lost the trick of communicating without words. But the skill was always there. They trusted that we'd get it back — and that maybe the next time, when we did, we'd get it right. So as much as I laughed at your Mother Ayahuasca and the collective unconscious bullshit, maybe you were sort of right. I mean, the Astrals did manage to peek into our world through your eyes."

"What the hell are you talking about?"

"Of course I'm *dead*, Meyer. Did your Heather ever talk about ancient societies and the collective unconscious?"

Meyer closed his eyes then rubbed them. He heard Heather laugh mockingly before he opened them again.

"Next thing, you'll ask me to pinch you. You're acting li—"

There was a minute buzz, and Heather suddenly stopped talking as if she'd been cut off clean. Her lips kept moving, but no sound came out. She spoke mutely for another thirty seconds or so, words buzzing and popping like a broadcast trying to break through interference. And then Meyer had it. He was speaking to the Pall, except the Pall didn't make sounds.

"I thought you didn't talk?"

"Please," the Heather/Pall said. "Did I *ever* stop talking?"

"You know what I mean."

"I —'e —lways know wha—" Heather's words buzzed in fragments. Then, her voice returning, she grimaced at what seemed to be leaving her mouth. "Well, *that* sounds like shit, doesn't it?"

"Why are you here? Where have you been?"

"Do you miss me?" Heather asked.

"Of course."

"Not Heather. *Me.*"

Meyer squinted, not understanding.

"I'm not always a plume of multicolored smoke, Meyer. And I'm not ever really Heather, or Piper, or any of the other forms I take. I sample them all. From ..." She made an all-encompassing circle in the air as if indicating the universe itself — or perhaps the collective unconscious the Astrals had trained ancient people into learning to use. "From *here*. But you know what I really am. Don't you, Meyer?"

"Kindred calls you a remainder."

"Hmm. A remainder of what?"

"I don't have a clue what that's supposed to mean."

*"Sigh,"* she said, actually pronouncing the word instead of making the noise. "And you used to be such a smart man."

Meyer forced himself to sit up, if for no other reason than to clear his head. The thing talked like Heather, like it knew things only Heather would know — right down to whom she had slept with. But how could that be, if Heather was gone, or if the Pall was reflecting Meyer back at himself?

Heather was speaking, but her volume had again been switched off. Every third or fourth word she seemed to clip back into auditory range, giving a snippet followed or preceded by a crack or sizzle or buzz.

She shook her head. "Fuck, is that annoying."

"Why is it happening?"

"Used to be, I couldn't speak. But now it's like I've remembered what sounds are like. Because we're closer."

"Closer to what?"

"Imagine a memory chest," Heather said. "Except that you can put anything that's ever existed inside it. This chest never fills up, and you can keep adding to it forever. It's not a jumble. You can find anything you choose the second you look inside. Your past is in there. Your hopes and dreams. Your friends, and *their* hopes and dreams. But sometimes you lose track, when you're away from the chest for a while. You forget what you've put inside. But then you take a peek to jog your memory and remember things you knew long ago, before letting them go."

"You mean the Ark. You're somehow sensing the Ark."

Heather sputtered and buzzed then smacked her head like a faulty television.

"But you don't always want to remember everything, do you? Amnesia is the great gift, like the universe's forgiveness. What's in there that we've all tried so hard to collectively bury?"

Meyer rubbed his head. He felt like he should have a headache, but he didn't.

"I don't even know where I am or how I got here."

"Relax. You'll find out when she gets here."

"The others. Where are the others?" He looked toward threshold and saw a broad white shoulder in the hallway: a Titan, keeping him inside despite the open door.

"You'll find out when she gets here," Heather repeated.

"Who?"

"Not long now."

Meyer waited for more, but Heather only crossed her legs and met his eyes.

"Whose side are you on, anyway?" Meyer was trying to remember the last thing he'd experienced before falling asleep, but there was only a slowly dissolving block of white. He couldn't recall details, only that there had been peril, and that they'd lost whatever had happened. He didn't think the Pall had helped. Just like it hadn't helped them through Hell's Corridor, which was a bit more vivid in his foggy mind. Just like the Pall had gone missing, how it hadn't raised a single smoky finger to assist them since the fall of Heaven's Veil.

"Yours. And the other side."

"Charlie says the Astrals aren't on a side, either. He thinks that what's inside the Ark will hang us or save us."

"The Astrals are neither side," the Heather/Pall said. "I am on both."

"It's splitting hairs."

"Is it? If it were, I wouldn't have spoken to Christopher."

"You ..." Meyer was remembering Hell's Corridor more now, and that meant he (and presumably the others) were in Ember Flats. But he remembered Christopher, and what had happened.

"You killed him."

Heather shook her head. "I encouraged him."

"Why?"

"Because I'm not splitting hairs," Heather said as if it were obvious. "The Astrals are on neither side. But I am on both."

"That's such bullshit."

"Is it?"

Meyer looked down, shaking his head. Then he heard footsteps approaching in the hallway behind him, and within two seconds of looking up found himself looking up at the long, white-gowned figure of an incredibly beautiful black woman with lean, exotic features and large dark eyes.

"So," she said. "The original Meyer Dempsey."

Meyer watched the woman for a beat then looked back at Heather.

But of course, Heather was already gone.

# Chapter Twenty-Seven

CAMERON WAS PACING, looking for weapons.

Piper was sitting in a comfortable-looking chair behind him, deeper in the plush, ornately decorated room. The place would have been luxurious if Cameron had chosen it for them to share — a belated honeymoon, perhaps, in a world without Astrals. But this wasn't a vacation even if Piper seemed ready to surrender and allow it to be one. The room was elegant, but Titans in the hallway made it politely clear that they weren't permitted to leave. There seemed to be every amenity but mints on the pillows, but on closer inspection the room was oddly sparse. There was nothing in the dark-wood dresser's decorative drawers; its mirror had a blue tint that suggested breaking it for shivs would be impossible. There were no toothbrushes in the private bathroom, bottles of caustic chemicals under the sink, or hairbrushes on the vanity. Lamps were secured to the tables. The only thing seemingly not bolted down were soft and squishy, like pillows and the comforter they'd woken beneath, expected to believe this was all so perfectly normal.

"You're working yourself up," Piper said.

"Is that a bad thing?"

"Cam, we've been here for hours now. You'll make yourself sick if you keep that up."

He turned, suddenly annoyed that Piper was sitting at all. Shouldn't she be trying to pry the frames off the wall so they could split them at the corners to use as spears? Shouldn't she be helping him find small items that could be made into keys to unlock the blue-tinted windows and run across the lawn beyond? It seemed as empty and innocuous as the room itself: a wide lawn of sandy, weedy grass that some clever landscaper had managed to make beautiful. Ember Flats was plenty irrigated; the taps all ran hot and cold. But whoever managed the grounds — those left behind after their courtyard arrest, along with the lawns and parks they'd passed on the levitating platform — had kept things native, using what the land provided rather than making things insultingly green. Perhaps it was a nod to where they were and where this place had been: outside the proper Nile delta, beside the ancient monoliths.

But no matter the amenities, they were being held against their will. And Piper was sitting in a plush chair. Reading on a Vellum.

Cameron softened his edge. Piper wasn't his enemy, even if she wasn't suitably infuriated. The enemy was … well, he didn't know who his enemy was, and that was the problem.

"So none of this bothers you? You're content to stay here?"

Piper met his eyes. Cameron could swear he heard her thoughts: *What are you complaining about? Those police and guards got you out of opening the Ark.*

Cameron wasn't sure what else to say in Piper's silence. They'd been discussing the same few topics since they'd opened their eyes in the enormous bed, and answers kept refusing to come. They both remembered being bound, loaded onto the platform, and led through part of the city. Then their memories ended until they'd woken in this room with no idea how much time was behind them.

Cameron could only gauge hours lost by the sun, but it seemed like maybe a quarter of a day gone since they'd regained consciousness. Their hosts seemed to have antici-pated a wait and had taken pains to give the guests some-thing to do in the interim. There were a pair of Vellum readers (too light to use as weapons) with access to some sort of a city network. Piper had found something to read easily and had shouted out several titles Cameron might enjoy before giving up. There was a screen recessed into the wall and a touchscreen control somehow integrated into the bolted-down coffee table. Piper had tried that, too, and for a while they'd watched some world news.

Building was underway in some capital or another in South America; Cameron had barely been paying atten-tion. They were building monoliths, and the screen had shown a few. To Cameron, they looked like sphinxes but without the pharaoh's cowl and more cat-like faces. They'd seen an update on some sort of summit, and that struck Piper as being business as usual, like the one scheduled in Heaven's Veil right before she'd run away with secrets in her grip. This one was in a city called Haunshoo, which seemed to have been built on a vaguely remembered spot in the south sea islands — somewhere Cameron recalled in a mental mishmash of places Benjamin had once dragged him to. The reporters were all humans, though much of the footage was of Astrals: Titans, mainly, shaking hands with human dignitaries as if they were pals. It made Cameron feel sick. And after the second loop of an iden-tical broadcast, he'd turned away. But the house — if, indeed, that was where they were — had a juke as surely as it had a Vellum server, and Piper had unearthed her old favorite shows. She'd settled on an episode of *Friends* Cameron had never seen, though his mother had always enjoyed streaming the show in days gone by. Piper was excited. "It's the one with Ross's couch," she said then quoted a line Cameron didn't know or care about — something about exchanging for a couch that hadn't been *cut in half,* complete with verbal emphasis.

Cameron had many thoughts about Piper's complacency but kept most to himself. He was especially bothered that although his thoughts were derogatory (Piper was deluded; Piper was gullible; Piper was too complacent and too easily pacified), he couldn't stifle a growing certainty that her reaction was the sensible one. *He* was being foolish, banging his head against a courteously provided and comfortably appointed wall.

The others were here, too. Or at least, most of them were. Jeanine's shouts had been echoing down what seemed to be a common hallway and through the open, Titan-guarded door. Cameron had heard Charlie arguing logically for something or other, perhaps appealing to the Astrals' analytical sides. Shortly after he'd woken, Cameron had thought he'd seen Meyer or Kindred (he wasn't sure which) walk past the doorway with a group of escorts, apparently unhurt. Piper had been most worried about Lila, but although Cameron hadn't heard her shout, Piper acted like *she* had.

"She's fine. They're both fine."

Cameron assumed she meant "both" to include Clara, though he hadn't heard Clara, either.

They hadn't heard from Peers — but Nocturne the dog had already come and gone three times. Their house arrest apparently didn't apply to the big black lab, who circulated like a visiting chaplain, come to offer comfort and take confession.

The second time Nocturne appeared, Cameron had scrawled a note and slipped it under the dog's collar. But the Titans at the door had stopped the dog for long enough to pluck the note out before sending Nocturne on his way.

There were feet coming down the hall. Cameron turned, and Piper looked up. After a few seconds of listening to the hypnotic plodding of shoes slapping tile, a dark-skinned man with a salt-and-pepper mustache appeared in the doorway beside a boy of maybe fifteen. Both entered the room, and the Titans moved from their guard posts, finally coming inside.

The man gave a tidy little bow.

"I am Kamal. This is Ravi." He indicated the boy. "Would you come with us, please?"

"Where are we going?" Cameron asked, unmoving.

"If you would please come this way?" he repeated, nodding toward the door.

"I'm not going anywhere until—"

Piper stopped Cameron with a gentle hand on his back. He looked over at her and was about to speak, but that same look on Piper's face stopped him and made his feet move. Piper wasn't just *willing* to go. Somehow, she knew that it was *right* to go, and Cameron — who felt none of the mental cache Piper seemed to have tapped into — was in no position to argue.

"Please," Kamal said, gesturing for Piper and Cameron to exit first.

They went.

The Titans followed.

# Chapter Twenty-Eight

As LILA ENTERED the enormous room hand in hand with her daughter, she found herself facing every member of the party she'd last seen when they'd all been in captivity, levitating their way through Ember Flats under guard. None had been killed or even seemed to have been beaten. Clara had told her as much, but Lila, deep down, hadn't believed it. She'd heard the others' voices calling out — all but her father's, or his duplicate's — but hadn't wanted to draw attention to her and Clara by doing the same. Maybe the Titans would forget her if she stayed quiet and pretended to watch the video screen's empty entertainment. And maybe Lila would forget what she knew about Titans: namely, that they could become Reptars, or God knew what else.

But no, they were all here. Waiting, all seated in posh chairs except for Kindred and a tall woman Lila didn't know, both standing by a fireplace that was dancing with bright purple flame and — at least from where Lila was standing — didn't seem to be generating any heat. Kindred seemed to be seeking command, making himself large and obvious, standing ramrod straight near the room's front, but the woman's presence dwarfed him. Her bearing was almost surreal, and effortlessly dominant. She was nearly as tall as Kindred and twice as magnetic.

She was dressed, appropriately enough, like an Egyptian queen. Like Cleopatra but with a skin tone more authentic to the region than Angelina Jolie. Her long, mostly bare arms were ringed, both above and below the elbow, with gold and silver bracelets. On the right arm was a skintight adornment made to look like a snake, its tail facing down, its head up, toward her shoulder. Her face was smooth and mostly natural, but her eyes were fixed like a cat's, dark black eyeliner wicking up at each outside end, lashes long. She had thin, delicate features and a chilly expression, her black hair swooped up and piled high, elaborately decorated with beads, jewels, maybe both. Even without the eyeliner, she seemed somehow feline, right down to the way she lithely moved her body in a flowing off-white gown.

"Lila Dempsey, I presume." The woman nodded to dismiss Kamal, and he gave a small bow before turning to go. Ravi seemed eager to do the same — to take her hand in a strange parody of farewell, but when Piper ignored him, he turned to Clara. Then Kamal's attention turned to Clara as well, and they both bowed again. It should have seemed absurd, but it wasn't. Lila had seen many strange reactions to her daughter over the years, and awe for Lightborn was hardly the strangest among them. The boy left, and Kamal moved to stand respectfully back from the woman, but Lila knew a guard when she saw one.

"Lila *Green*," she corrected, looking back up at the woman. There'd been no way, after Astral Day, to make her name change official (although the Heaven's Veil government had managed it when she'd become Lila

Gupta), but she'd still taken Christopher's name in mind and heart. And with that thought, a wall of sadness hit Lila with an almost crippling force. She'd been widowed twice, and was still closer to twenty than thirty.

The tall black woman nodded slowly, came forward, and as every head turned, approached Lila and took her hand.

"Your husband. Yes. I'm so sorry. I'd forgotten." She gave a sympathetic smile. "My name is Mara Jabari. I'm viceroy of Ember Flats. We have an unsteady peace with the clans outside our gates. They know not to enter the city but usually serve a valuable purpose outside it. Security, so that we are not forced to divide our forces and send them on patrol. The arrangement works because we do not receive authorized visitors arriving by land. If we'd known you were coming ..." Jabari trailed off, perhaps unwilling to deepen Lila's wound by implying that Christopher and Aubrey's deaths were her own group's fault.

*She's lying,* Lila told herself. But somehow she didn't think so. She looked over at Clara, who gave her an almost imperceptible shake of the head.

Lila smiled a polite but perfunctory thanks then slipped her hand from the viceroy's smooth-skinned embrace. She reminded herself that this person wasn't a person: a duplicate of a human woman, not a real one. But looking in the woman's almond eyes, it was hard to believe. The Astral mimic had even taken on a strange, region-inappropriate accent that Lila could almost place: Australia, perhaps.

"Your father and his friend, I've been speaking to for a while now," Jabari said, verbally brushing her hands to clear the uncomfortable air. Both Meyer and Kindred locked eyes with Lila. "Everyone else has been resting, and we've only now gathered. You haven't missed a thing."

Lila surveyed the room. Jeanine held her body rigid, as

if she planned to spring up at her first opportunity. Peers was mostly by himself, the dog sitting beside him, his eyes unreadable as they darted between the viceroy and Cameron, staring back with distrust.

"Kamal you've met," Jabari continued as if seeing none of this — none of the tension, none of the apparent murder lurking in Peers's dark eyes. "Kamal assists me in my duties here. And the others will not be staying with us."

Lila turned to see whom Jabari meant, but three pairs of Titans, near the room's trio of doors, were already leaving, shutting the doors as they left. Locking them in, Lila assumed.

"It's a great pleasure to meet you, Lila. Please. Be seated."

Lila looked to the others for a cue, got only uncomfortable stares, and finally moved to sit. Clara didn't follow, and found herself alone in front of the viceroy where Lila had been standing.

Jabari knelt in her long gown. The simple movement was elegant and effortless, no tremor of muscle apparent as she balanced low, now eye to eye in front of Clara. "And *you*, Miss Clara. I've been very eager to meet you: born under the first of the motherships, kin to the famous Meyer Dempsey."

Jabari took Clara's hand the way she'd taken Lila's. The minute skin touched skin, the strangest look crossed the girl's face. Clara looked from the viceroy to Lila, to the viceroy, to Lila. Finally she looked at Meyer, whose eyes flicked toward his double before he nodded with a small frown.

"Go ahead," Jabari said, seeing Clara's look aimed at her mother. "You can tell her."

To Lila, Clara said, "She's human."

# Chapter Twenty-Nine

Piper watched Mara Jabari as she stood, gave Clara's hand a parting squeeze and smiled, then moved to sit in the throne-like chair near the cool fire. Only Meyer and Kindred seemed unsurprised by what Clara had said — but then again, when Kamal and Ravi had brought Cameron and Piper into the room, the two Meyers had been sitting with the viceroy and gave the feel of a long conversation already nearing its exhausting end. They must have been through this already. Piper could only wonder what Meyer thought about his being replaced by a Titan while Jabari hadn't been.

Cameron looked like he was about to ask for more, but Jabari pulled a device from inside an end table cabinet before he spoke and set it on an ottoman in the room's middle. Cameron's eyes, seeing it, grew saucer wide.

"Where did you get that?" he demanded.

"I built it."

"*Bullshit,* you built it!"

Meyer spoke up. "Cameron, calm down."

But Cameron was standing, his manner agitated.

"I said sit down, Cameron!" His voice carried anger, but Piper thought he seemed more tired than anything.

"I've seen it before. In — !"

Meyer cut him off. "Yes, and if you'll stop and think for a second, you'll know there's no way that's the one Terrence used to own."

"You didn't even know Terrence," Cameron said.

"*I* did, though," Kindred said, his voice carrying the same weary, *will-you-shut-up-and-listen* tone. "He tried to use it once with Heather so they could speak in private, inside a bubble like this one." He ticked his head upward. Piper glanced up to the shimmering air and had to assume the thing on the ottoman was encasing them in some kind of a dampening field so they could speak without being overheard — though by whom Piper wasn't sure.

"And what? The Astrals took it? Gave it to her?" He glared at Jabari.

"No," Kindred said, still forcibly patient. "I wasn't … *ready* yet when I first saw it. At the time things were all so confusing. I only knew I had to take it away, to separate them, to keep a closer eye on Terrence. This was before Canned Heat. So apparently I didn't keep a close enough eye." He glanced at Meyer. "Or maybe I was finally waking up after all."

"What's your point?"

"Astrals don't have problems with privacy," Kindred continued. "Terrence's device was useless to them, so I destroyed it. Personally."

Cameron looked like he might challenge Kindred — maybe accuse him of lying — but it would be a stupid, rash thing to say. Kindred had been with the group for five long years. If he was going to stop being human in spirit and betray them, he'd have done it long ago. But at that thought, Piper had another: that the Kindred sitting with them might be a *different* duplicate. Wasn't it possible that the Astrals had created a bunch of Meyer copies and had only now — just before this meeting — swapped Kindred out for another with different allegiances?

*"No,"* a voice whispered. Piper looked over to see Clara two seats down, shaking her head, reading her mind.

"So … ?" Cameron began, but the question went nowhere.

"I built it from Terrence's plans," Jabari said. "Which he sent to me."

"Why would Terrence send plans for a privacy jammer to—"

"Through the resistance," Kindred said. "She's on our side."

Peers said, "Bullshit."

Lila's head turned. Peers stood from his chair.

*"Bullshit,"* he repeated, taking a single step closer. "She's not resistance. Or human."

"She's human," Kindred said.

"And they just don't know? We're supposed to believe that?"

"Sit down, Peers."

"They'd *know!* They'd know if she were human! I don't care what your Lightborn says or what you say." He glared at Kindred. "You're a fool if you believe she's just been able to trick the Astrals all along. What happened to you, Meyer? They abducted you, right? So who did they abduct if she's human? How did she get back down to Earth from the mothership? And then, what … she just killed her copy?"

Meyer answered with a heavy sigh, and Piper could see the effort it cost him.

"There *wasn't* a copy."

"What?"

"They didn't abduct me, Mr. Basara," Jabari said. "They ran me through a battery of tests. When the tests were over, they gave me the office."

Peers looked like he might explode. His eyes were on fire. *"More bullshit!* We've studied every one of the nine capitals! We've studied *all* of the viceroys! They were all like Meyer, like *you.* A strange compulsion drew them to a place, and—"

"That's exactly how it was for me," Jabari said.

Peers jabbed a rock-solid finger her way, accusation heavy in the air. Jeanine and Charlie were between Peers and the viceroy. Neither seemed to know where they should look. But if Peers had a straight shot, Piper felt sure he'd already have leaped at her.

*"Shut your fucking mouth.* I don't know what you are, but this … this *farce* is insulting to every one of—"

*"Sit down,* Peers!" Meyer bolted to his feet and moved toe to toe with the dreadlocked man, locking eyes until Peers finally returned to his chair, looking away.

"We've been through all of this," Meyer said, looking at Jabari and Kindred. "Five hours, at least. I'm convinced that what Mara says is true — and more importantly, so is Kindred. We're both tapped into the Astral mind — its *feel* and *intention* more than its informational content, at least — than any of you. Kindred can sense the mothership here. I can feel the collective on both sides."

*"Sensing. Feeling,"* Peers mocked, but nobody paid him more than a glance.

"We've run through the logic. We have an Internet backup from Cairo before Astral Day, and we've been here forever now, comparing and figuring, plotting scenarios. I believe her, as does Kindred. And more important: *Together,* with our combined mind, we believe her. I'm too goddamn tired to engage in debate." Meyer glared at

Peers then briefly at Cameron. "What we say *goes*. Got it?"

Nobody nodded, but Meyer met every eye in the group just the same. Watching him, Piper found herself transported effortlessly back in time, to when she'd met and married that dominant man. *Nobody* owned a room like Meyer Dempsey. It was his way or the highway — a lesson Raj had learned the hard way, again and again, on the road.

"Piper," he said. "Do you remember Astral Day? I called you at Yoga Bear as the news was breaking."

Piper nodded, still gobsmacked.

"I was watching a news program. The interview guest was a man named Bertrand Delacroix — I remember because I knew a *Brian* Delacroix and had this vertigo moment where I thought it was the same person. We also heard him on the radio a few miles outside Morristown. On the program, Delacroix was talking about government cover-ups. His whole thing was that if not for the Astral app, the public wouldn't have known about the ships until they were visible to light telescopes, and even then the field would have been limited and the panic contained. Most people wouldn't have known until they were visible to the naked eye."

"Benjamin and I saw that program," Charlie said. Then he did a double take and stared directly at Jabari. "Wait. You're—"

"What, Charlie?" Piper asked.

"I never made the connection. *You're* Dr. Jabari? Under Bertrand Delacroix?" He looked toward Cameron. "Jesus, I guess I just assumed you were a man. Did you know this, Cameron?"

"What the hell are you talking about?"

"Benjamin used to joke. Don't you remember? He'd

say, 'The da Vinci Initiate has a PhD your age. Why don't you get your PhD, Cameron?'"

"Sounds like my father's idea of humor."

"Benjamin Bannister — Utah, Walker Ranch — he was fascinated with you," Charlie said, now goggling at the viceroy.

"I was the Initiate's media contact," Jabari said. "*I* should have been giving that interview on Astral Day, and I'd have said all the same things. It made sense, to urge disclosure. Governments are always killjoys, aren't they? Bertrand only filled in because I was gone. I'd lined up all sorts of contingencies in place, just like Meyer said he did. A private jet on permanent standby at a tiny airstrip in Auckland. We had a refueling stop in India at a similarly remote airstrip. We ignored all the no-fly restrictions and took our chances. Fortunately, things went well." She looked at Piper, and Piper wondered if Meyer had already told her how terribly their own cross-country trip had gone despite similarly well-laid plans. "Cairo was hell, but nobody was going into the area, and only a handful of excellent guessers — nuts, most of them, rather than informed — went to the monuments at Giza. I was ready when they came. But they didn't take or replace me."

"If you're on our side," Jeanine piped in, "then why were we arrested?"

"You were running around my city with a machine gun in plain sight," Jabari said. "What did you think we were going to do?"

"*They* thought ..." Jeanine trailed off, but Kindred was nodding at her. "They thought we were *supposed* to go to the archive. That the ... the Astrals, I guess, but the humans too ... wanted us to reach it, and would let us walk right in."

"That's correct. That's what they want you to do. You

particularly, Mr. Bannister. But we're on a razor's edge here. Ember Flats has been a peaceful city for years, but it's a fragile balance. The Astrals provide all we need, acting as friends to the city and collaborators to the human government. They respect our administration and understand PR enough to let us be as long as we don't cause them trouble. The people of Ember Flats live a fine existence. One might even call it *privileged*. All thanks to the Astrals' help. But people have long memories, and most here remember how Giza *was*. They remember events like Moscow's destruction, before our peace. It wouldn't take much to hurl this city into chaos, and if we hadn't acted, that might have triggered it. So we had to stop you — though make no illusion, I'll let you unlock the Ark in time."

"But not now."

"Not yet," Jabari agreed.

"That's convenient," Peers said.

"*Enough,*" Meyer growled.

Peers stared back. Jabari rose from her seat and approached him.

"Mr. Basara," she said. "I don't believe you like me much."

Peers sputtered, suddenly at a loss for words. Nocturne licked his lips.

"I don't need to read minds like young Clara to read you. Meyer told me your story. And for it, I'm sorry. The city was not always so peaceful. There were days when harsher methods were required. I could not oversee every member of my security forces, and as you know, those were paranoid times. We all did our best. I would not have allowed what happened had you been brought to me rather than troops taking matters into their own hands. But it is not an excuse. I cannot and will not expect you to simply forgive me and my people. But I offer you my most heartfelt regrets nonetheless."

Peers looked smacked. He looked at Piper as if waiting for orders.

Cameron cleared his throat. "You said, 'Not yet.' You want it opened … but later."

"My people — when they were in better touch with the resistance, before the Internet fell — believed what I'm told Charlie does: that the Ark is like a jury. That it's still collecting evidence but already has a record of everything that's happened since the Astrals were here last. When it's unlocked, the information-gathering phase will stop, and the jury will take its recess. Then once the Astrals and the Ark are finished with their deliberations, judgment on humanity will be rendered."

"And if we're found *guilty*?" Jeanine asked.

"Then the human race will be eradicated," Charlie answered. "They'll save a representative group of survivors to start over and try again next time — plus a few new gods left to tell the stories," Charlie answered. "Just like every other time the aliens have come to Earth."

Piper's eyes went to Clara, but the girl seemed unfazed by Charlie's casual description of armageddon. In the most important ways, she was more adult than all of them.

"Oh, well … let's hurry and open it up, then," Cameron said, sarcastic.

Nobody answered.

Piper finally broke the silence. "But you said, 'Later.'"

"I need you do to something for me first," said Mara Jabari.

"What?"

"Ember Flats makes a monthly State of the City address that's broadcast to all the capitals. The next one is in three days. I need Meyer to appear onstage during the event and introduce himself to the world."

"That's it?" Peers chuckled. "Everyone already knows Meyer Dempsey. Even over here, we knew him before Astral Day."

"That's true," said Kindred. "But this time, there are two of us."

## Chapter Thirty

LILA FOUND her father still sitting beside the fire that wasn't a fire. Mara Jabari and her attendants were gone, just like all of the Titan guards in the hallways. They were apparently free to mill about wherever they pleased now that stories had been told. Whether they were true, Lila didn't know. And Clara, now asleep, wasn't talking.

Meyer was alone. Kindred was back in his room, with Jabari, or strolling the place as she had been. Strangely, Lila realized she'd be formulating words differently if Kindred were present. Both men loved her like a daughter because Lila *was* a daughter to both minds. But Kindred had remained very Meyer Dempsey while the true Meyer had evolved into something else. Perhaps the way Lila felt more comfortable with the real thing these days was a betrayal. Was it a better expression of love to appreciate the man as he was or as he'd always been? For most people, the distinction was one of present versus past, both sides housed in the same body. But for Lila, the choice between her father's two personalities was literal.

"You're still up," he said as he saw her, his eyes flicking to the big clock on the mantel. "It's almost midnight."

"I couldn't sleep."

"What about Clara?"

"She didn't have the same problem."

Meyer smiled and patted the chair beside him. He seemed too near the fire for Lila's taste, but it generated no heat. It was less an energy source than art on display. Would it ever burn out if it didn't truly blaze? Lila had watched Kamal feed it ordinary logs when they'd been here with Jabari earlier, though where they went once swallowed by the purple flames seemed a mystery.

"Has she told you anything?" Meyer asked. "Clara, I mean?"

"About … ?"

"About what Mara said."

Lila looked around, but the jammer — apparently a bit of Terrence that survived past death — was still in place on the ottoman, apparently on and granting them privacy.

If they believed Jabari. Or any of it.

"No. I don't think she knows much." Lila didn't go on and say the rest: *But she definitely knows* something *about* something. Lila was afraid that Clara knew more than she let on about the archive, or about what might be coming. But she didn't want to ask, and face the answer.

Meyer shook his head, looking toward the fire.

"What is it?" Lila asked.

"We keep going back and forth on this thing. This appearance Mara wants us to make."

"You and Kindred, you mean?"

Meyer nodded. "Usually, we can reach an agreement. This time, we can't. Kindred thinks we should refuse, but I'm inclined to do what she says."

"Why?"

"We both think she's telling the truth about her intentions. Just like we know she's telling the truth about who she is. They *didn't* duplicate her. She's *not* a Titan. There is no 'Kindred' for Ember Flats like there was for Heaven's Veil."

Lila watched her father's eyes. It was strange to think that not only did she have two equally valid fathers, she'd also lost one that everyone had forgotten. He'd been her father, too. In that first copy's mind, he'd been Meyer Dempsey. He'd built an empire, raised two children, had twice been a husband. And yet he'd died without anyone knowing until later — swept under the rug until Kindred's Astral memories could give them all the grisly details.

The newest shift in Meyer's eyes was hard to pin down, but to Lila it resembled defeat. Was it crushing to know the Astrals had found him unfit to lead a capital as himself but had no such compunctions about letting Mara Jabari do the same?

"If she's telling the truth, why don't you agree?" Lila asked.

"You know how Kindred is. The first time we found the Ark, it barely fazed him. He and Charlie have been saying we made a mistake from the start. But you want to know what I think, princess?"

Hearing him use the long-dormant term of endearment, Lila felt something shatter inside her. Whatever it was had been teetering on an internal shelf — a glass figurine, saved from her nearly forgotten childhood, when this man had been more dictator than father.

"What, Dad?"

"I'm starting to think that Cameron is onto something. Maybe we shouldn't open the thing at all."

"And just delay things forever?"

"Why not?" Meyer shrugged. "Forever is a very long

time. The Astrals here aren't like they were in Heaven's Veil. I watched one of the Titans remove the key from Cameron's satchel, inspect it, then return it to his bag. Kindred says they know what it is and what it's meant to do, but they gave it right back. I think Peers is right. They stopped *chasing* us a long time ago. Now they only *follow* as if keeping tabs. Because they're content to wait. Nobody knows how long the Astrals were around in previous epochs. Did they decide humanity's fate right away or take decades? Centuries? Even Charlie can't say. So is it terrible that I wonder if we should just never open it? The Astrals will wait, long past our deaths. Then it will be someone else's problem."

Lila watched her father. This wasn't the man she grew up with, and the beard wasn't the only difference. Something had wormed under his skin. Meyer Dempsey, both before and after captivity, faced his problems. This fatalism was as disturbing as a confession.

"The Astrals don't care, princess. They don't care if we keep going as a species or are wiped out. They don't even care if we're judged one way or the other. As far as they're concerned, humanity's case file can stay open forever."

"They killed Cameron's dad to get the key. They destroyed Heaven's Veil to find the Ark. So what's changed that now they don't even care?"

"They found the Ark. They know where the key is. Someone shuffled their deck, but now everything's back where it belongs."

To Lila, the explanation tasted funny. They'd spent years fearing and running from the Astrals, certain that what kept them coming was a desire to steal the key and activate the archive. The notion that they'd wait an eternity for someone to decide whether or not to pop the thing's top didn't sit quite right. They'd been nudged along the way, always suspiciously guided into the right spots at the right times.

"What about the thing Mara Jabari wants you to do?" Lila asked.

"Same argument. Kindred wants to open the Ark, and I want to let it be. He wants to stir the world's peace, and I'm inclined to let that be, too."

"What does she want, Dad? Specifically." Jabari had been vague on the details. Kindred and Meyer would both be surprise guests at the State of the City address, and the fact that there were now two Meyer Dempseys would, seemingly, shock the world. But how, and why? Lila was unconvinced, and that was just one of a dozen topics on which Clara seemed suspiciously silent.

"What is the Ark, Lila?"

"An archive. Of humanity's ups and downs while the Astrals have been away."

"What else?"

Lila shrugged.

"It's a symbol," Meyer said. "Everyone who's ever been to church — or, hell, who's ever seen *Raiders* — knows about the Ark. Charlie's told me some whoppers as far as alternative theories, where the Ark was a weapon as we first thought, or a machine, or a source of unlimited power for humans to harness and use. But the fact that we think it's so many things is what makes its mystery so compelling. Makes it fertile ground for new myths and the revitalizing of old ones. Nobody — except maybe the Astrals — knows the truth. Mara says they've deliberately said nothing, conveyed no messages about the Ark for Jabari or anyone else to reveal. They put it up on that platform in the middle of the courtyard and built a cupola around it. They've lined the walls of its enclosure with massive stone tablets written in an unknown script. Nobody's ever seen writing like it, so no one knows what it says. We couldn't tell from a distance, but Mara showed us close-up photos, and it's obvious that the Ark is missing a piece — that key Cameron is carrying. So everyone in Ember Flats walks by, drawing their own conclusions based on all they've ever heard and learned, wondering at the keyhole without a key. The Astrals don't need to say anything, Lila. That's the trick. Humanity's said it already, rumors and hearsay perpetuated over thousands of generations: the legend of the sword in the stone, the Ark of the Covenant, the Ten Commandments, you name it. And the flood, of course. The flood that wiped the world clean when God became angry, so Earth could try again."

"I don't understand what you're saying."

"Mara doesn't just want us to appear, Li. She wants us to tell our story."

"And?"

"It'll collapse all the myths. Think about it. Humanity knows there's a golden object on display in Ember Flats, smack-dab among the pyramids. But nobody's told them what it is or means. Which is fine because we all think we already *know*. Catholics think it's one thing. Muslims think it's something else. Atheists and agnostics have their opinions, just as steeped in myth as those of the religious folks even if they pretend they're being objective. The ancient aliens people think it's something else: maybe a nuclear weapon, displayed to quietly threaten us — or, conversely, as a display of the changed relationship between humans and Astral: a bomb turned into a monument as a gesture of peace. No matter who you are, you have an opinion as to what that object is and what it means. But everyone is guessing. Except for us."

Lila looked up, met her father's eyes.

"It's been here for five years, Lila. They built their city

around it. And because Ember Flats is the *Capital of Capitals*, where all the global broadcasts originate — the center of the new world, which the other cities look to for guidance — that means the entire world, in one way or another, has been built around that golden box. Even the wanderers, outposts, and gangs we've run across know about the Ark. Everyone's formed their opinion, and those opinions — all different — are safe and stable until someone establishes a definitive truth. The Astrals aren't talking about the Ark. But *we* can. And because of who we are — the viceroy much of the world assumed was dead and an apparent duplicate — they'll be inclined to believe us. I'm sure the Astrals — or even the human city authorities — will kill the world feed the minute they see us on it, but Ember Flats will see us. It'll start chaos, and the chaos will spread like a virus."

"And Kindred still wants to do it?"

"I think it's more that he feels we *need* to."

"I thought he felt that we *needed* to open the Ark."

Meyer exhaled. "It's complicated, Lila. That's why it took us hours to talk it all out before Kamal and Ravi got the rest of you from your rooms, and hours after you all went back. I promise it makes sense in Kindred's mind. Mine too, really. The trick is that although we agree on what's being done, we disagree on the damage it will cause."

"Or *won't*," Lila added.

"Oh, it causes damage even in the best-case scenario."

Lila didn't know how to respond, so she simply stared into the purple fire.

"So what are you going to do?" she finally asked.

"I don't know."

"The viceroy needs both of you. So if you don't want to do it ..."

"It's not that simple. You know how it is with Kindred and me."

Lila didn't, but she'd heard this before and had tried to understand. Her father wasn't really one man anymore. His strange mind sharing with Kindred — the conjoining that turned them into a logical machine, neither Meyer or Kindred but instead a third thing — made him more like a consciousness with two bodies. It wasn't literal, but that was as close as Lila's mind could get to grasping the concept. Both men described the shared portion of their memories as being more "in the cloud" than on either brain's hard drive. It was a different breed of psychic, a process that turned two things into one. It meant that while they were separate men, they were sometimes like two projections of a single being.

"If you don't do it, will she let us go?" Lila asked.

"I don't know. She may not feel she has a choice." He gave a bitter chuckle. "Just one more way we can refuse to decide, and let a stalemate continue forever."

"So we're prisoners."

Meyer looked around the room then gestured at their posh surroundings for emphasis. "It's not a bad way to be incarcerated, is it? Before Peers convinced us to come here, we'd been searching for a place to settle. Derinkuyu has nothing on Ember Flats." He wagged a sarcastic finger at Lila. "Now get back to your cell with its king bed and private bathroom before the warden knows you're gone. You're just *asking* for the guards to catch you out then pin you down and give you a massage."

Lila tried to smile, but it just wasn't funny. Prison was prison. Plots were plots. And as wrong as her father felt about what Jabari had in mind for him and Kindred in a few days, she was already reasonably certain he'd do it.

There was a knock at the open door, across the large

room. Lila and Meyer both turned to see Piper standing in the entranceway. Meyer tapped the privacy jammer, dropping the bubble — and for a half second a thought occurred to Lila: Were the Astrals so easily fooled? They were in the middle of a public room, discussing subversion. She thought of Cameron's suspicions of Peers, suddenly sure this was all a setup: a double-cross inside a double-cross inside a plot inside a misleading assumption. Her brain spun with reversals too thick to track.

"Piper. Come over, and join us," Meyer said.

Piper knotted her hands at her waist, not moving. She looked at no one in particular, then at Lila.

"Have either of you seen Clara?" she asked. "I can't find her anywhere."

# Chapter Thirty-One

Nocturne nudged Peers's hand, waking him. He felt momentarily disoriented then looked at the bedside clock. It was 12:04 a.m. A hair after midnight. Had he really gone to sleep just two hours ago? But then, they'd all been exhausted after the day's events, and sleep — for Peers, at least — had descended like a hammer. Jabari had said they could go wherever they wished within the viceroy's mansion — and the Titan guards were gone — so at first, Peers had planned to use his new freedom to snoop. He'd find where Jabari was hiding the secrets he felt sure she had buried. He'd find evidence of her nefarious plans just as she'd urged Meyer and Kindred to reveal evidence of the Astrals' iniquitous schemes.

Was this truly about the Ark?

Was it truly about Heaven's Veil — about informing the populace of the real reason the old American capital stopped broadcasting just before the Astrals had miraculously found a way to track their lost archive?

Or was it about power?

Peers had his doubts. He'd sat there all night, stewing,

watching Ember Flats's benevolent leader. He'd never met her, true. Nobody else had, either; according to Lila, there'd been an ambassador banquet in Heaven's Veil, but it had been presided over by the first Meyer duplicate, now deceased. Had Jabari been at that banquet, or just her ambassador? Peers certainly didn't know, and ultimately it didn't matter. Any familiarity with this woman came secondhand at best.

The only things they knew about Mara Jabari came from two sources.

The first, of course, was Jabari herself.

But their bigger body of knowledge about Ember Flats and its viceroy came from common knowledge. Supposedly other capitals these days knew Ember Flats to be the peaceful, cooperative paradise it was, but that information hadn't leaked into the outlands. To the non-capital cities — and to every wanderer they'd encountered outside of formal borders — Ember Flats was the pit that Peers had encountered all those years ago with Aubrey and James. And to that overwhelming majority of the population (the one Peers had encountered, anyway), the woman who ran such a hell could only be a demon herself.

*Bloody Mara,* the outlanders called her.

Sure, it was rumor. Sure, rumors always twisted out of control. And sure, Peers had heard the axiom about how when you *assumed* things, you made an *ass* out of *u* and *me.* But he'd also stood, helpless, while the Ember Flats guard executed his son in the viceroy's name.

Nocturne seemed to understand none of this. He'd licked Jabari's hand when they'd been gathered around the fire and was licking his now.

"Traitorous hound," Peers said.

The dog made a snuffling noise then rubbed his head

and body against the bed's side before flopping awkwardly onto the floor.

Peers rolled over, grunting with annoyance. He really was exhausted.

Nocturne buried his nose in Peers's armpit, nudging him.

"G'way."

The nose vanished. It returned a moment later, feeling decidedly thicker between Peers's upper and lower arms, spreading the angle of his elbow. He craned back to look and saw that the dog had retrieved a tennis ball, and that the larger object Peers felt was the dog's muzzle with a fuzzy green thing in his mouth. There'd been a bin of dog toys when he'd woken in the room the first time just as there'd been a plate of cheese and fruit waiting for Peers on the dresser, high enough to be out of dog's way. Someone had appointed the room for them both, but it'd been a big laugh between them (canine and human joking privately that the great viceroy apparently didn't know everything) that the box had so many balls and pull-toys. Nocturne didn't like tugging or fetching balls. He'd chase a stick, but he'd only enjoyed other toys while in Damascus, in the company of other animals. *Then*, he'd loved balls. A human throws; two dogs scramble to see who can reach it first. The game just wasn't any fun when you were alone in the chasing.

"Piss off," Peers told Nocturne.

The dog sat. He dropped the ball then stared at Peers with his mouth open and panting, tail wagging.

"It's bloody well after midnight," Peers explained.

When Nocturne didn't respond, Peers rolled back over and said, "Tosser."

The dog nudged him again. Peers felt the slobbered-up tennis ball drop onto his bare arm then roll onto the covers. Peers knocked it away. The dog patiently retrieved the ball (humans just don't understand such things) and set it back by his elbow, wet and disgusting.

"I'm not playing fetch right now, you fucking idiot."

Nocturne barked.

"Go to sleep!"

He barked again.

Rubbing his face, Peers sat up. He gave the dog a long, serious look, which Nocturne broke by licking his lips. Then he stood without further remonstrations, figuring that Nocturne had decided to be an asshole and wouldn't be talked out of it now. Stupid artificial daylight. They'd spent most of the past five years in the wild, sleeping whenever the sun was down no matter what the clock might have said. Now they were in a place with electricity — with goddamned *streetlights* in the courtyard and roads past the drapes. If he were to go outside now, there'd be enough light in Ember Flats that he'd be unable to see the stars — just the mothership's big, knobby belly hovering a mile or so away. The light was twisting their circadian rhythms. Damned dog's internal clock thought it was daylight.

Peers visited the restroom, relieved himself, and splashed some water (hot from the tap; Ember flats had everything) on his face. Then he removed the ball from the sheets, using only his index finger and thumb in deference to the slobber. The ball went back to the bin, and Peers traded it for a chew toy. Let the damned dog gnaw. It'd mean gross chomping sounds all night, but what the hell, Peers was plenty tired enough to sleep through it, and "chew" wasn't a game that required a partner.

Nocturne watched Peers set the toy on the floor. Then he ignored it, returning to the bin for the ball. He set it down and barked again.

"You don't even like balls." Then, because it was late and he felt lightheaded, he added, "Just like my ex-wife."

Nocturne retrieved the ball again then ran out into the hallway. Which was good enough. Until he returned, left, then returned again, tail wagging, dropping the ball long enough to pant, retrieving it, dropping it to woof and play-growl and bark.

"What the piss is wrong with you?"

Nocturne barked.

"There aren't any other dogs here, shitbox."

Another bark, now wagging his tail while backing toward the open doorway.

So Peers left his bed again, wrapped himself in the soft, fragrant robe provided by the household, and plodded toward the doorway to see what the hell the dog had up his butt. Halfway there, he retraced his steps and put on a pair of big, puffy slippers. They were posh but black enough for Peers to consider them manly.

He stuck his head out into the hallway, half expecting to find one of Jabari's assistants walking some froufrou breed of terrier, possibly with a pink bow in its hair, around the house for late-night exercise. That would be funny; Nocturne was large even for a lab, and chances were he'd annihilate a little dog if they played the race-to-the-ball game together.

But the hallway was empty.

Nocturne looked up at Peers. Then, likely anticipating more profanity, the dog trotted away, glancing back over his haunches, begging his owner to follow and join in the fun.

"No," Peers said.

Nocturne barked halfway — a quieter noise than usual, perhaps in deference to the late hour, and the likelihood that others were sleeping.

"I said no."

Another bark.

"I'm going to have you skinned and made into a wallet, you shitter."

Nocturne had reached the short hallway's end, where it met another perpendicular hallway. The dog ignored Peers, glancing off to the right, and barked in that direction. His big black head turned to Peers, ears flopping. His mouth dropped open, the ball falling to the floor with a disgusting smack. He dropped his front half down, elbows on the floor, elevated ass wagging feverishly: "downward dog" to human yoga aficionados; "play crouch" in dog parlance.

Before Peers could shout more epithets, the dog sprang from the crouch and ran off down the other hallway.

Peers mumbled to follow. There was nothing around the corner, but Nocturne kept going. Peers walked to the new hallway's end and found himself facing another, also empty. The halls were like a hotel in Wonderland, endlessly lined with anonymous rooms, crisscrossing and intertwining in a configuration that Peers, exhausted, found impossible to follow.

"Fine," he said at the next intersection to nobody in particular, hearing the now-distant scraping of dog claws and what sounded like a quiet human voice too low to hear. "But you're out for the night."

And that at least was something. He could close his door, and Nocturne wouldn't be able to bug him again, unless of course he scratched at the door to be let in. Which he almost certainly would.

He turned and took the first step back toward his room, but that was all he managed before hearing a new sound behind him. He peeked back around the corner and saw small feet, small swinging arms, a mass of little-girl hair.

"Clara?" Peers said, finding himself suddenly spooked by the uncertain sound of his voice.

But Clara was gone, marching on to more exciting places in the dead of night.

He was about to follow, but then something caught his eye and he squinted, bending forward at the waist.

And said, again to no one in particular, "What's this, then?"

# Chapter Thirty-Two

THE BIG BLACK dog ran ahead then sat in front of the wall, waiting for Clara, his tail wagging.

Clara's memories of the Heaven's Veil viceroy's mansion were clearer than her mother liked to believe, and it struck Clara now how similarly they'd been constructed — on the inside, if not out; in the details, if not the overall scheme. Heaven's Veil had been like a Roman palace, and this place was a fittingly Ancient Egyptian one with a kooky modern interpretation, but both were stone and wood, and the wood was always elaborately carved, sconces on the wall distinct but similar enough to have been born from the same basic mind. The floor plans echoed each other (Clara sometimes still walked the Heaven's Veil mansion in her mind; she'd read once about a memory technique called the "memory palace" and used their old home as her place to mentally place things she ought not forget), and the room sizes were too consistently repeated to feel like coincidence. To Clara, the echoes felt like two places designed by the same architect using distinctly different styles: an artist could change her mode but never hide her own, innate voice.

Two mansions created by the same mind.

Which, considering what Clara could see in the Astral collective (not much, but she caught a sense the way she did with most things), made perfect sense. They had many bodies, and one shared mind.

It was different from the way humans had many bodies and one shared mind. But, like the mansions, similar at root.

The wall where Nocturne had sat himself was wood-paneled, carved and polished, bookended by crown molding and a five-inch baseboard. The floor was hardwood, not tile like much of the rest of the house or carpeted like others. They'd descended a flight of stairs, and windows vanished from the walls. But even without looking out into the dark, Clara's internal compass told her she was a breath below ground, in the part of the house facing the Ark's courtyard, way across on the far end. Viceroy Jabari had given them that virtual tour, showing them around the local area without actually needing to show them around. Clara knew the others found this suspicious — being *shown around* while still inside. Clara could feel by probing at Ms. Jabari — it was true, they weren't permitted to leave. But she also sensed conflict inside the viceroy, and it was ordinary, everyday discord like Clara felt coming from her mother. Mom sometimes forbade Clara things she wanted because it was best for her, not because she wanted to be mean. Viceroy Jabari's feelings were like that. Clara liked the viceroy and believed even the parts of what she said that Clara, by tuning in, couldn't objectively prove true or false. She wouldn't lead them into danger no matter what Mr. Peers might think.

Nocturne was still sitting by the wooden wall, his tail

slapping the floor. The hallway died at the wall, and Clara knew that when she reached it, she'd have to decide between right and left. This pretty much had to be an outside wall, with the courtyard beyond it.

"Which way should we go, boy?"

The dog barked, not moving.

"You can pick," Clara said.

Clara liked following the dog. It was definitely more fun than aimless wandering. She'd lain in her bed for a long time, pretending to sleep because Clara sleeping would make Mom feel most comfortable. But she hadn't been sleeping; Clara had been in her internal space, talking to any who came from outside, exploring her memory palace back in Heaven's Veil's echo, gathering objects that her mind (except for the deep-down parts) had forgotten she'd once put there. But the minute Mom had risen, sleepless herself, and wandered back to find Original Grandpa, Clara had popped out of bed. She could roam without worrying her mother if she kept tabs on Mom's mind, just to make sure she didn't return while Clara was gone. So she'd shut out the others she usually tried to hear — Kindred, Grandma Piper, Mr. Cameron — and focused. And with her mother's emotional presence buzzing in the back of her mind like the fluorescents had buzzed in the bunker when she'd been inside Mom's belly, Clara had set out, exploring, led wherever her guide chose to take her.

But Nocturne wasn't choosing a direction, so when Clara reached him, she ran a hand from his slick head and down his back, pausing to scratch under his ears. And then she pointed for him, spinning a little as she indicated right versus left.

The dog faced the wall.

"You can't go that way, silly. There's a wall."

Nocturne barked.

Clara stepped off to the left. "How about this way? I think the kitchen is this way."

The dog didn't move, staying where he'd sat. He looked at Clara, panting happily.

"Maybe they have bacon in the kitchen."

No movement.

"Come on." Clara patted her leg.

And still no movement. Until the dog stuck his butt in the air and rubbed against the baseboard moulding.

"Hey, hey! You'll scratch it!"

She ran over to pull the dog away by his collar. Nocturne weighed more than Clara for sure, but he backed away willingly, panting at her with a dog-smile, as if he'd done well and she should praise him.

"Look at this, you bad boy," Clara said, running her fingers along a series of dull scratches in the hardwood. They were faint, but noticeable once you really got in there and looked close. And there were plenty now that she saw them. More than should have been caused by a few seconds of digging at a corner. The damage was barely there, not much more than the normal scuffs in the rest of the hallway. But it was strange because these scuffs ran right into the baseboard.

Where, now that she looked, there appeared to be a recessed button. It looked like a little half-moon shape carved into the molding's pattern, but there was clearly, on close inspection, a tiny gap around its edge.

*A secret door?* Clara's heart raced at the idea. She suddenly fancied herself inside Mr. Cameron's most cherished memories — the ones he kept hidden deep, and even a few that he hadn't given Clara permission to investigate. Mr. Cameron and his father had found secret passages when they'd been exploring together. Those old memories usually came with arguments — father saying one thing, son insisting another.

*You're absolutely sure you want to go in there?* Clara heard in her head.

But it was a ghost voice. Cameron's dad from long ago — prelude to yet another boring lecture about how Cameron always insisted he knew things he didn't because he was too proud. One of those memories Clara probably shouldn't really go into because Cameron wouldn't like her seeing, but to Clara it was all so mundane. He liked to be right. Was that really so bad? Clara liked to be right about things, too.

She pushed the tiny button. The dog nosed the wall as something clicked, opening a passage.

Clara's internal compass had been right about one thing: this was an outer wall, and there really was just the courtyard beyond.

That's probably why, with a mere three feet of clearance, the passage descended on a ladder.

Clara hesitated. She really shouldn't go down there. It must be one of the passages Ms. Jeanine had said must be here somewhere, connecting the Ember Flats government buildings in case of emergency, but Clara wasn't a viceroy running from bad guys. She was a bored little girl with an itch to explore.

Nocturne had no such compunctions. He leaped down into the tunnel, dropping six feet and landing lighter than he should have, like a cat.

Well, she couldn't exactly leave Nocturne down there alone, could she? He'd found the passage, but Clara had opened it for him to drop into. She could go back and get help, but was there any point in waking Mr. Peers? He'd had a rough day, with almost changing his mind about killing the viceroy.

The tunnel had to come up somewhere. And if the only ways up were ladders that big black dogs were unable to climb? Well, that particular bridge could be crossed when she reached it.

She sent her mind out to her mother. With the others shut out, seeing Mom was easy. She was still talking to Original Grandpa, discussing the aliens' memory bank and whether opening it was smart. It was good that particular decision wasn't hers — of course she'd open it without thinking twice. Who could resist the lure of a big, gold mystery box? It had freaked her out the first time, just like Mr. Cameron. But it was okay now. Little wounds never lasted long.

Clara was fine. She could be gone from her bed for a bit longer, and Mom would never know. And if she had to leave Nocturne here and go for help getting him back up, she could do that later. The tunnel wasn't all that scary-looking. There were at least a few small electric lights. The walls were concrete and tile.

Nocturne barked, and Clara climbed down to follow him as he walked off into the dim.

Some time later, the passage through the wall automatically ratcheted closed behind her.

# Chapter Thirty-Three

BELOW THE DOORKNOB, and a plate that read *Utility Closet*, three small triangles were carved into the wood. Peers probably wouldn't have noticed them if he hadn't been so tired — if the damned dog hadn't dragged him out of bed. But he'd yawned at the right time; he'd let fatigue drag his footsteps down the hallway, and his lazy eye had grabbed the pattern. Even then, most people would have moved along, but not Peers. For him, the pattern of triangles was as instantly evocative as the scent of alcohol can be for those who've suffered a long hospital stay. Or, in the days before the Astrals' arrival, the automatic alarm that screamed in people's heads when a red-and-blue light flashes in their rearview.

He felt his heart quicken. It took less than a second before he felt himself tumbling backward in time, to his boyhood. He wasn't in a mansion hallway; Peers was in a room sifting dust from the vaulted ceiling pouring sand like pounding rain. A kid with his hand on an ancient trigger, realizing he was deeper than he'd thought, or feared, or arrogantly decided. He was a little boy knowing he'd done wrong and fearing his father's wrath. Knowing the stories of exile, that his own days among family and friends were truly numbered. He was a kid who'd always done mischief but who'd finally managed to do something irredeemable.

Peers blinked the torrent of emotions away. He'd buried all that. Long, long ago. He'd moved on. There'd been London. There'd been university. There'd been studies, always meant to replace what he'd once known in more intimate ways. There'd been the quest. He was a goddamned adult man now, with a Ph-fucking-D. Nobody was coming after him. He no longer needed to fear the belt, or the Tribunal.

But the symbol was there, true as the moon.

Peers looked down the hallway, toward where Nocturne had run off, then back the way he'd come. He was near enough to the last corner to step back and peek around it — the way was clear there, too. The house was quiet. He knew, based on what he'd heard after waking from his stupor, that the others' rooms were near his own. But those rooms were now a full hallway back, not even visible. And during their brief tour, Kamal had told them most of the rooms were for visiting dignitaries, and thus were empty.

Still feeling watched — by a hidden camera or Astral device, perhaps — Peers squatted. He ran his fingers along the pattern, which at first he'd taken as dirt in an otherwise immaculate hallway. The carving was perfect as if stamped into the wood.

Three small triangles, upside down, arranged in a loose triangular pattern overall, with the tip pointing toward the floor.

He hadn't seen that pattern in more than twenty years. After his exile to London, he'd seen its cousin. Kids around the world would have said the symbol looked like an upside-down, stretched-out version of the Triforce: a symbol from video games Peers hadn't known, seeing as he'd grown up in tombs and sand dunes, playing hide and seek in ancient ruins. Today he'd say the symbol on the door looked like the Triforce. But back then, he'd wondered if it was coincidence that the good folks at Nintendo had created a symbol so similar to that of the Mullah. Mullah were everywhere, so why couldn't they be in Japan?

Peers stood, feeling vertigo. The door was wood, not stone. It looked fresh enough to have been carved yesterday, not thousands of years ago. The mansion wasn't ancient, or cobbled from other ancient sites.

No, whoever had carved that symbol had done it during the building — or perhaps the city's — construction.

Whoever had carved it was almost certainly still here. And knowing the Mullah's infiltration and placement tactics (like those of all the world's great secret societies), that person would be someone in a position of authority, someone with sway and access. Perhaps even Mara Jabari herself. It was possible. Peers had been a kid back then, more interested in causing trouble than networking. He'd known only his clan.

It was too ironic. Peers had thought he was following Cameron Bannister, the way he'd followed his father. But maybe he was the one who'd been shadowed all along.

He stood. Looked around again. And opened the door.

The room, with the door closed behind him, was true to its word. It wasn't a tiny broom closet with scant room to maneuver, nor was it palatial. There were some valves for water mounted to the concrete with half-round metal brackets, plus a mess of wires snaking in and out of network hubs. Even with the Internet dead, Ember Flats had its own little network. But like those in the other cities, Peers was willing to bet the system was deliberately antiquated, obsolete even by the standards of ten years before occupation. The Astrals could have wired Ember Flats to the nines, but that would defeat the purpose. This place had been built by human hands, possibly with Astral assistance. And so its tech capacity had been purposely retarded. You don't strengthen a leg by offering a stronger crutch.

Inspired, Peers closed his eyes and tried to think of the others in his group. But no, his brain was still just an old hunk of wet flesh. It'd take a lot more than slow web access to force his mind to consider the collective unconscious as a viable alternative, if there even was such a thing.

But other than the pipes and valves and wires and a few mops, buckets, and brooms, the place was ordinary. Maybe the marks on the door had been a coincidence. Maybe someone *had* been trying to draw a Triforce, and the door had been mounted upside down.

Swallowing, Peers scanned the room. The Mullah did nothing by accident. Someone had marked that door just as someone had authorized the marked door being discreetly set into place. Just as someone had laid all the bricks; just as Peers — if he knew his old fellows at all — was certain the house must have concealed passageways and tunnels.

*Don't be stupid. The Astrals would know if tunnels were being put in.*

But according to the story Clara had told Peers that first day, the Astrals hadn't known when the Templars and Mullah worked to relocate the Ark. Sure, it had been moved centuries ago while the Astrals were away, but it made no difference that the mansion had been built right under the Astral eye. The aliens stayed out of human political affairs; Kindred had confirmed as much from his time running Heaven's Veil. Once the roof was on the building, the Mullah and their famously tight-lipped workers would have been able to do as they wished. The Astrals could have forced their way inside for inspections, sure, but that would have made for bad human-Astral public relations — an even trickier balancing act this visit than in their prior ones.

The feeling of being watched escalated, and sent a chill up his spine.

Being watched by Mullah — who, being Mullah, would know exactly who Peers Basara was and had always been.

But also being watched by Astrals, the way the aliens had (again, according to Clara's story) seemed to allow Cameron's group to reach Mount Sinai then watched them discover the Ark.

Watched their approach.

Then watched them leave without doing what they'd come to do, off to wander the desert for five years rather than ever return.

*What had happened that day? Why had they run?*

Curiosity dug at his insides, but Cameron's latest bout of suspicion meant it would be a while before Peers could ask anything without Cameron suspecting ulterior motives.

There was another Mullah symbol etched into the concrete block, just below a heavy-duty metal shelf bracket.

Peers touched it. Pressed it. Rubbed it like Aladdin summoning the genie from his lamp. He was tempted to say, "Open sesame" but thought he'd heard something elsewhere in the house a moment ago — maybe someone stirring for a late-night snack. He hadn't done anything but felt intensely guilty. Old guilt, like bile in his throat.

*I'm just standing around inside a utility room. Nothing wrong with that.*

But whatever was bugging Peers was deeper down, under his skin like a parasite. He couldn't place the reason, but staring at the symbol in the bricks made it worse. The last time he'd seen that symbol was …

Was …

Peers remembered his father. He remembered the fury. He remembered a sinking sensation that not only had he angered his family and friends but that what he'd done — however unwittingly — went even deeper. Toward betrayal, like a traitor.

He'd never understood what he'd done so wrong other than causing one hell of a mess out of (let's face it) a bunch of stupid old rocks.

But then he remembered the blue disc.

He remembered his father's face when he'd realized what Peers had done.

The hand — not the belt — had gone up to correct the disobedient boy. The flash of Father's Mullah ring as the hand swung back for the strike had been indelibly engraved in Peers's memory.

*The ring.*

There was a box of nails on one of the higher shelves. Peers reached in and retrieved three. Maybe he was wrong about this, and the strangely precise rings were merely symbols of membership in the secret society and nothing more. Or maybe the rings *were* keys, but the locks they opened couldn't be fooled by picking tools as crude as nails.

But Peers didn't think so. The Mullah had always been more about symbolism than practicality, more about ritual than rationality. Twenty years ago, he'd managed to open a door he shouldn't have been able to open, and with no ring to do it.

He pressed the nails into the three triangular indentations, at precisely the same time.

There was a hard click, and one of the cinderblocks jumped forward an inch — revealing not the back of a cinderblock but a small, concealed drawer.

Inside the drawer was a perfectly round, perfectly smooth sphere of what looked like brushed aluminum. The size of a cricket ball covered with fine blue lines like a magnified circuit.

Feeling the same sense of *I shouldn't do this* that he'd felt touching the blue disc two decades earlier, Peers took the sphere in both of his hands, finding a single pulsing tentacle-like wire protruding from its back, attached somewhere at the drawer's rear.

"What are you, friend?" Peers whispered to the sphere, only half his mind noticing the rush of feet passing beyond the utility room door.

The lights went out.

The sphere answered.

# Chapter Thirty-Four

"Cameron. Come on, Cam, wake up."

Cameron blinked. Piper was above him, dressed in a robe, her face flushed and bothered.

"What?"

"Get up. Grab your robe."

"Why?"

"Clara's missing."

*"Missing?"* His eyes darted to the hallway past Piper. He spied Lila at the door, arms crossed, Meyer beside her.

"We don't know where she is."

"You don't know where she is, or she's missing?"

*"That's the definition of missing, Cameron!"*

Cameron held up one hand, all at once seeing the depth of emotion around him. He sat on the bed, with a nod to Meyer and a meaningful look to Lila, then stood. The cobwebs were intense. It felt like he'd been sleeping deeper than he had in years, and swimming to the surface from a dead slumber now was like rising from the ocean's floor, fighting narcosis.

"Tell me what happened." He said it to Meyer,

knowing it was a sexist thing to do. But Piper had been thinly stretched for a while, and Lila, if she truly thought her daughter was in trouble, wouldn't be sensible. Kindred, Jeanine, and Charlie would all have been rational and clear, but for now, the gentler-and-kinder Meyer would have to do.

"Lila and I were in the main room, talking by the fire. Piper came in and asked if we'd seen Clara. She'd gone to peek in on Lila, next door. But she was with me, and Clara wasn't in her bed."

"That doesn't mean she's missing," Cameron said.

"There's something about this place I don't like, Cam," said Piper, again composed. She hugged her elbows, subconsciously mimicking Lila, and sent her eyes to the room's corners. "I feel like we're being followed. Or watched. I just got this itch. That's why I peeked in. I even felt stupid doing it, like I was being ridiculous. But the door was ajar, with enough light from the hallway to see that Lila's sheets had been thrown back. So I went in. You know how Clara sleeps: like a brick. So I went ahead and turned on the lights. I just wanted to tuck her in. I … I just kind of had the shivers." She laughed to show the situation was all silly and stupid, but Cameron could tell from the laugh's artifice that in Piper's mind, at least, it was anything but. "I just wanted to run my hand through her hair, you know? The way you'd pet a dog or cat to feel better." And she laughed again, this one decidedly manufactured. Cameron could see her fingers shaking and somehow felt sure they'd been shaking before she'd opened Lila's door.

"I left her in bed. I couldn't sleep, but she was conked out." Lila seemed ready to say more but merely hugged her elbows tighter. Cameron could see Lila trying to keep herself together, maintaining sensible tones and stifling her speech against a clearly creeping panic.

"She's probably just wandering," Cameron said.

Meyer nodded to indicate agreement, but even his mannerisms struck Cameron as phony. "We've already been up and down the big hallways. Pretty much everything on this side of the palace with the lights on. But yes, you know how Clara is." He forced himself to add, with a tiny artificial smile, "Curious like George."

In the beat after Meyer stopped speaking and before Cameron answered, the mansion's stillness struck Cameron like a physical thing. They'd spent most of the past years either in ramshackle shelters, in small outpost towns, in co-opted vehicles, or out in the open. All of those places were full of sounds. But despite the way city light filled the windows of the bedroom, the night's silence, inside these four rock-solid walls, was absolute. Cameron spoke because Meyer required a reply — but even more because without sound he felt suddenly deaf.

No wonder Piper was so edgy. No wonder Lila seemed panicked despite a normal incident of childlike wandering off. It was the silent night forging the perfect slate for waking nightmares.

"Did you check with the others? Maybe Clara went into their rooms."

"Why would she go in with Charlie? Or Jeanine?"

"I don't know; I'm just making suggestions," Cameron replied, a trifle perturbed. Even his own annoyance came out of the blue. Piper was right: it was this strange place, this luxurious captivity.

"The doors are all closed," Meyer said. "I'm not even sure which rooms everyone is in."

Cameron wanted to roll his eyes. Kindred would have known. For the first time Cameron had ever seen, Meyer and Kindred had parted ways for the night with issues unsolved between them. Kindred had gone to bed with the others, clearly irritated with Meyer's obstinance. If Kindred were here, they'd know which rooms were whose. And if Kindred and Meyer were firing on the same cylinders as the combined logical entity they often became, they'd know the whole damned palace's layout, right down to having concocted an action plan for possible escape.

Cameron sighed, seeing that he would have to be in charge. He didn't like it but always ended up leading any group he joined. That was why he'd always preferred to travel alone — or, sometimes, with a trusted companion like Dan had been, who understood Cameron's past and individual quirks. But there were only four of them awake right now, and the trio of Lila, Piper, and Meyer had felt sufficiently unable to solve things on their own that they'd woken Cameron.

"Fine," he snapped.

Cameron pushed past Piper without warmth then between Lila and Meyer. He was still tired, logy, and missing his bed. Why did everyone have to ask him which way to go all the damned time?

A cool finger seemed to press itself against his neck. Facing away from the others, he closed his eyes and breathed deeply.

*It's this place. It's Jabari. It's our predicament. It's what they keep telling me I have to do whether I want to or not. You can be calm. You don't need to be on edge, or irritated.*

"Come on," he said.

# Chapter Thirty-Five

THE TOTALLY DARK, silent, and sensorily disconnected place Peers found himself should have been terrifying but wasn't. He'd been here before.

The Mullah elders called it "the vestibule." They trained for immersion, knowing that its total absence of stimulation could cause panic — and that panic, in a mental space disconnected from a very real but unfelt physical reality — could quickly unravel even the sturdiest mind. So the elders took their vision quests into the desert alone, sometimes building sweat lodges and smoking psilocybin, often wandering with nowhere to go and no way out. There were places deep in old ruins and converted caves where the elders had built voluntary confinement chambers, constructing shallow pools to float for hours or days in solitude with their ears plugged and eyes covered, breathing through reeds. Peers had always been curious about those nether realms as a child, and after moving to Oxford had sought sensory deprivation chambers to feel what it must have been like. But word among the Mullah was firm, and the rule — like all tenets in the clan — was unbreakable: only the elders entered the vestibule, and only those elders who'd prepared their minds for the nothingness they found inside.

The kids all had their secretly whispered beliefs, the way boys on the outside had covert theories about where adults hid porn. The children all talked about the practices and about the space and about what probably happened inside. *You could go mad,* they'd say, *because the vestibule is nothing, and it's what you think that controls what you see.*

And still they'd try to sneak in. Even when the secret box was heaved from place to place, they'd plot to find its new location and touch what should never be touched. It was the same feeling Young Peers had while standing over a nest of asps, knowing he should back away but still wanting to reach out and nudge the hissing mother with his foot. The same feeling he'd felt, years later, at the top of Dubai's Burj Khalifa tower, looking down, thinking of how if there was no glass, the devil inside him might not be able to resist the urge to jump.

*We all have darkness inside,* Jacob, the Mullah wise man, had said. *Our need to destroy ourselves is the reason we are not yet ready. Although that time is coming. And in the day we reach the vestibule untempted, each of us will be ready to heed the Horsemen's call.*

Well, if you were wise, Peers had always thought. If you were wise, you could face the vestibule and find out if you were ready — whether you were a man pure of heart or still a kid with reckless tendencies. Peers had once asked Jacob if he could ever enter the vestibule. If he'd ever be sufficiently controlled, adequately mature. It was a right of passage he'd never face, a test he'd never be allowed to attempt.

And, he'd thought even as a ten-year-old, *Fuck that.*

But in the end, who'd had the last laugh? Peers, now a proper adult despite Jacob's high-handed condescension, was back in the vestibule. It hadn't destroyed him the first time and wouldn't destroy him now. He hadn't needed training after all, either time. His exile wasn't so bad. Providence had given him another chance to prove himself, and now here he was again: in a Mullah place, seeing through the Horsemen's eyes. What he thought, he'd receive. He knew what to do, no matter that Jacob had ultimately called him an unworthy disgrace.

He floated in the black space, seeing, hearing, and sensing nothing. He couldn't even feel the heavy brushed-metal sphere in his hands, in the real-world utility closet inside Mara Jabari's palace.

His mental eyes seemed to look down. He realized that he still had hands and that there was a silver sphere with blue lines across its surface nestled in them. There was a pulsing line leading from the sphere's back, but in this place the thick wire vanished into nothing rather than being anchored in back of a hidden drawer.

He wondered, *Is this the same place? Is this the true vestibule, the way I visited it in the past? What is this object, and how did it come to be here?*

The sphere lit in his hands then vanished. The room changed around him, becoming a building under construction. Much of the surrounding landscape was arid nothing, and Peers found himself realizing that the sphere's artificial reality had placed him very close to his body's current position. He was seeing Jabari's palace before it had become one, seeing Ember Flats when it had still been a speck in the desert.

Ahead, in hot sun that Peers seemed to feel on his skin, he saw a tall, muscular, bare-chested Titan. In the alien's hands, the sphere looked tiny. The Titan handed the thing to a woman covered head to toe in black. She slipped it beneath the fabric, and it was gone. But then Peers saw a man very near where he seemed to be standing — someone he recognized: Akeem, whom Peers had known when they'd been children together. He'd changed as he'd grown, but Peers knew it was Akeem because the sphere knew it was Akeem, just as the sphere knew the Titan was being watched when he'd handed the memory sphere to the human.

Understanding came, dripped into his cortex as if from above.

*The sphere holds Astral memories. Like the Ark, except that it records a subsection of alien experiences rather than human ones.*

*It creates a space like the portal vestibule, but it is not the same as the portal.*

*It was given to the human leaders to facilitate understanding of what came before so they'd understand what must come next.*

*But the Mullah stole it. Connected it. Kept it hidden because they controlled construction.*

And that all made sense, Peers thought, considering that the relationship between Astrals and Mullah had always been complicated. The two sides of universal detente shook hands across distance then spent their time apart stabbing each other in the back. It had been the Mullah's idea to hide the Ark, though only the elders knew Sinai had been its destination until Clara had divulged the secret to Peers. It had been the Mullah's idea to remove the key and hide it in America. The Mullah had left the tablet under Vail, where the Ark had been last set by the Astrals. So double-dealing was nothing new, though they'd always had the small blue disc that nobody outside the elder circle even knew *was* a small blue disc — until Peers, of course.

But something itched at Peers as he watched the scene

— the answer the sphere had given to his last question — slowly dissolve and return to black. If the sphere held Astral memories, and if they included Akeem watching the Titan's handoff, didn't that mean the Astrals had known Akeem was watching and planned to steal the sphere?

Peers felt an abiding sense of complacency surround him as if the air itself had smugly smiled.

The black vestibule seemed to nudge him, to ask what he most wanted to know from the sphere.

Well, that was easy.

*What happened at Mount Sinai, when Cameron and his group went to find the Ark?*

It felt like a question the sphere couldn't answer, seeing as Cameron's group wouldn't have approached their quarry if they thought they'd been followed. But Peers felt himself slipping into a memory as if seen from above, and at a distance. A simple, no-nonsense understanding slipped into his mind, and Peers knew he was seeing from the eyes of Divinity.

Events unspooled as Peers felt himself slip into the skin of experience — as if he'd been there, and this was happening now. Cool, wet air kissed his skin, and he felt hard rock underfoot. He was inside the mountain's heart, down a corridor the Mullah had excavated and hidden. He must be inside a human mind (or at least steeped in the weak, underdeveloped mental network that had so surprised the Astrals on arrival) because somehow Peers, even now, five years removed from the events before him, felt certain that they were alone. There were no aliens here. They'd beaten the Astrals, and found the Ark first.

"It's this way," said a voice.

Peers looked over his shoulder. As the memory solidified, it was becoming impossible to tell reality from artifice. He was here, now. In a biblical mountain's ancient cave.

And now was two years after Astral Day, not the seven he'd so recently believed.

*It's not real,* Peers told himself. But the Cameron Bannister who'd spoken — a bit younger and less weathered by experience — looked plenty real. Peers was a member of his party. As solid, true, and in the moment as the others. Just like Cameron, the Meyers (one emaciated, half-dead), and Piper. Just like Lila, carrying a toddler because she'd chosen exploration over the more perilous option of staying behind in the shuttle. Just like Jeanine, Christopher, and Charlie. There was another girl, too: someone Cameron didn't recognize — tall and athletic-looking, pretty despite her dirty face and hands, wearing plain shorts and an old tee, blonde hair pulled back into an unraveling ponytail.

"Are you sure?" Piper asked.

Cameron looked back at the group, and Peers could see false certainty climbing onto his lips. No, he wasn't sure, but he was unwilling to admit it.

Two-year-old Clara, shoving out of her mother's arms to balance on chubby little toddler legs, answered in a curiously adult voice.

"He's sure."

Cameron nodded at the girl, and Peers felt some odd sense of understanding pass between them as if she were reading his mind as faithfully as (or more faithfully than) he was reading it himself.

They found the Ark at the short passage's end. It seemed to glow even in the gloom. Throbbing as if overfilled. Peers could sense electrical menace in the air as if someone, somewhere, was violently angry.

"There," Charlie said, pointing. "That's where the key goes."

It seemed almost too obvious. Cameron was carrying a

different satchel, but its purpose was the same. His hand slipped beneath the flap and removed the ceramic key, then he stood frozen with trembling hands.

"Go ahead," said the blonde, seeing him hesitate.

"Something's not right."

"This is what we came here to do," she said.

Cameron turned to Charlie, but Charlie only said, "Grace is right. Let's get this over with."

"So you feel it too," Cameron said, interpreting Charlie's *Let's get this over with* as meaning they all felt the same odd sense of sickness that Peers felt in his gut. It was like stepping into a place that's borne witness to murder. A horrible deed hung in the air like a corpse dangling unseen from a hook above, its tongue black, body bled dry, eyes desiccated so they dangle from their optic nerves like tiny piñatas.

Charlie said nothing. He looked at Christopher, who turned to Jeanine.

"Who brought this here?" Cameron said. "Why is it unguarded? The Astrals can fly so much faster than we can. Why aren't they here yet?"

"You remember what we talked about, Cameron," Charlie said. "It's not a bomb, but it's still going to go off if you don't turn that key."

"Why have they stopped chasing us now that they're zeroing in on this archive? They could take the key. They could start it up themselves."

"It's about choice. We decided it's about choice."

Cameron's face firmed. The key slipped back into the satchel. He licked his lips, bug-wide eyes staring at the golden chest.

"Whatever this does, I don't know that I want it unlocked. I can feel it."

Something slid from the Ark's upper corner and dropped to the floor. It looked like a tiny drop of light, like a leak not entirely contained. The drop formed a tiny pool, and the pool shot into the group's center, scattering them like roaches. They moved back, toward the small chamber's edges. Peers lost track of some of the party as he himself, falling for the illusion, staggered back as well. And then in the room's center, the tiny pool spread. Twin geysers seemed to spew upward, and the spray became the shimmering shape of a human. A moment later the shape became a solid man, dressed in black with coal-colored hair, a prominent nose, and hawklike eyes. In the middle of his forehead, a dripping red wound the size of a golf ball.

Cameron staggered back, tripping over a protruding rock. The black-jacketed man came forward, his eyes hard, his face running red with seepage from the open wound.

"What is it, Cameron?" The man had an accent that Peers, who'd spent most of his life in the UK, easily placed — Irish through and through but tempered by time away from the homeland. "Didn't you hear what Charlie said? It's about *choice*, isn't it?"

Cameron fumbled at his side, drawing a gun.

"Oh, but you already did that, didn't you?" The specter indicated his head wound. "You knew that Christopher was going to shoot me from behind, like a coward, didn't you? And yet you chose to do nothing. Are you sure it was the right choice, Cameron?"

Peers saw the absurdity yet wasn't surprised when Cameron still raised his weapon.

"You wouldn't have gotten to these people if it weren't for me," the man said. "It was thanks to me that you accomplished your father's little mission. Nobody cared who Cameron Bannister was; you could have shouted it from Dempsey's roof, and nobody would have given a damn. No. But you were able to use me just fine, weren't you? Because *everyone*, by then, cared who Morgan Matthews was."

"You're not real," Cameron said, crab-walking back to his feet, weapon still raised.

"I'm not, am I?" the Irish man said with slow, almost drawling disbelief. "But I wouldn't have been in there if I weren't." He ticked his thumb toward the Ark. "The fucking aliens just stuffed a bunch of other people into my box, and that after I'd taken the time to make myself known. But if *you* didn't put *me* in there, who else would have?"

Cameron looked at Charlie, his skin paper-white. The ghost of Morgan advanced slowly in his strangely fine dress shoes, no hurry at all.

"There are no surprises in there," he said, again indicating the golden chest. "It's not the unknown that bothers you. It's the *known*." He touched his nose thoughtfully then cocked his head. "You already know what's in your past, boyo. The only question is whether you're sure you rid the righteous cause of a threat ... or if you let some fool shoot a man *in the back of the fucking head* who protected you and got what you needed to fulfill Daddy's quest!"

"Ignore him, Cameron," said Piper from halfway around the circle. But she, too, seemed drained of blood.

"Yes, *ignore me*, Cameron. Just like you've *been* ignoring me. Just like you've been ignoring Dan and Vincent and the others dead by your indifferent hand. Just like you turned your back on your father, before your actions killed *him*, too. Just like you've been ignoring the truth that you took a woman who lost her husband into your bed. How after you thought he'd returned, you kept right on fucking her." The dead man put a splayed hand on his chest and affected a serpent's smile. "Now, I'm not judge and jury here. But if I were, I'm not so sure you come out clean and washed when the balance is tallied."

Jeanine Coffey was to one side, making frantic gestures. She seemed to want Cameron to circle the ghoul or at least slide the key in her direction. But Cameron could see only the man in black. He was swallowing, blinking, blind to everything else. His gun was still held up at the end of a trembling hand. Then the man walked forward and pressed the barrel of Cameron's gun into the center of his chest.

"Come on, boyo. If you're so sure you've done right, do it again — but be a man and do it yourself this time. I'm just a jack-in-the-box. You know I'm not actually here; I'm just something you put into the file for later consideration. You watched me drip from the corner like snot. So if I'm not a man, why not do it again? Why not remind yourself why you did what you did in the first place, like a couple renewing their vows?"

Peers watched Jeanine gesture more wildly then start forward when Cameron's foot kicked the satchel backward. It skidded two feet on the smooth floor, but there was no way Jeanine could reach it without moving into the open. Peers watched as the others started to creep forward: Christopher, Piper, even terrified Lila. But the blonde girl, Grace, was the closest, and Peers waited, knowing the key would be recovered, that they'd already been scared off. He kept his eyes on Cameron. Watched the dead man push him back farther.

"Do it, Cameron! Your pathetic indifference was righteous the first time. You never act rashly, do you? You always think first. And you're also *so good* at admitting when you were wrong, or that you don't know." The man gave a sinister little grin. "If you're so sure it was right to let Chris kill me in cold blood, prove it to yourself. This is your chance to do it all over again."

Cameron backed up. The dead man matched him, pressing him against the wall. Bits of blood and gore from his head wound dripped on Cameron's fist as the gun pressed into his belly.

"Do it, Cameron! Show me that you're a man! Show it to yourself!"

Cameron's mouth was working, his breath coming hard. The man reached for the weapon with both hands, cocked the hammer behind the slide, gripped Cameron's hand as if meaning to squeeze it down on the trigger.

"Do it."

"Fuck you," Cameron muttered.

"So you *do* have balls!" He laughed. "Then do it. Or are you second-guessing yourself? Do you have regrets? Because I'll warn you, there's a whole lot more where I came from ... if, that is, you're not quite as sure as you thought that you've always done right."

He nudged Cameron again. "Do it, Cameron."

"No."

*"Do it!"*

Peers jumped as the gunshot echoed through the tiny chamber. Blood spurted from the man's back, but before he fell and burst back into light, he smiled.

"One last regret for the road, then," he said.

The man was gone.

Beyond him — between Cameron's smoking gun and the Ark, which was beginning to leak light and shake on its platform — Peers could see what the man in black had meant when speaking of final regrets.

Grace was clutching her chest, bleeding from the gunshot.

The air began to fill with mist leaking from the archive.

And an appetizer's worth of judgment followed.

# Chapter Thirty-Six

THEY WALKED THE HALLWAYS FIRST. Cameron took the lead while Lila stayed back a few steps with Piper and her father, keeping a respectable distance from her husband's emotional balancing act. They were in a strange place, in someone else's home, in the middle of the night. They didn't know where anything was, or where people stayed or slept. Yet they were on the trail of something that a panicky voice inside Lila — more a *knowing* than the usual kind of meaningless *worry* — insisted more and more convincingly was worthy of panic. Cameron made sense, logically speaking: Clara liked to explore, and the girl, from a young age, had always shown a healthy disrespect for the rules. *Of course* she'd gone wandering, and of course it was no big deal. But Lila could tell it somehow was. And *worse*, she knew Cameron and the others could feel it, too.

But Cameron was keeping his face straight and his steps reasonably paced. He wasn't raising an alarm in deference to the hour and their status as guests. Still, tension hovered above their little troop like a storm cloud. If Cameron didn't break his sensible mask and start panicking soon, Lila thought she might go ahead and do it for him, until someone tied her down.

The hallways were empty. Clara might have ducked into a room, but none were open other than their own, which they double checked before leaving. They found the kitchen (one of them, anyway; Lila got the feeling there were several), but Clara wasn't there, either. The kitchen was fully stocked with snacks — and yet no boxes were disturbed, no cabinets open, no crumbs on the floor. They passed four marked public bathrooms, paired in two sets of men/women, and they peeked into each, calling Clara's name in urgent whispers. Lila thought she heard noises over and over, but each turned out to be only nerves, and once she thought she'd seen a blue light beneath a door that looked like a control room or a broom closet, but when she looked back it was gone and Cameron was still striding ahead, feigning confidence. Her mind was playing games.

And worse, her usual ability to sense emotions was making the soup of sensation thicken around them. She could feel Cameron's conflict: pushed into command of this excursion from a dead sleep, trying to keep fear at bay while doing his expected job. She could feel Piper's wariness, and feel her father's concern, touching in a most curious way. And she was sure, somehow, of what the others were feeling as her antennae raised: Charlie, studious as if he were asleep and dreaming of research; Jeanine, uncharacteristically surrendering in her unconsciousness — perhaps, Lila thought with embarrassment, to a sex dream she'd never admit upon waking. And Peers

...

And that part was curious.

Lila kept looking at Cameron, Meyer, and Piper, shocked each time she made the circuit that Peers wasn't with them. Because her mind kept becoming convinced that he was. She felt his absence in their quartet as if he'd been as stolen away as Clara.

She looked back. No, Peers still wasn't with them. And yet part of Lila had been so sure he'd been back there, looking over her shoulder.

Cameron stopped when they entered the fireplace room from its other end and realized they'd made a big circle. They couldn't have toured the entire mansion; they hadn't gone nearly that far. But they'd seen neither hide nor hair of Clara, and the panic in Lila's throat had brimmed to a fever pitch. She couldn't feel her daughter at all.

"What now?" Piper asked Cameron.

"I don't know."

"We have to find her, Cam. Even if it's nothing." Piper turned to Lila and added, patronizingly, "I'm sure it's nothing."

Cameron was looking around the dim, quiet room. He had no idea what to do, how to raise an alarm. Lila had something simple in mind: if nobody proposed an alternative in the next thirty seconds, she'd start screaming.

"Where's Jabari's room?" he asked.

"I don't know," Piper said.

"Meyer?"

"How would *I* know?"

"Kindred. Would Kindred know?"

"Why would Kindred know?"

"Can't he talk to the Astrals? Can't he sense things?"

"Not like that, he can't."

Lila felt her fist strike an end table. A crystal decanter clattered, its stopper jarred loose and almost hopping away. She wasn't aware of moving her arm or her fist. It just happened, and everyone looked at her.

"Do something."

"*What,* Li?" Piper asked.

"Cameron. Do something," she answered. There was an acid taste in her mouth. Her vision was swimming.

"I …"

"He doesn't know, Lila. Give him a minute."

"Kindred. That's as good a place to start as any," Cameron said, staring at Piper as if she'd said something offensive.

Lila turned back to bedroom-lined hallway. "Well? Let's go!"

"Which is his room?" Piper asked Meyer.

"I have no idea."

Lila marched to her father, grabbed his arm hard, and dragged. When Meyer resisted, Lila trotted off on her own, her face set and her composure barely held in check. She made it halfway down the hallway and was about to start yelling for Kindred, for Jabari, for guards that might come to put her in chains — it didn't matter, as long as this stupid goddamned house woke up and found her little girl.

"Miss Dempsey?" said a voice.

Lila turned. Kamal, Jabari's attendant or assistant or whatever, was standing behind her. He'd popped up out of nothing, like a ghost, fully dressed as if for business as usual rather than a restful night, in a sober gray suit over an open-throated white shirt, his dark skin a deep contrast beneath.

"Oh thank God. Mr. …" She didn't know his last name. "Kamal, my daughter is missing."

"Missing? Oh, dear."

But he didn't move. His hands were clasped behind his back as if waiting on her at a fancy restaurant rather than skulking the hallways in the dead of night.

Meyer, Piper, and Cameron arrived from the rear.

They were rushing, and piled up one against the other when they saw Kamal facing Lila. His dark, bushy eyebrows drew together. Seeing harried faces on four of the viceroy's guests at once, he seemed confused.

"Is everything okay?"

"No, it's not *okay*," Lila spat, her impatience coming out as rudeness. "My daughter is missing!"

"Please. Calm down. I'm sure she's simply gone wandering. I assure you, the home is thoroughly monitored. We will find her."

"Monitored? I haven't seen anyone!" Lila felt herself slipping into panic. The further she slid, the less she cared about her composure, about embarrassing herself. "Where are the guards? How could a little girl possibly just—"

Kamal raised a hand to stop her. "Please. Allow me to alert security." He pulled a small device from his pocket, tapped something on its surface, then returned it. Banked lights flickered around them, and within seconds Lila heard stirrings knocking down the long hallways.

Cameron moved beside Lila. "Did you know we were looking for her?"

Kamal shook his head. "No, of course not."

"What are you doing out here, then?"

Piper put a hand on his shoulder. "Cam ..."

"It's all right, Mrs. Bannister. I'm not often out and about at night. I'm tracking down a power outage."

"I didn't notice any power troubles," Cameron said, looking around at the still-multiplying hallway lights.

"No, of course you wouldn't. It's a contained circuit. I was alerted to a surge in this area, and just recently a ... hub? ... seems to have failed. But I don't want to bore you."

Cameron looked like he was about to ask more, but Titans and human guards were arriving from both in front and behind, fully dressed and carrying sidearms, called from hidden bunkers like ants in concealed pockets. Kamal explained that Clara seemed to have "wandered off" but did so with a clear implication of urgency. Then he pointed and barked orders until the troops were off again. Kamal slipped the device from his pocket, glanced at its screen as if following his people's movements, then stowed it again.

"We will find her for you, Miss." Kamal tipped his head slightly, almost a half bow. "The west wing is under construction, accessible past the kitchen. Nothing dangerous, you understand — no boards filled with screws lying around, no nail guns hooked to running compressors, nothing like that. I assure you it's quite safe. But if I had to guess, she may have gone that way. The in-progress work is very ... *cool.*" He said the word as if it were foreign to his lips. "Even Ravi isn't immune to its charm." He gave Lila a small, warm smile.

"Thank you." And as she said it, here in the light, Lila felt suddenly stupid. Of course Clara was investigating the construction. They hadn't seen the passage off the kitchen; they'd looped back and ended up in the living room or sitting room or whichever room held the fireplace. But it made sense. Much more than Clara vanishing into thin air or being abducted by people who needed their group's cooperation and trust, who hadn't even bothered to lock their doors.

"It's no problem." The device in Kamal's pocket blipped, and he took it out to look.

"Did they find her?" Piper asked.

"No, this is an alert from the engineers. The power-surge incident I mentioned. I'll send someone to your room to update you on the search for your daughter the minute we have one to give. Or you can retire to the grand room by the fire if you'd like." He tipped a nod. "If you'll excuse me."

He turned to go, leaving Lila still baffled but feeling calmer beside her father, Piper, and Cameron. But after five or six steps he turned and faced them again.

"Actually, if you'd like, there's an access point for one of the house monitoring systems in the same room where I'm headed now. It's an Astral design, quite ingenious. I can't guarantee that anyone saw your daughter because this part of the system taps into Astral minds and none may have spotted her, in which case we have other means. But if you're interested … ?"

Lila was. Only once moving did she stop to wonder what the Astral record might show if something really had gone wrong … and the Astrals had been responsible. But the thought barely had teeth. For weeks now — and especially since they'd entered Ember Flats, where Titans and humans worked side by side like friends — she'd shed much of her fear. The Astrals hadn't truly threatened their group for months, maybe years. During that time, the Mullah had been a much bigger threat — and thankfully, there'd be no Mullah here in the Capital of Capitals, let alone in the viceroy's home.

"This way." Kamal turned one corner and then another, not stopping until they reached the door where Lila almost thought she'd seen light earlier, the one marked *Utility Closet.*

# Chapter Thirty-Seven

THE ALERT BLIPPED on the big screen in Peers's room, across from his bed. It could be used to watch videos or even that compelling news stream (some raw, some stylized and filtered), but in their half day in the palace, he'd seen alerts as well, like the one that had summoned him to the fireside discussion with Jabari. If the alerts were specific to a room's occupant, you could tap the screen or speak your acknowledgement aloud. If you didn't respond after a while, the alert would make itself more obvious with an audible reminder.

But Peers wasn't asleep. He wouldn't need a chirp to wake him so he could read the alert. He was still breathing heavy, sweating, wondering if he'd actually got away clean. But he still didn't acknowledge receipt of the message because the alert was summoning him back to where he'd just been. And if he appeared before Cameron, Meyer, Kindred, and the others with a sheen of nervous sweat, eyebrows would raise. Particularly Cameron's. He already wondered how Peers had ended up with such clever devices and was able to understand Astral technology so

"

well. *Because I grew up studying it like my life depended on it* probably wouldn't dampen suspicions.

He moved quickly into the bathroom, knowing he could blame some of the time required by a reluctance to wake. But if the alert were true — if Clara really had run off and the whole damned house was rising to search for her — he wouldn't have long. Eventually, they'd knock on the door, if for no other reason than to see if the girl was in his room.

Peers was in the bathroom when he heard a light scratching.

He went to the hallway door, cocking his head, then recognized the sound and opened to Nocturne. The dog slipped inside, wagging his tail, panting up at his master.

"Run yourself out, did you?"

The dog sat.

"Go to bed, idiot."

So he did. But as Nocturne made three small circles to knead the dog bed conveniently provided by the house, Peers remembered the flash of limbs and hair he'd seen just before entering the utility closet, just around the corner ahead, where the dog had gone. Had that been Clara? Almost for sure. So she was fine, and with any luck they'd find her before Peers even finished composing himself. Then they'd broadcast a retraction alert and he could get some sleep, his telltale flushed skin and gobsmacked eyes safely hidden under covers until morning.

He returned to the bathroom, ran water, and splashed his face. With his eyes closed, he saw the cave in Sinai's belly. It had all been so real. He'd smelled the gun smoke, heard the wheezing involuntary exhale as Grace died from Cameron's gunshot — leaking lungs drowning in her own blood — and been as awed by what followed, he supposed, as the rest of them.

The bursting energy from the Ark as it recorded a new deed in need of judgment: a man killing a girl — by accident, yes, but the shot had been fired in defense of a previous murder.

The mental, timeless replay of events as Grace died: the Ark showing them all (not just Cameron, it seemed) the events in which they'd been complicit. Another nail in their coffins. *The bullet entering the girl's chest, exploding out the back. Her shocked, almost betrayed expression as she felt the kiss of lead. The panic in her eyes. The loss of focus as she expired.* All of it played over and over on a loop, ten times at least, in the space of a second. Everyone in the cave that day carried those internal visions — and now Peers, thanks to the sphere's immersive memory, would as well.

And most of all there was the surety Peers had felt, seeing that vision within his own, that he was being watched from above by the icy eye of absolute impartiality. You couldn't argue your case to that eye. You couldn't say *It wasn't his fault* or *We're all really good people, promise.* Peers felt weighed, measured, assessed the way a butcher appraises meat. There'd been neither vindictiveness in that gaze nor rancor. Nor had there been a molecule of sympathy.

Peers glanced at himself in the mirror. So what if it looked like he'd washed his face before joining the group? That was a sensible thing to do when knocked out of bed, bleary eyed and exhausted.

The screen chirped.

"Fine, fine," he muttered. He left the bathroom, crossed to the screen, and tapped to acknowledge. The clock was ticking now. Officially, Peers Basara had been roused. If he took too long to show up, people would wonder.

Something made him look up. Did they monitor the

rooms? He'd seen it before — tiny BB-sized surveillance drones that could follow a person and hide just about anywhere. But he dismissed the thought upon arrival. The sphere was an Astral device, but whoever had assembled the room — and built the palace, it seemed — were his old brothers and sisters. It was still tapped into the Astral hive mind, recording their side of at least this part of the story.

He thought of what he'd seen in his vision: Akeem preparing to steal the sphere, but seen from an Astral's eye. If the aliens had known Akeem was there, how had he managed to steal — unless they'd allowed it?

It didn't really matter. The device had been hidden by Mullah, which meant it was being monitored by them as well. They had to be in the house, even now. If there was surveillance, it would be Mullah eyes upon him.

And given that the Mullah, too, operated in secrecy, Peers didn't think they'd chance overt observation. They'd probably built other secret rooms, secret systems, and secret drawers to hold who knows what. They'd probably designed tunnels from the start — or more likely, so they could do it on the sly, branched unknown tunnels off of legitimate ones, like those linking Ember Flats's government buildings.

And besides: If anyone had seen him yank the sphere from its tentacle-like tether and smuggle it back here, he was already fucked. No point in worrying further.

Before Peers left the room, he picked the sphere up from where he'd set it on the entrance table — careful not to activate the thing with his palms; he'd do that later — and tucked it into the back of a built-in dresser drawer. They'd know it was gone, but with any luck, since it was Astral, they'd only be able to use simple human investigation to try and find it. And because the Mullah couldn't show their hand, Peers doubted they'd search in public or even admit anything had gone missing.

He'd have time.

After they found Clara, he'd have time to peruse all the sphere's Astral memories and find what he needed to find.

In the meantime, it was safe. And so was *Peers*.

Because given all he'd done over the years, there must be evidence somewhere on the thing that Peers Basara had once been Mullah, and that his knowledge of things unknown had managed to grease many questionable wheels. Someone in the house knew how to access the thing even though Jabari might not even know it was there.

Peers took one final look around the room, noting that Nocturne didn't raise his head as he opened the door. Exhausted by searching for whatever, it seemed.

"Stay," he said. The dog did not respond.

Then Peers left to join them, hoping his still-racing pulse wasn't too visible in the hollow of his throat.

# Chapter Thirty-Eight

THE UTILITY CLOSET'S screen remained blank, showing nothing of Clara.

Piper watched Kamal with a strange certainty that he was agitated but unable or unwilling to articulate why. His actions were expected for a man in his station, facing something that had malfunctioned or broken: He tapped the touchscreen on the multipurpose room's wall, more a by-the-way access point than a proper surveillance station. He touched the device in his pocket, which Piper couldn't see properly but that seemed to be responding in unexpected ways. There were wires in one corner leading to a stack of human-tech computers on little racks. Kamal went to them too, wiggling wires the way her great-grandfather used to slap the side of his ancient television to improve its reception, even after everything had gone digital. Everyone was watching Kamal, assuming the man knew what he was doing, trusting that in minutes his ministrations would cause the dead screen to flicker and show the many rooms and hallways, Clara safe and playing somewhere she shouldn't be. Piper scanned the room's faces to see expectation and barely held patience.

Piper wondered why her own expression was surely different. Because although Kamal was doing all the expected things, it struck Piper as kabuki.

*He knows why it's not working. He's just putting on a show and will seek the real cause once we're no longer watching.*

Piper closed her eyes. Opened them. She was so tired.

But the feeling came stronger and stronger, radiating from Kamal, the way Piper sometimes swore she sensed Cameron's moods better than she strictly should, the way she knew more often than not when someone was lying. The way, when Christopher had gone missing on the bus, she'd been momentarily inside his head, not seeing what he was seeing but hearing the intensity of his mood, feeling his fear and an overwhelming sense of grim, determined duty. And the way a pocket of strange emotion always seemed to orbit the group, disembodied, whenever the ...

She blinked away from Kamal, frowning. Where *had* the Pall gone to, anyway?

"This station isn't working; I'm sorry," Kamal said.

*It certainly isn't. And you don't know why, but you haven't checked what you think is actually the problem. Why haven't you checked, Kamal?*

"I've already sent someone over to the under-construction wing," he said, looking sympathetically at Lila. "I'm sure that's where your daughter is."

Lila gave a grim little smile that Piper didn't buy at all.

There was commotion from behind. Charlie had arrived and was standing like a statue. Jeanine and Kindred were still absent, but Piper saw Peers arriving, his face wet, looking intensely awake.

"What's happened? I saw the alert in my room." He stopped then added, "Heard it, I mean."

Cameron said, "Clara's gone."

"Gone?"

"She's just wandered off," Meyer said, putting an arm around his daughter. Lila sniffed, burying her face against his arm. Her shoulders hitched.

"No, no, I'm sure he's right," Peers said, watching Lila. "She's just out in the hallways."

Piper felt another of those strange, forceful emotions. She looked up to see Kamal looking directly at Peers. When Kamal looked away, Peers craned his neck in a way that was probably supposed to be subtle and eyed the wall beneath the screen, near the floor. There was nothing there, but Peers's gaze lingered until he saw Kamal looking at him. He flinched and turned, swallowing again.

With his eyes on Peers, Kamal said, "Mr. Cook — you haven't seen Clara since last night, have you?"

"No," Charlie said.

The rest of Kamal's attention turned to Peers.

"What about you, Mr. Basara? Have you seen her?"

"No. Of course not. I was sleeping."

"Hmm. I'm sorry. The alert woke you?"

"It woke everyone. Wasn't *everyone* sleeping?" He looked around the small group. Some nodded. Kamal did not.

"Of course," Kamal said. "I'm very sorry. And I'm sorry our systems are malfunctioning. I don't suppose any of you knows anything about Astral technology? Many of the systems in Ember Flats are hybrids of our two worlds."

A few in the group mumbled. Kamal bit his cheek, still looking at Peers. His eyebrows reset, then he sighed and turned his hands palms up, again the eager assistant.

"Well, it is what it is. I'm very sorry if this has caused you concern. We will need to wait for the teams to report in. But I can assure you, this house is very safe. I wanted to station Titans outside your doors to prevent …" He paused, searching for the right word. "*Accidents*. But Viceroy Jabari declined my suggestion. She said it would make you feel confined rather than like guests. And perhaps I shouldn't have raised the general alarm. I tend toward overcautiousness. Those of you who wish to stay and search may, and the rest can return to bed. It will be fine. But before you go: You're all positive that you haven't seen Clara? Nothing at all? You haven't heard anything that may have been a girl running past your door, seen shadows in the hallway in the gap under your threshold, anything at all that might help Lila find her daughter?"

Heads shook. Lila wiped her eyes. Peers stared at his feet.

"Please, then. Return to your rooms. All is well. We'll summon you in the morning."

But nobody moved.

"Really, it will be fine. We will handle what needs handling."

Still, nobody moved.

"Very well." Kamal sighed, tapped his device again, then extended a hand toward the great room. "I suppose we'll have midnight tea while we wait."

Lila wrenched herself from Meyer's embrace and pushed back through the knot of people, past Cameron and Charlie. Piper watched a flash of motion beyond, then Charlie staggered back a step, now struck by Lila from the other side as if she were a pinball and he was a rebounder.

There were six Titans outside the room, blocking the hallway.

# Chapter Thirty-Nine

MARA JABARI PUT a hand on Cameron's shoulder. It was almost sensuous, not like the annoying tap of someone mining his attention. He turned to see her perfectly smooth dark skin and exotic facial features then watched her slowly nod and purse her lips, putting one finger of the other hand in front of them.

Cameron nodded to acknowledge her request for quiet then tipped his head toward Piper and Lila, who'd finally fallen asleep — collapsed from nerves and exhaustion.

*What about them?*

Jabari's nod was equally simple, but Cameron heard her oath as if spoken: *They will be fine.*

It was a meaningless assurance, seeing as Cameron was easily as emotionally threadbare as Lila and Piper and only awake due to adrenaline and a sense of duty: If the girls must sleep, he must stay on guard. They were all in a strange place under decidedly strange circumstances, and Cameron trusted nothing. Ember Flats wasn't the bloody, chaotic dictatorship they'd all been led to believe it would be, and Mara Jabari wasn't the dictator portrayed. Even

Peers had stories of the woman standing above him, and only providence or uncertainty seemed to have kept him from finding something sharp to slit her throat. But then again, he didn't entirely trust Peers, either.

Of all the people Cameron shouldn't believe about who'd be fine under which circumstances, the Ember Flats viceroy was top of the list. But something in Jabari's soft brown eyes swayed him. He *did* believe her even if he shouldn't. And though he'd never admit it to anyone, her simple touch was reassuring in a way nothing else could have been. The woman had elegantly managed this fucked-up situation. Clara had been gone for hours, now certifiably missing. And yet Jabari's hand on Cameron's shoulder said, *Clara will be fine. They will be fine. You will be fine. All of it, Cameron, will be fine.*

He looked up at her before finally rising, reminding himself that even if circumstances had changed with much time passed, this was a woman his father had admired. A prodigy. She'd studied the Astrals, same as Benjamin had, and Peers at his London institute. She claimed to be on their side. It was probably folly to believe her — but honestly, was believing Jabari any worse than any other option?

Cameron stood and followed the viceroy, leaving Lila and Piper slouched in their side-by-side easy chairs by the cool fire, their hands on adjacent armrests, fingers touching. His eyes found the clock. It was after 5 a.m., and he'd barely slept.

The palace was graveyard quiet. Jabari's feet were bare, and she made no sound on the plush rugs or hard wood. Cameron was in socks, padding behind, feeling chronically underdressed next to the elegant viceroy.

They entered a medium-sized room with a desk. Jabari closed the door. Kindred and Meyer were already seated in enormous plush chairs that made even the large men appear small.

With the door shut, Jabari sat behind the big, dark-wood desk and spoke in her normal voice. It took several words before Cameron's ears adjusted to what sounded like sacrilegious volume in the early hours.

"I'm very sorry. I'd have come to you earlier, but Kamal decided to let me sleep. With the State of the City address coming up, I've been too thin. He promised that the situation was handled and that my presence would have added nothing. But I'm sorry nonetheless. We should have spoken hours ago."

Cameron looked at Kindred and Meyer. They seemed less disoriented than Cameron felt, but not by much. This wasn't like last time, when she'd spoken to the pair at length before summoning anyone to join them. But they both looked beyond exhausted. They acted half-Astral sometimes, and Kindred often struck Cameron as void of emotion — not because he'd once been a Titan but because that's how Meyer Dempsey, according to Piper, had always been. Without two years of wrenching captivity, the real Meyer would probably have still been the same way.

"Spoken about what?" Cameron asked.

Jabari's eyes flicked around the room. She seemed to be deciding whether to speak frankly. Cameron noticed a shimmer when he followed her gaze then spied the privacy jammer already idling on the desktop.

"I'm concerned about Clara's disappearance."

"We are, too," said Meyer.

And Kindred added, "Obviously."

"It's more than what you're probably thinking. Kamal told me that guards have searched the house, and the grounds, though I can't imagine how she'd have slipped out considering there are sensors on all the windows and guards at every door. I know he's told you there was one left unattended by mistake, during a shift change."

"He said she may have been waiting and watching then run out into the city after they left," Cameron said.

"It isn't the truth," Jabari said.

Meyer sat up. "What? Then why would he say it?"

"Because you needed an answer. *Lila* needed an answer. Even if Clara wasn't found right away, she had to have some idea of where the girl might have gone. But we know she didn't leave the house, or the grounds."

"Because of surveillance?"

"No," Jabari said. "Because there are only so many ways out, and they were guarded at all times, completely accounted for. There are motion-sensing lights across the grounds, and none were triggered. Surveillance is suspiciously out. We have no record, and nobody has any answers."

"Then we'll go to wherever the videos are recorded," Meyer said. "We'll check them even if we have to copy the raw logs over and watch them on a tablet, one at a time. How many cameras are there? I know it will take forever, but ..."

Jabari sighed. "That's just it. There are no cameras. Only the tiny droids used by the Astrals, and I suspect the Astrals themselves."

"*'Suspect'?*" said Cameron.

"Ember Flats has an excellent facade. It seems like a place of harmony, and for the most part, it is. We do work hand in hand with the Astrals. The new monoliths, the terraforming and irrigation, even our Apex — all handled cooperatively. Everything but our government buildings, which they allowed us to construct ourselves, either to establish trust (proving they don't want to peer over our shoulders into delicate affairs) or because they want to create the illusion that we remain in control. They let us have our government, and they stay out of it. But there are some matters they do not let us handle, and their position is absolute. Surveillance is one of those matters. Kamal and his people are usually able to operate everything fine despite not being entirely sure how it works or where their eyes are watching. So no, we don't know what replaces the cameras, but Kamal has theories, and he says it seems almost like experience and memory — of the Titans, of our few Reptar guards, or maybe of those like you, Kindred, who've been transformed."

Meyer shifted in his seat. The topic of *why* he'd been replaced by a Titan while Jabari hadn't didn't seem to sit well with him, but so far he'd said nothing.

"Any of this ringing true for you?" Cameron asked Kindred.

"I don't know. I only get a feeling, but it makes sense."

"And your combined mind? The two of you working together?"

"It's not a question we've asked," Meyer answered, his arms crossed and eyes hard.

Jabari waited for the Meyers to say more. When nothing came, she continued.

"Now the system isn't responding. It's like trying to access a computer with a missing hard drive. Kamal can't tell me more. I only know we have access to *nothing*. The house has gone dark, and we have no record of anything Clara may have done or where she might have gone. I'm sorry. But she could be anywhere."

"You said she didn't leave the house," Cameron said.

Jabari nodded.

"So …"

"There are tunnels. They connect each of the buildings

in our government center. These tunnels aren't secret; you've seen their entrances on our tour. But it's curious about the tunnels, and these buildings in general: I don't know exactly who built them, how, or when."

"You said humans built them," Cameron said.

"Yes. But which humans? And when? I came to Ember Flats immediately, same as I understand you went to Vail, Meyer. I felt the same pull. Back then, it was Giza. Nothing but desert. Lawless. The only people who came — and more all the time — were apocalyptic types, appropriate given that the end times seemed to have arrived. The first year was hard. The first occupants required a firm hand. An iron fist, perhaps. And what your friend Peers describes having experienced was, I'm afraid, not terribly uncommon. I moved around a lot back then. I think the Astrals *kept* me in motion. Sometimes I wonder if they were deciding whether to abduct me or not then create a clone — no disrespect intended."

"None taken," said Kindred.

"Why *didn't* they clone you?" Cameron asked.

"I don't know. As far as I can tell from meeting each in person, the other seven viceroys are all copies. There are subtle ways to tell, having to do with the way their memories handle emotion. I'm the only one they allowed to assume the position as a human."

She took a breath, glanced out the window, and continued.

"By the time I was finally returned here, to the city's center, the buildings had been erected, including the tunnels. But you hear things inside them. The echoes are a bit off. It makes me feel like there must be hidden branches."

"Why? The Astrals can move about wherever they want. They have their ships."

Jabari looked at Cameron.

"Cameron. Your necklace?"

Cameron looked down. The coin and its lanyard were under his shirt, and even the lump was hard to see. "What about it?"

"Would you mind telling me where you got it?"

Cameron looked at the Meyers. There wasn't a reason not to tell her given that Jabari's pointed way of asking suggested she somehow already knew. Still he hesitated.

"Then may I guess?"

"Go ahead."

"Here. In Giza. From one of the pyramids. If my orientation is right, it's that one right there." She pointed, and Cameron could just make out the monolith's sloping side in the city's light.

"My father gave it to me. We were … exploring."

"Do you know what it is?"

"A coin?"

"It's called a *mau*, after the ancient Egyptian word for cat. If you hold it up so the square cut in the middle is like a diamond, it looks a little like a cat's eye."

That sounded familiar; Cameron seemed to recall his father looking it up after their return to the States. But that had been the beginning of the end between father and son, and ancient objects hadn't mattered much to Cameron at the time.

"But they're not Egyptian. They were used — though nobody's sure what for — by a sect called the Mullah."

Cameron felt a chill. He looked at Meyer and Kindred, who seemed equally surprised.

"As you know, we had a strong alien focus at the da Vinci Initiate. It's fascinating to look back through the historical record and see that the times between alien epochs didn't resemble invasions. It's obviously impossible to know how it happened thousands of years ago, but we've always imagined it as *arrival* instead."

"It was an invasion this time around," Cameron said.

"Maybe. But maybe not. I have theories about that, too, but if you remember, all the panic in the first months came from humans reacting to the approaching ships and then taking up stations. Eventually they began their abductions, and narrowing the field to people like me and Meyer: the Nine. They destroyed Moscow, and the shuttles caused a lot of smaller destruction. But I don't think that was them 'invading.' I think they expected something different, and what they found surprised them. They had to adjust on the fly."

Cameron thought of his long-ago trip to Heaven's Veil. About the shuttles and BB devices responding to wires carrying bandwidth for the Internet.

"Still," Jabari went on. "An *arrival* required different steps, taken in advance, than an *invasion*. Invasions are about brute force and do not require more preparation than loading weapons and massing troops. It was our theory, at the Initiate, that the way was always paved. Earth had previously prepared for their arrival in advance."

"What does this have to do with my ..." He touched his upper chest, felt the bump there. "My necklace?"

"Do you mind if I ask *when* you got your mau?"

Cameron shrugged. "Twenty-ish years ago?"

"There was a cave-in about that time. We've excavated a chamber that—"

Cameron raised a hand. "I know. I was there."

Jabari paused. Then, deliberately: "You were there."

"We were looking for a chamber, too. My father and I. We didn't find it. The ..." He trailed off then decided there was no point in evasion given that Jabari had already said the word. "*Mullah* came when we were inside. Then the structure shook, and sand fell from above. I was sure we were about to be crushed. We got out fine, but the Mullah didn't come out behind us. We counted ourselves lucky at the time, but they've been following us since Heaven's Veil was destroyed."

"Do you know why?"

Cameron shook his head. He assumed it had to do with the Templars, with the Ark, with some duty the Mullah had to defend against both. He'd chalked up meeting Mullah back when he was sixteen to coincidence, to a simple case of *go to the same place, see the same faces*.

"We theorized that the Mullah have always handled that advance preparation. They guard something — something we heard rumors about but never found anyone willing to divulge. They might be like emissaries. They could be with the Astrals, or they could be their enemies. We only felt sure that the Mullah had deep knowledge of the aliens and preserved some sort of records they passed down from endless generations. They were somehow in contact, however distantly. When we learned that the Ark had been stolen and hidden, the Mullah seemed the obvious culprits. That made us think they were trying to thwart the Astrals, seeing as the aliens apparently needed the Ark before they could do what had to be done. We knew a key had been removed, and it made sense that the Mullah would follow them, to try and recapture it. But we didn't know why. Did they want to steal the key to open the Ark and help the Astrals, or keep it safe and assure that it was *never* opened?"

Cameron thought back to their years-long game of cat and mouse. They'd spent as much time hiding from the Mullah as from the Astrals. He hadn't stopped to ask why each was following or why. They only knew it was time to run whenever they saw either at the rear.

"The Mullah are in everything, Cameron, the way food acquires the taste of the air around it. I was never a random woman chosen to head a city. I was a student of ancient aliens theory like your father, and Peers Basara. I knew all about alternative archaeology and the epochs and the Astrals. I knew about the Mullah. So when I returned and saw that someone had built me a palace, I knew whose hands were behind it. And most importantly, I am not so naive as to believe there are no Mullah here today."

"Here in Ember Flats?"

"Here in my employ. In the house where I welcome friends, eat my meals, and lie down to sleep."

"Is that where you think Clara went? Into the tunnels? With the Mullah?"

"They wouldn't be so bold as to take her from bed, not with such a mix of humans and Astrals about. But if she went to *them* for some reason? Then yes. The Mullah would not look a gift horse in the mouth. They are not proud and will accept any advantage or point of leverage that offers a shortcut to the upper hand."

Cameron felt something off about what Jabari had just said but couldn't quite place it. Meyer seemed to have no such trouble.

"*Shortcut?* You make it sound like there's something they wanted to do all along, and Clara is a shortcut."

Jabari nodded and met Cameron's eye.

"Tell me something, Cameron. Be as honest as you can possibly be."

Cameron hesitated then said, "Okay."

"The Ark must be opened, by you. So if we hadn't stopped you yesterday, would you have done it? Once finished with the errand I've asked of you—" She nodded to Kindred and Meyer. "Will you do it? Are you convinced it must be opened? Tell me, honestly, with your heart: *Will you open it as the others have said you must?*"

In his mind, Cameron saw the ghost of Morgan Matthews, his hole punctured with the slug Cameron delivered in Vail.

He saw the dark cave, heard the gunshot.

He saw Grace gripping her chest, looking at him with eyes that pleaded, *Why?*

And he heard Morgan's echoing voice, calling him to judgment: *There's a whole lot more where I came from … if, that is, you're not quite as sure as you thought that you've always done right.*

The visions that followed. The replay of Grace's death. The heavy feeling of his hands and the slipping sensation of draining time, wishing he could rewind the clock. The iron sensation that gripped his chest. The Ark's prying tentacles entering his heart, his soul, his mind — the very core of every one of them. The cold certainty — *the absolute, total, bones-deep* surety — that if he was judged, he'd be found guilty … and that the same would, of course, be true of humanity.

If he never turned the key, the jury would never go out for deliberation. The current epoch would never end, and they'd hang in the balance forever. The Astrals might stay, even if they had to enslave the planet. And if Cameron was truly this time's King Arthur but died too soon? Well, the deed might *never* be done.

But if he *did* open the Ark?

He'd live an unending nightmare, confronted by his every deed. And the race would be found as guilty as Cameron. The Astrals would shake the cosmic Etch A Sketch and start every clock over.

"Tell me the truth, Cameron," Jabari said. "Would you open it?"

He sighed. He shook his head then let it hang.

"No."

"That's what I was afraid of," Jabari said. "You won't open it on your own. So if it's to be done, you'd need a very good reason to do it."

Cameron looked up. Jabari was holding a piece of what looked like parchment, but its ink seemed fresh. Cameron saw only squiggles: some language he'd never learned but felt certain his father would instantly know.

"I found this on the pillow beside me when I woke to the alert," Jabari said. "Someone entered my room as I slept and laid it inches from my head."

Cameron blinked at Meyer and Kindred, saw no understanding on their faces, and returned to Jabari.

"What does it say?" he asked.

The viceroy drew a breath, then: "It says that if the Ark is not opened, the little Lightborn may never be found."

# Chapter Forty

"I DON'T UNDERSTAND," Cameron said. But he seemed to be the only one; Meyer, Kindred, and Mara Jabari were all trading glances. "You're saying Clara was … taken? By the Mullah?"

Although maybe, contrary to his words, Cameron understood fine. He felt a chill as he spoke and had to suppress a shiver.

Jabari's face seemed troubled. "I've studied the Mullah enough — in theory at the da Vinci Initiate and in real life ever since — to know their hand when I see it." She tapped the parchment. "I have many enemies, as do you. But only the Mullah would have written such a note."

"But right here … in your mansion!" Cameron wasn't sure anger won out against his agitation or alarm. His felt a helpless sort of rage — the kind that curses fate even though it changes nothing. Then, trying for a modicum of calm. "Your security …"

"Was put mostly out of commission when surveillance inexplicably stopped working. I've sent word to our Divinity on the mothership, but there's been no reply. If you watch Ember Flats for a while, you'll believe that the city is a union between humans and Astrals, but that's a lie. They work with us to the extent that it suits their needs and desires. They help us when it aids them. They are not our adversaries and do not repress or control the city as they did in Heaven's Veil. But they are not our friends. We are permitted our government, and they do not interfere. But it's always been clear — to me, at least — that the Astrals only allow what is of no consequence to them. They are neither on our side nor against us here. They are indifferent. So I do not expect a reply … but without Astral assistance, my people don't even know how the system works or why it's no longer functioning. I've already tripled human guards — those I feel I can trust. But as far as last night, my people are blind."

Cameron looked at Meyer and Kindred. They kept glancing meaningfully at each other, and he'd heard a few chatters in their strange private language while Jabari was talking. Even those few words probably paled compared to what the men were surely sharing in the privacy of their hybrid mind.

Plotting.

Planning.

Working the numbers, finding the logic, weighing the variables.

It dawned on him: why the Meyers were here, with him, with Jabari.

"This helps you," Cameron said.

"I want to find her as badly as you do."

"But it helps you." He looked right at Meyer, who until now had wanted nothing to do with Jabari's plan for a dual-Meyer public appearance. One had immediately warmed to the idea, while the other stayed reticent.

There'd been a schism between them, but judging by their cooperative chatter now, that discord was gone.

"It's true that it makes the matter more urgent," Jabari said. "The Mullah are slippery. They could be operating in the city, but they could also be people I trust. I can't know and couldn't do anything about it if I thought I did. The people of Ember Flats are used to how things are here, and that's made them complacent. As the saying goes, people can get used to everything. Of course we heard about Heaven's Veil when it happened. It was an *unfortunate accident*. Nobody considered what it might mean, or knows the connection between Heaven's Veil and the Ark."

Cameron glanced at Meyer and Kindred. They'd apparently explained it all at some point: the city's destruction, the way the Astrals had triangulated on the misery streaming into the hidden Ark and used that homing beacon to locate its resting place.

"So?"

"If Meyer and Kindred appear at the State of the City address, that balance will be upset. It's the peace, more than anything, that allows the Mullah's operation in silence. If we stir the pot, there's a chance to flush them out."

"There's more to it, Cameron," Kindred said.

*"Really?"* Cameron felt his control slipping. He'd always been angry under the surface but thought he'd grown past the worst of it. But in recent days, that barely checked anger had reasserted itself, and now he felt it threatening to explode. "She laid out something she wanted you to do, and took us prisoner to do it." He looked around, gesturing sarcastically. "Oh, *sure*. It's a *nice* prison, but we're not allowed to leave, are we? They bound our wrists. Knocked us out for the trip, and did God knows what while we were sleeping. Then we heard all about this plan, for you to

upset the power balance in Ember Flats so the people turn against the Astrals. Who would benefit from something like that, Meyer? Kindred? You've got those big brains, don't you?"

"This isn't about my power," said Jabari. "I hold my position because at least as viceroy, I have some control over—"

"And what will you have control over if people have a new reason to hate the Astrals?"

"Cameron," said Meyer.

"Let's call Peers in here," Cameron said. "What do you say, Mara? He's the only one in our group who's had any interaction with your people. Let's ask him what he thinks of this plan. 'Hey, Peers, the woman responsible for killing your son has a plan that would eliminate her competition and give her a civilian army. Sound like a good idea?'"

"As I explained to Mr. Basara, that was a long time—"

"Meyer ..." Cameron shifted his attention and cut Mara off. "Lila said you were unconvinced and were fighting Kindred on this whole 'public appearance' scheme." He met Kindred's eyes for a half second, meaning no animosity. His animus was for Jabari, the Astrals, and the universe for concocting this unreasonable brew. "Before Clara went missing, you didn't want anything to do with this. But now, you're on board? Think about it for a second — Clara vanishes into the hands of an enemy we've not seen for weeks, right out from under our noses, in the Capital of all Capitals, and nobody saw it happen or has any clue where to start looking? Oh, the *Mullah* are to blame. And yet *she* benefits." Cameron concluded with a finger rigidly pointing in Jabari's face.

Meyer drew a deep breath then ran a hand over his beard. His eyes took in the room for long, painful seconds.

Then he exhaled and said, "We think it might be the only way."

"How convenient."

But inside his mind, Cameron felt the tiniest of pushes — foreign at first then deeply familiar like a long-forgotten memory. Ever since he and Piper had begun hearing each other's thoughts on their first journey from Vail to Moab, some sort of psychic itch had stayed just under the surface of his mind, dormant but present, able to be awakened by strong emotions and oddly powerful hunches. But this time it felt like Kindred had stuck an elbow deep into his mind from across the room and nudged him with it.

*Even if she's behind this, it's still the only way … so trust us,* the nudge seemed to say.

"It kills two birds with one stone," said Kindred, his eyes on Cameron's as if willing him into understanding. "I don't know how to explain it without insulting my human half, but the Astral knowledge within me has always insisted that the Ark must be opened. The Astrals won't force us — and in one sense, even Charlie thinks they don't care if we do. They are impartial. The judge, not the opposition."

"Everything that's pushed us toward or away from putting the key in the Ark has come from the outside. Never the Astrals." And in Meyer's downward glance Cameron thought he could see — or maybe sense, via that same dormant mental wavelength — additional context behind his words. "The Astrals have kept an eye on us, but they haven't actually done anything since Cottonwood."

"Derinkuyu," Cameron said.

"They blocked us in at Derinkuyu. Nothing more."

"Why would they block us in?"

"Ask Peers," said Kindred.

Meyer glanced at Kindred. "The Mullah have nudged

us in one direction or another ever since Sinai. Peers talked us into coming here. And the Pall ..." Meyer trailed off. In the second it took to resume, Cameron realized he hadn't seen the Pall in what felt like forever.

"Point is, it's never been the Astrals. And still, it's like the way has been greased. Not easy but obvious. We've never really had a choice. There's always been one way to go: inexorably *here*. Most of you should never have escaped Heaven's Veil, and yet somehow you did, even before we showed up with shuttles from the mothership. After Heaven's Veil, we might have wandered forever — but then we ran into Peers, who turned us around. We'd never have made it through Hell's Corridor if not for Christopher. You'd already refused to open the Ark by the time the capital guards appeared, and we'd have left if Jeanine hadn't needed to be separated from her weapon, keeping us inside the city. Even if we were free to go now, there are *literally* barbarians at the gate. And now Clara's been taken, and the demand for her ransom is that you ... well, that you do what we came here to do in the first place."

"So this is all kismet? Are you telling me the unflappable Meyer Dempsey suddenly believes in fate?"

"Fate, force, coercion," said Kindred, his voice more like Meyer than Meyer. "He's saying it doesn't matter. You didn't even know where the Ark *was*, Cameron. Look at the string of coincidences that led to our discovery. Your father gave you a vague hint. Then, after Benjamin was gone, the thought kept rising in your mind, of a place you'd seen once decades earlier. You powwowed with Clara and figured it out as if it were obvious. We homed right in on it without undue delay or opposition. Despite the Astrals causing the Heaven's Veil scream and us knowing we were racing them to the finish line, we still managed to get there first at our oh-so-human sub-light speed. And where were the Astrals when we arrived? How about the *Mullah?*"

"We saw dead Mullah guards," Cameron said, thinking back. But he didn't want to think of that day ever again. The emotions were too intense, still so raw after five long years.

"Killed by who, Cameron?" said Meyer. "And where were the rest of them? The Mullah's *mission* is supposedly to curate our connection to the Astrals. Together with the Knights Templar, their job was to shepherd the Ark. So wouldn't you think there should have been more of them?"

But none of this was making sense. "The Mullah have been chasing us for the key. My father and I first ran into them when …" Cameron glanced at Jabari then touched the *mau* under his shirt with tentative fingers. "Years ago. They've *always* been in the way. Always tried to stop or capture or kill us. *Five years,* Meyer! For five years, they've blocked us at every turn. They don't want us to open the Ark. They want to keep us from it."

Jabari picked up the paper then spoke once Cameron's confused and angry glare seemed to grant permission.

"At the Initiate," she said, "we had a slightly different conception of the Mullah. They weren't protectors of the Ark so much as custodians. Their purpose wasn't to *prevent* Astral contact so much as *facilitate* it. So yes, they stole the archive. They tried, perhaps, to take the key from you at the beginning. But recently our feelers have the impression that the Mullah's position has shifted — again from preventing to facilitating."

"What does that mean?" Cameron asked.

"It means that once upon a time, I think the Mullah would have felt it was their duty to stop you. But now, they'll do anything to help you turn that key — or, if you try and turn away, to *force* you."

"But why now? What's changed?"

Jabari looked from Cameron to Kindred and Meyer. The two men subtly nodded, affirming Cameron's impression that all of this had been discussed, and that once again he was late to the party.

"If I had to guess, I think things may have gone past a point of no return," she said, "and now, it's too late to stop the inevitable."

# Chapter Forty-One

PEERS WAS on the dusty lawn, at night, with a great white
light above, when the knock came. He could feel cool air
on his scalp, where it was exposed by his dreadlocks. He
could feel the grit of sand underfoot, though it was held
mostly in place by stubborn desert grass. The light was
blinding: a cone of brilliance in the middle of an otherwise
black night. The grass beneath the light seemed bleached
white. The woman entering the light wasn't even covering
her eyes, gazing up at the mothership as if spellbound.

The knock repeated. From the house behind him?
Peers wasn't sure. But it broke the vision, and for a second
he could feel something heavy in his hands even though
he was looking down, at the nighttime ground, somewhere outdoors, and could plainly see that his hands were
empty. The woman was still looking vacantly upward at
the Astral mothership's opening belly. And now there was
a young man running toward her, panicked, his feet
moving full out. He tripped and fell. The woman rose
into the air, her arms stretched out like Christ on the
cross.

Piper Dempsey, back when she'd been using that name.

And the man on the ground, looking in this particular memory like little more than a kid? That had to be Cameron Bannister — his body thinner and almost adolescent-looking, his hair long on top in a way that was probably once a hallmark style, his skin not as desiccated by arid wandering as it was today.

Cameron yelled out for Piper as she ascended. The sound was raw, real, visceral down to the marrow. Peers was *there*. He watched Piper vanish, the mothership close its belly, the giant sphere move away. Then it was dark again, and on the open lawn between the house and a building bunkered inside a cliff, it was just Cameron and Peers. And the intrusive sound of knuckles rapping on wood, which didn't even make sense.

"Shit," Peers muttered, his empty hands coming up, weight seeming to fill them. The sensory dissonance was baffling his brain, knocking it about like a violent kick. Finally he found the trick of perception that allowed him to see past what the memory sphere was showing him, and then again he was a man sitting cross-legged on the bedroom floor, cradling a metal ball in his open hands.

"Peers?" a voice called from the door, knocking again.

"Just a second!"

He scrambled upright, wondering how long his visitor had been knocking while he'd been sitting, exploring the recorded past. He'd been trying to learn how to use the sphere as much as he'd been specifically snooping through its records. He had to pose a question before it could answer, but Peers didn't know what he wanted to learn. So far, about two-thirds of the memories had shown himself, Cameron's group, or both. The thing might hold a disproportionate number of Peers-or-Cameron scenes, but it seemed more likely that Peers could mostly only think in terms of his current group. He didn't know what the Astrals may have done outside of what he already knew as touch points and didn't seem to have total control of his mind. He kept unintentionally inserting people he knew into the inquiries, asking questions more specific than he'd intended.

And the thing had definite limits. He'd asked a few of the obvious big questions: *What happened when you visited the Ancient Egyptians?* and *Did you build Stonehenge?* among them.

But each time he asked something beyond the Astrals' current visit, he came up empty. It was a record of *this* visit, and possibly only a subset of the total memories. Perhaps a sensory library that was common to other such spheres, Ember Flats history, and some random stuff that — at least as far as Peers's inquiries had managed to plunge — seemed to revolve quite a lot around Cameron Bannister and his journey since Astral Day.

Was it because Peers was incapable of thinking outside his own questions, on a subconscious level?

Or was it because Cameron Bannister was more important to the Astrals than most people?

"Peers? We need to talk. Can I come in?"

It was Jeanine Coffey. And of course she couldn't come in. He'd locked the door so he could sphere-gaze in private. Now he was scrambling to stash the thing like a teen boy hiding porn with his mother at the door.

"Hang on! I'm … um … not dressed!"

Peers scampered to his bed, where he'd used the spin rod for the blinds to pry back a bit of molding covering what seemed to be an unused electrical access. He crawled low and ducked under the bed. Fifteen seconds later the sphere was satisfactorily buried. He stood, his heart pounding and feeling exhausted. He hadn't slept, other than the few minutes he'd managed before Nocturne nosed him awake to roam the hallways. The house had gone quiet a while after he'd excused himself from Clara's vigil (after the Titans had made it clear that they could go to their own rooms but nowhere else), but instead of sleeping Peers had found a new hidey-hole for his prize and had memory-walked through the rest of his night. There was so much he needed to see. So much he wanted to uncover from within the sphere, and so little time.

He glanced at the clock.

Jesus, it was already after 8 a.m.

Peers yawned, brushed nonexistent dust from his clothes, then shot into the bathroom, glanced in the mirror, and saw that he looked beat to hell.

He opened the door. Jeanine was in a large blouse he'd never seen, immaculately clean and ill fitting. At first he thought she wasn't wearing pants, then he saw a small pair of loose shorts when she moved, concealed below the dress-like tee.

"Wow, you look like shit." It wasn't a judgment. Jeanine sounded almost concerned.

Peers considered countering. Although he hadn't slept by choice — feeling the sphere's clarion call through all five of the minutes he'd considered drifting off — chances were that everyone would look haggard today. Lila had been nodding off when Peers left and Charlie had returned to his room minutes after the general call. But Piper and Cameron had looked almost caffeinated. The Meyers seemed to have reconciled and were running calculations. Pointing out how strange it was that Jeanine didn't look as bad as he did was tantamount to Peers saying she was a cold, callous bitch who could sleep no matter the crisis — a perspective for which, Peers thought, an argument could surely be made.

"Thanks," he said instead.

"Rough night?"

"I've had better."

"I was going to look myself. For Clara, I mean. Tell you the truth, I don't entirely trust Jabari's people to thoroughly search. They're the ones who lost her, right? *Inside* the damned house. How does that even happen? Did you know they still haven't found her?"

Peers hadn't, but he wasn't surprised. The Mullah had Clara. He had no proof, but to him it was obvious. They had built the mansion; they had stolen and then repurposed the sphere, which seemed to have kept right on recording Astral thoughts even once in human possession. There were Mullah in the house right now. Peers was even reasonably sure he knew who one of them was. So yes, if Clara had gone missing and Jabari seemed honestly shocked, the Mullah had probably taken her. Of course even sincere searches were coming up empty. Peers knew better than most how well the Mullah could hide.

But looking at Jeanine, Peers thought it was good that she was practicing this little update routine on him before delivering the news to anyone else. She was as delicate as a dull jigsaw. If she'd announced Clara's still-missing status to Lila in the same dropping-a-rock way she'd announced it to Peers, the poor girl would be in hysterics.

"I didn't know. That's terrible."

Jeanine's gaze moved to the right and left, as if she might spy Clara in the corner, where everyone had conveniently forgotten to look. Her tongue moved below her lower lip, exploring.

"I just walked past Lila's room. Doesn't sound like she's taking it well. So, can I come in?"

Peers stepped back.

"You don't have any pants I could borrow, do you? Or shirts?"

Peers eyed Jeanine up and down. She managed to look stunning despite her rat's-nest bedhead and ill-fitting wardrobe.

"I don't know if they confiscated my backpack because they thought I had weapons hidden in my clothes or if they just wanted to do my laundry, but all I had was what I wore in … and then when I woke up, after sleeping in this stuff I found, even those clothes were gone."

"So you came to borrow pants?"

Jeanine sat in a chair beside the dresser, where Peers had temporarily stored the sphere before running back out the night before. "I don't know who to talk to."

"Piper and Lila, maybe? They both seem about your size."

"Not about pants, Peers."

"Oh." Apparently that issue was closed without a solution.

Jeanine seemed more agitated than usual: less distant and hard, more jittery. Maybe this was what she looked like in captivity. It sure wasn't what she was usually like when nervous, as far as Peers had seen during their brief time together. But then again, she didn't have her guns or her knives or anything with which she might fashion a shiv. Even the mirror and window glass couldn't be broken into a blade — he knew; he'd tried, with thoughts of Jabari's throat in mind. That left Jeanine mostly defenseless, with only feet and fists for protection in the face of an unseen, unacknowledged threat.

"Look me in the eye, Peers. Will you just … *here?*" She pointed at her eyes.

Peers looked. Her eyes were brown and surprisingly soft.

"Can I trust you?"

"Yes, of course."

"Are you lying to me?"

"No."

"Promise?"

"Would you like me to cross my heart? Or pinky swear?"

"Don't fuck with me. I'm serious."

"Of course. Yes, I promise."

She sharpened her gaze. Seemed to bore her glare through the back of his skull.

"You and me. We're going to be straight with each other."

"Certainly."

She watched him for another few seconds then sighed as if he were an impossible buffoon who simply didn't get her.

"What?" he asked.

"I hate this."

"What do you hate?"

"You're all I've got. You're it. Or Charlie. Maybe Charlie. But I've allied with him before, and it's like being on a softball team with one of the dugouts."

"I don't understand that metaphor."

"Fine," she said as if he'd begged her and she was finally relenting. "Cameron, Kindred, and Meyer are in on what's being planned. Have to be. They kind of have a forced hand, or at least Cameron does. And Kindred and Meyer? Well, you know how they are when doing their Sherlock thing."

"No," Peers said.

"Lila's messed up over her daughter, and Piper's messed up over Lila. Normally I'd go to Piper. She's had a real pulse on things lately, but right now it's like she's all

Lila, all the time. Which I can respect, but it doesn't exactly leave her head clear. So it's you or Charlie or your dog." She turned and raised her pitch an octave. "Hey, boy."

Nocturne, in bed, raised his head and licked his lips.

"What are you talking about, Jeanine?"

"Why are you here?"

"*You* came to *my* room."

"I meant here in Ember Flats. Why did you come here? Why did you *want* to come here?"

"I reached the same conclusions as Benjamin's group — about the Astrals and the Ark, even when we all thought it was Thor's Hammer. I've been keeping tabs on you using the Astral equipment I found in the Den. Grabbing your group and redirecting you here, where you should have gone from the beginning, on the mission you should have undertaken all along, just made sense from my perspective — and Aubrey's, God rest his soul."

"You knew we already went to Sinai?"

Peers couldn't parse his lies from truth. He tossed the dice. "Yes."

"And you followed us to Derinkuyu."

*Maybe?* Sure, why not.

"Yes."

"So this is all about the Ark for you. About the research because you've studied all this ancient aliens shit, too."

And now, a test. She pierced him with her stare.

He sighed heavily. "I also wanted to kill Jabari."

"Still do, or no?"

"The jury is out." He watched her stand, sit, then cross her legs in the space of ten seconds. "Why don't you just tell me what's on your mind?"

"Do you believe Jabari?"

"About what?"

"That she's *on our side*?"

"Like I said — the jury is out."

"Or that she's part of a resistance."

"She did build a privacy jammer. I suppose she could have lifted it from someone else, but my gut says no. And she's human; I do believe that much. Kindred and Clara said the same. So if I have to answer ..." He sighed, unwilling to give the woman he'd been so angry with for years any benefit of the doubt but finding himself unable to honestly do otherwise. "Then yes, I suppose I believe it. Why?"

A final assessing stare: Jeanine trying to decide if she would take Peers into her confidence or keep whatever was bugging her private. Finally the last wall crumbled, and she sat still, wary, composing her words.

"I just talked to Cameron, after he talked to Meyer and Kindred, along with Jabari. They have a plan in the works."

"To find Clara?"

"Sort of."

"What does that mean: *Sort of*?"

"It's a roundabout thing. It's ultimately for Clara, the way Cameron tells it. But ... I don't know, I just wonder if that's the main thing or a side effect. I asked Cameron if he honestly thinks it's wise. He said yes. He's thought about it and is totally sure. He's 'convinced this is the right thing to do.' But I don't think he's sure at all. I think he's justifying because that's what Cameron does. He's 'sure' about everything even when he's not. I think he's trying to be strong, but it's obnoxious because it closes him to other opinions. Like mine. But he didn't ask me what I thought. He *informed* me and then got pissed when I tried to argue."

"What's the plan he's so sure about? Or *not*, as the case may be?"

"Do you know about the Mullah?"

Ice chips slid down his spine. Peers stiffened then forced himself to relax. "Somewhat. From my research."

"The Mullah have been after us since Sinai. They've been trying to get Cameron's stone key, at what seems like any cost. Hell, since we left Heaven's Veil, it's been more about running from the Mullah than fleeing the Astrals. Although we managed to lose them a bit — or maybe they backed off — after we'd run far enough from Ember Flats and made it clear that we weren't going back."

"Why Ember Flats?"

"Cameron and Charlie say the Mullah guard the Ark, and the Ark was moved here shortly after we found it at Sinai."

That wasn't entirely true, about the Mullah guarding the Ark. In Peers's childhood, Mullah children had all talked about the mythical archive, and they'd all known how popular myth had distorted around the Ark the way it had warped around so much else: the great flood, the plagues, the reason for the pyramids' shape. But the Ark wasn't his old family's major preoccupation. Much more pressing was the portal, the vestibule, and maintaining balance with the Horsemen.

"Okay."

"But those knife-happy freaks are everywhere, Peers. *Especially* this close to the lion's mouth, with the Ark right next door. I guess we made a mistake by coming back, and pissed them off. One of them must have been watching us all along. Here, on Jabari's staff. Because Cameron says the Mullah took Clara, and that's why this 'plan' is necessary."

Peers feigned shock. Now that the plan had been mentioned a second time, he wanted to ask about it, but expressing surprise about this Mullah "revelation" seemed more important. Pretending he hadn't seen hints inside the alien sphere pointing to Clara's abduction by the Mullah, Peers said, "What makes you so sure it was them?"

"They left a note. On Jabari's pillow, while she was sleeping."

"Maybe it's a hoax."

Jeanine shook her head. "I don't think so. Cameron believes it, and so does Charlie. They both know a lot about stuff like that. Jabari apparently knows ancient aliens too, and she believes it. More importantly, Piper, who has a knack for assessing emotion, says that Jabari really *does* seem to believe it, meaning she's not bullshitting about the note. The Mullah don't fuck around, Peers. Count yourself lucky you've never run into them. They don't give up. Or bluff. They have people everywhere, like a network of spies. Someone told them about us, or they've got an agent right in the goddamned middle of our group."

Jeanine was watching Peers, but he saw nothing more accusatory than the severe expression she regularly wore.

"What would a spy tell them about our group to make them take Clara?"

"That Cameron has the key. And yes, I asked. He says he still has it, that Jabari's people didn't take it when they brought us in." A sour look claimed her face. "Apparently a vital Astral doomsday artifact wasn't worth confiscation like my pants."

"I don't get it. Why take Clara? Why not take the key if that's what they care about?" This time, Peers wasn't pretending, or hiding the truth. Only the elders knew *why* the Mullah did what it did. The group's position on the Ark, its key, and so much else was a crapshoot even for a man raised in the secret society.

"Charlie and Kindred say that *Cameron* needs to do it. No one else."

"Well, yes, of course, but ..." Peers felt himself tripping

over his words. Yes, Cameron probably needed to open the archive, but Jeanine's assumptions were backward. In the absence of true elder insight, Peers had been operating for decades on the same body of evidence as Cameron and apparently Jabari. The conclusion was clear: The Mullah weren't trying to open the Ark. It was their duty to make sure it stayed closed.

But before he spoke, Peers thought of the portal. Of the secrets. And of what he'd often heard among the Mullah in whispers. The children could never understand the elders' thoughts — even the most loyal adult knights couldn't fully interpret them and would never question their conclusions no matter how strange they became.

"But what?"

"Well, when I talked to Charlie … I mean, Benjamin Bannister knew it!"

"Knew what, Peers?"

"Haven't the Mullah been chasing you to get the key? To *prevent* the Ark from being opened?"

"I'm just telling you what I know. The note says that if we want Clara, we must open the Ark."

"So how are they planning to get her back?"

"By opening the Ark."

Peers went cold. You didn't open what the Astrals had sealed. You weren't supposed to shake the wasp's nest. He'd told the group that *this* was their mission in Ember Flats, but it was only a means to get inside and exact his revenge on the viceroy. But those old lessons and prejudices still orbited his brain; they'd been drilled in so deeply that they'd never come out. The children weren't to respect what the Horsemen touched. They were to avoid those things at all times — look the other direction and never turn back unless duty called.

"I know you told Cameron he had to open it," Jeanine

said, apparently missing what was surely a horrified expression. "But has anyone told you what happened when we found it the first time?"

"Sort of," Peers said, figuring a vague answer offered plausible deniability.

"Something … *happened* when we were there," Jeanine said, suddenly seeming cold, arms crossing over her chest. A girl who used to travel with us … she was killed. Shot. There was an accident. But the thing is, the Ark? It …" She sighed, now pacing, clearly disturbed. "It *showed it back to us*. I saw her die in my head, over and over and over. And there was this clear feeling of someone poring over every detail. Weighing it. Like a judge looking over an accident's details. It didn't matter that there wasn't any fault. Someone was dead, and thus someone had to pay, the way a police report is used to determine whose insurance should cover the damage. We were *all* at fault. I could feel it in my bones."

Peers looked at Jeanine, sympathetic. He'd felt something like that, once.

"Whatever's in the Ark … it doesn't like us. Maybe the Astrals are more evolved than we are, and maybe that makes us animals to them. Maybe they think they're being fair, if the point is to judge us. Maybe they even think this is all for our own good. But I know two things, Peers: We all felt the Ark's advance verdict when we saw it at Mt. Sinai, and based on everything I've ever heard anyone say, whenever the Astrals have come to this planet in the past, there's always been some sort of extinction. They come. They judge us. And we fail. Every time."

Peers watched Jeanine finally sit, no longer strong and bold, no longer the leader, no longer the angry grunt with a high wall around her. Now she was only a girl. One more human being in a sea of unworthy souls.

She'd come to him. The others were either committed or temporarily unfit. It came down to Peers — the one man who, if she truly knew him, Jeanine would trust least of all.

"We can run," he said. "We'll let them open it. We'll take Clara, and run. We can hide, deep in places like Derinkuyu. There have always been survivors. There must have been, if there's to be a human race to judge again later."

"There's no way to run," Jeanine said. "Nowhere to go and no time to do it even if there was."

Peers sat across from her.

"All right. So what do you propose?"

"We don't bow to the Mullah and open the Ark. Instead, we cut to the chase, and solve the problem at its source."

"How?"

Jeanine fixed Peers with a dire stare.

"We find out who the Mullah are," she said, "and we kill them ourselves."

# Chapter Forty-Two

The next day passed.

Then the day after that.

Clara still hadn't been found.

Piper stalked the halls, searching for remnants of emotion. Sometimes she took Meyer with her because he'd walked the fine line between Astral and human. Sometimes she took Kindred because he was even more plugged into the Astral collective (or at least, he felt it at times even if it defiantly barred him), and walking with Kindred awoke a different part of Piper than time with Meyer. It was odd: The men were identical in every measurable way besides temperament, and Piper had bedded down with and been married to both — individually at first, then in the strange but also strangely fitting three-way bigamist's paradise they'd tried after she'd found herself with duplicates. And yet her relationship with each now felt distinct, like a before and after, though neither was better or worse.

Sometimes, she walked the halls with Lila, and often felt the strongest clues. Even with Lila, what Piper felt of Clara was like little more than a scent left behind —

cinnamon tea brewed long ago in one spot, with its aroma still lingering — but finding those clues was better than nothing. Better than lying around in bed all day; better than watching videos in her room or together with the others in one of the lounges; better than accepting the staff's offers of massages and time in the hot tub to release tension. Better, even, than sex — though Cameron dealt differently than Piper, and she didn't blame him. Their few tumbles had taken her mind from troubles for a few minutes even if she'd been too distracted for climax.

There was a time when Piper would have sat back and accepted the situation: Clara was being held by unfriendly forces; those forces couldn't be found or reasoned with, in part because everyone felt sure there was a traitor among them; the chance to fulfill the ransom and free Clara was still a day away, so there was, practically speaking, no point in fretting. But that was then, and this was now. Piper was no longer that woman. She'd been little more than baggage when Meyer had dragged the family across the country to his Axis Mundi, and she'd been a mostly complicit dishrag during her two years as queen of Heaven's Veil. For five years after she'd faced lean living, deathly challenges, heartbreak, and horror. Some of the people once dearest to her were dead. And she'd reached her limit: no more would join them.

Maybe Clara was unreachable. It certainly felt that way when she prowled the palace, entirely unimpeded by Jabari, her people, or the Astrals. But she wouldn't just sit and wait to see what happened. She wouldn't accept massages and mud-cake facials. She wouldn't betray that little girl by giving up, or sighing and saying, "We'll have to wait and see" like everyone else seemed to be.

Piper seemed able to extend her emotional antennae — that curious sense of extended empathy she'd been growing while Kindred and Meyer were nurturing their hybrid mind — further out when she walked with others. But mostly, she walked alone.

Piper stopped. Inhaled. There was nothing, literally, on the air, but she closed her eyes and allowed herself to feel the breath sliding inside her. She tried to empty her mind, to let the sense/scent come to her. And she thought, as Piper always did in the wing where they all stayed, that she could indeed feel a lingering trail of Clara's essence. But it might also be all in her head; she might be fooling herself into believing something she desperately needed to.

But with her eyes closed and her mind on her breath, Piper could almost feel a sense of Clara passing, as if she were scampering by on silent feet. And a feeling of …

*Companionship?*

*Fellowship?*

But no, it was subtly different. This was sort of like a game. Maybe like a game of leading and following. Like hide and seek.

But the feeling was already gone.

Piper resumed walking. Through the kitchen. Through the second entrance to the kitchen and into the construction area. The project wing was very human. Piper saw boards and cinderblocks and bricks and compressors and buckets of cement and compounds. There was a large padlocked tool trailer just beyond the window, accessible through a closed door. The kind of thing she might have seen on any construction site before the world had ever heard of the Astrals. Before —

*(It's this way)*

Piper stopped midstride, then slowly turned. The sense of something nearly heard or seen or felt, like an apparition's whisper, called her back into and through the kitchen. Back to the hallway. But it wasn't just Clara's emotion — someone else had left something behind.

*Two people.*

The first was at an angle, at a featureless wall. The feeling Piper seemed to sense was as flat as the wall and floor beneath it. If sensations had color, this one was black. Or white. Or perhaps colorless and clear like a glass of distilled water. She could almost feel it, and yet its vacancy offered presence.

Confused, Piper followed the other, all too aware that she was probably full of shit and grasping at straws like an idiot. Meyer hadn't even understood why Piper did yoga beyond its physical benefits, so she'd explained the sense of integration or spiritual calm it gave her. He'd definitely never have understood Piper's preoccupation with her many New Age interests, so she'd kept them out of sight on her Vellum. But sometimes, at night, she used to swear she could rise above her body. It was mind-trick bullshit, but she'd always wanted to believe, and often chose to. The difference, Piper suspected, might be semantic.

This felt like that. Like something the old Meyer would laugh at — something that was nothing. But still she walked, trying to calm her mind, reminding herself that she'd guessed correctly more often than not in recent months, about hidden emotions and motives. And hey, wasn't that what all those New Age authors said? That we were all one, in a big energy collective?

And if that was too hard to believe, hadn't she and Cameron shared thoughts after passing through those twin lines of monolithic stones? Hadn't Lila sworn she could hear unborn Clara speaking from the womb back at the Axis Mundi, and hadn't Heather been sure she'd been able to hear Meyer — or possibly Kindred? Didn't the Astrals communicate with their minds? And hadn't Cameron and

Charlie both said that ancient societies — of humans, not Astrals — were supposedly psychically connected?

If all of that could be true, Piper wasn't about to beat herself up for trying to help — even if it meant hoping to find Clara using what amounted to Scooby Sense.

But this wasn't fear Piper thought she could feel. This was interest. Almost *obsessive*. And really, the intensity of that compulsive, shocked curiosity was a bit much for a seven-year-old girl, even as precocious as Clara was. So it was someone else. Someone adult, who'd felt something strong and compelling in this very same hallway.

Was Clara the object of that obsession? A chilling thought. Piper could almost imagine some creep stalking the girl through the halls, mere feet behind her without the girl knowing, his arms finally reaching out in disturbing lust when she was most remote and vulnerable and …

But no. She'd stopped in front of the utility closet. Where Kamal had taken them to peruse security footage, before he'd realized the surveillance system was down.

"Hello, Piper."

Piper almost jumped. She turned around, heart racing, hand on chest, unable to hide the depth of her scare. She felt suddenly guilty and ashamed, as if caught masturbating.

But the man behind her was unmoving, standing with his arms at his sides, a somehow-still-intact, somehow-still-unfashionable short-sleeve dress shirt tucked in over brown slacks. His hair had grown long during their wandering but now was freshly cut, trimmed back to something horridly boring. His glasses were perched in their normal place, bug eyes assessing her from beneath them.

"Charlie. You scared me."

"What are you doing out here?"

Charlie looked like he was trying to speak, but no

words came out. Then there was a curious electronic sound — like an amplifier experiencing feedback issues — and Charlie started mid-sentence.

"Really does know what she's talking about."

"What?"

"You don't trust her, do you?"

"Who?"

There was another of those curious noises. Charlie blinked, then said, "Jabari."

"I trust her enough."

"But not all the way."

"You've heard what she wants Kindred and Meyer to do. Do you really think that's wise?"

"I don't honestly have an opinion," Charlie said. "I'm impartial."

"Cameron told me the Mullah note said he needed to open the Ark. But what have we done? We've just been sitting around."

"Waiting for the State of the City address."

"One doesn't have to do with another."

"They all feel that the best chance of opening the Ark without undue … interference? … is to make sure attention is focused elsewhere. All of Ember Flats turns out for the State of the City."

"But we're wasting days."

"The Mullah will wait. They'd agree with Jabari's thinking."

"How could you possibly know that?"

Charlie touched his chin. "Funny thing. In the past, the amount of information the Ark has needed to collect must have been much less than it is now. Not just smaller populations but smaller minds. The way it's had to work this time must be so inefficient, don't you think? These days you keep so much of your brains out on the Internet."

"The Internet is gone."

"True. So where are your brains now?"

Charlie was always strange, but this was particularly odd. Where did he keep *his* brain, if he was going to talk in second person?

"If I were the archive, I'd be confused," said Charlie.

"What's that mean?"

"I don't know. I'm confused."

"Charlie …"

"When you went to the Ark before, did it surprise you what came out?"

"Did it surprise *you?*" Piper said, tiring of his posturing. He'd always been like this. Superior, putting himself one step ahead.

"Actually, yes. I felt almost vindictive. Which is strange."

"What do you want, Charlie?" Piper wanted him to leave her alone so she could go into the utility closet and spend some time feeling its aura. Chances were excellent she'd simply leave ten minutes later feeling like an idiot and knowing nothing, but it beat double-talk with King Awkward.

"You've been to court, haven't you? With Meyer."

"Once. Why?"

"The judge. Was she … stoic?"

"She was normal. She was a judge."

"Hmm. If you'd gone in and she'd been wildly emotional, do you think that would have mattered?"

"What?"

"Would you have pled your case differently if the judge was manic? If she was depressed?"

"I think we'd have requested a new trial date if the judge had been unstable."

"Do you think she'd have made mistakes?"

"You mean in the verdict? I don't know, Charlie; it was an intellectual property thing with Quirky Q, and it took half the 'trial' just to explain what the hell my business was about, and even then—"

"I'll bet," Charlie said, finger to lips, "a judge who was used to being calm and impartial — but who suddenly found him- or herself dealing with too much emotion and too much confusing evidence … I'll bet that judge would render a … *sloppy* judgment."

"Okay." Now literally tapping her foot. "Did you need something?"

Charlie's eyes blinked back from thoughtful to present. He opened his mouth, but again nothing came out.

She rotated to the utility closet. "We'll talk later, Charlie. Go get a glass of water."

"Jabari wants Kindred and Meyer to make their appearance in front of Ember Flats while Cameron is sneaking over to open the Ark," Charlie said, his voice forcing Piper to turn back toward him. "But if the archive reacted with anger before, maybe it's best not to give it a big, loud background of emotion elsewhere in the city. She wants to create a distraction, but maybe instead all that commotion will be like a bunch of noisy kids screaming while you're trying to think. And maybe …" He began losing his voice in spurts, like intermittent laryngitis. "Works so that … Meyer and Ki … tomorrow."

"What's wrong with you?"

Charlie said nothing, not smiling. Very like Charlie, but at least he was finally leaving her alone.

"And yet the more riled up it is once Cameron opens … sure, it'll be tense and furious, but maybe it'll be like that judge having a bad day, and make unfortunate mistakes."

Piper didn't know what to say, so she turned back to

the door as if to remind herself that it was still there. She touched it then decided she was no longer feeling all that woo-woo. Crusader or not — determined not to quit like the others or not — Piper still got plenty tired, and Charlie's infuriating, obtuse presence had, as always, exasperated her into a puddle. She wanted to take a brief nap and come back later.

She turned back to Charlie.

"Charlie, I'm going to ..." But then she stopped, her mouth still open.

Although she was on an empty stretch of straight hall with no open doors, Charlie was gone.

# Chapter Forty-Three

LILA WATCHED her fathers ready themselves, aware that she had two of them now more than ever. They'd both played that role; they both cared for her and her daughter; they'd both, in real time, loved her mother. Both had memories of Lila's first steps, her first words, her childhood's trials and tribulations. Right now, they were almost impossible to tell apart.

With the State of the City address scheduled within the hour, Meyer had shaved his beard in order to look as much like Kindred as possible. If they planned to shock Ember Flats, they'd do it all the way. He was the old Meyer again, like Kindred beside him. The face mattered. Even before Astral Day, Meyer Dempsey (movie magnate, change maker, reluctant philanthropist) had graced the cover of international magazines. He'd been a breed of famous that Mara Jabari had never been, as she'd quietly built her reputation — first with a prodigious rise through prestigious universities then with the da Vinci Initiate — proving herself to be a prodigy and authority worthy of notice. And that, Lila thought as she watched them prepare, gave her father some small measure of comfort. Sure, Jabari had been allowed to rule her city as a human, whereas Meyer had been abducted, held captive for two years, and slyly replaced — twice. But at least she'd never been in *GQ*.

"Hand me that tie, will you?"

Lila followed the man's fingers, honestly unsure which one he was. Only when he shifted enough for her to see a recent shaving nick did she know; Meyer had cut himself while trying to clear beard detritus on his own, having refused the palace barber. That and the wedding ring were all that gave him away. Meyer still wore the band from his marriage to Piper, whereas Kindred (just as stubborn, just as wifeless) had re-donned Heather's ring, pulled from some hock Lila could only imagine after she was gone.

She took the tie from the bedspread and handed it to him. It was blue. Kindred had grabbed the other tie on his own and was fashioning a full Windsor. Kindred's was red. Lila found the colors fitting. The time Meyer spent starved, weak, and steeped in the thought collective had cooled his temperament, whereas Kindred's personality was still piping hot.

"Thanks," he said, taking it.

Lila sat back, watching them primp, saying nothing.

"It'll be okay, you know," said Kindred. Lila looked over, her equilibrium fighting to make sense of the room. If not for Kindred's red tie, she'd have looked away from one thing to see the exact same thing somewhere else. Their suits, shoes, and haircuts were identical, all tailored for maximum shock value.

"I know."

"I know you know. But I really mean it. I'm not just saying that to make you feel better."

"Have you run the scenarios?" she asked.

"Of course we have," Kindred replied. Lila had been kidding, but of course the answer wasn't a joke.

"It was probably always inevitable that we'd eventually clash with the Mullah," Meyer said — and when Lila looked into his eyes, she could finally tell the difference between them. The two men had identical genetics, yet Meyer had taken additional scars that showed when you looked deep. "We even thought it likely—"

"Almost for sure," Kindred interrupted.

"That Mullah would be in the city. The great, ancient societies have always embedded themselves in positions of power. But this time we'll give them what they want, and everything will be fine."

*"Fine,"* Lila repeated.

"You don't believe us," Kindred said.

"I'm just worried, Dad. It's unreasonable if you actually expect me not to worry."

"Trust us."

"I do. It's just that …"

"What, Lila?"

"Well, you didn't know they'd take Clara, did you?"

Kindred looked almost affronted, but Meyer sat on the bed beside her.

"No. We didn't. But they shouldn't have. We're getting more data in Ember Flats than we've *ever* had. Kindred can sense the nearby mothership, which knows the citizens' mood. Just walking around when we came in, I got a million little details. There's Jabari, her staff, and simple common sense. Putting all that together, it seems ridiculous for them to have taken her. They want something from us, clearly, but showing their hand — exposing the entire Mullah operation inside the city — isn't the solution. The only way they'd even *consider* taking Clara would have been if she'd walked right up and asked for it. At least that's the way we figure it."

Lila considered a rebuttal. When Meyer and Kindred combined minds, they were right a lot more often than not. But she could think of many times they'd erred, and this struck her as a mistake. Logical or not, the Mullah had snatched her little girl.

"It doesn't even make sense. Charlie has always said the Mullah wanted to take the key away, not invite us to use it. Or *force* our hand."

"I guess Charlie was wrong."

Meyer watched Lila for a long moment. Then, seeming to decide she was as okay as she was going to get, he stood.

Lila recrossed her legs, running an idle finger along her knee, trying not to fret, failing miserably.

"What are you going to tell them? When you get up to speak?"

"The truth," said Kindred.

"Don't you think that the Astrals will stop the broadcast to the other cities if they have a problem with what you're saying?"

"We're sure they will. But Ember Flats will see and hear it."

"Unless they shoot you."

"Shooting us makes our case even stronger, don't you think?"

Lila didn't like the way Kindred had put that. It implied that if both Meyers were shot and killed, it was a fair trade for their message. And all this while Jabari, who'd insisted they do it, sat clear of harm.

"They won't stop us, Lila," said Meyer. "Only in 4 percent of scenarios do they stop us. We will have our say."

"Then what?"

"Unrest."

"That's what Mara Jabari wants, you know."

"It's fine. It's what we want, too. It draws attention from the Ark. We have guesses as to what might happen when Cameron opens it, but of that, we're the least certain. Fewer variables is better. There's usually a lot of pedestrian traffic around it. This will make sure there's none — not once word gets around that not only is Meyer Dempsey alive as rumors have claimed but that there are now two of him. So Cameron can open it quietly."

"And then?"

"The clock starts."

"Cameron is afraid of what it will decide about us. The Ark, I mean." She said it with eyebrows raised, waiting to see if either man would offer their calculations as to the Ark's judgment. But neither spoke, either not hearing or knowing or wanting to say.

After a quiet, collar-straightening moment, she said, "Do you really just expect me to sit back here while all this happens? While you rile the city, Cameron opens that damned box, and my daughter stays missing?" Lila hadn't realized she was angry, but now her cheeks were burning, and her eyes were starting to water. "Is that really what I'm supposed to do? Just sit on my ass and twiddle my thumbs. *Wait and see?*"

Meyer and Kindred shared a glance.

"Not at all, Lila," Meyer said.

"She doesn't understand," Kindred added.

"Lila …" Meyer raised a hand as if preparing to make a very important, very precise point. "When we say what we must and the Ark opens, there's an excellent chance that all hell will break loose. Perhaps literally. We can't calculate what the archive will decide. We can only break the seal and see. To get Clara back and for a dozen other reasons, breaking that seal is something that needs to be done. But anything could happen, and we must be prepared."

"Okay," Lila said.

"You're staying back for *only* one reason. Same as Piper, and everyone who's not us or Cameron: *protection.*"

"If today is judgment day," Lila said, "I don't think the viceroy's palace will protect anyone."

"I'm not talking about the palace," Meyer said. "It's staying close to Jabari that matters."

"I don't care about her! I care about you!"

And Kindred said to Meyer, "She still doesn't understand."

There was a knock at the door. Kamal stuck his head inside and said, "It's time."

# Chapter Forty-Four

Cameron sat on the carved stone bench in the western palace garden, not more than fifty feet from the gate. Beyond the open gate the courtyard was ringed, at comfortable, open distances, by the other gray stone Ember Flats government buildings. Somewhere in the middle, obscured, was the Ark's place of honor, bordered by fountains, its soundtrack the chirping of birds and the bubbling of running water. It was as if someone were pretending the thing was in Eden, as if it promised only blessings to those who greeted it.

Looking through the open gates (unguarded; the Titans had been called away and replaced by human guards, who'd already left on Jabari's orders), Cameron felt his legs flexing and trying to make him rise. Only, he wouldn't stand and dash toward the Ark to do his duty. He'd run out of the courtyard, out into the city — into the cannibal-strewn wastelands beyond if need be. Anything but face that cursed thing again. Anything to avoid its horror show and the wrath he felt certain it stood eager to unleash.

"Are you listening to me?"

Cameron's attention snapped back to Charlie, looking at him like he was an irredeemable idiot. He was the opposite of drunk. Why Piper had thought he'd adopted a substance habit was beyond Cameron. He didn't want to contradict her, but it seemed far more likely that she was lying for reasons unknown (or at least badly mistaken) than that Charlie had ever waxed philosophical with her. Yet she'd said he'd been strange and aloof, somehow disturbing when surprising her in the hall. When Cameron had asked him about it, Charlie said that he'd been sleeping at the time. He wasn't sure whom to believe, but ultimately it didn't matter.

"Pay attention, Cameron. Honestly. You're just like your father."

"Thanks."

"It's not a compliment."

Yes, this was Charlie, all right: no drugs or booze required. Benjamin had been the closest thing Charlie had ever had to a *best friend* as far as Cameron knew, yet this was the plainspoken way he honored the man's memory. Sure, Benjamin could be a pain in the ass; Cameron knew that better than anyone. But right now it felt like disrespecting the dead — and a jinx on the moment given what Cameron would be doing next.

"Jabari kept most of her da Vinci Initiate data. She seems to have been far better prepared than Meyer. Maybe that's because her preparations were based on research while Dempsey's were based on an acid trip. She—"

"Ayahuasca. Not acid."

Charlie glared at Cameron, who suddenly felt like he should apologize. For everything throughout the history of time. Then he continued.

"She had a private plane on permanent standby. Right where she lived, down the road, not a state away. If she'd had to drive, Jabari wouldn't have gone right the hell through Chicago like Meyer. The only thing that got him past doomsday was probably dumb luck and the fact that the Astrals seemed intent on making him one of the Nine. Regardless, she'd backed everything up remotely, in scads of locations and locally on an array of drives. The woman seems to do nothing that isn't phenomenally thought out. Just one more reason I wish Benjamin had done more to poach her from Delacroix instead of admiring her work from afar."

Cameron thought there might be an insult lurking somewhere in Charlie's words. Maybe another reminder of how Mara would have been a better offspring for Benjamin than Cameron. He said nothing.

"Culling Jabari's comprehensive Initiate research, I'd have to agree with what Peers has been saying all along: *You have to do this.* There's a strange organic matrix that seems to be just below the surface of that key you've been carrying. I'd have to break it open to be sure — and without proper equipment, I can't look inside the thing — but it fits some of what Delacroix found about biological imprinting. You touched the key, and it somehow mated itself to you. Carrying it for five years has likely only strengthened the bond. Maybe it would work if someone else used it, but I doubt it."

"Great." At least this wasn't something he didn't already know.

"What I don't understand is that Delacroix's and Jabari's research on matrices like the ones I think your key uses shows that it should require a hell of a lot longer to imprint. Kind of like a waiting period. Like the Astrals figured a lot of humans would touch the thing, so it needed to wait a long time to 'activate' on one particular person. To be sure that person was its match."

"What, am I dating this thing now?" Cameron looked down, but the key in his satchel didn't respond.

"Be serious, Cameron. And just tell me. When you take the key out, does it almost seem to adjust to your fingertips?"

Cameron shrugged. Though he'd never once come close to dropping the thing, as if his grip was infallible.

"And when you used the key back in Heaven's Veil to turn off the 'spotlight' inside the Apex pyramid …"

"It worked, yes."

Charlie assessed Cameron as if perhaps he was lying.

"I've had it for five years," Cameron said. "Isn't that enough?"

"Delacroix was predicting it would take fifteen or twenty years for bonding to occur. It could be non-continuous exposure, but the math says the time required after first contact is nonnegotiable."

"I don't know what to tell you, Charlie. I haven't had it that long. Maybe I'm not the Chosen One after all."

"Neither here nor there, I guess. If you used it in Heaven's Veil, there's no reason you couldn't use it now. You understand the importance of timing?"

"Just that I should open it when Meyer and Kindred are on stage. Not before or after."

"Correct. It will ensure you have privacy and minimize the chance that someone will interfere. Jabari says she'll put a few people at the entrance points to the courtyard but that most of her guard will be across the square. After she's done her bit and stepped down to let Kindred and Meyer take over, she'll be coming back here, and those guards are required to keep her out of harm's way."

"How brave of her," Cameron said. Charlie eyed him, but Cameron knew he was deflecting. He was so terribly scared. He knew all the reasons for Jabari hightailing it back to the palace, and he did, in the end, mostly trust the viceroy and her plan. But he didn't want to do this — not one tiny little bit — and all delays and distractions were welcome.

"The square isn't that far. You'll hear Jabari's address in the air, but you can also monitor it on that mobile she gave you."

Cameron patted his pocket. It was almost like the time before Astral Day, watching live entertainment on a phone.

"It's not like the old cell networks or the Internet," Charlie said.

"I know. I understand."

"No, I don't think you do. This is *the Internet, Astral style.* It's what all the ancient societies used to do: mind-to-mind communication. Only, we're so retarded and disconnected today that we can't always tune into the thoughts of others, even with rock monoliths around all the capitals and the big statues set up as focal points, antennae, and repeaters. We need clunky devices like the one I gave you. It's not a perfect system, it goes: thoughts, rebroadcast, reception … then the person 'receiving the thoughts' by watching them on one of those little screens has to take an extra step and process the information visually as if it were happening in front of them. That extra step leads to dissonance."

"Give me the short version, Charlie."

"What you see on that screen isn't video from a video-camera. It's an average of the way all of the eyes across town will see the event. If you could get the vision right inside your mind, it would make sense to your brain. But it doesn't."

"Shorter," Cameron insisted.

"Don't trust what you see on the screen. Listen and trust your hearing instead, if you can. You'll hear Jabari finish, there will be a lull, and then you'll probably hear a collective gasp or commotion. You should be able to hear Meyer, but it's possible the humans running the show will have already killed the amplifiers. So you'll have to take a guess. Open the Ark then. Immediately. Don't wait."

"I know what to do, Charlie."

*"No,"* Charlie insisted, his voice finding uncharacteristic anger, "you *don't.* You thought you knew what to do when we went to Sinai, but you weren't prepared when the Ark fought back. Now here we are again. You said you knew what you were doing when you took us into Damascus, and I'm sure you remember how that turned out."

"You want to lead instead of me? Any time, Charlie."

"Stop acting so goddamn righteous," Charlie snapped. "And most of all, stop acting so goddamn *sure.* You think it's confidence, but it's actually arrogance. I remember it from way back when I first met you, when you were a jackass kid with a chip on his shoulder. You had your problems with Benjamin, and I get it. My father and I weren't the best of friends either. But if you presume this time and get it wrong because you're still fighting daddy issues and feel the need to always be right and never admit when you aren't certain, it won't be someone getting shot by mistake. This time, the whole damned planet will suffer."

Cameron felt himself wanting to fight back — or at least to call Charlie on his cheap shots — but the most frightened part of him was sure Charlie was right. He *wasn't* sure. He had no idea what was next, and the uncertainty was worse than any punishment. Maybe opening the Ark would free Clara like the Mullah promised, and maybe they'd welch. Maybe the Astrals would judge humanity as worthy even though Cameron felt that the verdict would swing the opposite way. Maybe, if armageddon came, some would be spared, and maybe Piper and Lila and the others would be among them. Or maybe not.

Maybe by turning the key only he could turn, he'd be freeing humanity from bondage.

Or maybe he'd be committing genocide.

"All right," Cameron said, his eyes watching the space beyond the gate, seeming to sense the Ark and its waiting keyhole somewhere beyond. "Tell me what to do."

Charlie did.

# Chapter Forty-Five

Peers paced.

He'd left the silver sphere traced with glowing blue lines on the middle of his bedspread, right in plain sight. If anyone were watching this room, it'd be obvious what he'd done, and possibly reveal the true nature of his intentions. But if he understood the catch-22, nobody could be watching the room because he'd stolen the device that did the watching. Or was it really that simple?

He stopped his feet. Stared at the sphere. Felt it calling to him like a compulsion. Just minutes ago, he'd watched Moscow getting annihilated during the first phase of the occupation, just after the motherships arrived. Peers, like everyone else, knew all about Moscow; it was the 9/11 and Paris terrorism of the Astral era. Moscow meant violence, intimidation, distrust, and an instinctual (if somewhat cowardly) impetus toward unconditional obedience. Moscow's destruction had been the alpha dog asserting his dominance; it was the new guy in prison beating the shit out of the largest inmate in the yard. Moscow had steeped in every human psyche as a brutal, uncompromising lesson in paying attention and doing what humanity was told.

And yet Peers had just watched Moscow's destruction through Astral eyes. Seen that way, it hadn't been so horrible. Somehow the sphere conveyed not just sensation but also thoughts and feelings. Peers, fully immersed, had felt shockingly blasé as he'd watched all those lives end. *It's just energy,* he remembered thinking. *Why fret the pieces when the whole lives on?*

And really, Moscow *had* been firing rockets up at the mothership.

And really — given the temperament of the strangely connected, technologically advanced, arrogant crop of humans the planet had grown during the last epoch — a statement *had* needed to be made.

And honestly, considered rationally, killing the millions in Moscow had probably saved hundreds of millions of lives because without that statement others might have kept right on fighting the motherships.

Peers had felt pretty reasonable about the whole thing by the time the vision ended, and then he'd shot up from the bed and dropped it, staring at the sphere like a clot of bloody mucus. Staring, he'd felt as if he'd done something awful. And he didn't want to do such a hideous thing again.

But then other questions had reasserted themselves.

Questions he'd never been given the answers to — answers he very much needed to know.

Questions about the Mullah elders and the secrets they kept. If anyone would know the answers to those questions, it would be the Astrals — considering they were supposedly on the other end of all the secret Mullah business anyway.

The Mullah called the Astrals "the Horsemen," and

now that Peers was staring at the sphere, feeling equal parts revulsion and desire to grab the thing and reimmerse, he understood why. Maybe the Horsemen would bring about the end of the world, and maybe they wouldn't. Perhaps they'd already done it dozens of times, as both the elders and people like Benjamin Bannister believed. Either way, they felt like executioners. They felt like dark riders, once you'd been inside their minds.

Only that wasn't quite accurate. When he'd been *inside* the sphere, he'd felt content, reasonable, and objective. It was only laying human analysis over Astral actions that made them seem dark or evil. Only seeing those things through a human lens made them feel horrible — and that, Peers thought, made it all the more disturbing.

He took two steps toward the sphere. He took one step back.

"This is ridiculous," he said aloud. Then, to Nocturne, "Isn't this ridiculous?"

The dog wagged his tail, still lying on his side, slapping the floor in rhythm.

He went to the bed, wrapped the sphere in the comforter, then used his feet to kick the padded package off the bed, onto the floor, and ultimately under the box spring.

There was a knock on the door, but it was perfunctory: one solid rap, and then the door was swinging open. Jeanine entered looking like she was ready to go hiking. She'd found shorts, a sensible T-shirt, and a backpack. She paused with her hand on the doorknob, looking at Peers while he froze, guilty at a near-catch for the second time in an hour. He'd been sure he'd locked the door. But then again, Peers hadn't thought he'd needed one. He was *going* to change the minute Jeanine left, and the rest amounted to tidying up and killing time. He hadn't meant for the sphere to leap out from its hiding place and into his hands. He hadn't meant to go memory-walking again.

Jeanine looked him over. Peers was still in shorts and a sleep shirt — miles distant from his desert garb, but even further from clothing he'd want to wear in public.

"What have you been doing in here?" Jeanine asked. "Are you even ready?"

Peers felt a thin mist of sweat on his forehead. "I just need a minute."

"Want me to step out?"

No, no, he didn't want that at all. If she went into the hallway, he'd pick up the sphere again. His only evidence of self-control — and it was a small thing — was the way he'd shoved the sphere away *before* Jeanine knocked, not *because* she had. A good thing considering the nil delay between knock and entry.

"I was just ..." He looked toward the bed and the comforter-wrapped bounty beneath it. Then he grabbed a wad of clothes and ran into the bathroom. Before closing the door, he saw Jeanine meander forward, her curious eyes absorbing the contents of his room. Each room seemed to have been customized for its occupant: Peers had a dog bed and toys; Piper and Cameron had a king-sized bed instead of a queen because they roomed together; Lila, now heartbreakingly, had a second small bed with pink sheets. And while Peers was changing, Jeanine would be exploring what made his room unique — what defined Peers as a person, through Astral (or at least Jabari's) eyes.

As the gap closed, shutting Peers in the bathroom, he saw Jeanine bending to pet Nocturne, squatting while the dog rose in greeting.

A board squeaked as she stood. Footsteps while she crossed the room.

"I got the clothes from Piper," she said, her voice clear through the door. "But of course, when I got back to my room, there were finally some clothes there for me, too. New stuff. But it was girly. What's up with this place? In what world am I girlier than Piper?"

Peers shuffled through his pile. A shirt peeked out; he dragged it on inside out. It came back off, a dreadlock snagging in the neck hole.

"I just kept hers. The backpack was actually in a supply closet. Oh, and I got this." Pause. "Oh, right. I guess you can't see it from in there."

He heard fabric shuffle. Probably Jeanine setting the backpack aside, sorting its contents, showcasing whatever "this" was to show him once he came out.

Then he heard a muffled *crump*, followed by a series of material groans as padding and springs shifted.

*Dammit, now she's sitting on the bed.*

"What were you doing while I was gone? Did you find anything at all?"

"Just a second!"

More shifting. More groans as she shifted on the mattress.

Jeanine was probably leaning forward. Wondering why the bed didn't have a comforter. Looking underneath, probably about to drag the thing from below, spreading the thing on top to be helpful.

"Jeanine!" But it came out alarmed, not casual as intended.

When she didn't answer, he said, "Nocturne likes it when you throw the ball for him. It's in the bin near the door."

"He looks tired to me," said Jeanine's voice.

Peers straightened his shirt. Found pants, jeans, and

succeeded in putting one leg in the wrong hole. The bed groaned again.

"He'll really appreciate it!"

His heart was beating. The sheen of sweat was growing thicker, wetter, almost dripping. It had never, in history, taken longer to put on a pair of jeans. And meanwhile, Jeanine was out there, surely on all fours, dragging the comforter out and noticing something heavy inside it, taking the sphere, touching it, realizing that they wouldn't have to search for Mullah because there was at least one of them closer than she'd thought.

*This* would be a gun. And when he came out, she'd shoot him.

But there was a noise outside: the flat *thunk* of a tennis ball striking the floor, followed by a mad scrabble of paws and claws.

Jeanine said to Nocturne, "Silly boy, look what you did. I don't want to fish it out from under there."

Peers got the other leg in his pants and knocked the door open, his fly still unbuttoned and unzipped. He saw Jeanine getting to her knees, moving toward the bed and the lump of fabric underneath, the green fuzzy shape of a tennis ball beside it.

"I'll get it."

And Peers did, flaps open and flying, his knee practically kicking Jeanine out of the way. He got the ball in his hand and nudged the comforter bundle back with his forearm, then came out with the ball held up like victory. Jeanine's eyes went from the ball to his crotch.

"You ... um ... missed something."

Peers set the ball on the bed. Nocturne craned his neck and took it, then squished it in his jaws. Peers had his hands on his waistband, on his zipper. The pants, like

Jeanine's explorer gear (a bit too Piper-short on Jeanine's long frame), were new. But they fit him like a glove.

Jeanine looked him over.

"You look strange."

"I'm just tired."

"I meant in jeans. I got used to the nomadic look."

"I used to wear jeans all the time in London."

Jeanine squinted. "You okay, Peers?"

"Peachy."

She watched him for another few seconds then turned to the bed. The backpack was atop the untucked sheets, open. Beside it was what looked like an iron pipe, made of wood.

"What is that?" Peers asked.

"Middle part of a lamp. The base was bolted down, but that unscrewed from the base." She hefted it. "Might break a skull, right?" Jeanine looked up, seemed to mistake his flush for concern. "Look, I don't want to hurt the wrong people. But we need a gun, and the guards are the only ones packing. We knock one of them out. Just one."

"Then what?"

"Leverage one gun into two."

"I meant, with whoever we cold-cock."

"I hadn't thought of it. Drag them into a closet? Tie them up?"

"This is a terrible idea."

"Look, we don't need to fight our way past an army or get lucky. I don't buy this *surveillance is out* bullshit. A house like this? They're watching it somehow. So we find the surveillance room and watch the tapes for that night. Then we go where Clara went."

Peers knew that wouldn't work, but wasn't sure how to explain why. He hadn't been seduced into meaningless immersion; the second time the sphere had captivated him, finding Clara had been his excuse. But no matter how he'd asked the sphere where she'd gone, he'd come up empty. It didn't feel to Peers like the footage wasn't there; there were clearly droids flying around to record memories when Astrals weren't present, and the other records seemed comprehensive. It was more like he didn't know how to ask or secretly didn't want to participate (where do a former Mullah's loyalties lie?) or — and this was the strongest impression — the sphere simply didn't want to show him. Maybe that meant this was something he was supposed to do, and maybe it didn't. If Jeanine would leave, dammit, he could unwrap the sphere and immerse then maybe find out. That would be *brilliant*.

"Peers?" Jeanine snapped her fingers. "You still with me?"

"We're not going to find anything."

"Like I said, this is the only way. Cameron is already gone, with Charlie. I think they're waiting for Kindred and Meyer. I saw them preparing to head out with Jabari. This is the only chance. They're going to do this, and it's going to be … bad. I can feel it."

"We don't have time," Peers said.

"We have to try."

But Peers wasn't so sure. He'd nudged Cameron to face his destiny, but half the reason he'd wanted to come was his now-on-hold desire to kill the viceroy — and once inside Ember Flats, the Ark's sheer *presence* had triggered his second-guessing. Seeing what had happened to the group at Mount Sinai had increased it, and he'd seen hints, in his journeys into the sphere since, that only worsened those impressions. They'd feared the archive's legend when they'd been kids even though nobody but the elders had seen it or knew where it was. Now he had experiences to back up those fears.

He'd seen CliffsNotes from previous visitations, extending beyond the time frame the sphere's main memories seemed to cover. Nothing detailed, only highlights, like a *previously on* reel at the start of a recurring show, to remind viewers what aired in the last episodes.

Floods.

Fires.

Plagues.

Earthquakes, storms, dust, death, darkness.

*Extinction* — for all but a few new gods and their disciples.

Yes, what was coming, when Kindred and Meyer stirred the pot while Cameron broke the seal, would be bad. But what could he and Jeanine do? Peers himself held the only security record in the palace (the sphere had already suggested that much), and that record offered no help. They had one man, one woman, one lazy dog, and part of a lamp. They didn't know where to find Clara, where she could have gone or where she'd been other than "in the hallways somewhere" (another thing Peers couldn't admit to knowing), and no idea who could have taken her. No clue which loose ends to pursue, where to start searching, whom to —

But: *Wait.*

Wait.

"Maybe we could—" Jeanine began.

Peers held up a finger, thinking. Jeanine stopped at the raised finger as if afraid she might break it.

Finally Peers lowered his finger and met Jeanine's curious eyes.

"What? Do you have an idea where we might find Clara?"

"No," he said, "but I know who we can ask."

# Chapter Forty-Six

Kindred opened his eyes. Mara was in front of him, waiting expectantly.

"Anything?"

"No."

"You?" she turned to Meyer, who was also opening his eyes.

"Nothing. I'm sorry."

Jabari stalked the tiny, curved chamber. Kindred recognized Astral fingerprints (if they had fingerprints, which he didn't think they did) all over the place. It was a vehicle but floated so smoothly that it seemed more like a stationary room. Intellectually, Kindred knew they were moving through the Ember Flats avenues toward the stage in Town Center, but with the half-round walls turned opaque and the sound dampening on, his mostly human mind was fooled. If he couldn't sense the nearby mothership or hadn't piloted a shuttle with the same technologies, he wouldn't have believed it. There'd certainly been nothing of the type in Heaven's Veil, during his own viceroyship, just as there'd been no giant monuments inside the city walls or vague lumps of sandstone that, if the viceroy commanded, might easily be built into enormous idols in her image.

"I wish we knew if the Astrals had any idea you were here," she said, uncharacteristically rattled.

"They know we're here," Kindred said. "But I thought that was obvious."

"I mean *here*. In this vehicle, headed to give a public address. I'd like to know if we'll be catching everyone by surprise or if they'll stop us the minute we arrive."

Kindred had been pondering that as well — he and Meyer, in their mindshare space, had hybridized to consider it as a combined being. Odds kept coming up roughly even. On one hand, the Astrals had completely ignored them since Titans had stopped guarding their rooms and, supposedly, started searching for Clara. But on the other hand, Astrals didn't always need eyes to see, and they only had the staff's word that the security system, when outside a jammer bubble, was no longer able to watch them. Kindred could feel nothing inside his internal space. No Titans at the periphery, no Reptars sent out to quell a coming disturbance, no background hum from Divinity as it laid odds and played its game. If there was a feel to the Astral presence inside Ember Flats, it struck Kindred as *detached observation*. Anything went, so long as they were allowed to watch.

That would change when a pair of Meyer Dempseys took to the airwaves and delivered their message. With the Internet mostly gone and satellites dead and jammed, the only real network left was the stone monoliths, jamming the round psychic peg into humanity's square hole. Modern-day humans could be forced into a collective, sure, but given their ineptness, the broadcast could be broken from Ember Flats to the other capitals with Divinity's flip of a metaphorical switch.

Their message would stay in Ember Flats.

And inside the city, Kindred felt sure it wouldn't be well received. But that was the point: a distraction and an instinctual psychic burst strong enough to shock the complacent human brain back into its ancient rhythms. If there was one way to get that collective humming — perhaps enough to prove humanity's worthy, and bode better for judgment — then this, ironically, was it.

"There's really no way to know," Kindred said. "We still come up indecisive."

"I thought you were calculating machines," said Jabari.

"Not with this many variables."

Jabari sat in an easy chair as the room's gravity seemed to subtly shift: the vehicle taking a slow turn, nearing Town Center.

"It's not too late," Meyer said, watching her. "We can still change the plan."

"No. No. I'm fine."

"Maybe there *are* too many variables," Meyer went on, looking at Jabari. "Cameron needs to open the Ark. The State of the City address will keep people's attention off him. But you can give it alone. We can stay in here then handle this part of things later."

"It's now or never," Kindred said.

"Don't listen to him, Mara. It's your city. We can wait until after—"

"*It's now or never,*" Kindred repeated. "You know that, Meyer."

Slowly, Meyer shrugged then reluctantly nodded. "Fine. With the Ark opening today, it's now or never. But it *can* be never. We don't need to make this worse. We can return to the palace. You mentioned having some plans."

Jabari looked up, reluctantly decisive. "They deserve to know. If we're about to be put on trial, they should be told what's coming, and what they're facing."

The room seemed to slow then hitch. On one wall, the view through a window began to change, no longer showing the view outside the mansion. Now they could see people, politely assembled beyond simple, civilized barricades. And they could hear subtle murmurs — the kind that unconcerned people make when going about their ordinary business, with no clue that doom is knocking.

There were no Titans guards. No Reptars. No signs of Astrals, save the moon-like gray bulk of the nearby mothership and Titan civilians milling among the humans: one big, happy family in the Capital of Capitals.

Okay," said Jabari, moving for the door. "Me first. And when I wave, you know what to do."

Kindred nodded and crossed his legs in the comfortable chair. Meyer sat in an identical posture beside him. Together they waited for it all to begin.

# Chapter Forty-Seven

PEERS'S COMMENT that they were running out of time was intended as a general public service announcement, but Jeanine took it differently.

He'd checked a clock, realized there were only ten minutes or so left until the State of the City was scheduled to start, and whispered that they'd have to hurry. Cameron was supposed to wait until the Meyers took the stage and said whatever before he opened the Ark. That meant ten minutes before the address began, maybe another five or ten until Jabari yielded the floor, and probably no more than another five until the shock of dueling Dempseys gave way to the big, uncomfortable announcement. That meant they had twenty minutes until the Ark's top was popped *at most*, and Peers worried it might be less. And even if there were twenty minutes left, it's not like they *had* twenty minutes. Somehow, if they meant to stop Cameron from opening the Ark, they'd have to get him word. Ideally, they'd also get word to Jabari because she might postpone or handle things differently if the Ark weren't to be opened. *And* there was the matter of commitment: Even if they figured out where Clara was in time, and even if they could get word out, there was no guarantee that would stop things. Jabari would be on stage. Cameron might be holding the metaphorical handle, ready to crack the seal.

Which all meant that they needed to hurry.

But rather than simply internalizing this and moving quickly and making mental notes, Jeanine took Peers's words as license to kick Kamal's office door open the second he cracked it, then hit him hard enough to spatter his desk's polished wood with blood droplets and pin him to the floor.

*"Jesus, Jeanine!"* Peers said as she climbed atop the man's moaning form, sitting on his chest, incapacitating his limply flailing arms with the weight of her knees. Kamal's head rolled back and forth, groaning, blood running from a superficial but freely bleeding scalp wound.

"Get his legs!"

Peers did as he was told, Jeanine rising above him like a cowgirl, the lamp-birthed weapon held high as if Kamal might rise and strike. But holding the viceroy's attendant's legs was like gripping dead fish, and Peers's biggest concern was that Jeanine would clout him again for spite, just because adrenaline had her intoxicated.

"You got him?"

"I didn't mean for you to—"

*"Do you have him!"* It came out as a command, not a question.

"Yes! I have him!" Peers forced his panic down as blood surged into his head and blurred his vision. If this went on for long, he might tackle Jeanine himself because fight or flight commanded it. Calmer, fighting the sense that time was slipping away, he said, "Did you have to hit him?"

"You said it yourself. We don't have time to ask him

nicely." She slapped Kamal's face, and Peers watched the man's head slowly wag, his eyes trying to climb into his brain. "Kamal! Where is she? Where is Clara?"

Kamal moaned. His eyelids fluttered, threatening to drift away. Knowing he was risking wrath, Peers moved up and abandoned the man's motionless legs, grabbing the cloth skirt over an end table, pressing it to his bleeding head. It came away only moderately wet, the wound already slowing.

"You nearly killed him," Peers said.

"You said he was Mullah."

"I said I *thought* he was Mullah!" Now, with Kamal semiconscious due to Peers's intel, the signs seemed suddenly dubious. Kamal had known about the sphere when it seemed even the viceroy didn't know how the system worked, but did that mean he was Mullah? Kamal had also raised eyebrows at Peers when he'd come to the group late. But did that mean he knew what Peers had taken and why, or did it simply mean Peers had probably looked sketchy that particular day, his eyes bugged with guilt, face wet after the nervous sweat had been washed away?

"Well, what's done is done." She slapped his face again, but the man was fading. "Kamal. Kamal!"

"Great. That's just great, Jeanine."

"What would you have done? Ask him to tea?"

"I wouldn't have tried to kill him!"

"He's not dead. He's just out."

"Which is perfect. Because he's sure as hell going to be a big help now."

"Maybe he has a key or something. If he's Mullah, he'd have a secret key to a hidden door somewhere, right? A place where he's stuffed Clara." Jeanine's face clouded in sudden concern, more practical than emotional. "Oh, wow, I hope she's not dead."

*"Jeanine!"*

"Don't just sit there playing nurse, Peers! Search his pockets! Search his desk!" Jeanine snapped her fingers in front of Kamal's face, tapped his cheeks, called his name louder.

Peers scrambled along Kamal's side as he rolled slightly on the floor, consciousness barely hanging on. Jeanine took the opposite side, moving to his other set of pockets. They searched pants, shirt, and suit jacket. But of course they found nothing. Because any keys he'd have, if the man was Mullah, would look like any other keys. Unless he had the ring key — which, come to think of it, he'd *have* to because there'd been a Mullah keyhole where Peers had found the sphere. The locks weren't *really* locks and were simple to pick with nails or pins, but a true Mullah would still own and probably proudly wear a ring that …

But there were no rings on Kamal's hands. No necklace or bracelets. Nothing hard at the seams of his clothing, nothing obvious in or on his shoes.

Peers moved to the man's desk, glancing at the clock, seeing they'd already lost nearly five minutes. In another five or so, Jabari's face would probably pop up on every quiet screen in the house, triggering the catastrophe that Meyer and Kindred would finish. A second scream of sorts — all that new emotion streaming across the plaza and into the Ark, distracting the thing as the speech sidetracked the people, urging the lid open as Cameron turned his key, the true clock ticking for the first time in thousands of years.

"Keys. Notes. Anything at all," Jeanine said, now standing above Kamal with her makeshift weapon raised. Kamal had mostly stopped bleeding below her, barely moving, his chest rising and falling in an almost empty rhythm.

"There's nothing."

"There has to be something. Look harder."

*"There's nothing, Jeanine!"* And there wasn't. The desk drawer was a study in minimalism. Peers saw a single pen, a pad of Post-Its, and a pair of paperclips. He yanked it out and held it up, furious, near panic, then threw it down near Jeanine's feet.

"You said he was Mullah."

"I said *it made sense* that he was Mullah! That's why we were going to talk to him! That's why I wanted to ask him questions!"

"And he'd just admit it? Just come out and say, 'Oh, you want to know if I'm Mullah? Why yes, sure.'"

Peers practically growled his answer, feeling impotent. "I had a way I wanted to ask."

"A special way," Jeanine mocked.

"Yes. A special way."

"And in just a few minutes, you'd get the answer for us. No violence required."

That was the plan, yes. He'd have pushed Jeanine back and talked to Kamal in private. They each thought they knew what the other was, Peers had thought. He'd confirm it, say a few things that proved his membership. *Then* violence might be needed, but even then Peers doubted it. The Mullah had never responded to threats. But maybe he could trick him, suss out where the girl had gone. It was a thin chance at best, but at least it *was* a chance compared to whatever this had become. And given what the sphere had shown him about the last times the Ark had rendered judgment, it was a chance worth taking, no matter how thin.

"Now we're fucked." His frustration broke. Peers took

Kamal's single pen from the desk and threw it hard at the polished wood surface. It bounced like a spring and rolled into a corner. "Thanks a lot. But in a way, it's a relief. Now we don't have to go through the effort of trying."

"Don't you blame this on me!"

"Oh, no. You're fucking commando. I'd *never* blame *you*. It was stupid of Kamal, to run into your head-clubber like he did."

"You were just going to sit in your room. You think this is such a big problem, what were you going to do about it? You weren't even ready when I came back! 'We have to hurry,' I said. 'Get your shit and be quick about it.' What did you do after I left? Lie down and rub one out to clear the dust?"

"Oh, that's so mature. So helpful."

"You're the one with the scary insights. How do you know who's Mullah anyway, Peers? More of that luck that always goes your way, winning you the horde of Astral technology, spying on them from your suspiciously well-furnished Den, always in the right place when—"

"I took a guess. I thought he might be Mullah. But now we'll never—"

A new voice interrupted Peers: Ravi, the kid.

"Kamal isn't Mullah."

Peers turned. Jeanine turned. The kid was standing in the doorway with a pistol leveled.

"But I am," he said.

# Chapter Forty-Eight

CAMERON CREPT CLOSER. He looked back once, saw Charlie squatting just inside the gate as if expecting something tall to come along and spot him, and decided not to look back again. Charlie's posture was one of someone who could easily come forward but was deliberately staying back — the posture of a man who feels he could help but is glad he hasn't been asked. The way the protected cower when the protector goes to see what went bump in the night.

The way Charlie was squatting made Cameron feel more alone than if he had been truly here by himself. Charlie had told him what he knew, but it was Cameron who'd have to face it without so much as a hand on his shoulder.

The courtyard was deserted. They'd watched this space through the windows during their stay in the palace; you couldn't see the Ark from inside, but you could see the space it called home. Normally, as Ember Flats went about its civilized business, people crossed this space all day long. No particular reverence was given. It had become a mundane presence in the city: a symbol of triumph and history rather than anything that might ever be relevant again. Peers had compared the archive in the courtyard to the Sword in the Stone, but as far as Cameron had seen or heard, nobody had come to the Ark to try his or her hand. They simply walked by as if the Ark were a bus stop.

The emptiness of this usually mundane, usually cheery space chilled Cameron to the bone. Evening was coming; light had mostly left the day, and the only sounds were coming from a few blocks away where the rest of the humans and Astrals had gathered in harmony. Everyone was invited to that party — everyone but Cameron. Even Piper, Lila, Charlie, Jeanine, and Peers, who'd spend the evening's events behind mansion walls, were more involved in the city's affairs. Screens would come on when Jabari took the stage; they'd watch events unfold as Meyer appeared, then Meyer, again, to follow. They'd be in wonder with the others, have their breath stolen again, feel the city's shared shock and awe of the secret revealed. Their focus was unified — and though he had had his earlier doubts, Cameron could feel out here in the dark that Meyer was right: There *was* a mind-share network in this city. Epochs ago, the Astrals had arrived to find human minds joined — or at least join*able*, with a bit of Astral teaching. In the days of cell networks and the Internet, the idea of a collective consciousness seemed strange — even to Cameron, who'd shared thoughts with Piper — surrogate grandfather to a Lightborn child. But he felt it now, the city's attention on the stage, seeming to anticipate a big change coming.

*Keep moving. Clara is counting on you.*

Cameron looked down, saw his traitorous feet now frozen. He resisted the urge to look back at Charlie, knowing it'd only make him feel worse, and forced his feet to move again. To take another few steps.

He'd wait to hear the crowd's reaction. He even had the cell phone-like device in his pocket to help him time the opening. But the gadget was pointless. Cameron had to fight the urge to take it from his pocket, to throw it away and be free of its weight. He didn't need to watch the broadcast to know what was happening.

Cameron could *feel* it.

The Ark was just ahead. It was lit at night, but Cameron could already see a sort of psychic glow: a light the Ark was generating rather than one shone upon it. The glow might be his imagination. But it was possible — likely, even — that it was something Cameron's mind was seeing more than his eyes: the visible interpretation of the town's ample attention, anticipation, foreboding.

Would Ember Flats truly be surprised to see Meyer Dempsey? Would it truly be surprised to see the same man a *second* time? Or had the group mind already figured all of this out, and it was only human obstinance barring obvious knowledge from the top level of their minds?

Cameron squinted at the golden box. The glow seemed to stretch out and climb out of the courtyard to arch above the surrounding government buildings, rising and falling toward the gathering like a monochrome rainbow.

Was it feeding something to the people or siphoning it from them? To the right viewer — one bonded with the key, if he believed Charlie — was this what it had looked like during Heaven's Veil's destruction? When the psychic echo of all its burning citizens had streamed back to the archive at Sinai, giving the Astrals a signal to home in on?

Or had it been a thousand times brighter? A thousand times worse?

There seemed to be a swirling of smoke from

Cameron's right, and suddenly his father was standing in the shadows.

"Not real," Cameron muttered, forcing himself to keep walking. "It's only an echo."

But Benjamin Bannister came closer. Into the light.

"I'm proud of you, kiddo."

"You're not my father."

"That's right. I'm not. But I'm not what you think I am, either."

"You're from the Ark."

"I've been with you all along."

Cameron watched the specter — it wasn't a phantasm leaked from the Ark. This was the Pall. It didn't speak, and yet somehow, now it could.

"You're still not my father."

The Benjamin thing gave a little half shrug accompanied by a smile. Behind him, across town, Cameron heard a low voice that, at its source, he knew would be loud. It was Jabari, starting her address. Time was short — and if this were the Pall, its strength seemed to promise the same. It was somehow connected to the Ark, rising with its power. More intelligible as the Ark's time to articulate grew near. It was of the Ark but not the Ark itself. A third thing, somewhere between the privacy of Cameron's authentic mind and the shared mind he could feel the archive, even now, trying to touch.

"I think you're splitting hairs," Benjamin said.

"You're the Pall."

A tick-like nod. "I am."

"But what are you really?"

He looked to the Ark. "I'm that." Then he looked at Cameron, at his heart. "And I'm that, too."

"You abandoned us. You've tricked us. You made Christopher—"

"I made a suggestion. Christopher did what was required to get us all where we needed to be."

"You want me to open it."

Benjamin nodded. "But only if you choose to."

"I don't have a choice. The Mullah—"

"There's always a choice, Cam."

"I can't just let them keep her."

"Mmm. So your hand has been forced. There is only one option."

"Of course."

"And it's not right that Clara go to the Mullah. You *have* to get her back."

"Of course!"

"You're saying there's no benefit of her being with them. Things aren't as they should be, so now you need … to fix it."

Cameron took another few steps. The Pall paced him until he had to stop again, feeling the Ark's power like an electrical field. Had it been like this before, the two times he'd been close? Cameron didn't think so. The air was different. Something had changed.

"Cam. Do you remember that day, in Giza? The first time we ran into the Mullah, when you read the map wrong?"

"You're trying to trick me. You're not my father. My father is dead."

"In a sense. But isn't he still alive in you? In your own box" — Benjamin nodded toward the Ark — "that your thoughts and emotions still hold open?"

"Meaningless," Cameron muttered. But it wasn't. He could feel the difference.

"Well," Benjamin said, shifting his feet companionably as if this were an everyday bull session, "*I* remember that day. I gave you a reminder. Do you remember what it was a reminder of, Cam?"

"How do you know all of this?"

"I told you it was a souvenir of your stubbornness. Of the way you always insist you know everything, even when you're only guessing."

"I'm not guessing about this. It's the only way to help Clara."

"I see. Because Clara needs help."

"Of course she needs help!"

"And you're *sure* of that?" Benjamin put a thoughtful finger to his chin. "But of course you are. You're Cameron Bannister."

Cameron took another step. Then another. He could feel the archive filling him up, surrounding him with raw, terrifying power. His hair wanted to stand on end; he felt as if his blood were imbued with a static charge. The court-yard felt electric. One spark could catch and blow it all to dust.

"I said I was proud of you, and I meant it," the Pall/Benjamin thing said in a lower, more earnest voice. "But it's not because you're doing what you feel must be done. It's because you don't have a clue. You might even think this is wrong. But still you're surrendering, just a little. Having some trust. Willing to put the key in the slot and turn it even though you're terrified it's the wrong call and that extermination will follow."

Cameron took his first step toward the Ark. Then a second. Three wide steps left. He'd never been this close. It was radiating something like heat, or wind, but actually neither. There was light in the air even though it was mostly dark. A thousand thoughts raced through his mind, all confusing.

Countless souls seemed to scream.

He looked over at his false father. And, feeling the words but unable to stop them, he asked, *"Will* extermination follow?"

"I'm proud of you, Cameron, because you don't know and are admitting your ignorance. Yet still, you're doing it anyway."

The air changed. Cameron somehow knew that Meyer and Kindred were taking the stage.

A flat compartment opened on the Ark's top: a keyhole awaiting its key.

The Pall was gone. Cameron was alone.

This was the right choice, and he was about to do what had to be done.

This was the wrong choice, and he was seconds from killing a planet.

The time was seconds away.

Cameron opened his satchel. He removed the key, and though it may only have been his imagination, the cold ceramic seemed to mold itself to his fingers and give his hand a welcoming hug.

*It's the right choice.*

*It's the wrong choice.*

He held the key above the horizontal keyhole and waited for a sign.

# Chapter Forty-Nine

MEYER ASSUMED that the monthly Ember Flats State of the City address was typically filled with platitudes and politics as usual: good-feeling but maybe not entirely accurate updates on the most important city issues, overly optimistic forecasts ("eliminating the cannibals outside our walls within six months!"), and vague positive statements that meant nothing.

Meyer assumed that's the way the address would normally unfold, but he wouldn't ever know because Jabari didn't waste time, or mince words. There was no business-as-usual run-up; there were no platitudes; there was no discussion of essential city issues.

Jabari took the stage. She told them about how Ember Flats had thrived under its spirit of cooperation and how it had — for years now — served as a shining example not just for the other seven remaining capitals but for the entire planet. The world had changed when the ships had arrived, and there'd been a lot of panic, fighting, over-throw, rebellion and mayhem. But Ember Flats alone showed Earth how the two species could work together, as things were meant to be. The time of turmoil was over. Now came the time of rebuilding.

Or at least, that's how things had been going until now.

Meyer watched from backstage as Jabari's tone changed. What she'd said until now was rhetoric. If Ember Flats had a department of commerce brochure, the viceroy just told the city something straight from its pages.

*Settle down in Ember Flats. Raise your children here. We promise, no aliens will eat them when they go out to play.*

The shift in her body language was subtle, but Meyer — together with Kindred — could also feel its echoes in her mind. And what's more, the people could feel it, too. There were monolith repeaters around Ember Flats, meant to capture and broadcast what was happening. Kindred said the system meant that humans weren't quite as divorced from the group-mind communication common to our ancestors as we believed, but Meyer had his doubts. Now he could sense the shift in the crowd's mind, knowing they could taste what was coming.

Not something sunny.

Not something bland.

Something terribly, horribly dark.

"Will they cut it off?" Meyer asked Kindred. "Will they stop the broadcast?"

"I assume so. But not yet. And she only needs a few more sentences before even cutting her off will cause unrest, because of what that might mean."

The two men were side by side, Kindred now close enough to smell. They'd each chosen their own aftershave from the mansion's surprisingly complete collection, and of course they'd chosen the same one. Meyer's eyes were on Jabari, but seeing Kindred in the corner of his eye made him feel like he was sidelong to a mirror.

"Ember Flats, ever since the arrival of our most precious artifact, has always stood as an example of what the new world is supposed to be," Jabari said, as the crowd watched her with eager eyes. "The Ark meant different things to each of us in the past. There were many beliefs, many myths. But today it's concrete; it's real; it's a true thing that you can walk up to and touch. Now it's our symbol of unity. Now we know what it's always been, through all the myths. What it represents. And what it represents, for us, is a promise from the past. The Astrals were here before. They left it behind. They've been watching us. It means we were never alone. All those years, we weren't wandering children lost in the universe after all. We had mothers and fathers. And so we brought the Ark here to remember one thing: *that they didn't forget about us, and that our mothers and fathers would always return.*"

Meyer hadn't heard this particular bit of propaganda. He looked at Kindred but didn't need to speak his question.

*Do they really believe this? Even after all the destruction and fighting and wars?*

*They believe it because they need to.*

"Ember Flats is the world's shining example of what's possible," Jabari went on, solid enough, though even across the distance Meyer could feel nerves coming off her like heat. "We've shown the world how we can all move on together once we get past the walls of prejudice we've built in our arrogance. But demolishing those walls is not always easy. We're stubborn and feel we know best. And that — as you all know, as you've duly been told — is why we've needed negative examples as well."

The crowd murmured. Inside his mind, a smooth continuity began to fragment. It felt like a domed ceiling flaking, threatening to crack, surrendering to pressure from above.

"When Heaven's Veil fell, I took to this stage and told you why. You all *know* why."

No one spoke, but Meyer half expected shouted responses like the riling of a medieval mob. Inside, he felt the sense of continuity fragment further. He hadn't heard any of this, either. He had no idea what Ember Flats or the rest of the world believed about Heaven's Veil. He'd been too busy running for his life to know.

"Heaven's Veil crumbled from the inside. It was rotten at its core. There was poisonous dissent. There was corruption. There was murder. The viceroy was crooked. Dempsey was *only human*, but in the worst possible way. Most of us, even if you're originally from Giza, knew Meyer Dempsey. We knew how he was, how he did things his own way and damn what anyone else wanted. He was ruthless and ruled Heaven's Veil the same way he ruled his businesses. He ignored and defied Astral leadership. He turned his nose at Astral help when things began falling apart. There was an insurrection. Rebels detonated a bomb, destroying their Apex." She gestured to the left, toward Ember Flats's own blue pyramid. "And that's when Dempsey turned on the city. He commanded his people in, and they met with the peacemakers. You all know what happened next."

Meyer felt Kindred flinch inside his mind before he moved in the flesh. Meyer shot his hand out and grabbed Kindred's arm. Still he tensed; still he tried Meyer's grip: to break free, to take the stage, and do to Jabari what Peers had always wanted to do.

*It's a double-cross!* Kindred's thought-shout screamed into Meyer's consciousness. *She brought us here as sacrifices!*

And Meyer thought back: *Wait.*

Jabari's eyes found Meyer's and Kindred's, then she resumed speaking to the crowd.

"For five years, we've lived in peace under the spotlight of those twin influences. On one side, we have the Ark: symbol of harmony, reassurance that the Astrals were here for us before and have now returned. And on the other, we have our memory of the failed experiment that was Heaven's Veil: a reminder of the importance of trust and order. A reminder of humanity's most base nature, and what happens when humans are given too much power — and hence why any arrangement like ours in Ember Flats, ruled in cooperation between my human government and Divinity in the mothership — deserves your absolute faith and obedience."

Kindred had stopped struggling. Meyer met his eyes and slowly nodded, their shared mind collecting the undertones.

"For five years, we've lived in peace. And for five years, we've believed a lie."

Jabari raised her hand, beckoning at Meyer. Feeling the uncertainty and latent, assumed hostility in the crowd, he came. The crowd must have recognized him before he spoke because murmurs multiplied, a slow gasp permeating the group.

"I'd like to introduce you all to Meyer Dempsey," she said.

Noise increased. Heads turned, fear percolating to join the uncertainty, freshly stirred hatred for the past.

Jabari raised her hand, now summoning Kindred.

"And to the viceroy of Heaven's Veil," she said.

The people looked from one man to the other as they approached the stage's front edge. Images from close up were rebroadcast on screens around the square, same as to the other capitals — still with communications curiously uncut.

One supposedly dead and deposed Meyer Dempsey.

And *another* supposedly dead and deposed Meyer Dempsey, standing right beside him.

Composure broke. The babble of a thousand simultaneous conversations was almost deafening, but it quieted in seconds as Meyer raised a hand and delivered the two sentences they'd rehearsed, exactly as written.

"All you've been told about the capital governments and your Ark is a lie. The truth is much simpler." Meyer held his eyes to the crowd, waiting for curiosity to force their quiet. Then he said, "The Astrals destroyed Heaven's Veil just to hear you scream."

# Chapter Fifty

THE SCREEN MOUNTED to Kamal's office wall came on, showing a blue background and a seal that Peers hadn't seen around but that obviously represented Ember Flats. One eye ticked to the kid, Ravi, but he hadn't flinched. If there was hesitation, Peers had already decided he'd try for the gun.

"Sit," Ravi said. "In those chairs there."

Peers looked down, decided that righting the spilled chairs before attempting to sit would be allowed, and did so. Jeanine sat first, but she was watching Ravi same as Peers, waiting for her moment. But Ravi would offer none.

The kid came the rest of the way into the office, peeked out into the hallway, then closed the door. He watched the screen, gun still rock-steady leveled at his two prisoners. The room was plenty large enough for him to control them without restraints; if either came at him or threw something, he'd have more than enough time, from where he was standing, to pull the trigger. And if the boy was who he said, there would be no hesitation. The Mullah were usually peaceful, but when important matters were at stake, there was no latitude. And this little incident concerned the most important matter of all.

Ravi watched the screen. Jabari approached a lectern and spoke. The volume was low, barely high enough to hear. Ravi didn't turn it up. Instead, he looked past Jeanine to the window. But Kamal's office faced the wrong way; he'd need to be in another room to see the Ark, and what Cameron would do when Meyer's and Kindred's faces took Jabari's place.

"Is she alive?"

Peers turned his head and saw a challenging stare on Jeanine Coffey's smooth features.

"The Lightborn?" Ravi asked, barely taking his eyes from the screen.

"Her name is Clara."

Now Ravi turned. He couldn't be much older than Peers just after his exile, and possibly younger.

"I imagine she's fine."

"Just tell us," Peers said.

Ravi fixed his gaze on Peers, more curious than acrimonious. Perhaps he'd taken Peers for a potted plant, and was shocked he'd spoken.

"Why would they hurt her? Like I said, I'm sure she's fine."

"*Why?*" Jeanine said. "You took her as ransom!"

"*I* didn't take her at all," Ravi replied, speaking as precisely as an Oxford grad; the Mullah prided themselves on infiltration, and infiltration required education. "Maybe you should check your assumptions before casting accusations like dice."

"You — !" Jeanine began, but Ravi cut her off.

"*I,*" he said, emphasizing the word by putting his free hand on his chest, "am merely keeping you here until this is over."

Peers looked at the screen then back at Ravi.

"Then what?"

"Then it will no longer matter *what* I do with you."

"But Clara …"

Ravi shifted, turning his affable (if gun-toting) manner on Jeanine. "The Mullah are very interested in the Lightborn. But there are none among us. All came from the sites of first encounters, though they've wandered since. Some among us say they are a kind of X factor: those who were affected from youth, with a new kind of mind. Past epochs created messiahs and seers, but this is different. With your girl in the house, wandering right into their midst, practically offering herself to the group without the need to so much as show our hand, it was too great an opportunity to deny. Believe me, *harming* her is the last thing they'd do."

"But the note …"

"I left the note."

"Why?"

"As I said, it's too great an opportunity to pass up."

"You … you defied the others," Peers said.

"'Defied' is so uncouth a word. I was *decisive.*" His big eyebrows rose then fell. He smiled like someone with a secret. "Come now, Peers. You of all people understand the impetuousness and arrogance of youth."

Jeanine looked between the two. "What's he talking about?"

Peers shook his head, brushing it away.

"It's interesting," Ravi said, watching Jabari speak to the crowd on the office screen. "We infiltrated Ember Flats to have our hands inside the human government. We took great pains. I was only ten when I came here with my father, and I remember the sense of it all: 'We will hide in their underbelly. We will make them itch with things that need scratching.' I've always considered the viceroy my enemy, or at least one to watch. But look at this." He pointed at the screen. "Now her plan for subversion has meshed with ours. Sharing a side, in the end."

"You want the Ark opened."

"This epoch has run its course. It is time to rip off the bandage so we can try again from a new beginning. There are many among us who believe the Horsemen were called early. They say humanity might have had a chance if protocol had been observed, but it was not. Another hundred years, maybe three, perhaps a millennium … the species might have been worth saving then. But even among those who believe we might have been judged worthy if given more time, *all* agree that we are not worthy *yet* — and will be judged as such. For seven years we've been in limbo because those who can end it refuse to act. Half my life spent in waiting." He shook his head, biting his cheek, watching the screen. "I'm tired of waiting. If my eternal reward is coming, I am prepared to meet it now."

"And the rest of the Mullah?"

"You know how they are, Peers Basara," Ravi said, his statement raising Jeanine's eyebrows. "They're like monks. They will fight terribly for what they feel is right or predestined, but it takes so long to decide on what those things are. They'd have taken the key from you, had you given them a chance, had the key not seemed so stubbornly determined to stay by Bannister's side. But if they'd taken it, they'd have placed it on an altar. It's all patience with them — seeing what will happen, and only forcing things so far. Eventually they decided to stop chasing you, to let Cameron decide for himself what to do with the key. That's when I started to think I'd have to wait forever and that my own action might be required. Because without a nudge, he'd never have chosen to open the Ark and trigger the process of judgment."

"Cameron kept his end of the deal," Peers said. "Now take us to Clara."

"He hasn't done it yet," Ravi shook his head, his eyes on the subtle unease crossing the faces on-screen.

"Please," Jeanine said, and Peers realized he may never have heard the word on the woman's lips. "If we get her now, maybe we can protect her."

"Nothing can protect her. Nothing can protect any of us."

"You have to let us try."

"You aren't listening," Ravi said, his tone suddenly sharp. "We're on the eve of the apocalypse. On the eve of extermination. You cannot simply *run*. They will not follow us one by one, pointing guns as I'm doing now. The Horsemen have done this many times before, and they know how to do it well. When judgment is over, only a handful will remain. Our history will be eradicated. After a few generations, the marvels of these times will be lost to history and remain only as legends. Like the mythical flying machines from the ancient past, so they will talk of our airplanes. Like the lost desert cities, so will they speak of our New York, Beijing, and Berlin."

"We could be part of that handful!" Peers blurted. "Jesus, we were just trying to save a girl who's been taken!"

"You know the legends, Mr. Basara," Ravi said, again drawing a confused look from Jeanine. "You know how it always unfolds. The end days come. The Seven reveal themselves: The Warrior. The King. The Fool. The Innocent. The Villain. The Magician. And the Sage. The followers are chosen at random, as if by lottery. You will not increase your odds of survival by taking her to flee now. If Clara has any chance, it's here with the Mullah, who at least have reason to understand her. And maybe her kind *is* an X factor; it is for the elders and not one like me or you to know. So tell me: How does handing her off to you assist anything? How could you possibly escape the city, surrounded as it is by tribes?"

Peers looked up, a thought dawning. "The tunnels. There used to be tunnels all over, deep down. Far under the sand, restored by the Mullah."

"How do you know that?" Jeanine asked.

Peers rushed on, ignoring her.

"I *know*, Ravi. The Mullah say they must be here when judgment comes, when the Ark is opened. But I can take her away. I of all people. I can take them *all* away, any who remain in the house. Even Dempsey if he returns. *Especially* Dempsey! You must see the signs; you know at least part of this has to be true. *The King*, Ravi! 'Out of two, one.' Meyer Dempsey and his clone, together, must be the King the scrolls speak of! The Mullah won't show him the old tunnels, but they're the only way out. He must escape. You *know* it! So how, if not with my help?"

"What the fuck are you talking about, Peers?" Jeanine said.

Peers was shaking his head, walking forward, all the old Mullah legends coming back like he'd read them yesterday.

"Let me take them, Ravi. You're serving destiny by forcing the Ark to open. So let me serve it next. Meyer and Kindred did all of this for Clara; they won't leave without the girl, so we need to find her before he returns. *The scrolls say the King survives!* Put the puzzle together, will you?"

Ravi looked uncertain. The gun lowered a little but not nearly far enough to leap for and grab. Jeanine was still staring as Peers let his Mullah all hang out. Still he pressed on, imploring the kid with hard eyes.

On the screen, Jabari stepped down. Meyer, with his

blue tie, appeared in her place, and in Peers's higher mind, the entire human race seemed to sigh.

"You can't know he'll be chosen as the King," Ravi said.

But Peers knew he had him; the kid was on the ropes.

"I was young and stupid once. I did something nearly as dumb as you're doing right now. It lost me my family and friends, all of whom turned away and cast me out. I know you think you're doing what's right, and that nobody else will do it if you don't step in. What's done is done, for better or worse. But don't make it worse. Tell me where to find Clara. Tell me where the other Mullah have her."

"You …" Ravi stuttered. "The tunnels out of the city. You won't be able to open them without an elder ring."

"I've opened those locks before. You just need three points of conductive metal and …"

"What locks? When? Where?" Now Ravi was unraveling. He was only a teenager, and now, as Peers kicked the bedrock out from under him, his panicked youth was showing.

"Here! In the palace!"

"The tunnel locks are ancient."

"And years ago! Twenty years ago, on the most ancient locks of all, in the temple!"

Ravi's frenzied expression gave way to one of study, of uncertainty.

"You opened a lock in the temple? Beyond the elders?"

"Yes! And I can get them through the tunnels if you'll just make up your goddamned mind to—"

Ravi was shaking his head slowly, in disbelief. "No."

"Don't be an idiot! Let us go, Ravi! It's done!" He jabbed a finger at the screen, where one Meyer Dempsey had joined another. The feeling of anticipation and warning in the air was like static, raising the hair on his arms. "You feel it, don't you? Cameron will put the key in the Ark any second. You won, okay? You got what you wanted. None of this matters anymore. *Now let us go!*" Peers nudged Kamal with his foot. With any luck, the man would die before he awoke, the lucky bastard.

But Ravi was just repeating that one word, his eyes wide. He wasn't denying Peers's request. He was simply refusing to believe the dawning realization.

"No. No."

"Ravi! Think!"

He went to the door. He opened it.

"*The Fool,*" he hissed.

Then he ran, leaving Peers and Jeanine alone with a snoring Kamal.

# Chapter Fifty-One

It began as a whisper. Then it came at him like a wave.

Cameron held the key above the round indentation, recalling his grandfather's ancient record player. Time to drop a platter, put the needle in the groove — then dance until the world ended.

But then he heard someone in the corner of his mind. It seemed to echo, doubled on itself as if shouted into a cavernous space, the reverberated shout then dialed down to barely audible. He remembered the monolith repeaters, remembered the way walking between lines of similar stones seven years ago had first connected Piper's mind to his.

It was the broadcast. Meyer and Kindred had told the city about Heaven's Veil, and the Astrals hadn't cut it off. They'd let it go out.

It meant that the twin Dempseys hadn't just told Ember Flats about the alien treachery, about the way viceroys had been replaced, about annihilating an entire capital to generate an emotional outcry that would let them triangulate on the Ark's hidden location.

It meant they'd told every capital all of those things.

The whispered shout doubled in Cameron's mind. It tripled. It felt suddenly like his hair was being lifted by a gentle breeze, though no wind was stirring. And still he looked toward the square with the key still mostly steady and held high, squinting into that invisible wind. It wasn't just a breeze. It was the sigh preceding a storm: a forecast of something much stronger on the way.

Then it hit him: all the fear. All the anger. All the betrayal and grief and anguish. All the dredged-up memories. The breaking of trust, shattered like china on the floor. A million voices spoke at once, all in reaction, trying to make sense of something insensible, lost and floating, no longer able to find the ground below them.

But the thoughts and whispers weren't for Cameron. They were for the Ark.

He could almost see it streaking past him now: faint veins of light soaring through the air — many in a gentle arc from the square; some from the sky itself, from half a planet away. They stirred Cameron's hair in their passage and dove into the chest, building its energy. Building its indignation and fright and anger.

Still the key hovered, held above the keyhole by Cameron's hands. He'd begun to shake, but he didn't pull the key away. Some deep part of himself held his limbs in place like an iron fist. He'd been here before; he'd run once, when things had gone bad, and yet here he was again. If he ran this time, a small part of him felt sure he'd spend more years wandering, chased and fleeing, only to end up in the same place a decade older, no more sure than he was now.

*Take a leap of faith.*

But it wasn't really Cameron's voice. It was his father's.

And not the voice of the Pall in masquerade but of Benjamin Bannister himself.

*It's the wrong choice,* Cameron thought, the key still unmoving, six inches from the platter-like keyhole.

*Maybe it's neither right nor wrong. Maybe it is what it is.*

*It's the wrong choice!*

A wave of incoming emotion jolted him. He almost dropped the key then nearly wished he had. But did it matter? If this was destiny, the key could never break. It'd grip his hands, holding on until the deed was done.

The jolt rattled Cameron's brain in his skull. Something clattered at his neck, and then there was a loose thing dangling just below his vision, tugging minutely at him.

Cameron looked down. It was the coin on the lanyard his father had given him: the thing Mara Jabari had called a *mau.*

And Benjamin's voice inside his head — a voice from something above, something Cameron might have thought came from the realm of souls if he'd believed — said, *Are you absolutely* sure *it's the wrong choice?*

He waited for something to happen as the world screamed around him. As the indignation and torment from the capital buzzed by, making the Ark glow and shake as if in fury. He waited for an unseen hand to grip the key, tug it into its slot, and force the unlocking. He waited for a blast of air to unseat him again, tossing the key away to shatter. But nothing happened. Cameron's arms were sure as they held the thing, neither urging him to mate key and hole nor pressing him away.

It was his decision alone.

The Ark was practically vibrating, reminding Cameron of furious hornets.

But he didn't quite want to run. He didn't want to

leave. He was terrified out of his mind yet frozen in place, in the no man's land between *this* and *that*.

"Tell me what to do," he whispered.

Nobody answered.

Nothing answered.

He watched the keyhole. A circle with ridges at the edges to match the key. Turning it in Heaven's Veil, Cameron often thought, had killed Heather. She'd sent him out, making his distraction. Then she'd stayed behind to die. Because of him.

This time, turning the key might kill nearly all of humanity.

And yet he couldn't go. The stone's faintly glowing circle shone up at his face, illuminating it, captivating him.

In his mind — this time as a memory — Cameron heard Benjamin's voice. It had been the Pall speaking and yet somehow his father, too.

*I'm proud of you, kiddo.*

Cameron pressed the key into the keyhole.

A skim of metal slid from somewhere and covered it, locking his decision into place.

The very walls of the buildings around the courtyard seemed to shriek as the world cried out, as the ground shook, as the air filled with an ominous hum. Cameron felt a new mind join the others, sifting data, weighing with a grudge, dealing through humanity's past with gritted teeth and absolute fury in its every mental movement.

He turned to run, but his hands seemed fixed to the Ark's top corners. Nothing seemed to be holding them, except that he couldn't pull them away. The glowing surface under his fingers felt like it was changing, molding itself to his touch in the same way the key had always felt so comfortable in his hands. His eyes saw no difference, but the feeling was that of new hands reaching out, inter-twining its fingers with his own, holding tight.

*It was the wrong choice,* Cameron thought.

He could already feel the archive's fury beginning to boil. He felt himself bleed into the Astral mind as the Ark held him, making him complicit, making him part of this. As his mind reached out, he realized something wasn't right. The archive wasn't supposed to *have* any anger. It wasn't supposed to be Morgan Matthews; it wasn't supposed to present in prejudgment at all. But it couldn't help itself, not now, not as the thoughts of the people across Ember Flats streamed into the thing he and the archive had conjoined to become. Inside his mind he watched oil mix with water, acid with base, fire with ice, matter with antimatter. The brew's percolations reached a fever pitch as Divinity seemed to watch it all from above, from over Cameron's shoulder.

The Ark was a wild animal stalked by a predator, terri-fied of the dark. A startled rattlesnake, coiled to strike. A roused mother, protecting its young. Its entire lid had slid into its sides, leaving the top open and churning, swirling down into an unfathomable void of human experience. To Cameron it looked like a brewing storm. Like death on her way.

*Now run,* the Pall seemed to whisper in Cameron's ear, though he saw it nowhere. The voice was somehow inside the Ark now, from its guts. From the primal infection that human emotion had wrought on what was supposed to be a simple, objective process. *Run back to Piper.*

But as Cameron held the Ark, snippets of truth kept flitting through his mind.

The Astrals knew about Jabari's exodus plan. They'd accounted for it. The Astrals knew whom they planned to spare and who would perish. There was no true future.

There was only inevitability in Divinity's mind. The balance of justice was weighted, and judgment — for most, at least — had been rendered while the archive's guts choked on human poison, well before the top had been opened.

*Guilty.*

Cameron would run to Piper and Lila.

The Dark Rider, as the Astral mind knew the Mullah called it, would come.

Then they all would die.

There was no need for deliberation. No need for the jury to leave the room to deliberate. The equation was already solved. The way was already decided, already blocked. The Astrals knew about the Messiah. They knew about the Cradle. And three little people who'd already served their purpose meant nothing.

The Ark let Cameron go, the connection suddenly broken. He was just a man again, standing beside an ornate box with the world shrieking around him.

*Run, Cameron!*

But instead of running, Cameron put his hands back on the Ark. He looked into its hurricane of a soul.

The Astrals had all they needed. Every bit of evidence was in place, judgment rendered in advance. The Ark had been making its case for thousands of years, and by now it knew all it needed to know.

Cameron looked down. The verdict couldn't be argued.

But all new evidence muddied waters and raised reasonable doubts.

Benjamin Bannister was standing beside him again.

"Cameron," he said. "Are you *sure about this?*"

This time, for once, he truly was.

# Chapter Fifty-Two

PIPER WAS REACHING for the doorknob, feeling a change in the air and watching light spill from around the corner of the otherwise dim courtyard, when her hand suddenly leaped to her chest. It happened involuntarily as if she'd been shot.

Lila, behind her, worn beyond her breaking point, yelped when she saw Piper startle.

*"What? What is it?"* She sounded panicked, almost out of her mind. Ever since the occupation, they'd all had a touch of extrasensory perception, and ever since the address had lit the screens, the psychic warble just under the world's surface had set Piper's heart to pounding. Unknown tension had ramped up on an exponential curve, each minute feeling twice as tense as the previous one. Now it felt like the room was packed with people, each holding a pistol with a hair trigger, cocked, aimed, eager to fire. Each step Piper took felt like it was on land mines. The very air around them felt like glass with jagged edges.

Piper wanted to answer but couldn't. She'd felt a low throb of fear for the past few minutes and recognized it as

Cameron's. Their bond had been mostly quiet, but in times of trouble she always seemed to feel him. And then there was this place. Maybe it was the monolith stones still around the Capital of Capitals that had made her so empathic lately, or perhaps the sheer harmonic convergence of all those hypersensitive citizens. Charlie had told her how the broadcasts worked: not over the air but through thought. Apparently modern humanity wasn't as inept as they'd seemed, now able to do the tricks the Mayans, Ancient Egyptians, and countless other ancient societies had been able to do with their collective minds.

But the thrum of Cameron's fear had been growing increasingly intense, clearly more in her heart than in Lila's — or Charlie's, or Jeanine's, or Peers's, wherever they'd gone off to. His fear had joined hers, twisting around it like a terrified braid. The combination made Piper feel heavy as if her limbs didn't want to work. She wanted to curl into a ball and wait for it to pass, like an animal in a hole.

But now Cameron was gone. Just like that. She'd felt a sense of falling, and of having done something important. But he was gone, just the same.

*"Piper!"* The word was drawn out, whiny, threadbare. Despite the pain, Piper felt her heart go out to Lila. Things were so much worse for her. Clara was gone, and they could only go on faith that the note-leaver would hold up his or her end of the bargain. Piper knew Cameron had opened the Ark; she'd felt the air thicken before he'd vanished with that final noble thought. But she could already feel the world unraveling. Would the Mullah truly keep their word? Or really, by the note's wording, had they even *made* a promise? They hadn't really, and Lila knew it.

She turned to Lila.

"What is it?" Lila asked. "You looked like ..."

"It's Cameron."

"What about Cameron?"

"He's gone."

"Gone where?"

But she wouldn't say it. *Couldn't* say it. Piper couldn't let herself acknowledge that he was dead. Not yet. Not until this was over, until the minutes of horror were behind them.

"Do you feel the change?" Piper said, looking up as if the answer were above.

Someone ran by outside the door. The footfalls were rushed, each striking the floor like a hammer. Some else ran after the first, a woman, shouting. Lila startled at the sounds like a bird, but Piper was still trying to feel the ephemeral thing she could almost sense. Relief among the doom.

"Where do we go to get her, Piper? Where do we go to find Clara?"

"I don't know. But I think we will."

Something seemed to detonate outside. A human sound — one large thing colliding with another. Through the window, Piper could see shifting light. Her mind showed her villagers running hither and yon with pitchforks and torches, metaphorical images of disintegrating chaos. There was still something streaming from the Ark's direction, but Piper didn't need to look out to see it. She could feel the stream pulse and hitch, choking, changing, adjusting its previously inevitable path. It was all happening in the pit of her chest, where Cameron fell through an endless void, his whisper not entirely quiet, his will a tangible thing.

"Come on," Piper said, obeying a heavy itch inside. There was suddenly no question about what they needed to do.

"Come on where?"

"We have to find your fathers."

"But they're still at the—"

"They'll be back in minutes," Piper said. "With Jabari. And Jabari has a way out. She has a plan. And ..." But she cut herself off. Because that wasn't all of it; the Astrals *knew* about that particular escape plan; they'd already cut it off. The knowledge came from outside Piper but not from Jabari or the Astrals or anyone else. It had come from Cameron.

But there was a way now. All over again, there was a way. Maybe not the same escape. Maybe not escape at all. But one way or another, she felt a dominant, pressing certainty that all of a sudden there was a way out that hadn't existed before.

A thought flashed through her mind in a half second: Charlie in the hallway behind her, yammering on about angry juries, distracted judges who made mistakes.

And in one gestalt leap, she understood.

*Charlie.*

*Cameron.*

*Jabari, Meyer, and Kindred.*

There was a way.

"Take my hand," Piper said, holding one toward Lila, the other reaching for the knob. "And don't let go."

# Chapter Fifty-Three

JEANINE CHASED Peers through the hallways, frustrated by her inability to catch him or even narrow the distance. Reaction to Ravi's flight had taken her a good ten seconds. She'd stood frozen, listening to Kamal's snoring, unsure which damned end was up and which was down. By the time she'd taken off after Peers, he'd had a big head start, and adrenaline-fueled legs to match.

*"Peers!"*

She caught a glimpse of his limbs at the end of one hallway as she entered it from the opposite end. She turned on her afterburners, tightly cut the corner, and saw more of the running man before he vanished the next time.

She had no idea what was happening. They'd gone to Kamal's office to beat a Mullah confession out of him, been cornered by the real Mullah, and then Jeanine had lost the thread. By the end, Peers and the kid had been trading unintelligible sentences like baseball cards. Ravi seemed to know something about Peers, and Peers seemed to know a hell of a lot about the Mullah. But why had he run, and why was Peers chasing him? Didn't the kid have a gun? Shouldn't they be counting their blessings? They weren't going to find Clara. Given all the noise that had erupted outside (not to mention the thickening of air, which felt too much like Sinai for comfort), this had to be the end. Meyer and Kindred had delivered their dual-Dempsey fuck-you to the world, Cameron had probably opened the Ark, and now shit was going down *hard*. It had been a while since the civilized parts of what remained of the world had seen anything worthy of true panic, but Jeanine remembered how the dread and terror spread on Astral Day and the week before.

She hoped Jabari wanted panic and widespread disorder in Ember Flats because the bitch was about to get exactly that.

*"Peers! Get back here, you asshole!"*

Peers was still hauling ass. Back toward the big room with the purple fireplace. But when they entered the big room, Ravi was nowhere in sight. Either he'd put a lot more distance between himself and Peers than was between Peers and herself, or the kid had vanished. And still Peers was hauling hard as if he could see his mark just ahead.

*"Where did he go?"* she shouted.

Peers ticked a chair with one of his legs, staggered as it dropped to the floor, and almost fell. Jeanine hurdled it five seconds later, now within yards of her quarry. But she still couldn't see Ravi ahead. How was Peers hoping to catch someone he couldn't see? And if he *had* seen him, Jeanine couldn't be sure where. They were in the middle of the large room, its entrances and exits like a rotunda. Peers was only halfway across. He could be headed for any of three exits on the opposite side.

*"If you'd just fucking tell me which one he went into—"* She

heaved, her breath beginning to fail her. *"I could cut him off!"*

No response. No turned head. Peers barreled forward as if the Devil were on his heels.

*"Peers!"*

Nothing.

*"PEERS!"*

When he didn't acknowledge her again, Jeanine went for broke. She leaped and missed Peers's foot by inches. Then he was regaining his lead while she scrambled to right herself. On the way to standing, she caught a panorama of the city through the big room's semicircle of windows. Mostly she saw palace grounds, but beyond the gates Jeanine could see low, dark, stalking shapes that could only be Reptars. *Lots* of Reptars. She saw wavering orange light, probably from fire. With her heartbeat pounding, it was hard to hear the world beyond the glass, but Jeanine was sure — even if it was inside her mind — she could hear screaming.

Jeanine was up, off again, fighting the acid burn in her legs, feeling a perhaps-unreasonable need to catch Peers. Did it matter? He wasn't going to catch Ravi, and without the kid, they'd never find Clara. Maybe the best course of action was to see what weapons she could find, hole up, and do what she'd done best since the world ended. How secure could the guns be, really? They'd taken them from her, but she hadn't been thoroughly searched. Not enough to find the tiny grenade she'd faithfully strapped back between her boobs. They'd probably found her original when they'd taken her clothes, but the other had been between the seams of her pack, right where she'd left it.

She startled. Jerked her head to the right, suddenly certain she'd see something. And she was right; a spherical Astral Shuttle was moving along outside the black iron fence, discharging its weapon at something she couldn't see. There were already more fires. More Reptars. The world was sliding into shit with sickening ease.

With her attention distracted, Jeanine didn't see the obstacle in her way until she hit it full on. The wind left her. She hit the ground, unable to tuck or roll, and barked her head hard on the leg of something large and heavy and made of wood. It took a few seconds to reorient, and when she did she saw Charlie Cook kneeling over her.

"Are you all right?" he asked, reaching down.

Jeanine's frustration and fear came out as anger. Peers was gone, and she hadn't seen which exit he'd taken. She was out of breath, had failed in her pursuit, had failed to find Clara, and frankly had no clue what to do next.

"Get your hands off me," she snarled.

Charlie looked back the way Jeanine had come. "What's chasing you?"

His hands were still too close. She slapped them away in a flurry of wild movements, knowing how ridiculous and unreasonable she must seem. She climbed upright, suddenly aware of how drained she was, unwilling to grip a chair for support. Charlie did the same. He stood patiently, awaiting an answer, as if the world weren't ending.

"Nothing's chasing me." A heavy breath. "I was chasing Peers."

"Why?"

"Where is Cameron?" she countered.

Charlie's face made a strange expression. It took seconds before Jeanine recognized the emotion as discomfort. She'd never seen Charlie uncomfortable. It took social awareness to be uncomfortable, or emotion in general. Charlie had always been light on both.

"He's gone."

"He ran off? Did he open the Ark first?"

"He opened it." A long sigh from Charlie. "Then he stood there for a long time, just looking at it. And then he jumped inside."

*"What?"*

Charlie's expression firmed. "He did what he needed to, okay? I can ..." He stopped, seeming to grapple with another moment of discomfort. "I can *feel* that it's what he needed to do. So now it's our turn."

"To do what?"

"Get Clara back. Get out of here."

"What the fuck do you think I've been trying to do?"

"I have no idea what you've been trying to do. Where is Piper? Where is Lila?"

"I don't know! Why should I know?"

"Perfect. Just perfect. We all head out to do a job, and you just stay back here playing tag."

Jeanine could tell Charlie was at his wit's end. He wasn't showing it, but the man was panicking, mourning, terrified, furious. It came out as stoic arrogance, like he alone knew things in the middle of a forest of idiots. Like Charlie always did because he was so damn superior. So Jeanine did what her own worn-thin impulses demanded she do by hauling back and punching him hard in the face.

He staggered, almost fell, and looked up, nose bleeding.

"Well, that's nice."

"I've got nothing better to do, Charlie. You have ideas? Let's hear them. But if you say one goddamned thing I think sounds too superior, I swear I'll—"

"Do you know what's happening out there? It's not just people looting because the State of the City made them a little short. The mothership is moving closer. It dropped about thirty shuttles while I watched, and they all flew over here and started making a mess. They didn't cut the broad-cast, Jeanine. Do you understand what that means? They don't particularly care if the capitals all fall apart because they're about to be swept under the rug anyway. What happened the last time we saw a mothership move into place over a city? Do you remember?"

"Stop treating me like an idiot, Charlie. If this is armageddon, I don't mind going out beating that look off your face."

"Smart. Very smart. Don't look for a solution. Don't try to find the others so we can get out. Just use your fists. Is that how this goes?"

"I *am* looking for a solution. If you'd just listen for a second instead of mouthing off, I could—"

Jeanine stopped when a dark, low purring sound split the air.

Followed by a dozen or more.

Reptars at every entrance, moving in from the outer walls. More spilled from behind, stalking forward like giant insects.

"Shit," Jeanine said.

Charlie raised his hands. "We're with the viceroy. We're with Mara Jabari."

"I don't think they care."

The Reptars circled. Moved closer.

She didn't have a weapon. There were too many to even attempt a fight. Every exit was blocked.

So she looked down at her chest. She unbuttoned her shirt.

"What are you doing?" Charlie asked.

"I'm sorry I hit you, Charlie."

"Why ... *what?*" He was staring at her exposed bra, distracted even from the presence of the Reptars, now only ten feet away.

She pushed aside a flap of fabric between her breasts. Charlie's eyes widened at the sight of the tiny grenade and its dangling pull-string.

"Go ahead," Jeanine said. "I'm sure you've never touched tits before anyway."

The Reptars purred.

Charlie looked at Jeanine's face then at the little black cylinder with its short, dangling cord. Then he met her big brown eyes again, and she nodded grimly.

Charlie reached.

He pulled the cord.

## Chapter Fifty-Four

PEERS FELT the whiff of air as Jeanine jumped for his foot and missed, falling to the ground in a loud mess. She'd been shouting at him about catching Ravi, but the kid was no longer the problem. He'd lost him a few turns back. Now Peers had a different destination in mind, and a single, troubling refrain kept knocking around inside his head as his feet pumped, knowing he'd have to hurry if he meant to beat the furiously ticking clock.

*The Fool.*

Peers knew all about the Seven. They had the same basic significance for Peers and his friends, back when he'd been part of the clan, as Saint Nicholas had for the kids he met after moving to London. Tales were told about all of the old legends, the ancient scrolls, the aura of prophecies. But the Seven, much like Santa, weren't folks anyone ever expected to meet. At a certain point, they became myth. Until Astral Day came, and Peers — much as Cameron Bannister must have done, for different reasons — realized that all he'd been taught was actually true. With his eyes open, the pieces all fit. The elders hadn't lost the thread of truth over time; the old stories fit the unfolding invasion shockingly well, nothing lost through telling and retelling of those legends. It was almost as if the elders *did* have an ongoing line to the Horsemen. As if the legends weren't from a disconnected past, but as the inevitable consequence of a long, contiguous present.

Which, of course, made sense. Outside the Mullah elders, Peers might know that better than anyone.

They'd all studied the scrolls like other kids study multiplication tables. Some were for elder eyes only, but there were things even the children should know. Legends made it into their bedtime stories and colored their world. And now Peers was beginning to see it. Like the coming of the ships, the emergence of the Seven would be a real thing, too.

There was the King. In the stories, he was a man with two heads. A man who could think as a pair, and as a single mind. The legend said of the King, *Out of two, one.* And to Peers, that spoke of the Meyers. Two bodies, not just two heads. But essentially the same.

The Warrior. The Innocent. The Villain. The Magician. The Sage.

And of course, there was the Fool.

A noise came from ahead. Peers had heard it many times, but not for a long while: the deep-throated purr of Reptars. He and Aubrey had left London before the siege, and once he'd started his wandering the Astrals had stayed mostly away. They'd parted before him like the Red Sea before Moses, taking to the periphery. That had always been convenient, and finding the Den and its horde of technology had been ideal icing on the ultimate cake. But looking back, was there a reason for it?

Peers stormed past Piper and Cameron's room. Then past Lila and Clara's. He felt a pang of guilt thinking of the girl, and what might have become of her. But if Ravi left the note rather than the Mullah as a whole, what did it mean? It wasn't the threat they'd taken it to be — the threat that had sent Cameron to the Ark, that had convinced Meyer and Kindred to go along with Jabari's plan to rock the city's complacency from its rut. And judging by the activity outside and the purrs ahead, they'd succeeded famously if unsettling people was the goal. Ravi had said the Mullah were *interested* in Clara. And considering that Peers had seen her in the hallway the night Nocturne had gone wandering, she must have somehow encountered their hidey-hole. Somewhere in the tunnels, apparently accessible near the place he'd seen Clara last, not far from the room in which he'd found the Astral memory sphere. *But where?*

Around a corner. And then there were two Reptars ahead, their large, black, insect/panther bodies entirely filling the hallway.

He turned. Another was behind him.

The Reptars purred. They came forward.

Peers backed against the wall, sweating, swallowing, his heartbeat like the thrum of a rapid-fire tympani. The single Reptar came closer, the blue spark in its throat churning as it exhaled, death on its breath. Peers pressed back harder as if he might go through the wall itself.

He closed his eyes, waiting for the end. He felt the huge thing press into him, rubbing him with its scaly skin. He heard the clattering of its claws, too close. Then more claws, more breath, more purring. But different now.

Peers opened his eyes. The single Reptar had squeezed by him, and now all three were moving away, toward greener pastures and more suitable victims.

He didn't stop to wonder. His own room was a few doors down, so he rushed to it, turning the knob, practically falling inside. Nocturne, dutifully in his bed with a chew toy, barked a greeting. Peers closed the door then clicked the thumb lock as if a small bit of wood and thin metal might keep Reptars, Titans, or even human guards at bay. Nocturne started to come forward, tail wagging.

Peers took two steps before the explosion knocked him to his knees, shaking the dog on his four legs, confusion entering his deep brown eyes.

*Jesus. Hurry.*

Whatever was happening out there was falling apart fast. It wouldn't take hours or days for Ember Flats to eat itself alive; it would be done in clusters of minutes. He shouldn't even be here. He should already be searching for the tunnels out of this place, ideally for Meyer and Kindred — who, he was now suspecting, were either his ticket out of here or his duty to shepherd safely away. But he could afford the diversion — or rather, he couldn't afford *not* to take it. The diversion would take only a second. Then he could find Jeanine, apologize, maybe let her punch him in the face. He'd almost welcome it. She could be the muscle for what came next; the Meyers could be the leaders; Charlie could be the brain. Peers would be happy to coast. To try and find a way out then sit back and let others get them away. Which, of course, they would.

Because everyone knew the King survived.

If a few Reptars ran into the King in a hallway, they wouldn't attack. They'd just … squeeze by him or something.

Same for any of the Seven.

Peers shook off a creeping feeling he'd been trying to shed by pouring all of his focus into catching Ravi after he'd inexplicably become afraid and run away. The feeling was the reason Peers followed. An itch that needed scratching even though he wanted to leave it alone.

He pulled a bag from the corner and fumbled under the bed while Nocturne recovered his wits and came forward, tail still wagging, wet nose investigating Peers's busy arms. The molding came away easily, and he had the sphere out in seconds. No point in covering his tracks; the device was now mobile, and if anyone learned he'd been hiding something under the bed, so be it.

He hefted the sphere, moving it toward the bag's open mouth.

He thought of Ravi. Of how he'd held them at gunpoint then turned and run. Why had that happened? Peers had been talking about locks, like the one he'd opened to get the sphere. It wasn't hard to open them even though the elders all had those fancy key rings. Poke three points in the inverted-Triforce keyholes, and doors opened easy as pie.

And sure, he'd been the only one of the kids who could do it, after he'd discovered how easy it was. He'd remained Mullah for two full weeks between realizing he could open those locks and being ejected, and during that time all the others he'd shown could never get the hang of it. Only Peers. But that was because he had the knack, not because there was something about Peers, in particular, that let him open locks that ought not be opened.

Just like there was nothing about Peers, in particular, that would cause angry Reptars to pass him by while similar Reptars were out in the streets, ripping people to shreds.

Ravi's wide eyes. The change in his expression, after Peers had made a few nothing mentions of events long ago.

Ravi's words. His shock. His fleeing feet.

Peers was setting the sphere in the bottom of the backpack as his mind wondered, *What made Ravi run? What was he afraid of?*

Peers felt a static charge rush through his fingertips, locking his muscles. He froze where he was, knowing he now couldn't drop the sphere if he wanted to. Not now that he'd asked the right question.

The lights went out.

The sphere answered.

# Chapter Fifty-Five

THEY HEARD and felt the explosion with Meyer, Kindred, and Jabari in sight. Lila barely knew where she was, but Piper seemed to have no such hesitation. After a few turns through the serpentine palace with her hand in Piper's, Lila had asked her why she thought to find the others at all, considering they'd been across town minutes before, and now the town itself was burning. Piper had said, "I can hear them." Funny thing was that Lila could almost hear them, too. But it wasn't quite auditory. Like a voice behind a curtain, far away, calling her forward. Her fathers' voices.

The trio ahead shook with the explosion, Kindred foundering and grabbing a hallway accent table for support. Lila staggered wide, barely staying upright. But Piper barely trembled; her face showed no surprise. She'd stopped and grabbed a doorframe a half second earlier, braced, absorbed the shock as if she'd known it was coming.

"They're here already," Mara said, looking toward the sound. "We may be too late."

Piper shook her head. "No. It was Jeanine and Charlie. They're gone. Whatever they did, they chose to do it. Cameron's gone, too."

Jabari looked like she might ask the most obvious questions, but there wasn't any time for mourning or regret. Instead she said, "Do we know if he opened the Ark?"

Piper nodded. "Can't you feel it?"

Lila broke free of Piper and rushed to the red-tie Meyer, unsure in the moment which it was. It didn't matter. She hugged him hard then switched to the other.

"Thank God you're okay. I thought—"

The man in the red tie — Kindred, Lila now saw — said, "Have you found Clara?"

Lila felt a second's intense despair, but Piper interrupted her moment to answer.

"Clara is fine."

"Did they let her go?"

"No. But she's fine."

"If they didn't release her …"

"It was a trick. The Mullah have her, but she's not in danger."

Jabari shook her head, eyes squinted. "Where are you getting this?"

"I can hear her."

"Where?"

"Everywhere."

To Lila: "What's she talking about? Did something … ?" Then the viceroy kind of ticked her head sideways, an uncomfortable expression on her face — one meant to ask if Piper was losing her mind.

"Cameron did something," Piper said. "That's all I know. Now, it's like I can hear everything."

Lila looked to Meyer, who came forward. He took Piper's hands, met her eyes, then nodded in a businesslike way and stepped back. He nodded to Kindred next, and Lila watched knowledge flow between them.

Jabari, observing the exchange, glared at each of the suited men in turn. "Don't you two play coy on me now."

Kindred answered. "I think all of Ember Flats has been able to sense the Ark on some level for hours now, maybe days. Maybe the whole world has been able to. But now that it's open, it's like the light's been flicked on."

"Meaning?"

"Every time in the past, the Astrals came expecting a planet that had learned to tap into its higher mind. This time, we surprised them. We hadn't developed a higher mind at all, at least not consciously. So they used the rock lines. The henges around the capitals. And now there's the Ark."

"I thought it was an archive."

"We gave Ember Flats something to be angry about. It's feeding the Ark, and the Ark feeds that energy right back at us, repeated out into the other capital cities as a broadcast the Astrals haven't bothered to kill. They're *letting* us do this. Humanity gets angry, sad, full of despair, whatever. But instead of thoughtfully planning a response after learning about Heaven's Veil, humanity chooses to fight and riot. You saw it. Hell, we barely escaped. It's Astral Day all over."

"What does Astral Day have to do with it?" Lila asked.

Meyer put a hand on her shoulder. It was almost condescending, but Lila let it be.

"Every time they test us, we behave poorly. We trample each other to get where we need to go. We fight and kill and steal. It happened that first day, when the ships came, and it's starting to happen again. If the Ark is meant to record our responses and weigh our fate, I don't know that we'll pass."

"Then why did you — ?"

Kindred interrupted, his eyes scanning the room, his tone decidedly less placating and sentimental than Meyer's. "Because it cuts both ways. Now that the tempest is out of the box, the stalemate is broken. Piper's already changing. Maybe, once the dust settles and humans find they're more connected than they thought, there will be something we can do. But I don't think things went our way. I can feel it from both sides: human, like Piper, and Astral. If this was a trial, we've already been found guilty. The lit-up human network seems to be pouring minds into the archive, but we can see each other more than ever through that same network."

"Come with me," Jabari said, breaking the mood that threatened to freeze them in place as the city burned. "We thought this might be coming." She waved at Piper, Lila, and both Meyers. "Come on. All of you."

"But Clara!" Lila said.

"She's safer than we are, Lila," Piper said.

Lila felt her arm yanked hard as they went back on the move, now running with Jabari leading in her long, formal viceroy gown. Through the windows, Lila could see groups of people swarming past, fires burning, Reptars on patrol, shuttles flying by like in the early days of Heaven's Veil. And what Piper and Kindred had said was true, now that Lila tuned in to her own heavy-handed intuition: She *could* hear the others out there; she *could* sense the mood; she *did* feel that heavy sense of a judgment gone wrong. Not as deeply as Piper seemed to, but the feeling was there. And below it all, she feared for her daughter. Not as a logical being but as a mother. No matter how you sliced it, Clara had been taken from her, and nobody knew where she'd gone.

They moved into an unknown hallway, through an

unmarked door. The room was filled with screens and computers. It was like a tiny version of Peers's Den, only in a room instead of a cave, using human technology instead of Astral.

Jabari was about to close the door when she paused, hand on the knob. Then, with the door still open, she walked slowly back into the hallway as if she'd spotted something and wanted to get a closer look. Across from the unmarked door was a gallery of windows. Outside, beyond a lush expanse of grass, Lila could see nothing but an outer wall and open sky beyond. There was nothing of the city from this vista. Were it not for the sounds all around and the murmurings in her head, this might be just another peaceful night in the Capital of Capitals.

Beyond, Lila could see something moving.

"Ms. Jabari?" Lila said, approaching her.

But Jabari was shaking her head.

"It's too late," she said.

# Chapter Fifty-Six

A TEEN BOY of about fourteen stood in front of Peers. It took a while to realize he was staring at himself.

There was a grating, a grumbling from somewhere behind him. A sort of shifting sound, nothing to worry about. Peers remembered it well, from when he'd *been* the boy in this vision. One of the big doors closing, or possibly opening. Judging by where they (both adult and boy) were standing, Peers was sure he remembered the day, and why the doors might be moving, though some typically stayed open and others closed, all seldom moved. Today the Mullah was rallying defenses, aware of an intrusion. The adults were scurrying about the tunnels like busy bees rallying to rise and sting.

And in so doing, they'd left the temple unguarded.

Well, *mostly* unguarded. Sabah, one of the elders, had remained at his station when the others ran off. Peers had watched him for a while, hidden, and only recently, as Adult Peers understood the timeline, had he taken a short break to relieve his bladder.

Watching now as full-grown Peers, he remembered his

thoughts on that long-ago day, now around two decades behind him. He hadn't meant to do anything, not really. But he'd been curious, as he'd always been, and you usually couldn't even *approach* the temple, let alone enter. There were all sorts of pain-in-the ass adults milling about and telling nosy kids to get away, to mind their parents and whatever dumb tasks they were supposed to be doing. The kids had many chores. Peers had spoken to children from the outside world, who didn't live in caves and holes in the ground, worshipping old scrolls and performing ancient rituals. He knew enough about the world beyond these stone walls to know that Peers was dealing with *slavery*, no more or less. Screw the adults and especially the elders. The soldier ants had to do all the grunt work, while those *in the know* held their secrets and chanted in circles, probably, laughing about how they ran things and could make others — most particularly Peers and his friends — do whatever they wanted.

All for the stupid temple. All for whatever was inside it. All because of the Horsemen — who, despite lots of rather over-the-top indoctrination, sounded like boogeymen. The kids were told that if they didn't do their chores or listen to their parents, they'd be taken away when the Horsemen returned.

It was all such crap.

It didn't help that Peers's father had been an envoy to Cairo, to Jerusalem, to Damascus. It didn't help that Father was an infiltrator, occasionally placed in high positions, meant to pull invisible strings for the Mullah. Father, when he was home, brought back stories. Said insidious, even blasphemous things that came to him from the world beyond the caves. Peers absorbed it all. He began to see the Mullah's way of life in terms of Haves and Have-Nots, the way Father sometimes spoke when he thought the children couldn't hear. And Peers, always curious, resented the fact that if he had to slave his days away, he couldn't even truly know what he was slaving *for*.

*Horsemen*. Horsemen, indeed.

So he'd gone to the temple entrance, just to see it. Just to be there without being bothered. And when Sabah stood and tottered his way off toward the latrine chamber, Young Peers had gone to the door. Touched it. Seen the way the stone had been perfectly milled so that door met jamb with no gap in between. Could you suffocate someone by locking them in the temple? Probably. But that was fine because as far as Father said, nobody ever went into the temple. *Almost never*. Once in a great while, one of the elders would go in to "consult the Horsemen." Peers had his own thoughts.

Seeing as the whole Horsemen thing smelled like bullshit, that *had* to be where the best stuff was kept. All the games the children weren't allowed to have. All the money for use in traveling and acquiring things, perhaps. All the forbidden material, which the elders kept for themselves. Maybe there were loose women inside, kept alive by air holes. And the elders entered to screw them.

Peers watched his young self creep forward, looking around for Sabah's return. Despite knowing the outcome, Adult Peers couldn't help a flutter of nerves. Sabah had stayed away long enough. Peers had got away with all of it — at least, for a while.

The boy pushed on the rock. Glanced back, pushed again. He'd even smelled at the gap, as if the good stuff in the temple might be sweets he could sniff from a distance. Eventually, the boy decided he'd seen enough, that the temple's guts had never been the goal and that the door and foyer themselves were boring. So he'd turned to go, then half tripped and smacked his back against the wall near the door.

Peers watched it happen. Beside the boy, the door slid sideways. Not open like on a hinge but into the wall. It shouldn't have been possible with stone.

The boy looked at the door, deeply puzzled and slightly afraid. The door's movement had been too quiet for stone on stone, and that meant he probably wouldn't be discovered by sound. But on the other hand, here he was, on the threshold, the door wide open. He'd be beaten if caught. Maybe expelled.

The boy looked at the open door, with nothing but darkness inside.

Maybe killed, for all Young Peers knew.

The boy turned, now noticing a small circular keyhole with a pattern that matched those rings worn by the elders. Then he looked at his belt, where he'd leaned against the wall. He'd tucked a cleaning pad into his waistband when the commotion started, when the outsiders had arrived and the Mullah stirred to find them, then either kill or force them to leave. He'd been scouring one of the tables using the pad, which was a big wad of twisted metal threads.

Watching now, it was obvious to Adult Peers what had happened. Just as he'd done when he'd retrieved the sphere from its original home in the closet, the metal on the pad had pressed into the key indentations. You didn't need a special key after all. You had to touch the points with something, maybe metal.

Adult Peers felt his heart skip, mentally urging the boy back. But of course, this had *happened*. This was history, already written.

He walked forward.

The temple was small. Far too small to be called a temple, not much larger than a walk-in closet at the viceroy mansion. If this were real, it would have been a tight fit for two people. But in reality he'd been the boy in this place, looking at the temple's sole feature: a blue disc on the far wall about the size of a large dinner plate, glowing in the dark, swirling like liquid.

Peers touched the disc and found it semi-permeable. It gave a bit when he pressed it, like taffy.

A voice in his head (just in the boy's head at the time, but now also echoed in Adult Peers's head) said, *Who are you?*

Peers remembered how unsure he'd been about how to answer — or, really, whether he should even try. He wasn't supposed to be near the temple. He definitely wasn't supposed to be *in* the temple. And holy of all holies, he *really, really* wasn't supposed to be in front of this disc thing, touching it, talking to who knew whom. Or what.

But the answer rose in Young Peers's mind, now echoed in Adult Peers's thoughts, without effort. A lie.

*I'm an elder of the Mullah.*

*You seem young. Even for a human.*

Young Peers stepped back. All the way to the doorway. Intellectually, he *should* be terrified. But curiosity was the stronger emotion. He'd *never* be here again. If he left now, too many questions would plague him. What was this thing? Who was the voice in his head? And how did this all work, anyway? He knew the voice wasn't really speaking his language. It was an instantaneous translation of both words and concepts, happening mind to mind.

This was too much. He had to leave.

But instead, Peers watched his stupid younger self step forward again.

*We were not expecting contact,* said the voice.

*Yeah, well.*

There seemed to be a pause as if the voice was waiting for something. Then it said, *The archive has been disturbed.*

And Peers, having no idea what that meant, said, *Okay.*

He saw a mental image, of a large gilt box in a cave. There was a cerebral relaxation, and he somehow knew that what the voice proposed — the thing he'd just agreed with — wasn't actually true. Peers intuited this as good; the archive, whatever it was, hadn't been touched. It was something else — related but different — that this little mind-meld felt was off.

Then the voice seemed to decide what that thing was. *The key. It has found a bearer.*

*Sure.*

*Is this why you've broken the silence?*

*I thought someone should know. About the archive and the key, I mean.*

*Why has this happened?*

Peers recalled one of the expressions his father had brought back from the outside world. It wasn't appropriate, but seeing as this was a mental thing, he was unable to keep it from slipping out.

*Shit happens.*

*Is it time?*

*Um, I don't know.*

*It has been millennia since the last epoch. Your kind has rebuilt. You know the rules. We will not decide. Only you can decide.*

Now Peers was uneasy. *Both* Peerses were uneasy: Young Peers because he'd trespassed enough and was ready to leave, curiosity or no curiosity, and Adult Peers because a slow creeping was summiting his spine.

*Epoch.*

*Rebuilt.*

*Only you can decide.*

And on the heels of those thoughts, he recalled Ravi's

words, before he'd run off terrified: *You opened a lock in the temple? Beyond the elders?*

Because that definitely wasn't supposed to be possible, not without a key, not even if you had steel wool on your belt. But then again, the way had always parted for Peers almost as if he had a role to play in destiny.

And Ravi's parting whisper, before he'd run: *The Fool.*

Aloud, even though he was inside a memory, Adult Peers said, "Oh, shit."

*The key has found its bearer,* said the voice. *The portal has been activated.*

But the boy was becoming worried. Worried about what this place was, whom exactly he was talking to, and most pressingly, when the elder guard would return. He'd been here far too long, and was in too deep. But the voice held his attention like a clenched fist.

*Are you ready?*

Young Peers didn't answer. He backed away. The voice held him, freezing his muscles. It wasn't going to let him go. He'd be held here forever. They'd find him here, tethered. He'd die in this place, his mind held prisoner.

*Are you ready?* the voice repeated, its tone calm and rational.

*Yes! Yes, just let me go!*

And then, it did. Young Peers reeled backward, his momentum strong enough to propel his memory body back through Adult Peers's own insubstantial presence. The boy emerged on his backside then stumbled out into the light. Clumsily, he pushed the steel wool pad against the lock, and of course the door closed. Peers remembered how easily it had shut, cutting the boy off from that strange, horrible blue disc and its resident voice. He'd been so relieved. For two weeks afterward, he was sure he'd gotten away with it. Only later had a kid named Fahim finked on him, reporting out of pious guilt that Peers Basara had gone to the area outside the temple door. He hadn't even seen Peers enter; just going to the temple and touching its closed door was enough to earn his exile.

Peers, shut in the dark chamber when the door closed, stepped through the wall and found his child self walking backward, afraid to move his eyes from the door. He remembered how terrified he'd been. How much he'd felt on the edge of a near-miss, almost having been caught, maybe trapped. But cogitation had been cut short when the floor trembled, its point of origin far in the other direction, where the intruders were being dealt with.

The room changed like a jump cut in a film. Suddenly Adult Peers — alone now — found himself back in his room in the Ember Flats viceroy's mansion. The room was still shaking, but now it wasn't from the rocks shifting in what the Mullah called the Key Room. It wasn't the sign of coming that he now realized it had always been. Now it was the sign of something else.

Past knowledge stitched with the understanding gained since. All the things he'd studied, both on his own and in concert with data sent from Benjamin Bannister's group, from other groups around the world, both before and after the Astrals' arrival. Mullah legends meeting science, myth, and findings from sites across the globe. And all of a sudden, everything seemed to fit.

*Are you ready?*

The Astrals viewed time differently than humans did. Even neglecting physics Peers knew nothing about, decades and even centuries simply didn't mean much to beings who lived nearer to eternity. From their distant home, mentally accessible only through the portal, it would take them forever to reach Earth. Hell, it might take more than a decade.

They'd arrive on their dark, spherical horses. *En masse*, to weigh humanity and lay judgment — but only once we were ready. That's what the Mullah were for. They were the keepers. Those who mediated the way. Kept Pandora's box closed until it was time to open it, when circumstances were finally right, and we'd had time to become what the keepers felt had a fair chance of succeeding.

And again, Peers heard, *Are you ready?*

And his own answer, blurted in childish fear: *Yes!*

He backed away from the Astral sphere. He looked up, toward the invisible sky, hidden behind the palace roof.

He'd done this.

He'd called them.

It was Peers, all those years ago, who'd brought the Astrals to Earth far, far too early, as only a Fool could do. He'd gone where he wasn't supposed to go. Touched what he oughtn't have touched. Transgressed where nobody was supposed to transgress. And eleven years later, the Horsemen had arrived.

Had the Mullah known? Peers wasn't sure. They'd exiled him without ceremony, not bothering to detail what damage, if any, he'd caused. But Peers thought they might not have known at the time, though they surely figured it out later. When Peers had been exiled, the concern had been all about the incursion into the Key Room: the key finding its bearer; Cameron Bannister finding his place in destiny, dooming himself to finish off the choice that Peers, too young to know any better, had triggered the process of choosing.

Coincidence? There was no such thing in the blessed, cursed life of Peers Basara, Fool of legend.

He remembered the desert. The shove from his own uncles and cousins and mother, telling him to never return.

The Mullah's was a sacred duty, and Peers had threatened it. If only they'd known how badly.

Sabah had said, *When the day comes that the Horsemen arrive, may the Dark Rider himself take your soul.*

The Dark Rider.

In the old legends, the Dark Rider rode at the rear of the Horsemen's pack. Lagging back, lying in wait. And given the way modern technological society had crumbled in the years since the occupation, that wouldn't be hard. If there was a Dark Rider, he could hang back, just out of obvious sight. There were no strong telescopes anymore. No telemetry, no radar, no satellite feeds out of Astral hands, and even those pointed only at the ground.

He had to find the tunnels. He had to get away.

Peers zipped the pack, slung it over his back, and rushed for the door, Nocturne at his heels.

They both stopped when the door opened. In his fugue, Peers seemed to have missed a major event at the palace: one that had ripped the house wide open, leaving his room door opening into open yard, chaos, and rubble.

But he barely saw the rubble, or the chaos beyond.

An all-black ship, its bulk spanning to the edge of each visible horizon, was sliding into place above Ember Flats.

**They know what we've done...**

Cameron Bannister and his group of survivors went searching for what they once believed to be a weapon … but found to be something else entirely. It's something that will decide the fate of all humanity if Cameron can summon the will to start the doomsday clock ticking.

Start reading Extinction today!

# A Quick Favor...

If you enjoyed this book, please take a moment to write a short review on your favorite online bookstore so other readers can enjoy it, too.

Thanks so much!
Johnny and Avery

# About the Authors

**Avery Blake** doesn't want you to know where she lives, or what she does. She travels the world, moving from place to place quickly to ensure she can't be tracked. It's safer that way.

When she's not looking over her shoulder, you can find her in the corner of a cafe, facing the exit, typing as fast as she can.

~

**Johnny B. Truant** is co-owner of the Sterling & Stone Story Studio, an IP powerhouse focusing on books and adaptations for film and television. It's the best job in the world, and he spends his days creating cool stuff with partners Sean Platt and David W. Wright, as well as more than 20 gifted storytellers.

Johnny is the bestselling author of over 100 books under various pen names, including the Fat Vampire and Invasion series. On the nonfiction side, he's also co-author of the indie publishing mainstay Write. Publish. Repeat. and co-host of the weekly Story Studio Podcast.

Originally from Ohio, Johnny and his family now live in Austin, Texas, where he's finally surrounded by creative types as weird as he is.

The Hidden

The Saved

**The Next Evolution**

Transition

Convergence

Evolution

**Stand-Alone Novels**

Analog Heart

Family Royale

Ruthless Positivity

Vicarious Joe

# Also By Johnny B. Truant

**The Dead World Series**

Dead Zero

Dead City

Dead Nation

Dead Planet

Empty Nest

**The Fat Vampire Series**

Fat Vampire

Fat Vampire 2: Tastes Like Chicken

Fat Vampire 3: All You Can Eat

Fat Vampire 4: Harder, Better, Fatter, Stronger

Fat Vampire 5: Fatpocaplypse

Fat Vampire 6: Survival of the Fattest

**The Fat Vampire Chronicles**

The Vampire Maurice

Anarchy and Blood

Vampires in the White City

**The Beam Series**

The Beam Season One

The Beam Season Two

The Beam Season Three

**Robot Proletariat Series**

En3my

Robot Proletariat

The Infinite Loop

The Hard Reset

Cascade Failure

Reboot

**The Invasion Series**

Longshot

Invasion

Contact

Colonization

Annihilation

Judgment

Extinction

Resurrection

**The Tomorrow Gene Series**

Null Identity

The Tomorrow Gene

The Tomorrow Clone

The Eden Experiment

**Stand Alone Novels**

Pretty Killer

Pattern Black

Burnout